E.R. PUNSHON
SIX WERE PRESENT

ERNEST ROBERTSON PUNSHON was born in London in 1872.

At the age of fourteen he started life in an office. His employers soon informed him that he would never make a really satisfactory clerk, and he, agreeing, spent the next few years wandering about Canada and the United States, endeavouring without great success to earn a living in any occupation that offered. Returning home by way of working a passage on a cattle boat, he began to write. He contributed to many magazines and periodicals, wrote plays, and published nearly fifty novels, among which his detective stories proved the most popular and enduring.

He died in 1956.

The Bobby Owen Mysteries

1. Information Received
2. Death among the Sunbathers
3. Crossword Mystery
4. Mystery Villa
5. Death of a Beauty Queen
6. Death Comes to Cambers
7. The Bath Mysteries
8. Mystery of Mr. Jessop
9. The Dusky Hour
10. Dictator's Way
11. Comes a Stranger
12. Suspects – Nine
13. Murder Abroad
14. Four Strange Women
15. Ten Star Clues
16. The Dark Garden
17. Diabolic Candelabra
18. The Conqueror Inn
19. Night's Cloak
20. Secrets Can't be Kept
21. There's a Reason for Everything
22. It Might Lead Anywhere
23. Helen Passes By
24. Music Tells All
25. The House of Godwinsson
26. So Many Doors
27. Everybody Always Tells
28. The Secret Search
29. The Golden Dagger
30. The Attending Truth
31. Strange Ending
32. Brought to Light
33. Dark is the Clue
34. Triple Quest
35. Six Were Present

E.R. PUNSHON

SIX WERE PRESENT

With an introduction
by Curtis Evans

DEAN STREET PRESS

Detective Stories, the Detection Club and Death:
The Final Years of E. R. Punshon

... but, they dead,
Death has so many doors to let out life,
I will not long survive them.

The Custom of the Country (c. 1619-23; 1647)
JOHN FLETCHER AND PHILLIP MASSINGER

WHEN IN 1949 E.R. Punshon published *So Many Doors*, his twenty-sixth Bobby Owen detective novel, the Englishman was seventy-seven years old, with nearly a half-century of published novels behind him and a comparatively scant seven years of life and letters remaining before him. 1901, the year of the appearance of Punshon's first novel, *Earth's Great Lord*, saw the death of Queen Victoria, the long reigning granddaughter of King George III for whom a regal age of European global dominion has been named; while 1949, a year during which a convalescent Europe was still bleakly recovering from a world war that had reduced much of its civilization to ashes and rubble, saw the testing by the USSR of its first atomic bomb and the proclamation of the formation of the People's Republic of China. The world was changing with a fearsome fleetness that not merely old men who had first glimpsed light in the Victorian era were finding hard to follow.

Rapidly changing too was the craft of crime and mystery fiction that E.R. Punshon had long practiced (this admittedly a minor thing compared to unsettling phenomena like armed revolution and atom splitting). Like the once seemingly imperishable British Empire, the hegemony of the between-the-wars "Golden Age" clue-puzzle detective novel was breaking asunder, under pressure from increasingly popular rival forms of mystery fiction, such as hard-boiled, noir, psychological suspense and espionage. Already stalked by Raymond Chandler's famous gumshoe, Philip Marlowe, as well as ill-humored and hard-drinking would-be Marlowe doppelgangers like Mickey Spillane's brutish Mike Hammer, Punshon's well-born English policeman Bobby Owen, along with other of his surviving gentlemanly detective colleagues from the era of classic crime fiction, soon found himself in the sights of no less deadly a professional killer than James Bond. Agent 007's creator, Ian Fleming, who cited as his literary influences Raymond Chandler, Dashiell Hammett, Eric Ambler and Graham Greene, published his first Bond spy novel, *Casino Royale*, in the United Kingdom in 1953, where it enjoyed immediate popular and critical success. In the United States, where the novel appeared in 1954, the same year as Raymond Chandler's much-lauded *The Long Goodbye*, *Time* magazine wryly declared that "Bond . . . might well be [Philip] Marlowe's younger brother, except that he never takes coffee for a bracer, just one large martini laced with vodka."

Upon the publication of *So Many Doors* in the UK and the US (in the latter country it would prove the last Punshon mystery published during the author's lifetime), crime fiction reviewers deemed the novel and its author representatives of a vanished era. "The twenties were the plotter's heyday (consider Freeman Wills Crofts, J.J. Connington, Dorothy L. Sayers)," observed the Democratic-Socialist *London Tribune* in its review of the "well-plotted" and "studiously told" *So Many Doors*, "and to the twenties, in spirit at least, belongs Mr. Punshon." In the United States, Anthony Boucher, dean of American mystery critics, allowed in the *New York Times Book Review* that the narration of *So Many Doors* was "leisurely"; yet, after noting the seventeenth-century English stage derivation of the novel's title, he approvingly added that there "is something Elizabethan, even Jacobean, about the obscure destinies that drive [Punshon's] obsessed and tormented characters, and about the frightful violence that concludes the story." Punshon, it seemed, still had something to say in the harried and hectic atomic age, when crime fiction reviewers and readers alike seemed increasingly to believe that brevity was the soul of death.

* * * * *

To his death in 1956 E.R. Punshon maintained a loyal following in the United Kingdom among readers who staunchly adhered to the strict standard of fair play puzzle plotting associated with Golden Age detective fiction. During the Fifties the aging but seemingly indefatigable author, who still lived quietly with his wife Sarah at their house at 23 Nimrod Road, Streatham, produced, through the medium of his prestigious longtime publisher Victor Gollancz, nine new mystery titles-- *Everybody Always Tells* (1950), *The Secret Search* (1951), The Golden Dagger (1951), *The Attending Truth* (1952), *Strange Ending* (1953), *Brought to Light* (1954), *Dark Is the Clue* (1955), *Triple Quest* (1955) and *Six Were Present* (1956)—that detailed the final criminal investigations of his longtime series police detective, Bobby Owen, now risen to the august rank of Commander (unattached), Metropolitan Police. Additionally Punshon continued to remain active in his cherished Detection Club, a London-based social organization of distinguished detective novelists, in which the author had been inducted, along with Anthony Gilbert and Gladys Mitchell, in 1933, three years after the Club's founding, joining such luminaries from the crime writing world as G.K. Chesterton, Dorothy L. Sayers, Agatha Christie, E.C. Bentley, Anthony Berkeley, R. Austin Freeman and Freeman Wills Crofts.

Like other British institutions the Detection Club from 1939 to 1945 bore the bitter burdens of war, including the devastating Nazi air raids known collectively as "the Blitz." When the Club revived its meetings and annual dinners in 1946, it became immediately apparent that time had wrought cruel changes with its membership. On seeing his brother and sister detective novelists again at the Club premises after the long interval of war years, John Dickson Carr, a comparative stripling at the age of forty, recalled that he had been "shocked" by their appearance, which he had found decidedly "greyer and more worn."

By 1946 eight of the original twenty-eight Detection Club members, including G.K. Chesterton, R. Austin Freeman and Helen Simpson, had passed away and many other members were now elderly and inactive. Several more members would expire over the next few years. Even the formerly quite engaged Freeman Wills Crofts and John Rhode (Cecil John Charles Street), now in their sixties and living in the country, became markedly less involved with Club affairs, as did an increasingly infirm Henry Wade (the landed baronet Henry Lancelot Aubrey-

Fletcher). For his part, John Dickson Carr, deeming British life under postwar conditions and the governance of the Labour party intolerable, would in 1948 depart for his native United States. Besides Punshon, only Christie, John Rhode and Henry Wade, among original members, and Anthony Gilbert, Gladys Mitchell, Margery Allingham, John Dickson Carr, Nicholas Blake, Christopher Bush and E.C.R. Lorac, among the smaller number of Thirties inductees, remained substantially active as crime writers into the 1950s. Of these Lorac and Wade, like Punshon, would not survive the decade, and another, John Rhode, would barely outlast it.

Clearly some new blood was badly needed. During Punshon's remaining span of life the aged and ailing Detection Club received transfusions, so to speak, from seventeen new members. Although with the deaths of Baroness Emma Orczy and A.E.W. Mason (in 1947 and 1948 respectively), Punshon became the oldest surviving member of the Detection Club, the author, who served as Club treasurer between 1946 and 1949, during the postwar years remained extensively involved in Club affairs, actively participating in hearty debates concerning prospective new members, like Christianna Brand, Michael Innes, Michael Gilbert, Elizabeth Ferrars and Julian Symons, as to whether or not they practiced fair play and sufficiently respected the King's (later Queen's) English, the Club's chief requirements for induction. (These debates are chronicled in detail in my CADS booklet *Was Corinne's Murder Clued? The Detection Club and Fair Play, 1930-1953*.)

In 1949 Punshon found himself at odds over the matter of new enrollments with the man who unquestionably was the Club's crankiest and most cantankerous member: Anthony Berkeley, famed author of *The Poisoned Chocolates Case* (1928) and, under the pseudonym Francis Iles, of *Malice Aforethought* (1931) and *Before the Fact* (1932), three of the best regarded British crime novels from the Golden Age. In April Berkeley wrote a provocative letter to Punshon in which he claimed that as the Club's "First Freeman" he possessed blanket veto power over prospective members, despite the fact that he no longer served on the membership committee. During the early days of the Detection Club, Berkeley had observed at a meeting that the

Club had two "Freemans" as members (R. Austin Freeman and Freeman Wills Crofts), and he pronounced that as the person who had originally suggested forming the Club he would be its "First Freeman." To this suggestion everyone else had laughingly assented, taking the office as a joke; yet now, nearly two decades later, it seemed that Berkeley had not been joking.

Incensed by Berkeley's gambit and the rude language in which he had couched it, Punshon wrote Sayers, enclosing his antagonist's "offensive" letter (which evidently has not survived) and warning that "[Berkeley] intends to make some sort of fuss." Punshon speculated that "possibly it is better to take no notice [of the letter], except perhaps as regards the absurd claim of his to hold some special position as what he calls 'First Freeman.' I have a vague idea that once before he put forward a claim to be a permanent member of the [membership] committee on the same ground." He noted dryly that while he had forborne responding to the specifics of Berkeley's letter, he had sent the notoriously tightfisted "First Freeman" a reminder that his annual membership fee was due, to which he had received no reply.

"Bother AB!" responded Sayers in a letter to Punshon that she composed the day after receiving his missive. "I do wish he was not so rude and silly." She entirely concurred with Punshon's recollection of the once comical but now rather annoying office of First Freeman and added resignedly: "If he tries to make a fuss at the meeting, the committee will have to cope; but I hope he will have more sense. I am sorry he should have written to you so impertinently."

By the summer of 1949 the First Freeman's irksome machinations had been checked--but only, Punshon feared, for the moment. With considerable skepticism Punshon wrote Sayers, "I gather the reconciliation with Anthony Berkeley is now complete and the hatchet well and truly buried. Until dug up again." Sayers, who soon would succeed E.C. Bentley as President of the Detection Club, advised members to tread carefully around Berkeley's tender sensibilities. "Let a (more or less) sleeping Berkeley lie," she urged. Nevertheless Sayers agreed with Punshon that the Club members would have to keep Berkeley off the membership committee, because were he to be on it the Club would "never get any new member . . . he turns them all down on sight." She lamented that "Berkeley is a difficult man to work with."

Sayers found working with Punshon, whose detective fiction she had enthusiastically promoted as a book reviewer for the *Sunday Times* between 1933 and 1935, to be an altogether more pleasant experience. Surviving correspondence between the two authors suggests that Punshon was, along with Anthony Gilbert (Lucy Beatrice Malleson), the Detection Club member with whom Sayers got along most amicably at this time. The two communicated fairly frequently during the postwar years, chatting not only about Detection Club matters, but more personal affairs as well.

As treasurer of the Detection Club, Punshon gave his attention to matters large--such as any taxes the Club might have to pay to a revenue-hungry British government ("we have to remember that we may be dropped on by the Income tax people")—and matters small. As an example of the latter, Punshon advised Sayers in December 1948 that the Club should give a "small Christmas present" to Mrs. Buchanan, caretaker of the Club premises at 12 Kingly Street, Soho. ("A room and loo in a clergy house," Christianna Brand bluntly recalled of the locale.) Although payment for services was included with the rent, Punshon pointed out that "services included are very often badly neglected and so far as I have noticed in this case they have been quite well carried out and the room always seemed neat and tidy." "[E]ven in this sordid age," he reflected with characteristic gentle irony, "a few thanks and expressions of satisfaction . . . often please as much as gifts—at any rate if accompanied by a gift." A few days later Sayers gave Mrs. Buchanan a £1 Christmas tip (about £32 today).

Sadly, Punshon suffered a serious setback to his health in August 1949, not long after a busy summer that saw the English publication of *So Many Doors*, his nettlesome skirmish with Anthony Berkeley and the annual Detection Club dinner at the Hotel Café Royal, Piccadilly. (Recorded treasurer Punshon of the latter event: "L87/9/9—Miss Gilbert paid L6/9/4 for after dinner drinks. I gave the head waiter L1. Total 95/9/1. Great success.") After writing Freeman Wills Crofts and John Rhode to inform them about the Berkeley brouhaha, Punshon went into hospital for an operation. In September Sayers wrote Punshon that she was pleased to hear from his wife that he was "making a really good convalescence," adding: "We will miss you greatly at the October meeting, but of course you must have a good long holiday and get quite fit."

By early November Punshon, recuperating at Christopher Bush's house, Little Horsepen, near Rye in East Sussex, was able to report that he was "very much better," though the same month he resigned as Detection Club treasurer. (Christopher Bush succeeded him to the office.) Later that month Punshon wrote Sayers from Bournemouth, where he was taking a "long rest." He wished her good fortune with the recently published Penguin paperback edition of her translation of Dante's *Inferno*, remarking, "I don't know any translation of Dante except the old one [1805] by [Henry Francis] Cary, and that was a fairly pedestrian performance." He also heaped praise on Penguin's ambitious paperback publishing scheme, deeming it a "very praiseworthy attempt to turn us into a nation of book buyers instead of borrowers. A Real Revolution—if they can bring it off." Punshon had particular reason to applaud Penguin's effort, as the previous year the company had issued a pair of 1930s Bobby Owen mystery titles as paperbacks. (Three more titles would follow in the next half-dozen years.)

Punshon remained active in Detection Club affairs in 1950, though he urged that Michael Gilbert be tapped to replace him on the membership committee. "Would [Anthony Berkeley] take the suggestion as an insult," he sarcastically queried Sayers, obviously still smarting over the events of the previous year. Punshon also participated in evaluations of the work of proposed new member Julian Symons (1912-1994), one of Britain's new wave of consciously self-styled "crime writers." Of Symons's recent *Bland Beginning* (1949), a novel based, as was Punshon's own *Comes a Stranger* (1938), on the Thomas J. Wise literary forgery scandal, Punshon wrote Sayers, "On the whole I should be inclined to say 'yes,' even though I think the character drawing deplorable and the construction and final explanation a bit shaky. But he does manage to produce a readable story and it is certainly an intelligent and clever book."

By 1952, Punshon's health had declined to the point where he felt unable to attend the Detection Club's annual dinner. "[A]s they used to say in the war, the situation on the (health) front has deteriorated," he mordantly wrote Sayers, adding ominously that he had scheduled an "appointment with a specialist." The next year, however, both he and his wife, now octogenarians, managed to make it to the dinner, much to the pleasure of Sayers, who promised, "you shan't be bothered with the [initiation] ceremony at all—there will be plenty of people to carry candles." Sayers promised the Punshons good seats at the High Table to hear philosopher Bertrand Russell speak, and in a contemporary letter Christianna Brand somewhat cattily reported observing Mrs. Punshon sitting "terribly close to the speakers so as not to miss a word, and sound asleep."

Sometime in the 1950s an increasingly fragile Punshon took a dreadful tumble down the landing steps at the Detection Club premises at Kingly Street, an event Christianna Brand vividly recollected many years later in 1979, with what seems rather callous amusement on her part:

> My last memory, or the most abiding one, of the club room in the clergy house, was of an evening when two members were initiated there instead of at the annual dinner [possibly Glyn Carr and Roy Vickers, 1955 initiates]. As they left, they stepped over the body of an elderly gentleman lying with his head in a pool of blood, just outside the door. . . . dear old Mr. Punshon, E.R. Punshon, tottering up the stone stair steps upon his private business, had fallen all the way down again and severely lacerated his scalp. My [physician] husband, groaning, dealt with all but the gore, which remained in a slowly congealing pool upon the clergy house floor. . . . However, Miss Sayers had, predictably, just the right guest for such an event, a small, brisk lady, delighted to cope. She came out on the landing and stood for a moment peering down at the unlovely mess. Not myself one to delight in hospital matters, I hovered ineffectively as much as possible in the rear. She made up her mind. "Well, I think we can manage *that* all right. Can you find me a tablespoon?"

The club room was unaccountably lacking in tablespoons. I went out and diffidently offered a large fork. "A fork? Oh, well . . ." She bent again and studied the pool of gore. "I think we can manage," she said again, cheerfully. "It's splendidly clotted."

I returned once more to the club room and closed the door; and I can only report that when it opened again, not a sign remained of any blood, anywhere. "I thought," said my husband as we took our departure before even worse might befall, "that in your oath you foreswore vampires." "She was only a *guest*," I said apologetically.

"Dear old Mr. Punshon," no vampire he, passed through a door to death in his 84th year on 23 October 1956, four years after his elder brother, Robert Halket Punshon. On 25 January 1957 the widowed Sarah Punshon presented Dorothy L. Sayers with a copy of her husband's thirty-fifth and final Bobby Owen mystery, the charmingly retrospective *Six Were Present*. "He would like to think that you had one," wrote Sarah, warmly thanking Sayers "for your appreciation of my husband's work during his writing life" and wistfully adding that she would miss her "occasional visits to the club evenings." Sayers obligingly invited Sarah to the next Detection Club dinner as her guest, but Sarah died in May, having survived her longtime spouse by merely seven months. Sayers herself would not outlast the year. As Christianna Brand rather flippantly reports, Sayers was discovered, just a week before Christmas, collapsed dead "at the foot of the stairs in her house surrounded by bereaved cats." Having ascended and descended the stairs after a busy day of shopping, Sayers had discovered her own door to death.

* * * * *

Dorothy L. Sayers's literary reputation has risen ever higher in the years since her demise, with modern authorities like the esteemed late crime writer P.D. James particularly lauding Sayers's ambitious penultimate Peter Wimsey mystery, *Gaudy Night*--a novel E.R. Punshon himself had lavishly praised in his review column in the *Manchester Guardian*--as not only a great detective novel but a great novel, with no delimiting qualification. Although he was one of Sayers's favorite crime writers, Punshon was not so fortunate with his own reputation, with his work falling into unmerited neglect for more than a half-century after his death. With the reprinting by Dean Street Press of Punshon's complete set of Bobby Owen mystery investigations—chronicled in 35 novels, five short stories and a radio play—this long period of neglect now happily has ended, however, allowing a major writer from the Golden Age of detective fiction a golden opportunity to receive, six decades after his death, his full and lasting due.

"Death on the Up-Lift"

E.R. PUNSHON'S 1941 radio play, "Death on the Up-Lift," is a major rediscovery (by mystery genre authority Tony Medawar) for fans of Golden Age mystery: not only a fine fair-play puzzle that makes most diverting reading (as it assuredly made most diverting listening for a war-stressed British audience), but also a forty-first criminal case for Punshon's most famous series sleuth, Bobby Owen, complementing the thirty-five Bobby Owen novels and five Bobby Owen short stories. Those vintage mystery fans who have followed the Bobby Owen saga as Dean Street Press has reprinted it over the last couple of years should be interested to know that "Death on the Up-Lift" takes place around the time of the cases chronicled in the 1941 Punshon detective novels *Ten Star Clues* and *The Dark Garden*, after Bobby Owen has left Scotland Yard to become an inspector in the police force of Punshon's fictional English county of Wychshire. The play technically joins the nine Bobby Owen novels, published between 1940 and 1946, that form what one might term Punshon's chronicles of Wychshire, though it takes place entirely in the West End of London, at the hoity-toity Hotel Elegance, where an extremely obnoxious British business tycoon, Sir John Briggs, holds court in a private suite on the ninth floor. In the play Bobby Owen has come to warn Sir John of a plot to steal his precious Blue John diamond, providentially putting Bobby on the scene when Sir John is murdered. The Blue John diamond, incidentally, made its original appearance in Punshon's fictional world as the eponymous bauble in the author's 1929 non-series mystery novel *The Blue John Diamond*, and the gem also makes a dazzling cameo appearance in the 1940 Bobby Owen detective novel *Four Strange Women*.

The unlamented Sir John Briggs's early background as a sailor ties in with Punshon's own family history. Not only had Punshon's maternal grandfather, David Halket, made much of his ephemeral fortune as a convict ship owner, Punshon's younger brother, Alfred Douglas Punshon--evidently as adventurous a soul as his immediately elder brother, who left a clerkship in the 1890s to roam the American West--had joined the navy at the age of sixteen in 1893, eventually rising to the rank of Chief Signal Boatswain aboard the renowned HMS *Hood*. Commissioned in 1920, "The Mighty Hood," as she was dubbed, was one of the world's largest and most powerful warships and the pride of the British navy until it shockingly exploded and sank during a Second World War confrontation with the German battleship *Bismarck*. Alfred Punshon served for only four years on HMS *Hood*, having died from a heart attack in Melbourne, Australia, in 1924, when he was but 46 years old, during *Hood*'s 1923-24 circumnavigation of the globe with the Special Service Squadron. He was described as an "excellent" officer who "carried out his duties with zeal and ability."

Curtis Evans

CHAPTER I
CONSTANT FRERES

BOBBY OWEN, on leave from Scotland Yard, and intending to spend that leave in touring the country with his wife, Olive, brought the car to a standstill and stared in rather a bewildered way at the scene before them.

"This is where the entrance used to be," he said, "and there's the old lodge-keeper's cottage, but it seems to be all wired off now and the grounds turned into a market garden by the look of them."

A little distance from where the car had halted stood the burnt-out shell of Constant Freres, once a fine old Georgian mansion till it had been destroyed in a disastrous fire towards the end of last century. The great pillared entrance had remained standing, and behind it rose a magnificent marble double stairway, apparently largely undamaged, though the gilt iron balustrade had long since vanished, and now it rose only to a desolation of fallen floors, crumbling ceilings, burnt-out rooms. Three-quarters of the roof gaped open to the sky, and what the fire had begun wind and rain were in process of completing.

But the great tower—Folly Tower as it was locally known—a landmark for miles around, a kind of annexe built on later to the east wing and, of course, entirely out of harmony with the rest of the old building, seemed also to have largely escaped damage. It still reared its sixty feet or more into the air, intact, ugly and defiant. Further away stood Constant House, a bleak, early Victorian building to which the family had retreated after the fire—temporarily as it had been hoped, permanently as it had proved. It stood at right angles to the ruin, at which, through its curtained windows, it seemed to be peering with prim disapproval.

"What on earth is that great tower for?" Olive asked, for though she had heard of it before she had not been prepared for the way in which it both dominated and fascinated.

"Goodness knows," Bobby answered. "No one else, unless it's my late respected great-great—or thereabouts grandfather, and if he did he never told. Folly Tower it soon got called. There is a story he wanted to have his coffin kept there after his death so he could have a kind of grandstand view of the Day of Resurrection when it came along. But his heir didn't approve and had him buried in the family vault, so I suppose he'll have to take his chance with the rest."

"He must have been a funny old man," Olive commented. "All the same, I rather wish it had come to you, ruins and all, and that horrid tower, too, instead of to your cousins. So swanky to be able to talk about your country estate."

"Not much swanking about it when it came to paying for the upkeep," Bobby pointed out. "Police pay doesn't run to playing at landed gentry—that's for stockbrokers. I don't know how Val Outers and Myra manage. I thought he only had his pension from the Colonial Service, and that won't amount to much. Pensions never do. Only what do we do next? As far as I remember, there's no way round for cars—only a footpath."

"Sound the horn," Olive suggested. "Someone may hear. I'm beginning to wish we hadn't come."

"Couldn't very well help," Bobby said. "After all, they're both cousins, though I've never even seen Outers. But Myra and I were kids together. She used to spend her holidays with us. Her letter rather sounded as if she were worried about something."

"Just as we were starting on our holidays," Olive grumbled, and Bobby said:

"I can't imagine how she came to know that."

Then he sounded his horn, shattering with its blast the quietude of that peaceful country scene. The sound died slowly away. From the one-storey, stone cottage which Bobby had identified as in former days that of the lodge-keeper—the family coat of arms was still visible above the doorway—there now emerged a bent and aged woman, crippled apparently, supporting herself on a single crutch. She stood there, quite still, staring straight at them, but otherwise taking no notice. Bobby gave another little, he hoped, apologetic-sounding hoot, and alighted, expecting the old lady to come to that odd wire barrier so that he could speak to her. Instead she retired into the cottage, closing the door behind her.

"Well, I never," said Olive indignantly.

"She may have gone to get someone else," Bobby said.

"The way she shut the door," Olive said.

"I think I saw a chap working over there behind those bushes," Bobby said. "He showed for a moment when I hooted," and then he tried again, wishing he could make it sound as cross as he was beginning to feel.

There was no result. The cottage door remained shut, the gardener stayed invisible.

"They don't mean to take any notice," Olive said. "Perhaps it's just that they hate motorists."

"Nice sort of welcome to the ancestral home," complained Bobby.

"There's a cyclist coming," Olive said.

Bobby moved round to the other side of the car and, as the cyclist rode up, spoke to him.

"Excuse me," he said. "I want to get to Constant House over there, beyond the tower. The entrance used to be here, but it seems to have been wired off."

"That's Dewey James's part," the cyclist answered, and he seemed slightly amused. "You ought to have taken the left-hand fork about five or six miles back. Your best plan is to go back there. It's rather a rough road, but it takes you straight to Mr Outers's place if it's that you want."

Bobby said it was and the cyclist looked as if he were going to say something, and then he changed his mind and rode on. Bobby began to turn the car. Olive said:

"That man looked funny when he knew it was Mr Outers you wanted."

"Did he?" Bobby asked absently, fully occupied turning the car on this narrow road without running into the deep ditch that bordered it on both sides.

The drive back and then on again by the left-hand fork did not take long. It was to the back of the house that the road brought them and they might well have passed the entrance but for an open gate marked simply with the word 'Freres'.

"I suppose this will be it," Bobby said, a little doubtfully, for of the house itself nothing was to be seen.

He drove through the gate, following an apparently little-used, weed-grown gravel drive. On his right was a path that seemed to be more used and to lead directly to the house, of which the chimneys were now visible above the trees that till now had largely concealed it. But that was only for foot-passengers or for cyclists and then a sharp turn in the drive brought them round to the house. Evidently their approach had been heard, for the front door was open and a tall girl was coming down the steps, guarded by stone lions, that led to it. Bobby halted the car and alighted as the girl came up.

"It is Cousin Owen, isn't it?" she said.

"It is," Bobby answered. "And you'll be Rosamund. And this is your Cousin Olive," he added as he turned to assist her to alight. "I'm afraid," he went on, "we both thought of you as quite a small girl."

"That's Mother," Rosamund explained. "She calls me 'That child' and makes people think I'm still in my cradle." As she said this she smiled faintly—coldly indeed and rather indifferently much as if it were just another of the absurdities life was constantly presenting and that you had to put up with as tolerantly as possible. She was handsome rather than pretty, dark of complexion with strong, well-formed features, her nose prominent, even thrusting above a firm-looking mouth and chin. Her teeth were magnificent, though the generally closed mouth seldom showed them. Her hair was a kind of shining darkness, as though an unseen light lurked within it, and her eyes so deeply black they seemed twin pools of light. Much more a Juno than a Venus, Bobby thought, and the impression he had of her was of one who held herself reserved and aloof, as though within her were forces she knew instinctively she must control. Even when she shook hands with Bobby her grip was firm rather than welcoming, and the kiss she submitted, as it were, to exchange with Olive remained formal and distant. "Here is Mother," she added as an older woman came running down the front-door steps.

Myra Outers was a small, plump woman, between whom and her daughter only slight resemblance existed. In her youth she had been extremely pretty, but it had been largely a prettiness of youth and colouring, of that 'school-girl complexion', and also of a certain quick, eager grace in movement. But long residence in Africa and the heavy passage of the years had robbed her of these, though of the last something still remained, and when she removed the spectacles she was wearing her eyes even yet showed clear and large and of a blue as deep and pure as Rosamund's were deep and black. Her greeting of her two guests was as exuberant and fussy as that of Rosamund had been contained. She fairly swept them both into the house under a barrage of questions, comments, and exclamations, while Rosamund with the aloof efficiency that seemed characteristic of her seated herself in the car and drove it to the adjoining garage, or, rather, cycle shed, for, as Bobby had noticed in passing, it held only three or four bicycles.

"I don't know where Val is," Myra was saying. "I thought he was in the study, but I looked and he isn't—oh, here he is now," she added as there came to the head of the stairs, and then began slowly to descend them, an immensely tall, immensely thin man, six feet and a half in height at the least, Bobby thought, though possibly his exceeding thinness might tend to exaggerate his apparent height, and then in this narrow and ill-lighted entrance it was not easy to see him or judge accurately.

But it was at least abundantly evident that this was the one of her parents from whom Rosamund derived her looks, even though the great black beard Mr Outers wore made it almost impossible to distinguish his features.

The likeness was there, though, all the same, but less perhaps in individual feature than in a kind of general overriding resemblance. The nose, however, in both father and daughter was similar, prominent and thrusting, a Roman conqueror's nose, in fact, and then too there were the eyes, deepest black in both, and in both showing something of that same elusive quality of a clear and hidden light deep in their darkness, even though with him this light in darkness had grown a little dimmed with age till now his eyes seemed withdrawn and hooded, as from long brooding over things beyond understanding. There was, too, in his manner as he greeted his visitors, much of that air of remoteness which Rosamund had managed to convey, as if they both brought themselves back with difficulty from their inner lives to the details of everyday existence. He was cordial enough, however, as he shook hands, and expressed, in what Bobby privately thought could have been suitably described as a 'few well chosen words', his pleasure in meeting relatives previously unknown in person.

"A quarter of a century—more—in deep African bush does rather isolate one," he said. "It is quite a change for us to have visitors. You understand?"

CHAPTER II
THE MEDICINE BAG

GIVING BOBBY no time to reply to this question—but probably no answer was expected—Myra bustled him and Olive upstairs to the room in which already their two suitcases had been deposited. An apologetic reference to them passed Myra by without response. It rather seemed as if she were so fully accustomed to finding necessary things done that she felt no comment was required. Then she withdrew, leaving them to themselves. Olive started to unpack—they were to stay the night—and Bobby said:

"Rosamund's doing, I expect. She must have taken them out of the car when she drove it off and carried them up here."

"Yes," agreed Olive. She finished getting out what she wanted and shut the suitcase. Then she said: "There's something about her—" but what she did not say and Bobby did not ask. Abruptly Olive said: "Myra's worried."

"You could tell that from her letter," Bobby said. "I wonder if it's Rosamund."

Olive made no comment and they went downstairs. Myra took Olive off somewhere. Rosamund did not appear. Mr Outers led Bobby into a room that was evidently his own special domain. It was long and narrow and looked the larger for being so sparsely furnished. A library table stood by the window at one end, the only window there was, so that the other extremity of the room remained in obscurity. The walls were bare except for a shotgun hanging above the mantlepiece. Two bookcases stood opposite each other, one on each side of the room, though on their shelves there seemed to be as many miscellaneous objects of one kind and another as there were books. At the room's further end, in the semi-gloom that reigned there, except on the brightest summer day, was a fine old mahogany bureau. Three rickety cane chairs were ranged before the fireplace, a brand new revolving office chair was by the library table and there were one or two other chairs. On the floor the only covering was a rug made from a lionskin. Altogether Bobby thought he had seldom seen a room in which there were so few indications of the occupant's character or interests. Strange then that it also gave such an impression of holding within itself a throbbing, concealed energy, such an impression indeed as Bobby had already received from Rosamund when she came out to greet them.

"I expect luncheon is nearly ready," Mr Outers said. He waved a hand round the room. "Where I work," he said, but gave no indication of what the work might be.

"Oh, yes," Bobby said, and for want of something else to say he went on: "You have a nice outlook here," for the room's one window gave a pleasant view over open country, a northern view, the house itself facing west and overlooking that market garden which once had been the great lawn and the shrubberies and flower beds that had composed the Constant Freres grounds.

From a cupboard under one of the bookcases Mr Outers now produced sherry. He poured out two glasses and Bobby, though no connoisseur, recognized at the first taste that the variety was that known as 'cooking'. He consoled himself with the reflection that it might have been cocktail or cocoa, both of which he detested.

"Folklore," Mr Outers said abruptly. "African folklore."

"That must be very interesting," Bobby commented, with the mental proviso that no doubt so it was to some people.

"Frightening," declared Mr Outers, glowering at Bobby over his great black beard. "You understand?"

"Well, really, I know so little about it," said Bobby, hurriedly warding off an attempt to fill his glass again with that rather trying sherry.

Mr Outers turned to fill his own glass, found to his apparent surprise that it was still nearly full, since so far he had merely tasted it, and then pointed to the bureau at the back of the room.

"I have a witch-doctor's medicine bag in there," he said. "I bought it from an African as he was dying. He didn't want to take it with him. He made me promise that I would never open it. You understand?"

"Oh, yes," Bobby agreed. "Promises should always be kept."

"I know. I have," Mr Outers said gloomily. "You're in the police, Myra says?"

"Quite true," admitted Bobby, and added as a precaution, "I'm on leave at the moment, at least as far as a policeman ever is on leave."

"I was a district officer," Mr Outers told him. "A district officer has to act as a policeman sometimes. You understand? Then he gets blamed. If he doesn't, he gets blamed again, only more."

"Oh, well, that's often the case everywhere," Bobby commented.

"A district officer," Mr Outers repeated. "I never got much promotion. My ideas didn't meet with approval. I was told I was giving support to the witch-doctors. They were unprogressive, opposed to our civilizing mission. The missionaries. They complained I was encouraging devil worship. It was the chiefs I ought to have backed. Chiefs all muddled with a Christianity they made no sense of, a college education that cut at the root of all their traditional knowledge, and a way of government that prevented them from governing in the only way they knew."

"It must be pretty confusing," Bobby said. "One can only hope it will all straighten out in time. You were interested in native beliefs?"

"Devil worship, the missionaries called it," Mr Outers said. "A wicked mistranslation. The early Christians did the same thing. Tried to make out that Venus and Mars and the rest of them were demons. Fiddlesticks, of course. The African word ought to have been simply translated 'power'—the hidden power. No good or evil about it in our sense. The hidden power that makes the world tick. So keep on the right side of it and the witch-doctor knows best how to do that and others had best keep out of it. Exactly like Christianity."

"Well, there are differences after all, aren't there?" Bobby suggested mildly. "Of course, I know nothing about what Africans believe."

"The science of the West," Mr. Outers said. "The wisdom of the East. The insight of the African. A synthesis of these might take us somewhere. Do have some more sherry?"

From this fate Bobby was saved by the sudden appearance of Rosamund.

"Luncheon's ready," she announced. "I'm sorry about the sherry," she added, looking doubtfully at the glasses on the library table. "Mr Baynton and Mr Manners both say it's poison, but we haven't got any whisky. It's so dear."

Bobby hastened to assure her that he seldom tasted spirits and never before night, but Rosamund didn't seem to be listening. She was looking at her father, frowning from under her dark, overhanging brows.

"You've been talking to Cousin Owen about the medicine bag," she said accusingly. "Or why is it so dark over there by the bureau?"

Mr Outers didn't answer. Bobby said, rather feebly:

"The sun has just gone in."

Rosamund took no notice of this remark. She moved towards the door. The two men followed her into the hall, past the foot of the stairs into a large, pleasant room, conventionally furnished with a dining-room suite evidently from Tottenham Court Road—though perhaps, Bobby thought, at one remove. He noticed, too, and with more interest, some paintings on the wall, sombre, dreamlike productions, where even a still life of fish on a large china plate seemed to convey its own mute warning. He felt he would like to examine these more closely. The window overlooked the market garden, as Bobby took it to be, with its neat orderly beds of vegetables and its rows of fruit bushes. On the left were the ruins of Constant Freres and its tall, adjacent tower. At the window Myra and Olive were standing together, watching a scene outside that apparently interested them. Olive was saying as Bobby and the others entered:

"I can't think how she possibly can."

"Rosamund," Myra said. "Teddy Peel's here."

"I know," Rosamund said, and did not look pleased.

Bobby joined Olive at the window. Mr Outers stood by the table already laid for luncheon. He was fidgeting with the knives and forks as if their arrangement did not altogether please him. Olive said to Bobby:

"Just look. How does she manage?"

This referred to the scene outside. Beyond the low wooden fence—almost a token fence, in fact—that seemed to mark the dividing line between the market garden territory and that still appertaining to Constant House was the old crippled woman Bobby and Olive had seen previously at the door of her cottage—the old Constant Freres lodge. She was now however using her crutch not so much as a means of support but for giving emphasis to what she was saying. She seemed to be talking with some heat to a smallish man in bowler hat and rain-coat, carrying a dispatch case and a badly rolled umbrella. Bobby guessed—quite wrongly as it turned out—that he was a travelling salesman of one sort or another, either trying to make a fresh sale or to collect instalments on what had been already sold. There was a second man there, too, but he did not seem to be taking much part in the lively discussion or argument or whatever it was, going on between the other two. Neither Bobby nor Olive could see him clearly, as he was half hidden behind a line of raspberry canes, though now and again he bobbed up under a cloth cap to say something or other, of which apparently no notice was ever taken.

"Oh, look," Olive exclaimed, for the crippled woman had just aimed a vicious thrust with her crutch at the little man in the bowler hat, before which he skipped away with an entirely justifiable prudence. From behind Rosamund said:

"That's Mrs James, Dewey's mother. She tries to do without her crutch as much as she can. She can't quite, of course, but she is more active on one leg than most people are on two."

"How did she lose it?" Olive asked.

"During the war, while she was at the B.B. works. Mr Baynton says she was an awfully good mechanic, just as good with her tools as any of them or better. Only then there was an accident. A wheel flew loose or something. Several people were hurt and Mrs James lost her leg. They started their market garden with the money she got in compensation. I don't think Dewey's an awfully good gardener," she added thoughtfully, "and then it's poor soil he says, all chalk underneath."

"Oh, look," Olive said, for now the little man in the bowler hat was fairly on the run and it almost seemed as if Mrs James would have started in pursuit had not the second man run out from behind the raspberry canes to stop her.

"That's Dewey; he's her son," Rosamund said, and add-ed, almost defiantly it seemed. "He's terribly deformed—a hunchback."

CHAPTER III
STUDENT OF THE OCCULT

THAT DEWEY JAMES was a hunchback was something to which it seemed hardly necessary to call attention. He was also, as those so afflicted often are, almost a dwarf, a full head and shoulders shorter than his mother. He gave also the impression of possessing great physical strength, with long arms reaching nearly to his knees.

The two of them, the crippled mother, the deformed son, walked away together; and Mr Outers, rousing himself suddenly from his apparent absorption with the placing of the knives and forks on the table, said to no one in particular:

"What about lunch?"

"It's all ready," Rosamund said. "You others sit down. I'll get it." She disappeared, returning quickly with a plump roast chicken, which Bobby regarded with highly apprecia-tive eyes. "We've no help," Rosamund explained, "except a daily who doesn't come as often as not. We practically live on chicken," she went on apologetically. "We did, too, out there, only they are so different at home."

"Skinny," said Mr Outers. "All skin and bone. Rosamund feeds these up. Grain. Milk. Scraps from the kitchen. Cod liver oil."

The roast chicken was followed by an egg soufflé and by coffee—tea for Myra—such as neither Bobby nor Olive had ever met before. Myra explained that it was sent direct to them from 'out there'.

"An African planter," Rosamund said. "Father knew him. He grows better coffee than anyone else. No one knows how he does it and he won't say. All the white planters are furious."

"Brings its own price," Mr Outers said. "You understand? Used for blending. You can't buy it retail. He sends us ten pounds twice a year. A gift."

"Because Father was interested in African ideas," Rosamund put in, "and he stuck up for the witch-doctors."

"I never drink coffee," Myra said; and said it with an unexpected emphasis that struck a sudden silence on them all.

It was an awkward silence, a silence to be felt as it were. One sensed that Mr Outers's mouth, hidden beneath his great black beard, was tightly closed. Rosamund was staring straight in front of her, but the knuckles of her hands, clasped in front of her upon the table, showed white with the force with which she held them. To break that silence, Bobby said something about those paintings on the walls he had noticed immediately he entered the room.

"Rosamund does them," Myra said, but not with much show of pride or appreciation.

"When she's not fattening up the chickens, she's painting," Mr Outers said. "Jolly good, too. Gets it all just as it is. You understand?"

"The dealers don't think they are jolly good," Rosamund interposed. "One of them said people didn't like nightmares. He told me to change my style and do flowers or jolly little landscapes with lots of sunshine—sunny glades in springtime."

"Don't change your style to please the dealers," Bobby warned her. "In art, always follow your own nose."

Rosamund received this advice in silence, evidently slightly puzzled by it. But by now luncheon was over. The three women set to work to clear the table while Mr Outers and Bobby took themselves out of the way to the room where they had been before. Now it had another occupant, that same little man Bobby had seen flee with such speed before the deadly thrust of Mrs James's crutch. He rose as the other two entered, clutching his bowler hat in one hand, his baggy umbrella in the other.

"Miss Rosamund said I could wait here," he explained. "It's about to-morrow night. Mr Owen, I presume? Pleased to meet you, sir. An honour."

"I'm afraid I don't remember you at the moment," Bobby said, searching his memory to see if among all those many others with whom his work was so continually bringing him into contact, he could place this little man with his small, pale eyes, his indeterminate features, his muddy complexion, his sharp, little pointed nose.

"Our paths have never crossed before to-day," the little man assured him. "But Mr Owen is well known. I also may claim the same in my more restricted sphere. I regret my own encounters with our wholly admirable but possibly at times rather too enthusiastic police forces have not always been so agreeable as I for my part could have wished."

"Oh, well," Bobby murmured, thinking this was at least candid.

"Twice," the other said. "On two separate occasions. But each time discharged without a stain, and on the last occasion with a definite expression of opinion that proceedings should never have been brought."

"Mr Peel—" Outers began, but was promptly interrupted.

"Teddy Peel," the little man corrected him. "Such has become, if I may say so, my professional name. So am I billed. So am I universally known. My cognomen. If you please."

"Mr Peel," Outers resumed as if he had not heard a word of this, "is a medium well known, I believe, among spiritualists, but not recognized by all of them, the most responsible ones. Caught out faking more than once."

"Not me. The power," Mr Peel protested. He lifted a hand, dropping his bowler hat in the process. He stooped to recover it. "Not me," he repeated. "And I'm not a medium, Mr Outers, sir, as I've said before. A humble student of the occult. That's me. But sometimes the power fails, it can't get through; then in its impatience it short circuits the message, so to say." He paused to shake his head reproachfully at such behaviour. "Or else it fades out and then mischievous, even evil influences rush in. But I can generally cope."

"What the witch-doctors say," Outers commented. "Medicine gone bad is how they put it."

"Is it too much to hope that Mr Owen will honour us to-morrow evening?" Teddy Peel asked, and, without waiting for a reply—possibly Bobby did not look very encouraging—he went on: "Mr Baynton is anxious to be present. I might say very anxious. Mr Manners, of course. He has shown himself greatly impressed. A substantial monetary gain he informed me."

"So he told me," Outers agreed. "Naturally. Money talks. Results." He turned to Bobby: "You understand?" He turned back to Teddy. "The witch-doctors, too. They produce results or they are believed to. The same thing. Settle it all with Mrs Outers, just as she wants. She's somewhere about. Wait in the hall, will you? I'll find her for you presently."

Teddy expressed his thanks and managed to edge himself out of the room without further talk. Bobby, a little puzzled, a little wary, more than ever determined to attend no meeting with which Teddy had anything to do, settled himself in the rickety basket chair Outers now pushed forward. A box of cigars was produced, but Bobby—a little afraid these cigars might be to other cigars as his before-luncheon sherry had been to other sherries—asked if he might have one of his own cigarettes instead. Mr Outers seemed to think some explanation of Mr. Peel was necessary. He said:

"I don't know exactly where Teddy came from. He's managed to impose himself. He seemed to know a lot, things he shouldn't have known. Myra's quite accepted him. So has Rosamund. It's the top room of the tower where we meet now. Things have happened. Ludovic Manners—Ludo they call him. A business-man from Midminster. Over there." He made a vague gesture in the direction of that famous city some twenty miles or so distant. "He and Rosamund are friendly and Myra says he wants to be more friendly still. Information he got through Teddy was worth a lot of money to him, he says. You understand?"

"I do indeed," Bobby admitted. "No getting away from money. But you have to take into account lucky guesses, co-incidence, scraps of information picked up somehow, that sort of thing. There's always the traditional test—who is going to win the Derby? I'm afraid I don't feel an awful lot inclined to trust Mr Teddy Peel any further than I can see him. Not quite so far in fact."

"A bit of a rogue, a bit of a charlatan," Outers agreed dispassionately. "But the power comes—sometimes. It's the same with the witch-doctors out there. Immaterial. A priest may betray his altar, but the altar remains. Teddy knew—" Outers paused, glanced towards the end of the room where the old mahogany bureau stood, resumed: "He knew about the medicine bag I've got, he knew where it was, he knew how I got it. He knew the man who gave it me said it had gone bad. He knew what was in it."

Bobby looked entirely unconvinced.

"Surely he could easily have got to know all that by entirely normal means," he said. "But didn't you tell me you had never opened the thing? So you can't be sure he's right about that, can you?"

"I never opened it and I never shall," Outers repeated and was silent for a moment or two, then resumed: "I promised. But I was told by the man I got it from. A dead man's hand. The hand of a man who had been buried alive. A sacrifice."

"Good God!" Bobby muttered below his breath. "What an idea," and in his mind buzzed confused memories of the Hand of Glory, that ancient, widely-spread, rather horrible superstition.

"Ludo is rather keen on opening it," Outers continued. "He'll never get the chance, not while I live. I think Rosamund would agree. Perhaps Myra, too. Ludo would like to go out there. Rosamund would, too. Not Myra. There's the uranium. Teddy knew about that as well."

"Uranium?" Bobby exclaimed, startled. "Do you mean there's uranium in this thing of yours?"

"Not uranium itself," Outers answered. "A map. A big field, it may be the biggest, richest in the world. The natives know, but the witch-doctors have warned them never to tell the white man, and if they do all their lands will be taken from them. It's in a native reservation. A white man did find it two or three years ago, so they poisoned him, but not before he had drawn a map. They didn't dare destroy that. They thought it was big medicine, so they put it in the bag I've got. That's what made the first medicine go bad, so now there are two strong medicines, both bad, each making the other worse. That's what they thought. You understand?"

"What are you going to do about it?" Bobby asked.

"Nothing. Why should I?" Outers asked in return. "Some day it will be found. Then the poor devils will lose their lands. Progress. You understand."

"There would be ample compensation," Bobby said, though with some hesitation.

"Oh, ample," Outers agreed, tugging fiercely at his big black beard. "Only thing, they would die of it. To a native, to lose his land is to lose his life. Ludo would like to get hold of the map. He won't. Not while I'm alive. Perhaps that's why he wants Rosamund. He has plans. Full of them. Shall we see if we can find the ladies? I expect Teddy is still waiting."

CHAPTER IV
THE DEATH WISH

However, in the hall there was no sign of Teddy Peel. Mr Outers muttered something about his having probably been picked up by Myra or someone, and he and Bobby went out to the front, where already Folly Tower was throwing its long dark shadow over flower beds and shrubs. Bobby made some complimentary remark, for indeed they made a pleasant sight, though of no great extent.

"Myra and Rosamund look after it between them," Outers explained. "Dewey James helps with the heavier work, the digging and rolling and so on. They oughtn't to let him. Rosamund says they try not to, but he won't take any notice. He has enough of his own work to attend to. There they are now," and this was said with a kind of undertow of strong resentment.

Bobby had already noticed them standing near Freres Lodge, talking and laughing together. Mrs James came round the corner of the building, swinging along with astonishing agility on her crutch. When she saw them, she paused, swung round equally nimbly and disappeared as swiftly as she had come. It was rather like a vanishing trick and one that did not seem to please Outers, who was tugging at his beard in a way he had when he was troubled or annoyed. Bobby, looking up at the tower, said:

"When we were kids, Myra and I used to have races to see who could get to the top first. Myra won as often as not. You get a fine view up there."

"It's where we meet," Outers said. "Teddy's idea. He said it helped being so high up. Myra and Rosamund. Mrs James. According to Teddy, her presence is necessary. She's not a medium herself, but she is a reserve of power. That's what he says."

"Can she manage the climb?" Bobby asked.

"As well as anyone—better," Outers answered. "You would be surprised. Then there's generally Bryan Baynham—B.B. he gets called. He's Chairman of the B.B. Agricultural Implement Manufacturing Company—the people Mrs James was working for when she lost her leg. But he's a sceptic. All humbug. That's what he says."

"What's he go for, then?" Bobby asked.

"Rosamund," Outers explained. "They quarrel about it. He tells her it's nonsense and she tells him it's no business of his. They're on speaking terms at present, but that's about all. If you would like to join us to-morrow, your wife too if she cared to—sometimes things do happen."

"I'm afraid we could hardly fit it in," Bobby answered somewhat hurriedly, beginning to suspect that to secure his attendance had been the chief cause and object of Myra's somewhat obscure but certainly appealing letter.

Well, if that had been the idea it wasn't going to come off. Of that Bobby was more than ever determined. He found himself wondering if it was because the same sort of gentle, indirect pressure was being put on Olive that she and Myra had remained so long invisible. Meanwhile, Rosamund and Dewey James were still laughing and talking together and Bobby, watching them, said:

"Does Mr Dewey James come with his mother?"

"No," answered Outers. "He doesn't approve. He tried to get his mother to stop away and he tells Rosamund she ought to give it up. He is the only one she'll listen to. B.B. she shuts up at once, but Dewey can say what he likes. She's sorry for him. You understand?"

Bobby said he did. Outers looked as if he didn't. From behind the house a man now appeared. He was young, sturdily built, handsome in a dark moody way with hair and eyes almost as black as Rosamund's that were like night itself. He walked with a light, swift step and then stood still suddenly, rather like a dog scenting game. Apparently he had not noticed Outers and Bobby, standing near the house, a little to one side. Instead he was staring hard at Rosamund and Dewey, and, though Bobby was not near enough to see his features plainly, he had the feeling that it was no friendly stare thus concentrated on those two standing and laughing in the sunshine by the old lodge. It was almost, Bobby thought, like a jealous lover watching a rival making unexpected progress in the favour of his mistress. But surely that could not be. This confident, well-dressed, prosperous-looking young man did not seem one likely to be jealous of a hunchback, an almost dwarf, a market gardener or smallholder not making much of a success of his job.

"It's Ludo Manners," Mr Outers was saying. "About tomorrow I expect."

By this time Ludo had become aware of their presence. He came towards them, but still with more than half his attention given to Rosamund and Dewey. Now Rosamund laughed again and ran off, turning as she went to wave a gay farewell. Dewey did not acknowledge that parting gesture, but there was something in his attitude as he stood motionless that made Bobby think of an acolyte watching disappear the vision of his goddess that had been vouchsafed to him. At Bobby's side Outers was saying as much to himself as to Bobby.

"You don't often hear her laugh like that."

Ludo had joined them now. He looked frowning and disturbed and his eyes were full of anger as they rested on the motionless Dewey still watching the disappearing figure of Rosamund. Even in his voice there was a kind of rumble of suppressed resentment as he exchanged greetings with Outers—whom he addressed as 'Val'—and expressed his pleasure at meeting Bobby, of whom, he said, he had heard so much from 'Val and Myra'. A young man very much at ease in the world, Bobby thought, and evidently a devotee of the new fashion of addressing all and sundry by their Christian names. A little inclined, too, to be rather patronizing towards others who he felt would never reach the heights he himself was so sure of attaining.

"Myra's hoping you will be joining us to-morrow," he was saying now. "I can promise you things do happen—things I own up I can't account for."

"I've been hearing about that," Bobby said. "A solid financial result?"

"That's right," Ludo said beamingly. "Though, mind you, it took working out. I'm an insurance broker and all out of the blue Teddy said he had a message for me about a Midminster firm being headed straight for trouble. No bis. of mine, I wasn't a shareholder or anything. Why should I be told? But what I say is, if you do get tipped off, follow it up. If it's all hunkadory, no harm done. If it isn't, take appropriate action. How come, you say, you having no standing. Bit of a problem, but I worked it out. I found a big Midminster man, a real V.I.P., had just put a sizeable bit of capital into the firm for developments. I managed to get an introduction to him and I talked him into letting me insure him at Lloyd's against any loss if the developments went wrong. Lloyd's thought the risk derisory, so was the premium, my commission the same, only more so, and then when the crash came, there was my V.I.P. sitting pretty, with a claim on Lloyd's to cover every penny of his loss. Nothing in it for me, you say? That's where you're wrong," and he smiled triumphantly at this rebuttal of an opinion that Bobby had neither formed nor expressed. "Sent my prestige away up. I don't need to go to people now; they come to me. And my V.I.P. hasn't forgotten I saved him thousands of pounds—thousands."

"Very interesting," Bobby said, still cautious, but undeniably impressed.

"And if you ask me how Teddy knew—well, I can't tell you," Ludo added. "Beats me. Flummoxed I am." And that anything should 'beat' him, or that he should ever be 'flummoxed' seemed to astonish him more than had done the happenings themselves.

"Do you know, I rather think I should like to climb the Folly again—there's a magnificent view," Bobby remarked to Mr. Outers.

"Not for me," declared Ludo promptly. "Too much of a fag by half. Folly—that's right," he added, chuckling throatily.

"Well, why not?" Outers said. To Ludo, he said: "Wait for us here, will you?" and received the prompt assurance that that young gentleman would be around.

"Mooch around till someone shows," he said. "I might see if I can find Rosamund," and for a moment a faintly complacent smile showed itself and vanished.

He strolled away then and the other two began their climb, Bobby telling himself that he rather wished he had not eaten quite such a good luncheon, but thinking also that to run up and down those interminable stairs two or three times a day would be excellent training for anyone. He noticed that what once had been a communicating door between the Folly and the first floor of the old house was still there, though now more as a doorway than as a door, this being represented by a few boards placed crossways in position, presumably to forbid its use as an entry to the old ruin. No doubt it was in a highly dangerous condition and should have been demolished long ago.

A little out of breath, he reached the top chamber, but it was not the view, the professed object of the climb, in which he showed most interest. He had indeed really yielded to a curious urge he had felt to visit the scene of Ludo's experience. Then, too, there had been Ludo's assurance that 'things'—unspecified 'things'—happened there. It was just possible, Bobby told himself, that he would be able to find something either to confirm or deny the doubts and suspicions he felt.

In his boyhood this upper chamber had been entirely empty: stone walls, stone roof, stone floor, four unglazed windows, north, south, east and west, through which the four winds of heaven blew unchecked, by which with his telescope the original builder of the Folly had been able at ease to survey the surrounding country—an inactive god high above all earthly things. In one corner a small winding stair led up to the flat roof, guarded only by a low parapet, so that to venture out on it was an ordeal some would not have cared to brave.

Now all that was changed. There were rugs on the floor, the four windows had been provided with glass, shutters, curtains: there were chairs and a table, against the wall stood an enormous gramophone. Doors had been fitted both where the steps from below ended and where those others led up to the flat roof. Before them, too, curtains hung.

Up here, the doors closed, the windows shuttered, the curtains drawn, one would be as private from the world as remote from all earthly influences as well could be. Outers, a puffing, panting Outers, had joined him now, and stood in the doorway, tugging at his beard with both hands, a sure sign that he was feeling troubled and uneasy. As he remained silent, apparently disinclined to speak, making no reply to Bobby's first rather banal remark about its being a long climb, Bobby added that it must have been difficult to get all these things up that steep stairway with all its twists and turns.

"We all helped," Outers mumbled in response, "Ludo, Dewey, B.B. too."

"B.B." repeated Bobby, and then, remembering: "Oh, yes. Bryan Baynham, another Midminster man. Was he impressed, too?"

"No. He only comes because of Rosamund. He proposed to her, but she put him off, and then they quarrelled."

"Over these meetings?" Bobby asked.

"Over both wanting their own way," Outers told him.

"It's a common cause of quarrels," Bobby commented, and thought that with Bryan Baynham proposing, Ludo Manners obviously courting, and Dewey James still more obviously worshipping, Miss Rosamund had her hands as full as any girl could reasonably desire. Yet she had in no way given him the impression that she was anything of a flirt. Secret depths in her, he thought, not easy to fathom, depths perhaps that neither she nor others should ever try to explore. When Outers offered no comment on what he had just said, but just pulled his beard harder and looked more gloomy even than before, Bobby went on: "There are plenty of ways of explaining the message Ludo got without calling in spirits."

"Not spirits," Outers mumbled in an interruption Bobby hardly heard.

"Coincidence, for instance," he said. "Or just a lucky guess. Or thought transference. Manners may have heard some bit of gossip, paid it no attention at the moment, stowed it away in his unconscious till it worked itself into Peel's mind and Manners got it back again."

"It proved true," Outers reminded him.

"Ideas sometimes work out their own truth," Bobby said; and now Outers looked at him so strangely from those dark, glittering eyes of his that Bobby was quite startled. It seemed he had said something that for Outers had a significance far beyond Bobby's knowledge or intention. He began to speak.

He said: "I mean—" and then paused, for indeed he did not know what he had meant.

"It is why Myra is afraid," Outers said. "It may be there is a death wish loose among us and she is afraid."

CHAPTER V
TRAGIC STORY

CONSIDERABLY STARTLED, Bobby looked at his companion for a moment or two in silence. Then he said sharply, frowningly:

"What does that mean? Whose death wish?"

Outers it was who this time remained silent. He had suddenly begun to look very tired, as if the effort of saying what he had just said had exhausted him. When he moved from the doorway where he had been standing to sit down on one of the chairs by the table in the centre of the room, he walked like an old man. Bobby repeated his question; and this time, but mumbling so that his words could hardly be heard, Outers replied:

"What you said yourself," he muttered. "Just now. The witch-doctors, too. They tell you that when a thought is born, if it is strong enough, it seeks instinctively to find a mind where it can come to life in action—just as a newborn child strives by instinct to become a man to express itself in deed. The Church warns against dangerous thinking. In the West, psychologists are beginning to ask if when a deed is done, is it done by the doer or is it done through him?" and Bobby, hearing this, remembered that once he had listened to almost those very words spoken by a man who had indeed acted suddenly, swiftly, almost without intention.

For a moment he had the impression that in this high lonely room unseen forces were at work. Angrily he tried to throw it off, but he found himself crossing to a window to assure himself that the sun still shone without, that the winds still blew. He came back and sat down opposite Outers, who once more had sunk into a dark silence.

"Tell me more," he said.

"We had two sons," Outers answered in the dull, flat voice that now had come to him. "They knew African beliefs. They had been born there, always lived there, they knew more than I ever did. The Africans told them things, said things before them that would never have been said before me—things the boys did not always tell again to me. There are initiation ceremonies when boys become men. You'll know that. Everywhere, in every age, always secret, secret and sacred. No woman is ever present, no European—above all, no European. It is death to try, instant death. Our two boys thought they would find out what really happened, for none would ever tell them that, neither their playmates nor those who had been their nurses in babyhood, their teachers and friends and daily companions since their birth. One night they slipped away to try. They did not return. Months later some bones were found. In the deep bush. Boys. European."

"They had been murdered," Bobby said.

"We do not know. We hope that was all. It depends on how much they had seen or heard. It may be that when they were discovered they were taken into the bush and left to find their own way home, but not before the initiation ceremonies were over. It might be like that. We shall never know."

"A tragic story," Bobby said, more moved than he cared to show.

"Rosamund has never been the same since," Outers said. "She used to be always laughing, but not now. She was older than the twins, but they were always together, she and they."

"Was it this Myra was thinking of when she wrote to us?" Bobby asked.

"I expect so. I dare say," Outers answered wearily. "I didn't know she had written till afterwards. They have never forgotten—she and Rosamund. It is always between us, though we never speak of it. Sometimes I think Myra still hopes the boys may even yet return. Sometimes I think Rosamund knows things she has never told me. I was blamed. I was held responsible. You understand? There was talk that I knew what the boys meant to do, it was said that I had sent them. People said I ought to have known and stopped it. They said it came of 'going native', as some called it. I was told it was my fault for trying to get at what the Africans really thought, giving them the idea there might be something worthwhile in their beliefs instead of teaching them their own ideas were all wrong, all evil, and they must learn European beliefs, ways, thoughts. The missionaries preached all that."

"What started this notion that there is a death wish loose among you?" Bobby asked.

"It was one evening," Outers answered. "We were sitting here. We all heard it. A voice—a thin, cracked voice. From near the roof, above the table we were sitting at. We had been a long time, sitting there. We thought nothing was going to happen. It was like that at times. Teddy Peel said communications seemed blocked, and he didn't think it was any use sitting any longer. Then it came, the voice from above, I mean."

"Teddy Peel," Bobby repeated. "I don't think I trust him much. I should want to know a lot more before I accepted anything that happened when he was there."

"Yes," agreed Outers. "There's that. You've always got to sort these things out. We all heard it—that thin, cracked voice, high up against the roof, very thin, very cold, distant."

"Ventriloquism can do a lot," Bobby suggested.

"It was spoken in Bantu," Outers said. "There are many different varieties of Bantu, but this was that spoken in the district where I was stationed. I don't suppose there are more than twenty or thirty whites in all the world who can speak it. Teddy Peel can hardly be one of them; he has never even been in Africa or near it."

Bobby was not convinced. He had experience of the strange bits of knowledge rogues and charlatans sometimes manage to pick up and use to convince others of their honesty. But he was deeply concerned and yet did not know what could be done. A little resentful, too, at being brought unawares into such a troubled situation.

"I must ask Myra," he said rather vaguely. "I still don't quite see why she wrote to me. Surely the best thing to do is just to ignore this 'death wish' as you call it, forget all about it."

"It is not easy to forget it," Outers said. "It is never easy to forget. And there may be some minds not willing to ignore it."

"Whose minds?" Bobby asked; and when Outers showed no sign of being willing to answer that, Bobby repeated: "I must speak to Myra."

"Thoughts may be forgotten or ignored and then they may die," Outers went on. "But they may be too strong for either forgetting or ignoring. They may be smothered at birth. They may be frightened into not even wishing or trying to be born into deed. To catch ill wishes before they grow strong is what witch doctors are for. They do it, or try to, by spells, incantations and so on, by ways they keep secret, by what they call their medicine. The Christian priest would urge prayer and penance. No doubt it is a better way. But it is not the African way."

"I am neither witch-doctor nor priest," Bobby said.

"Ideas, death wishes," Outers continued unheedingly, "can be checked or destroyed, whichever word you prefer, by fear. Fear is a great preventative. All religions have a hell. Myra may have thought that with you you would bring fear—a fear that the death wish would feel and no longer try to grow into a mind and then it would wither away into nothingness. And then perhaps Myra and Rosamund would find release, the release they need, though they don't know it."

Bobby got to his feet. He felt he only understood half, or less, of what had been said, yet that half was enough profoundly to disturb him. Was it possible, he wondered, that Outers had been hinting that his wife and daughter, or both, brooding over the loss of sons and brothers, might seek a dreadful reparation? Did they believe—or know—that Outers had in fact encouraged, more than encouraged, the two unfortunate boys to undertake their disastrous quest? He might conceivably have done so, believing that as his sons they would be immune. Or was this 'death wish' warning, if it had in fact occurred as related, perhaps concerned with something else altogether, some other rivalry or strain? For that matter, Outers might be aware of hidden impulses, pressures, in himself that he needed help to combat. This strange primaeval African 'medicine', as he called it, that he had apparently studied so deeply, had it affected him more than he had realized?

"Shall we go down again?" Bobby asked, putting these doubts and fears aside.

"I thought you ought to know," Outers said.

They made the long descent in silence. Bobby at least was glad enough to leave a room that was beginning to seem to him full of dark and angry menace. It was a relief when he found his feet once more on firm and solid earth. In the shade of some trees in front of the house, a trolley table was now in position. Rosamund was busy arranging cups and saucers on it. Bobby had had no idea that the hour had grown so late as to warrant preparations for tea. He experienced an odd sense of relief as he watched Rosamund so busy with so homely, so pleasant a task? What could be further removed from the dark mysteries of the deep, African bush than afternoon tea on an English lawn? It seemed to put him once more in touch with the solid realities of everyday life, to sweep away the cobwebs that primaeval fancies had left over from a dreaming, superstitious past that had no possible concern with this scientific, technological age where all nature dances to our tune. He began to feel quite cheerful again, and to feel, too, that it had been rather silly of him to have taken Outer's story of the thin, cracked voice from the roof and the warning that there was a 'death wish' loose among them quite so seriously.

"Anyhow, one thing's plain," he told himself cheerfully. "Teddy Peel's a fraud."

STANDING NEAR that inviting-looking trolley which had served to recall Bobby to the realm of common sense were two young men, both looking exceedingly sulky, both with their hands in their pockets, neither speaking. The one to the left was the Ludo Manners Bobby had already met. The other was tallish, youngish, rather untidy, wearing horn-rimmed spectacles with thick lenses, behind which his eyes were hidden. He was beginning to grow bald and he would have passed unnoticed in the crowd in almost any Western country. Only a second glance would perhaps have taken count of the thrust-out chin, a mouth set in firm lines, and a certain suggestion in his stance of restrained, even violent strength, all ready to leap into action if required.

Rosamund came out again carrying a stand laden with cakes. Both the young men watched avidly, but neither of them moved to help her. Bobby had the impression that both had been, so to say, 'warned off the course', and he noticed that the two of them were scowling at each other even more openly than before.

"Punch-your-head-for-you wish trying very hard not to be born into deed," Bobby told himself, and giggled in a way that betrayed how much his nerves had been affected by that long, strange talk in the upper chamber of the Folly Tower.

From behind, Mr Outers, who had now come up to join them, called out:

"Oh, B.B., you've got here, then. You haven't met my cousin, Mr Owen, have you?"

"I've heard of him," B.B. answered, moving forward to shake hands.

"Cousin Olive and Mother are just coming," Rosamund interposed. "I told them tea was ready. They've been talking all afternoon."

Myra and Olive had in fact just emerged from the house; and Bobby needed only a glance at Olive to tell him she, too, was troubled and disturbed. He guessed she had probably been listening to the same sad story he had heard. Myra, on the other hand, seemed much more composed, even lively, than she had been earlier on; and Bobby got the impression that this did not altogether please Rosamund.

"I'll pour out," she announced, seating herself before the cups and saucers; and Bobby saw her look an invitation at Ludo to take the chair by her side, which he did with alacrity.

"Now we are all hunkadory," he said, not without a triumphant look at B.B. Her mother and Olive, Rosamund placed with the same authority, putting Bobby next to Myra and Olive next to Mr Outers. The result of these manœuvres was that B.B. was left rather on the outskirts of the little group, with only a very small, rickety chair to sit on. He looked at it doubtfully, picked it up and put it down again. He said aloud:

"I don't think I had better risk sitting on that—might break my neck. I'll squat on the grass instead," and he established himself almost at Rosamund's feet. "I can still pass the bread and butter," he announced.

"Don't trouble. Besides, there isn't any," Rosamund said icily; and Ludo, at whom Bobby took a quick glance, looked—well, the phrase that came into Bobby's mind was 'like murder', but that was silly and only showed, Bobby supposed, how badly frayed were his nerves. No wonder he had been told he needed a holiday.

"No. I see there isn't," B.B. was saying, answering Rosamund's remark and looking very hard at the plate in the middle of the trolley table.

"Margarine," said Rosamund briefly.

"Such nice margarine," put in Olive; and now it was Rosamund who flushed and looked away, for she knew from Olive's tone that Olive had tasted it and had recognized it as real country butter, freshly made, too.

It was a piece of nice, polite homely comedy with Miss Rosamund playing off one young man against the other; and in it Bobby found such refreshment and relief he almost forgot that long talk in the Folly Tower with its dark African background.

It was considerably later, not till the two young men had departed, Rosamund and her mother vanished into the kitchen, and Outers himself to the brooding solitude of his own room, that Bobby found an opportunity to be alone with Olive. They knew each other sufficiently well to be sure at once that each had heard the same strange tragic tale.

"It's rather a horrible story," Olive said.

"I don't see why we had to hear it," Bobby grumbled.

"Myra is frightened," Olive said; and Bobby nodded a gloomy assent, for he knew well what strange things people can do in fear.

"It's why she started those sittings, up there in the Folly Tower," Olive went on. "She half believes the boys may be still alive. She was hoping to get something. She's been hinting that Rosamund knows things she won't tell."

"Why not?" Bobby asked; but to that question Olive made no answer, for she did not know.

"It always lies between them, what happened to the boys," she said.

"I can't imagine there's the least chance of their being alive," Bobby told her. "And if they aren't—" And he left the sentence unfinished, for what else was there to say?

"Myra talked a lot," Olive went on, and she shivered slightly. "These secret rites the two boys were trying to get a look at are rather dreadful—sacrifices of living creatures are offered. Human sacrifices," she said after a long pause. "On special occasions. To propitiate the gods if deep sacrilege had been committed—or attempted. Like strangers trying to look. Myra's nightmare, though she won't admit it, is that if that happened, then the two boys may after death be in some way entangled with or under the control of these gods or whatever they are to whom they were offered."

"She must be going off her head," Bobby said angrily; and perhaps himself a little frightened, too, at this glimpse into the dark hinterland of the unknown. "Val never suggested anything like that. He did say he was blamed—held responsible. By everyone apparently—Myra and Rosamund, too. That may be what Rosamund knows and won't tell. That he did in fact encourage the poor kids to take a chance. Nothing to be done about it."

"Just your being here has helped already," Olive told him. "Rosamund said so."

"Oh, she did, did she?" grunted Bobby, quite unappeased. "In the interval of flirting with her three admirers?"

"Three?" Olive repeated questioningly.

"Well, there's a chap they call B.B., and the Ludo young man. And then there's Dewey James."

"But he's the hunchback," Olive exclaimed.

"Doesn't prevent him from having feelings, does it?" Bobby asked. "Doesn't prevent her from being sorry for him, does it? And when a woman gets being sorry for you, it's the very devil. I saw them laughing together and I saw the way he looked after her when she went off—his face shone so he might have just swallowed the sun."

"I never thought of that," Olive said and looked more troubled even than before. "Anyhow, I don't think it's fair to say she was flirting—it's not that. It's more she feels set aside, doomed in a way, by what's happened—and perhaps by what may happen, for I think that voice they say they heard has frightened her as much as it has the rest of them."

"Did you know she was a potential heiress?" he asked abruptly.

"Rosamund?" Olive asked in return. "Why? They've nothing but Val's pension and this old house they're trying to sell only no one wants it."

"Well, she is, all the same," Bobby insisted. "An heiress, and a whacking big one, too. Val has got tucked away a map showing what he says is probably about the biggest uranium field in the world."

But Olive looked more puzzled than impressed. "Well, then, why doesn't he do something about it?" she demanded. "It would give Myra something else to think about."

"Well, that's one way to look at it," Bobby agreed. "It's all mixed up with this witch-doctor medicine business, and then it's in the middle of a native reserve. Val says if it was known it was there, the natives would soon be out."

"I don't see why," Olive protested, but at this point Outers appeared from the house and came across to join them.

He seemed in an entirely different mood now, excited and jovial. Bobby was inclined to suspect that he had retired into the privacy of his own room for a drink or two—or even more. Anyhow, his change of mood was very marked, even though the same heavy gloom remained in those deep-set eyes of his, where this new rather febrile joviality found no place. Possibly, Bobby thought, the telling of his story to one who was both a relative in blood and yet a stranger, too, had brought him the kind of relief often experienced after confession.

Olive managed to slip away while Outers was talking about the book he planned to write on ancient Bantu civilization as exemplified by those imposing ruins at Zimbabwe, at one time attributed to the Portuguese, but now believed to antedate the arrival in Africa of the white races by many hundreds of years. Bobby was interested and listened with attention. "At a time when the Ancient Britons were running about dressed in woad. You understand?" Outers said more than once, and Bobby made no attempt to controvert this last somewhat doubtful statement. But he was equally interested to notice that Olive had been joined by Rosamund, now escaped from the kitchen. They had crossed over together into the James domain and were chatting with Dewey in what was apparently a kind of conducted tour under his guidance. But a call from Myra to come in to dinner cut short both Outers's discourse and this conducted tour.

It had been arranged that Bobby and Olive should leave fairly early next morning, and though the usual polite hopes were expressed on both sides that their visit would be soon repeated, yet somehow there was a general feeling that this would not be, unless indeed in very different circumstances.

Bobby, however, had now discovered that there had been no need for that long drive back on the day of their arrival to the cross-road and thence back again to Constant House. Tucked away on the south side of the Folly was a track, certainly rough and unmade and in wet weather extremely muddy, but avoiding all that long detour to the cross-roads. The next morning, accordingly, Bobby took it, and when all the farewells had been said and they were fairly on their way, he told Olive that he was going to take the opportunity of talking to Mrs James.

"I want to hear what she thinks of this voice they talk about," he explained. "I told Val I wanted to. I don't think he liked the idea, but he didn't object. Teddy Peel, as they call him, strikes me as a fraud, and I have an idea he and Mrs James may have fixed it up between them. I should like to be able to form my own opinion of her."

"Well, I can tell you one thing," Olive said. "There's nothing of the vulgar cheat about her. She hates Dewey because he is deformed, she hates herself for having borne him. She loves him because he is her son, and there is nothing she would not do to make amends for the wrong she did him in giving him birth as he is."

"How do you know all that?" Bobby asked, carefully steering his car over the bumpiest apology for a road he had ever come across.

"Well, I do know, that's all," Olive retorted, "and not from anything she said, either. From how she said it and how she looked. She came out to join us when Rosamund and me were talking to Dewey yesterday evening." She added slowly: "You were right about Dewey. He is in love with Rosamund because she is sorry for him and never shows it or that there is any reason why she should be. He knows that with her he stands on his own feet and there is nothing he would not do for her—it is the sort of love that gives everything and asks for nothing, and you are all the better for having met with it."

CHAPTER VII
HOSTILE MRS JAMES

Not until they were safe once more on the high road, axles and springs still intact, did Bobby make any comment. Then he said:

"You don't mean you think there could be any question of marriage between them, between a hunchback, almost a dwarf, and a girl like Rosamund?" He did not wait for an answer that seemed to him self-evident, but went on: "What about Val and Myra? Have they any idea?"

"I don't think so," Olive answered. "I'm sure Val hasn't. They both take Dewey as a kind of freak to be sorry for. They didn't mean to, but they've let Mrs James see that—that they hardly think of Dewey as human at all. Val once said that among the Bantu anyone like Dewey would have been smothered at birth, and that was the best way. Of course, he didn't mean Mrs James to hear, but she did."

"Well, of course, she would be sure to," Bobby said.

"You can imagine how she felt," Olive said presently and Bobby nodded. "Anyhow, Dewey never wants to do anything but worship at a distance," she concluded, and this time with a slight note of relief in her voice.

By now Bobby had brought the car to a halt outside the old lodge. No one was visible. He alighted and knocked at the lodge door. There was still no answer. He thought, however, that he could hear sounds, as of some one hammering, coming from the back, where he knew there were various sheds and outbuildings. There he found Mrs James at the bench in what was evidently the tool and repair shed. She was working with a file and vice at what seemed some kind of lazy tongs, to which apparently she was trying to affix a spring. Her crutch was at some distance, leaning against a chair and she gave Bobby the impression that she was both startled and discomposed by his appearance. Hurriedly she pushed the lazy tongs contraption she was working at into the midst of a huddle of tools and so on nearby on the bench, wiped her hands on a dirty cloth and then flung it on top of the heap. Bobby began an apology for disturbing her. She did not listen, but with one of those odd, prodigious leaps of hers, balanced on her one leg, she reached her crutch. As if now she felt safer, reinforced, so to speak, she turned to face Bobby.

"You're the murder man, aren't you?" she demanded.

"Well, that's not exactly how I describe myself," Bobby answered; a little startled by the undisguised hostility with which this remark had been hurled at him. "The fact is I'm very interested in what happened the other night when you were in the Folly. You all heard a voice?"

"There was something," she admitted, though Bobby felt she would have liked to deny it if possible. "Sounded gibberish to me. Like the quacking of a duck with a bad cold. What about it?"

"Didn't Mr Outers say it was an African dialect he understood?"

"I didn't," she snapped. "Ask him if you want to know what it meant?"

"Oh, he's told me," Bobby answered.

She made no reply. She shifted her weight on her crutch as she stood. Bobby thought it might be because she found standing irksome or her crutch misfitting in some way. Adjusting it, might have been the task she had been engaged on when he appeared. He glanced at a chair and made a move to get it for her. It seemed she noticed his movement, but misinterpreted his intention. In the same sharp, angry tone she said:

"If one leg can stand, so can two." Then she added: "It may all have been Teddy Peel."

"You think it possible he faked it?" Bobby asked. "You don't trust him?"

"No. I don't," she snapped. "I don't trust him. Or anyone else. Or you either."

"Well, I'm sorry for that," Bobby said. "I don't see why. You don't know much about me, do you?"

"Poking your nose into things that don't concern you," she said.

"But they do," Bobby protested. "And everyone else for that matter. We would all like to know what these things mean."

"Nobody knows what anything means," she retorted; and as this was an incontrovertible statement, and as by this time he had decided that Mrs James was determined not to talk, he apologized for troubling her—an apology of which she took not the least notice—and retired to where Olive was waiting for him in the car.

"I'm afraid Mrs James doesn't like me," he said in an injured tone. "I can't think why. All I got out of her was a hint that Teddy Peel is probably a fraud."

"Well, then, why does she go on being there?" Olive demanded; and Bobby said that was what he wanted to know, but there might be any one of a dozen reasons or more.

"She may be more impressed than she admitted," he said. "Or she may merely want to keep on terms with Val and Myra because of Dewey's friendship with Rosamund. If you're right about that."

"Oh, I am," Olive assured him with complete certitude in her tone. "You don't mistake absolute pure devotion when you see it."

Bobby started the car then and they drove on. Their first call was to be Cranmer, formerly a remote and picturesque village in the midst of lovely though not very fertile country, but now become a kind of exclusive dormitory for the wealthier inhabitants of booming, smoking, bustling Midminster and also for a few of the less wealthy who had established themselves there before land values shot up to astronomical heights. In this latter class was Mr Nixon, the West Midshire Chief Constable and an old colleague of Bobby's, with whom he and Olive were to lunch. The happy uncertainty of English country roads nearly doubled the map distance and kept Bobby's attention fixed on the problem of finding his way. Not until presently they came to a signpost that condescended to mention Cranmer and gave the distance to it as a mile and three-quarters did he relax a little. Then he said:

"Remember what I told you about Val having a map showing the position of a big uranium field somewhere in a native reserve in South Africa?"

"Oh, yes," Olive said. "I've been wondering. Isn't he really going to do anything about it? If he doesn't, someone else is sure to."

"Well, of course, he knows that," Bobby agreed. "Needs must, but not through him. He didn't ask me to keep it quiet and he must have known I should be likely to tell you if he thought about it at all. All the same, it's rather worrying. It really is tremendously important—much more than a new gold mine or two or a new diamond field stuffed with Koh-i-noors. Every government's dream in every country is to find a nice new fat uranium field in its own territory. All the same, it's Val's secret, not ours, and I don't feel we have any right to give it away, and yet I feel it's too big a thing to keep quiet about. If it got known, Val would be under tremendous pressure—official, Press, public. I don't think he or anyone could stand out. If they tried, they would probably be driven mad. Well, have I any right—?"

"Certainly not," interrupted Olive in her most decisive tone.

"But have I any right to hold back anything of such importance to the country? Val didn't make any sort of suggestion that what he said was meant to be confidential—perhaps on purpose so as to push off part of the responsibility on to me."

"I don't think Val's like that," Olive said.

"I don't either," Bobby agreed. "All the same, if I keep quiet it may be the end of me. Think of the rage in the City, the pompous articles in all the papers deciding that I acted from admirable but wholly mistaken motives, and so I had better have the sack."

"Oh, dear," Olive exclaimed, and considered this. "Oh, dear," she said again. "What a nuisance it's always so wrong to do what's right. I expect you could get another job, though.

I'm sure I could. We could be caretakers at some ducal mansion, showing people round. It would be rather fun."

"Nothing doing," answered Bobby with decision. "Ducal families keep that job for themselves. No wonder. Remember the tips. I'll write to Val or go to see him again and try to persuade him he oughtn't to trust his own judgment in anything so big and important. It ought to be decided at Government level."

"I wouldn't trust any government one inch further than I could see it," announced Olive firmly; and, as Bobby had no comment to make on this most natural and proper sentiment, he drove on in silence.

The so carefully measured mile and three-quarters to Cranmer was soon covered, nor had Bobby any difficulty in finding Mr Nixon's home. An excellent luncheon provided the background for an enjoyable gossip, in the course of which Bobby managed to turn the conversation to the Folly Tower.

"Mr Outers is a far-off cousin of mine," he explained; and it was impossible to miss the air of slight embarrassment that now showed as Nixon and his wife looked at each other. "He was a district officer in the depths of Africa," Bobby went on. "Not a policeman, he said, but he often had to act as one. Ever come across him?"

"I called there once," Nixon answered. "There were some rather funny stories going about and I drove over to have a chat and see if he knew anything about it."

"Did he seem to?" Bobby asked.

"Just sat there glowering and pulling at that great black beard of his," answered Nixon. "Thanked me for coming and got out the whisky and all that, but wasn't talking and, of course, I couldn't press him. I tried to drop him a hint about a man named Peel. Slippery customer. He's been through our hands once or twice, but we've never been able to pin anything on him. He calls himself a student of the occult. Has the impudence to print it on what I suppose he calls his business cards. The Midminster chaps have tried to get him for fortune-telling, but that was no good. We've had a se-

ries of burglaries, you know, at the big houses in this neighbourhood. Very worrying. Peel's name keeps cropping up as
having been a visitor doing his stunts just before. Of course,
there may be no connection."

"Reconnaissance?" Bobby suggested.

"That's right. What we thought," agreed Nixon. "Then he
was a dewy-eyed, innocent witness after a gang fight on Midminster Racecourse a year ago. One man got a knife pushed
into him and died of it. It couldn't be brought home to anyone, but we had a good idea Peel was the knife-pusher."

"We saw him at Freres when we were there yesterday
afternoon," Bobby said. "I shouldn't have taken him for the
knife-happy type."

"In the back," Nixon said, and Bobby nodded comprehen-
sion.

CHAPTER VIII
THE WISH FULFILLED

"It wasn't exactly what you would call a police matter I
called to see Mr Outers about," Nixon resumed presently in
rather an apologetic tone. "But worrying. And then you never
know how things will turn out, do you?"

"Never," agreed Bobby. "Except that it's generally the way
you don't want."

"One of my chaps," Nixon continued. "Youngster, but
seems reliable and sticks to his story. He was on night patrol, and near Freres he claims he saw a little old man sitting
by the roadside. It was late, and dark except for a bit of a
moon, but he says he could see plainly enough. He thought
it queer, so he got off his motor cycle to question him. He
heard the old man say something he couldn't understand,
but when he looked again the old man wasn't there, and nowhere, my chap says, where he could have got to. I shouldn't
have thought so much of it, but for a lorry-driver coming in
later on with the same sort of yarn. Shaken, he was all right.

This time it was early in the morning, soon after daybreak. Little old man sitting by the roadside near Mr Outers's place. The lorry driver says he saw him plainly and thinks he was a Negro. He was quite naked except for a cloth round the middle and a kind of necklace of polished bones. The lorry chap slowed up to have another look. The old man said something in what the driver called 'a kind of foreign lingo', and then he wasn't there any more."

"There's such a lot of gossip goes on in Cranmer you can't believe a word you hear," interposed Mrs Nixon. "I get it all from our daily. Her sister started going to the Outers to help, but she stopped. She complained Miss Outers went about looking fit to scare you."

"They had a tragic experience in Africa," Bobby said. "I don't think they've ever got over it. Their two boys were killed by natives—a kind of ritual murder as far as I can make out."

"I didn't know that," observed Mr Nixon, and looked as though he thought someone ought to have told him. "And now mysterious natives hanging about."

"I thought Rosamund a very nice, quiet girl," declared Olive. "I expect she didn't gossip enough. Some dailies seem to think that's all they come for—a nice cup of tea and a gossip."

Mrs Nixon, all bubbling sympathy, said "I know," and for a moment or two the conversation seemed about to develop into a duologue on the iniquities of 'dailies'. But then she reverted to an earlier theme and said instead:

"I don't think I've ever seen Miss Outers, but she seems attractive to young men. There are two of them in Cranmer never off the Freres doorstep—Mr Baynham and Mr Manners. They used to be friendly enough but now they never speak except to scowl at each other. Daggers drawn. And Dewey James as well," and at that she and her husband exchanged glances of sly amusement.

"He's a hunchback," Mr Nixon explained unnecessarily. "Runs a market garden in what used to be the Freres grounds before the old place was burned down. Not making much of a success of it by all accounts."

"People say it's because he spends all his time running after Miss Outers," Mrs Nixon told them. "And Mr Outers doesn't like it, but can't stop it and I do think he ought to—a hunchback. Only it's just wicked to try to make a joke of it, as some do."

"They'll be more careful about that now," Nixon remarked. "One man tried to be funny in a pub and Dewey picked him up and took him outside and threw him into the old horse-pond there. When he tried to get out, Dewey threw him back again. I had to send a chap to warn him against taking the law into his own hands. I wouldn't like to answer for him if he got really worked up."

"I always say it's what started these silly stories about little old black men," Mrs. Nixon put in. "It's really been Dewey wandering about, trying to walk it off. If it was too dark to see properly he would look all bent up and small like old men are and all the rest is just the way stories grow. Tell someone you've found a safety-pin in the road, and it'll be a fur coat before you can turn round."

Mr Nixon nodded agreement, and Bobby said it was time they were getting on their way if they were to get to Bristol, where they had arranged to spend the night, before dark.

They started off accordingly and not until they had driven some considerable distance did Bobby rouse himself from the silent and abstracted mood into which he had fallen and remark on how pleasant it was to meet an old colleague and have a chat with him. So Olive said, "Yes, wasn't it?"

"Not that I think for one moment," Bobby told her severely, "that there's anything to worry about in those stories of talkative old Negroes sitting by the roadside. What's happened is plain enough. Teddy Peel's bit of ventriloquism in the Tower Room has got about and been fathered on some harmless old tramp whose one idea, of course, was to make himself scarce as soon as he saw a police patrol. Then the lorry driver heard about it and wasn't going to be outdone. All quite normal. I shouldn't be surprised if some more of the same stories don't come in soon."

"I shouldn't either," agreed Olive.

"Soon be forgotten," Bobby said, staring angrily at the signpost, which told him he was on the right road to Bristol. Then he said: "Very disturbing. I've half a mind to turn round and go straight back to Val's to have it out with him."

"Oh, you can't do that, dear," protested Olive, startled into housewifely sympathy with an unprepared Myra. "Have what out?" she asked.

Bobby made no attempt to reply, and not till he had driven on another mile or two did he speak again.

"I don't much like it, that's all," he said. "There's Rosamund looking like a thunderstorm except when she's talking to a hunchback Nixon thinks is capable of anything if he gets worked up—which is what you say he is already. There are two other young men hating each other like poison because of the girl—and are they capable of anything? You could think so when you see them glaring at each other. And what does she feel about the death of her brothers? Does she think her father's to blame? There's Myra brooding for ever on what happened to her boys, both before they died and afterwards. There's Mrs James hopping about on that crutch of hers and fiercely angry with Val for what he said about her son. What's in her mind? There's Teddy Peel who is certainly a rogue and possibly a murderer. And what's he up to? No good probably. Behind it all, Val, knowing he's thought responsible for the tragedy and holding back the secret of this uranium field that may be worth millions in money and much more in other ways. It's a position that may develop in almost any way. Explosive."

"I suppose it could," agreed Olive, "but there's nothing you can do, or anyone as far as I can see. They must work it all out for themselves as best they can and we must hope they do. Only I wish that silly old tower had been burnt down with the rest of it."

Without incident, without much further talk, Bristol was reached, an hotel found. Dinner and bed followed, and next morning Bobby was called away from his breakfast to the telephone, an interruption both he and Olive deeply resented.

"I did think we could get away from that horrid thing for just a few days," Olive lamented.

"I can't imagine how anyone knows we are here," complained Bobby. "We didn't know ourselves where we were going to stop." He added apprehensively: "Nixon knew we were making for Bristol."

"It's a local call, sir," said the waiter.

Bobby went off then to the hotel 'phone booth and returned, wearing what Olive sometimes called his official face. Olive looked up at him and said at once:

"It's broken then?"

Booby nodded.

"Nixon on the line." he said. "The local chaps put me through to him. He had asked them to try to find us. They've been calling all the A.A. hotels in this place. He wants me to go back there at once."

"Who it is?" Olive asked.

"Val." Bobby answered. "During their sitting last night in the Tower Room. Stabbed and died immediately. Nixon says I seem to be the only man relative they have in the country, and he thinks I might be able to help. He'll have to know about the uranium field map."

"I hope that's all," Olive said.

Bobby went away to get ready. He drove her to the station and saw her into the London train. Then he drove back to Freres, where he found Nixon and a bevy of assistants, all of whom had been up all night, asking questions, taking statements, searching, measuring, photographing, going through the whole of the careful established routine, designed to make sure that no existent clue escaped discovery.

So far apparently none had been found.

Neither Myra nor Rosamund was visible. They had retired to their own rooms, and Nixon suggested to Bobby that he would like to hear what Bobby could tell him before letting the two women know of his arrival.

"I promised to send for you," he explained. "They both seemed to want it. And then, of course, they've had a terrible shock and been up all night as well. In a way it's a perfectly simple case. They were holding one of these meetings of theirs up at the top of the Folly Tower and they all agree the killing must have been done by one of them. They were sitting round the table—big circular thing. I don't know how they got it up those stairs—in bits probably and then put it together again. Outers had his wife on his left, his daughter on his right. Next to Mrs Outers there was Mr Baynham, and Peel was next to him. Peel seems to have been acting as a kind of chairman or something of the sort. Then there was Mrs Dewey James, almost opposite Mr Outers, and then Mr Manners, next to Miss Rosamund. The room was in complete darkness. It was getting late, about nine o'clock, and there were heavy curtains over the windows. The doors, the one at the top of the steps and the one by which you went up a few more steps to the roof, were locked and bolted. There was a gramophone going full tilt and there was a high wind blowing with occasional gusts of rain. They all mention the noise the wind made and apparently there had been some suggestion of putting off the meeting till a quieter night. No one seems to remember who made the suggestion, but anyhow it wasn't taken up. Peel told them a strong wind helped what he called developments. He said a high wind often meant that powers were abroad that lay quiet on quiet nights. He got his developments all right."

CHAPTER IX
BOBBY STAYS ON

AT THIS POINT there was an interruption. One of Nixon's men appeared to say the ambulance was there and would it be all right if the body were now removed to the county mortuary? Nixon said it would and went off to see to it himself, promising Bobby he would be back immediately. They had been talking in the room that had seemed more especially the dead man's domain, the one in which he and Bobby had had their long conversation less than forty-eight hours before. Now Bobby, left alone in this long and narrow room, went to its further end, where stood the old mahogany bureau he had noticed previously. It had two long drawers. He tried them. They were both locked and he noticed now that the locks seemed modern, as though they had been added recently. He returned to his seat and almost at once Nixon came back.

"There's a crowd beginning to gather," he said discontentedly. "Reporters as well—two of them. I've told my chaps to keep everyone out for the present."

"You said the two ladies were in their rooms, didn't you?" Bobby said. "What about Mr Baynham—B.B., he seems to be called—and Ludo Manners?"

"I asked them to stay around," Nixon answered. "I told them I had to know a lot more before I could let them go. They were both quite reasonable about it. Badly upset, of course. You can't wonder."

"And Mrs James?" Bobby asked and Nixon smiled faintly.

"Oh, yes," he said. "Wonderful the way she hops around on that crutch of hers. She's been very busy, takes it more lightly than the others. A bit excited and nervy. Of course, she's not one of the family. I sent for sandwiches for the men—you've got to eat, haven't you?" Bobby nodded agreement; remembering how he had been told at the very beginning of his career that the most important part of an investigator's equipment was always his sandwiches. Nixon went on: "She made tea for them, and she's been trying to get the two ladies to have some breakfast—tea and toast. She's even been seeing to the poultry, giving them their feed and hopping around in the hen-run on the look-out for eggs."

"There's the son, Dewey James," remarked Bobby. "Hunchback, poor chap. You haven't mentioned him. He wasn't at the Folly Tower meeting?"

"No. Never did join them, they say. Went to bed early, he says, as always, and knew nothing about it till he woke this morning. It has to be one of the six who were present."

"Yes. Yes. It looks like it," Bobby agreed. "Yes. But we must not forget there may be other possibilities. Have to think of everything. What about the man they call Teddy Peel?"

"Oh, yes," Nixon said. "Yes. Peel. Teddy Peel. There's him all right. In a blue funk. He would have done a bunk if he had seen half a chance. But so far no more against him than anyone else, and no motive that I can see. He must have known he would be the first suspect."

"You haven't mentioned the murder weapon," Bobby said. "I take it, it's not been found?"

"We'll turn it up in time," declared Nixon confidently. "First thing we thought of. First thing the murderer would think of, for that matter. The trouble is, they were all under each other's observation all the time. Except Mr Baynham. He rushed away at once to ring us up. Was that because he kept his head while the others didn't, or was it because he had it all thought out beforehand?"

"It's a point to remember," agreed Bobby.

"Another thing," Nixon went on. "Outers was killed by a thrust delivered with great force from directly in front, sloping slightly upwards, penetrating the heart. The doctor says death must have been almost instantaneous. But there was no one directly in front of him except Mrs James, and she could not possibly have reached across the table to deliver a blow like that. No one could for that matter, according to the story they all tell."

"In other words," Bobby put in, "Outers was killed by a blow and in a way that couldn't possibly have happened?"

"That's right," admitted Nixon. "I can handle most things, but this is getting me down. They all back each other up, and it's against reason to suppose they're all in it and all lying— wife and daughter too. Three men and three women. One of the six guilty and five innocent. Yet the evidence of all of them clearing each one of them. Screwy."

"Do you know if they were linking up round the table, holding each other's hands? I believe that's usual."

"That's right," agreed Nixon again. "Teddy Peel kept talking about that. Said none of them could have moved without the two sitting next knowing it. Another thing, owing to the noise—gramophone going and the wind and rain outside—it took them some time to realise what had happened. Outers was certainly dead before they knew. Bloodstains no help either, they had all got it all over them. Except Mrs James. She's a cripple, of course. Says in the first panic she got knocked over and someone had to haul her up to get her back in her chair again."

"Has anyone said anything about uranium?" Bobby asked.

"Uranium?" repeated Nixon, looking as if he thought that Bobby, too, had gone off his head, and now nothing was wanting to complete the general madness of the set up. "Uranium?" he repeated. "For the good Lord's sake, that doesn't come in, does it?"

"Outers told me when we were here the day before yesterday that he had a map showing the position of what he claimed was probably the richest uranium field in the world," and Nixon stared as if he could hardly imagine Bobby was serious. "Oh, he meant it and believed it, too," Bobby assured the still incredulous, staring Nixon.

"But—but," Nixon stammered. "Well, then," he asked, "what was he doing about it?"

"Nothing," Bobby answered. "Thought it had better stay where it was, perhaps. He said it was in native territory and development of the uranium would mean developing the natives out of their lands. Also—" And then he went on to repeat the tragic tale of the fate of the two young Outers boys, as probably the victims of a ritual murder, of what strange and dreadful fears, doubts, and suspicions had been aroused in the bereaved mother's mind, of her contradictory, lingering hopes that they might still be alive held captive somewhere in the deep African bush, and of her terrible haunting dread that in some way the dark African magic might have pursued them even after death.

"What a nightmare," Nixon muttered, more to himself than to Bobby. "You don't take all that seriously, do you?" he asked, rather with an air of trying to persuade himself not to.

"I thought you ought to know," replied Bobby, evading the question, which indeed he hardly knew how to answer. "Apparently," he went on, "Outers was blamed by many people. There was an idea that he had encouraged or more than encouraged the two boys to try to get him information about secret African rites. I shouldn't think it likely, but I suppose no one will ever know for certain. But there was considerable local feeling at the time."

"See," Nixon said. "These stories going the rounds. I mean about old fellows sitting by the roadside and then disappearing. Can they have anything to do with it? I mean trying to get this uranium map back."

"I suppose they've got to be traced, if possible," Bobby agreed, "but I shouldn't myself attach too much importance to them—or the stories either. In any case, how could they be implicated in the murder?"

"I know," Nixon agreed in his turn. "Bribed one of the others perhaps. Or, it sounds mad—but, then, so is the whole set-up—could one of 'em have been hiding in the Tower room? Pitch dark and black men wouldn't be seen so easily. Did Outers show you the thing or say where he kept it?"

"In there," Bobby said, pointing to the mahogany bureau at the other end of the room. "Both drawers are locked and neither show any sign of having been opened."

But he did not mention the odd affair of Rosamund's apparently instinctive knowledge that the medicine bag said to contain the map had been talked about by her father to Bobby. Nixon got up and went to the bureau and stood staring at it for a minute or two. Then he came back to his seat looking very worried and said:

"Have to put one of my chaps to keep an eye on it. I'll send in a report to the Home Office. They ought to deal with it.

Probably just shove it in a pigeon-hole and tell me they're awaiting further information before taking action." In an even more troubled tone he said: "Do you think Mrs Outers can have been brooding over this notion that her husband sent their boys to fish out native secrets, knowing the danger?"

It was a question Bobby had been dreading but that he knew must come and that he must answer it.

"I think that's very possible," he answered slowly. "I don't know. I don't imagine it's ever out of her mind."

"And the daughter?" Nixon asked. This time Bobby did not reply. He felt it was not necessary. "When you start brooding," Nixon went on, "God knows where you'll get to—or the Devil. Wife and daughter, too," he said and lapsed into a silence Bobby had no desire to break. Rousing himself, Nixon continued: "Wife and daughter," he repeated gloomily. "I did think I could leave them out of it. Now they're right bang in the middle of the picture. There was some story I didn't pay much attention to about a voice they all heard. I put it down to Peel up to some of his tricks."

"Outers told me of that," Bobby said. "Spoken in an obscure native dialect very few people know. It was a warning that there were thoughts of murder floating about."

"And now murder's been done," muttered Nixon. "The set-up is the dead man's wife brooding over the loss of her boys. And was he responsible? And the daughter going about looking like a living nightmare. Is that the way she thinks, too? Have you seen the things she paints? Wouldn't have them in my house if I were paid for it. Then there're the two men—B.B., as every one calls him, well known in Midminster. So is Ludo Manners. Both after the same girl. For me, I would as soon marry a thunderstorm. Those pictures—working it off or not working it off? Which?" Bobby offered no opinion. "From all accounts, those two young men never did like each other. B.B. says Manners is a bit too sharp, and Manners says B.B. is a humbug. Sort of a test between them which gets the girl, but hardly matter for a murder there?"

"No," agreed Bobby, and then the door opened and Rosamund came in.

CHAPTER X
ONE OF SIX

ROSAMUND DID NOT look at the two men; she did not even seem to be aware of their presence, nor of how intently they watched her. With stiff, unnatural steps, a little like those of one walking in sleep, she went to the mahogany bureau. She stood looking at it. The silence in the room was profound. Bobby watched, as motionless as the girl herself. Nixon moved restlessly in his seat. Once or twice he seemed inclined to speak, but did not. They heard Rosamund say, very quietly but very clearly:

"It is not there any longer."

"Where is it, then?" Bobby asked.

Startled, she turned round, and looked at him in a vague, questioning way, as if trying to remember who he was. Then she said slowly:

"Are you staying here the night? I must see about your room, if you are."

"What is it that's no longer there?" Bobby asked again. "Is it the medicine bag?"

"You knew about that?" she asked in return. "Did Father tell you? Now it's gone and he is dead."

"Have you any idea where it can be?" Bobby asked next, and at that she shook her head.

"Somebody may open it," she said. "It is bad medicine." She moved from where she had been standing and came slowly down the room. "It's my head," she said, and added, as if in explanation: "Father's been killed. That's why you are here, isn't it?"

"Yes," he agreed. "Have you had any sleep? Or any breakfast?"

She appeared to be considering this.

"There was a cup of tea," she answered at last. "Someone brought it me. I think it was Mrs James."

"And your mother?" Bobby asked, in the same quiet even tone he had used throughout.

"She is asleep," Rosamund answered. "You must not wake her. She hasn't slept like that for years. Not since—"

But there she stopped, leaving the sentence unfinished, for now there was a knock at the door. None of them answered. The door opened and Mrs James came in, carrying in her free hand, a tray with toast and tea on it. She put it down, and, ignoring the two men, went to Rosamund, taking her gently by the arm and leading her to a chair.

"You must eat something, dearie," she said. "Or you'll break down. That won't do any good. I got this for your mother, but she's sleeping like a newborn babe; and a good thing, too. I didn't want to disturb her."

"No. You mustn't. No one must, no one. Let her sleep," Rosamund said, a strange intensity in her voice.

Bobby had joined them now. He went to the tray, poured out a cup of tea, added a drop of brandy from the small flask he always carried and gave it to Rosamund. Mrs James saw what he was doing, and nodded approvingly.

"That's right," she said. "Needs it, the way she is."

"Drink this," Bobby said.

Rosamund obeyed and coughed a little. She looked up at him and said.

"Father's dead and mother is asleep, but you mustn't wake her." She was still looking at Bobby. "Are you staying?" she asked. "You are, aren't you? You put something in that tea, didn't you?"

"Yes," Bobby answered. "I don't know if I can stay. It depends on your mother. Only if she wants me to. If she does, you and she must understand quite clearly that it will be to help you in the only way I can—that anyone can—by trying to discover your father's murderer, and, though that doesn't matter so much, what has become of the map of the uranium field he told me was in what you call the medicine bag. I shall have no official standing, of course. I shall be here simply as a man doing his best to help two women relatives left alone." He turned to Nixon. "I hope you won't object. I hope you won't mind."

"Only too glad," declared Nixon, thus appealed to. "Need all the help I can get—a case like this."

"Thank you," Bobby said with real gratitude, for he knew that Nixon could easily make his position in the house impossible, kinsman or not. "I'll keep you informed." He turned to Rosamund and said to her: "You knew this map might be of very great value, politically as well as financially?"

"Father said so," she answered. "He told me once. He said it could make us all rich and turn him into a knight. Only it would mean betraying people who trusted him, and he wasn't going to."

"Even though it was they who had murdered his sons?" Bobby asked and paused. Rosamund remained silent and her eyes were proud and aloof. She did not speak. Bobby said, slowly, deliberately, perhaps cruelly: "Your brothers."

She got to her feet and stood, but unsteadily, as if no longer very sure of her footing. She was looking straight at him.

"I must go," she murmured in a voice so low he could hardly hear it.

"No," he said with authority and motioned to her to sit down. She obeyed, but whether because of what he had said or because she found it difficult to stand, he was not sure. In a milder tone, he continued: "You must help me if I am to help you. It was his sons' murderers he was keeping faith with. Was that because he felt himself equally to blame with them? Did you think that?"

"What does it matter?" she asked in return. "What do you want to know for? Why are you asking these questions?"

"Because your father is dead," he told her and saw her wince, as if he had struck her. He went on more slowly: "If I ask the right questions, I may presently get the right answer. Did anyone else know about this map or where your father kept it?"

"He told you, didn't he?" she said. "He may have told others as well. I can't say. Generally he didn't talk much, but sometimes he did."

"The medicine bag, and the map in it, was kept in that mahogany bureau. You said just now that it wasn't there any longer. How do you know? The drawers are both locked."

"I knew as soon as I came in," she told him then, suddenly excited. "I came to see and I knew. It was bad medicine. I always knew it would bring bad luck. I always knew it would do harm if it could, and now it has. I meant to burn it so that nothing should remain—only ashes I could throw away. From the top of the tower. In the wind. Or bury it. Deep. Very deep. That would be better. In the fire it might escape when the bag began to burn. But if it was buried, deep, deep, deep, before it had a chance, it and bag together, the bag never opened, that would be safer."

Nixon stirred uneasily in his seat by the window. Bobby knew what he was thinking, for he was thinking the same himself: How would all this sound in an English court of law? He could imagine how the hard, stiff, legal mind would react. He could imagine the small cynical smiles, the amused jests passing from one to another before the world of precedent and man-made written law was returned to. Never mind. He went on:

"I am afraid all that is very difficult to follow. I don't understand very clearly. What is this 'it' you talk of as if it were something alive, something in the medicine bag, something that was trying to get out?"

"You think it all childish superstition, don't you?" Rosamund flashed, still speaking with the same sort of only half-suppressed excitement. "Everyone does. Here. Not if they have lived in Africa. Not if they know the deep African bush. Even if the settlers don't believe it, they are afraid. They invent all kinds of explanations. Perhaps they are right. They can't bear to think the Africans they call savages and look down upon so much may know more than their civilized selves, more about unseen things. But the Africans live close to Nature, very close, and why should they not know what Europeans may have known as well once but have forgotten because they have become such busy little people, bullying her, making her do what they want? It may be she has her secrets still that the scientists know nothing of and never will."

"You have thought a good deal of these things," Bobby said, and she answered in a tired voice from which all emotion had vanished:

"Haven't I good cause?"

"Does it help to tell us who murdered your father?" he asked.

"It was you keeping asking questions," she retorted.

"There will be many questions to be asked," he warned her again. "Till we know who killed your father."

"I suppose so," she agreed listlessly. "One of us six," she said. "That's what you are thinking all the time, isn't it?"

"Isn't that what you are thinking, too?" he countered.

"And that Mother and I were sitting next to him? You haven't forgotten that, have you? Very well. Very well."

"Unless you help me, there is little I can do," Bobby repeated.

But she showed no sign that she had even heard what he had said. She got to her feet once more. This time he did not motion to her to sit down, nor would she have obeyed if he had. She went to the door, her step much firmer than it had been, as if in a way she had been purged of uncertainty and fear. At the door, her fingers on the door handle, she turned and said to him:

"You are a hard man. I think you could be a cruel man, a bad man. I don't think you are."

"I hope I'm not," Bobby said, more than a little disconcerted by this sudden transformation of suspect into judge.

She did not hear, however, for she had already opened the door and gone out, closing it behind her.

"Rather a back-handed compliment, that," Nixon commented. "What do you make of all that guff? Is she off her head? Or putting on an act? In my view, it's as likely her as anyone. Thinks her father as good as killed her brothers and so . . . Eh? He knew what she was working herself up to, and he and Teddy Peel faked that voice they heard to head her off. Easy. The mother knew too. Or guessed. Why she got you here. To frighten the girl and it didn't, only made her hurry up. It's like that sometimes."

"So it is," Bobby said.

He opened the door. There was no sign of Rosamund, but Mrs James was standing at the foot of the stairs. She was supporting herself as much by the newel post as by her crutch. It looked to Bobby as if she had just made one of those prodigious hops of which she seemed to have the secret. And he had another idea—that perhaps she had been listening at the door while he and Rosamund were talking. But she was speaking now. She was saying:

"I've just this minute been in to see how Mrs Outers was, poor soul. Still asleep, thank God, but a little restless now and talking to herself."

"What did she say? Did you hear?"

"I could hardly catch a word, not to make sense. Something about blood washing out blood. Everyone in the room got blood all over them. Except me. I got knocked down instead, and it's a job getting up again when you've only one leg. Everyone knows it's only cold water washes out blood."

"Yes; I know," Bobby said with a friendly smile. "If I may say so, you get about wonderfully—stairs and all."

"Well, I've plenty of practice," she told him; and not as if the remark had much pleased her, but rather as if she were sensitive, though she had not hitherto seemed so, to her crippled condition or any reference to it.

"I've been asking Miss Outers a few questions," he said next. "I wonder if I might do the same to you?"

"There's not much I can tell you," she answered. "I've made one statement to the other gentleman already. Of course I don't mind if that's what you want."

"Thank you," Bobby said and led the way back into the room he had just left.

CHAPTER XI
'ELECTRIC MAGNETISM'

NIXON WAS COMING out as Bobby and Mrs James entered. Nixon went on his way. Bobby found a chair for Mrs James and another for himself and said:

"I've read your statement. There are one or two small points I would like to mention, so as to get things a bit clearer in my own mind. For instance, what was your impression at the time of the voice you all heard—didn't you?—at one of your sittings a week or two ago?"

"Teddy Peel," she answered promptly. "Up to his tricks. Mind you, things do happen, and if it's always him, he's a wonder."

"You didn't understand what the voice said?"

"Gibberish," Mrs James declared. "Didn't sound like any Christian talk. Mr Outers understood. Mind you, I don't know, but he looked as if he did."

"Did his wife and Miss Rosamund?"

"I didn't notice. It was him I was looking at."

"In your statement you say no one else could have been in the room, only those sitting round the table. You still feel sure of that?"

"Stands to reason. How could they? There was a hullabaloo going on, what with the gramophone and the wind howling and the rain. All the same we should have heard, all listening as we were, ready for that voice if it came again. Besides, if anyone had crept in—which he couldn't—how could he have leaned over the table with us holding hands. One of us six did it, stands to reason."

"We have to try to consider everything," Bobby said. "Everything however improbable or far-fetched. Things do happen, as you said a moment ago. You have no notion of who it could have been? You noticed nothing unusual? Even the tiniest detail might help."

"I have my own idea," she told him with a little nod, as if challenging him to make what he could of that. "I'm not saying anything. I was never one to scandalize people without being sure."

Bobby asked a few more questions, not very important ones, and to them received equally unimportant replies. Mrs James began to get restless.

"I ought to be seeing to things," she said. "There's no one else with those two poor souls not fit to do a hand's turn. Meals have to be got ready. They don't do it themselves."

"No, indeed," agreed Bobby. "I'm sure it's more than good of you to help as you are doing."

"It'll have to be cold," she said. "And not too much of it, either. No time to do any cooking and very little in the house. Only mostly the few eggs I found in the hen-run. A lot of hungry men."

"You needn't bother about them," Bobby told her. "Mr Nixon has sent for sandwiches and beer."

"Oh, has he?" she said, and he thought she sounded slightly disappointed. "I'll be off then and get a little something at home. Dewey will be wanting his. He can get it all right for himself if he wants to, only he never does."

"Oh, well, men always do expect to be waited on," Bobby remarked smilingly. "By the way, you've never heard anyone say anything about a map, have you?"

"A map? What sort of map?" she asked, and with obvious suspicion as if she felt this question, so suddenly shot at her, might conceal some sort of trap.

"Oh, just a map: that's all," Bobby said, and went to the door to open it for her.

She swung away on her crutch. Bobby got the impression that she felt less sure of herself than she had been before, but he could not think why. He went back to his seat by the window and became lost in rather worried meditation. Presently Nixon came in again.

"Want anything to eat?" he asked. "Meat-pies, sandwiches, ice-cream. Beer if you like the stuff. I don't."

"Well, I can put up with it on occasion," Bobby confessed.

"Mrs James is in the kitchen," Nixon said. "Hopping about the way she does. Making toast and boiling eggs for Mrs Outers and the girl. She says they've had nothing to eat yet. Very useful old lady. Did you get anything out of her?"

"Nothing," Bobby answered. "Except a personal impression, and that's useful at times. A strange old woman. Warped, I think. Partly the loss of her leg and then her son."

"What about him? You mean his being the way he is? She can't help that, can she?"

"It may have left her with a sense of guilt that she didn't," Bobby remarked.

Nixon made no comment. Apparently he thought it irrelevant to the problem they had to solve—that of finding the one guilty among the six who might be. Bobby went off then to claim his share of the meat-pies and the sandwiches before they were all gone. Of the ice-cream and the beer he had not much hope, nor in this expectation was he disappointed. That duly accomplished, he went on to examine the ground by the Tower. It had already been carefully inspected, but all the same he wanted to see for himself, as he held strongly that the officer in charge of an investigation should always make a point of doing. True, here he wasn't the officer in charge, but old habits prevailed.

He soon satisfied himself that the inspection had been made with skill and care. Nothing fresh to be learned here. He turned away and almost at once was joined by a little man in whom he recognized Teddy Peel.

"You're the boss, aren't you?" Teddy demanded, his mouth full with a last bite from the last of the meat-pie he had been holding in one hand. He had had three in all and now had just been warned off the course. "What's the big idea, keeping us blokes hanging around? Not legal if you ask me. I've got my appointments to keep. See?"

"I'm not in any way in charge," Bobby explained. "I'm not here as a police officer. Only as a friend of the family. Both ladies are suffering from shock and there's hardly anyone else they know."

Teddy did not seem much impressed by this disclaimer.

"I call it a bleeding shame," he protested. "Quite free to go, no compulsion at all, they tell you. Only if you do clear out, it will look a bit suspicious, won't it?" He made a sound expressive of extreme disapproval. "Statement taken and all," he said.

"I'm sure Mr Nixon won't ask you to stay one moment longer than he thinks might help," Bobby assured him. "I wonder if you would mind telling me what you thought of the voice I understand you all heard at one of your meetings?"

"Nothing to do with me, if that's what you're getting at," declared Teddy. "Knocked me flat. Scared me, too, and that's a fact. See?"

"Did you understand it?"

"Not me. Not like anyone's voice either, not of them sitting there. More like a parrot with a bad cold—regular croak. See?"

"Did any of the others seem to understand what was said, do you think?"

"Mr Outers looked as if he did. Upset, too. I don't know. Afterwards I thought maybe it was him what worked it. But funny things do happen, and that's a fact. Not spirits; that's bunkum. Electric magnetism, same as what makes some write poetry and such, and some talk so you can't help falling for it—the con. men or them as sells you what you don't want and never meant to buy. My old dad was like that. Fair drove the three-card men out of business. As soon as they saw him they packed up."

"How was that?" Bobby asked, more than willing, if Teddy was in the talkative mood that nervousness and a sense of tension often induce, to let him run on as long as he wished, since, the more he talked, the more he would say, and some of it might be useful and all of it would help to an understanding of his character and personality.

"He always knew where the 'lady' was," Teddy was explaining now. "'That one,' he would say, pointing, and there it was. Or else, 'Not on the table at all. Up your sleeve', and sure enough it was. A kind of tingling he felt and then he knew. Did well at it for a time and that's a fact. But then the three-card men tumbled to it."

"Rather a wonder he didn't get beaten up," Bobby remarked.

"They didn't dare," Teddy explained, "see. They weren't too sure how that electric magnetism mightn't work. They made it up once for him to go to the Derby and spot the winner. N.B.G. Cards one things, see, and horses another."

"That's very true," agreed Bobby. "All very interesting, but not much help in what's happened here. You were all sitting round the table, holding hands, weren't you? I believe that's usual? So that no one could move without those sitting next knowing. That is so, isn't it?"

Teddy's nervousness became more apparent still; it was even beginning to approach panic, as if he felt this was probing altogether too deeply. He hesitated for a moment or two and then seemed to make up his mind.

"Seems like you've been there," he grumbled. "Nixon, he never went into that, didn't never have heard of it, most likely. Gives confidence if you're that way with your fingers locking. Easy enough, if things don't seem like moving and you have to put the skids on with your clients getting impatient, expecting value for money, as is only honest and fair dealing they should have, to give the table a jolt. Makes 'em lose grip, but they don't notice, being all worked up, and you bring their hands together right and left so they hold each other, but think it's still you. That leaves you free. See? But you can't fake a voice that way, same as we heard, and that's a fact."

"No," Bobby agreed. "No; but it might help to explain what happened last night."

"So it might," Teddy agreed unexpectedly. "But it doesn't. Even Mr Nixon, who would give his ears to pin it on me, said it didn't look possible for any of the six of us to do the job the way it was. Took a mighty strong man to drive in a knife like that, even standing in front, and not possible, leaning over.

So it must have been someone else, but there wasn't anyone else, and that's a fact."

"I know," Bobby agreed. "It couldn't have happened, only it did. So we've got to find out who and how and why."

"It might be that girl, if it's anyone," Teddy suggested and continued: "Women being able, when worked up, to do more than any man. Only what for should she, him being her dad? But looks like she might, anyone, any time. There's times I've thought I could see a sort of cloud of darkness all round her. That's when the little old electric magnetism begins to tick, so I feel the tingle all over me."

"You liked Mrs James to be present at these meetings, didn't you?" Bobby asked.

"Seemed as if the electric magnetism got going quicker when she was there," Teddy agreed. "I always like to get results that way without having to work it. The poor old geezer got knocked down, and there she was, squawking on the floor and him dead in his chair, and the rest of us pretty near off our heads. What with this and that and the storm outside, I don't rightly know what did happen, but did my best to say in the statement the coppers took. Same with you. See? I own up: all I did was stand and gape and then run round the room, trying to find someone else, but there wasn't anyone else—only our six selves."

CHAPTER XII
CIGARETTE END

ON THIS SOMEWHAT unsatisfactory note the interview ended. Teddy wandered away, muttering that he had a duty to his 'clients' and that he wasn't going to hang about any longer, not to please all the coppers in the country. Bobby started to climb the Tower, anxious to see for himself the summit room where this apparently impossible murder had taken place. It was an arduous climb, arduous enough even for one, like Bobby, sound in wind and limb, let alone for the crippled Mrs

James, though, indeed, she seemed able with her one leg and her crutch to be as active as anyone.

The summit room had already, he knew, been thoroughly examined, tested for finger-prints, measured, photographed, so on. Even the walls of solid stone had been tapped and scrutinized. The locks of the two doors, the one at the head of the stairs, the one leading to the flat roof, showed no sign of having been tampered with. The shutters covering the windows had been opened, the heavy curtains drawn, and the possibility that, when these last were in position, the unknown assassin might have been hiding behind them had been considered and dismissed as manifestly out of the question. Bobby opened the second door and ascended the short flight of stone steps that led to the roof. It was surrounded by a low parapet, and from it there was a lovely view over the adjoining country—lovely at least except towards the west, where hung that great black cloud which proclaimed the bustling prosperity of Midminster. Not that Bobby took much notice of the view, or of the smudge of smoke either, for though he stood for long looking at it, of it he saw nothing, his thoughts so busy were they elsewhere. He had been wondering if by any possibility the murderer could have been lurking there and afterwards have escaped by lowering himself by a rope to the ground below. Not worth considering, he soon decided. On this smooth stone surface, surrounded by a smooth, intact parapet, there was nothing to which a rope could have been fastened, nor, if it had been, any way of removing it again. Nor had the ground at the foot of the Tower, reduced to a morass by the night's heavy rain, shown any sign of the tracks such a descent must inevitably have left.

"It must be one of the six of them," he told himself without satisfaction, "even if it can't have been."

Having arrived at that contradictory conclusion of 'must' and 'can't', he returned to the summit room, took another and now somewhat aimless look all round it, and then began the long but easier descent.

At the level of what had been the first floor of the old house there still remained, as he had noticed before, a doorway which had once provided direct communication between house and Tower. The door itself had long since vanished and the doorway closed by a barricade of boards easily removed and replaced.

Bobby paused for a moment, and presently, ignoring an ancient painted warning 'Danger', on one crumbling wall, crossed into the shell that once had been a human habitation.

The first thing that happened was that he displaced what was left of a party wall by not much more than brushing against it. It went crashing through vacancy, for all traces of a floor had long since disappeared, down to where rubble lay in heaps below, undisturbed apparently since the day of the fire. After that he proceeded with more care, noting with some relief as he did so that the outer walls seemed still sound. The solid stone of which they were constructed had resisted well both fire and weather. Even the slow, inexorable hand of time had not as yet had much effect. Further in, too, the destruction wrought by the fire had been less complete. Some of the party walls had survived, much of the roof and a good deal of the flooring were still in position, and now he stiffened to attention as in one place, where the flooring seemed secure, near the emptiness of an old hearth, he saw a cigarette butt.

Moving cautiously, for he did not much trust this flooring and held himself in readiness to jump at the first hint that it might be giving way, he went nearer. It could not have been there more than a few hours, but proof that someone had been recently, probably about the time of the murder. Not one of the six evidently, since they had all of them, all the time, been under each other's observation. Who then? And Bobby's thoughts turned instantly to Dewey James and his claim to have been asleep in bed all that night.

But if he had lied, why? With what motive?

Moreover, the puzzle still remained how he, if he were guilty, or anyone else for that matter, could have obtained admission through a locked, bolted, heavily curtained door into a room plunged in utter darkness, been able to locate the exact position and place of his proposed victim and strike a blow with such force, from directly in front, all without the others sitting round the table having any notion of what was going on.

Wholly, even preposterously impossible, Bobby decided.

All the same it still remained that from these twin impossibilities there had emerged the grim, inescapable fact of murder.

Leaving the cigarette butt lying where it was, still holding its secret of how it came to be there, Bobby moved slowly forward.

He was hoping that presently he might find a safer means of descent than return by the somewhat precarious route he had so far followed. A little to his relief he came presently to the great central double stairway, which had remained, as so often had been the case in the bombed houses of London during the war, firmly in position while all around was ruin. Desolate now, robbed of its great gilt balustrade, leading nowhere, it stood in marble serenity, like a warrior wounded to the death, yet still upright and firm.

Cautiously, Bobby tested it with one foot, next with his full weight, and then heard quite plainly, in the silence of that place of ruin and desolation, the sound of rubble falling. He stood, intent and listening. Now the silence was again complete. The rubble might have fallen simply because a precarious balance had been disturbed by some trifling natural cause, as an avalanche it is said can be started by a puff of wind or the passing of some animal. But also it might mean, and probably did, that someone else had decided to go exploring here. If so, was the object to remove the cigarette butt and with it the evidence that, in addition to the six, another person had been that night in the vicinity?

Bobby decided that there was no great object in indulging in a game of hide and seek in this old ruin where evasion would be easy and an incautious step result in a fall likely to cause serious injury or even death. The intruder could probably be identified by easier means if he was not made aware that this excursion of his, whatever its reason, had been noticed.

Carefully, therefore, for he was even yet not fully convinced of its stability, Bobby descended the stairway, by no means sorry to be in the open air again. He did not go away, but stood there, waiting to see if his fellow explorer would presently make his appearance, and then he heard himself called as Nixon came towards him.

"I've been wondering where you had got to," Nixon said as he came up.

"I've been having a look round," Bobby explained with a nod towards the ruin.

"In there?" Nixon asked doubtfully. "You didn't expect to hit on anything, did you?"

"I didn't, but I did," Bobby replied. "The place isn't anything like so completely done up inside as you would think. The outer walls seem sound enough, and it wouldn't be too difficult to patch up the interior again."

"It's been talked about, I believe," Nixon told him. "Cost too much. Too expensive to restore, too expensive to pull down, so it's just been left. You said you made a find? Interesting?"

"Not very, as far as I can see," Bobby admitted. "But you never know. It may come in somewhere. For one thing, I found I had a fellow explorer doing a prowl. I don't know who or what for. And I found an old cigarette butt that can't have been there so very long, and that does seem to suggest there was some other unknown person hanging around about the time of the murder."

Nixon made no answer for a time. He was trying to take in this information and to relate it to what had happened. Presently he said:

"Does that help? I don't see how. Do you?"

"No," Bobby admitted. "I think my fellow explorer is coming."

He had heard what he thought were footsteps descending the marble stair. The footsteps became louder. Through what once had been a fine, portico entrance there emerged Baynham. He saw them and came briskly towards them.

"There's a chap in there," he said. "What's he up to? I only had a glimpse, but I saw him plainly through that gap." He pointed to one near the Tower, by which Bobby knew he himself must have passed. "Who was it? What's he think he's doing up there? Jolly suspicious, people prowling about like that."

"Up to no good, anyhow, you may be sure of that," Bobby pronounced. "Wouldn't be one of your chaps, would it?" he asked Nixon.

"I'm sure it wasn't," Nixon answered. "They're all busy packing up. Done about all we can do here, and that's precious little. I was looking for you, though, Mr Baynham, and for Mr Manners, too. I don't think it's necessary to ask either of you to wait any longer. I must tell you frankly I feel it's certain it was one of those at the meeting, but nothing to show which."

"Well, it can't have been, all the same," Baynham retorted.

Neither of the other two tried to answer this dictum, to which indeed they knew no reply. Instead, Nixon said he must see how his chaps were getting on and tell Mr Manners there was no reason now why he should not leave at once if he wanted to. He went off then, but Bobby remained, for he felt it might be a good opportunity to see if Baynham would be willing to answer a few questions.

"Of course," he explained once more, "you understand I have no official standing here. I'm only present as the nearest, I think the only, male relative, in the country."

"You're a policeman, aren't you?" B.B. asked, and without waiting for a reply, went on: "Not six of us. Mrs Outers and Miss Outers don't count. Mrs James is out of it, too. She was on the floor. Knocked over. I remember thinking for a moment she had been killed, too. That leaves three of us. Three, not six. Peel, Manners and me. One of three."

"One of six," Bobby corrected him. "Nobody who was present can be freed from suspicion as yet."

"Well, you've got to use common sense," B.B. said impatiently.

"There isn't any in this affair," retorted Bobby, and got the unexpected reply:

"What about the map to a gold-mine somewhere in Africa Mr Outers was supposed to have got tucked away. Did you know about that? Can that come into it?"

CHAPTER XIII
FINGER-PRINTS

"GOLD-MINE? Gold-mine?" Bobby repeated, taken aback, for this was indeed a complete surprise. Was it possible Mr Outers had chosen to talk about uranium as camouflage for the possibly more universally attractive gold? He didn't think it likely. Just one more complication in this baffling case. "In Africa?" he asked. "No. Why? Have you?"

"Or about strange, wandering coloured men appearing and disappearing round about here?"

"Well, yes. I've heard something like that," Bobby admitted. "Mr Nixon told me. I don't think he took it very seriously. I'm sure I didn't. We will now. You mean you think there may be some sort of connection between the vanishing Negroes, this gold mine map, and the murder?"

"Well, I think it might be worth while making a few inquiries among the Midminster coloured people. A very decent lot on the whole, and I'm sure they would give you all the help they could. We employ quite a number, and glad to get them."

"I've no doubt Mr Nixon will take that up if you speak to him," Bobby said. "Can you tell us anything more? How did you hear about it?"

"I don't really know," B.B. answered. "I didn't pay much attention. Gold-mines are not in our line. Talk at the Club, chiefly. About how rich the mine was, but Outers wouldn't do anything about it. Thought the natives were better off as they were, and anyhow if it was developed they wouldn't get much of a look in. That's all. Of course, if it's all true and someone wanted the map showing where it was and Outers wouldn't part—well, there's a motive."

"So there is," agreed Bobby.

"Limits it to someone who knew about the map," B.B. said, and added defiantly: "Like me. I thought I had better tell you."

"Much more sensible," Bobby told him. "Much. I'll pass it on to Mr Nixon. I don't see that it helps much though. It may answer 'Why?' but not 'How?' or 'Who?' If it was talked about at the Club, many people might know. What Club?"

"The Midminster Conservative-Liberal-Unionist—the C.L.U. Add a 'B' and you get 'Club.' It's for Midminster top business-men. I'm not tops by any means, but my grandfather was a founder member—'Old B' he was always called. That's why I get called 'B.B.' even by people I've never met before. And one reason why Ludo Manners doesn't like me, as you may have noticed. He isn't a member. Got turned down."

"Oh, why?"

"Well, he's more or less on his own—insurance broker and not long established. Also it got about that once when he was there as a guest he tried to do business. Sort of blasphemy. You may talk business as much as you like, you may treat a client to a swell luncheon on expense account, but you mustn't actually do business. So he got turned down when he put up."

"Then it's altogether likely Mr Manners knew about this gold-mine map if it exists?"

"He might. Anyone in Midminster might, for that matter. You could ask him. I've no idea. The *Midminster News* got to know and sent one of their chaps to try to interview Mr Outers about it. Mr Outers wouldn't talk. All he said was that he wasn't responsible for the chatter of a lot of old women who ought to be out doing an honest day's work for a change. It didn't endear him to the Club."

They parted then, B.B. to avail himself of the official permission to depart and Bobby to wander into the house to see if he could find Ludo Manners. In that he had no difficulty, for on his side Ludo was also looking for him.

"Just been having a turn-up with Nixon," he said. "I can't stand cocky official blokes. I took it to mean he thought it was all hunkadory when he said there was no need for me to hang around, but now he's claiming everyone's suspect. Me, too."

"Everyone who was present at the time," Bobby corrected him. "Necessarily so, till the situation's clearer. Have you heard anything said about a gold-mine?"

"Gold-mine?" repeated Ludo; and he, too, stared in amazement, in which, however, with him, a certain amount of relief seemed mingled. "No," he said with emphasis. "I've never heard anything about gold-mines. What have they to do with it? Never," he repeated with even greater emphasis.

"I gather," Bobby explained, "there's been talk about Mr Outers having known where there was one, but kept it secret."

"Doesn't sound likely," pronounced Ludo. "If you know where there's a gold-mine, you develop it, don't you? Why not? No good keeping it up your sleeve. Outers was a queer, secretive sort, and so this gold-mine yarn got about. If he was secretive, there had to be something to be secretive about, and why not a gold-mine? Filled the bill all right. That's all. He wasn't really secretive, but he always had the murder of his two boys on his mind and he knew he was blamed for it. His own fault, mixed himself up with a lot of beastly native superstitions, silly Stone Age stuff, cannibalism and all."

"I've heard something about that, too," Bobby agreed. "I suppose there isn't anything else you can say? I'm not here officially, you know. Officially, I'm on leave. In a way, you may feel you can talk more freely to me. Nixon probably kept you to facts. I'm more keen on impressions. I could follow up what you could hardly put in an official statement. Of course, if I did turn up anything relevant I should have to tell Nixon at once."

"Hand in glove with him, you mean, don't you?" Ludo grumbled. "I made a statement to Nixon as long as your arm. It didn't amount to anything. We all more or less lost our heads. Running around in circles. I didn't even notice old Mrs James had been knocked over. I must say that monumental prig of a B.B. was a bit more sensible than the rest of us. He rushed off at once to ring up your Midminster chaps. I own up I was so muddled I started to think that was how the murderer got in when B.B. opened the door till I remembered poor old Outers had had his already."

"It may have been how the murderer got out," Bobby said.

Ludo shook his head.

"Couldn't," he said. "I had switched on the electric lamp by then. There were the two oil lamps we use as well, and someone else had got them going, too. Light as day."

"Did Mr Baynham help in that?"

"No. I told you. He rushed off immediately first thing to give the alarm."

Ludo spoke with a considerable show of impatience, but also with an oddly satisfied air, and Bobby got the impression that he felt he had succeeded very well in drawing attention to the fact that B.B. was the only one among them who had had the opportunity to dispose of the murder weapon. And the man who had done that must, of course, by necessity, be the murderer—or need he? Might he have done it to save someone else? A disconcerting thought. But then the young man seemed strongly attracted by Rosamund and might risk much to earn the gratitude of her and of her mother. Bobby left these doubtful considerations. To Ludo, who, at the moment, was busy lighting a cigarette, and, at the same time keeping an observant eye on Bobby himself, he said:

"You were one of those who heard a voice that didn't seem to come from anyone present, weren't you?"

"That's right," Ludo said. "Teddy Peel. Cunning little devil. Cheat his dead mother of her shroud if he got half a chance. He didn't murder Outers, though. Not him. He might slip a knife into you if he knew he could get away with it, but not when he was sure to be suspected. Besides, why should he? Outers was a jolly good client—five guineas a sitting. And you don't kill your best clients. They're your bread and butter."

"There's always that," Bobby agreed, though reflecting that for a sufficiently big prize—such as a gold-mine, even a Teddy Peel might take a desperate risk.

Now Ludo announced that he must really be getting off, if only he could fight his way through the crowd of newspaper men and others gathered together outside and kept at bay only by the extreme and unremitting efforts of the police on duty.

"You won't talk to any of the journalists, I hope," Bobby warned him and Ludo gave a knowing smile.

"Nixon started to lecture me about that," he said. "I told him I knew my onions. But I don't say that if I happen to call on some of my prospects to-morrow to make up for losing to-day, I shan't find it a bit easier to see some of the top rankers, if they think I can give them the low down on it all. Bit of a sensation you know. We don't have so many murders in Midminster as all that."

He departed then, and Bobby watched him go with some distaste. Unreasonable, no doubt. No real reason why he should not use his momentary notoriety, as witness of a mysterious murder, to advance his business interests. All the same, Bobby was not sure that the aura of suspicion surrounding all the six of them would be as helpful to Ludo in his business relations as he seemed to think. In any case, Bobby felt he preferred the young man who might conceivably have made himself an accessory after the fact to help others to the one who planned to turn such a tragedy to his business advantage.

But now Nixon, who had been watching from afar, made his appearance.

"I saw you talking to Manners," he said. "Did you get anything out of him?"

"Nothing much," Bobby admitted, "except that he was trying to make sure we realized B.B. was the only one of them with an opportunity to smuggle the murder weapon away. He did it quite cleverly. But it would have been cleverer still if he had taken it for granted that we could see that much ourselves. Then we wouldn't have to wonder whether he had any reason for throwing suspicion on someone else."

"Well, just possibly he has," Nixon said. "I've got something at last, but I'm blessed if I know what it adds up to. Our dabster" (Nixon's name for his finger-print expert) "has identified Manners's finger-prints on the bureau in the room Mr Outers used for himself."

CHAPTER XIV
AN ANCIENT RIDDLE

BOBBY REMAINED so irresponsive to this piece of what Nixon regarded as startling, and indeed 'vital', information that he began to think Bobby had not taken in its full significance. In reality Bobby was trying—and failing—to relate it to the vague fleeing, fleeting, glimmer of a theory that was beginning to try to shape itself in his mind.

"Well, what was Manners doing there?" Nixon was saying now. "What call had he to fiddle about with Outer's bureau immediately Outers was dead and out of the way? How about his being after that uranium field map you told me about? The girl said there was something missing. Not there any more, she said. Well, how did she know?"

"Nothing to show the locks have been tampered with, was there?" Bobby asked.

"No. They look new—good quality, too," replied Nixon. "I asked Miss Outers where her father kept his keys and she said he always had them on him. Well, they weren't on him when we got here. One of my chaps reported that at once. Most men keep their keys in their pockets, so he noticed it immediately. Well, who has them? Manners?"

"If he has, not in his pockets now," Bobby remarked. "Baynham says there's been some talk in Midminster about Outers knowing where there was an undeveloped gold-mine. That may mean the uranium field story getting changed into a gold-mine yarn, gold-mines being more picturesque and exciting—and more familiar—than uranium fields, though uranium fields are much more important. Did Miss Outers say anything else?"

"Well, no. I asked her what made her think something wasn't there any more, but I couldn't get anything out of her. Then I asked her if it could be what you called a medicine bag, and she just looked at me like—well, like thunder and blue lightning. Then she said if it were it had been better left where it was. Not good enough," Nixon pronounced, looking very firm and determined. "The young woman will have to be a bit more open or there's going to be trouble," but for all the firmness and determination in his voice he managed to give the impression of not being altogether sure on whom this threatened trouble was likely to fall.

"Did you take statements from the women?" Bobby asked. "There weren't any among those you showed me, were there?"

"Well, not from Mrs Outers. She was in a state of collapse. The doctor wouldn't let us. He put her to bed and I put a man at the door till we got a policewoman out to help search for the murder weapon. Not a sign of it, of course. We did get a word or two out of Miss Rosamund, but she kept rushing off to see to her mother. You couldn't rightly call it a statement. In a general way, a knife's easily hidden, but how it's been managed this time I can't think. What did you say?" for Bobby murmured something Nixon had not caught.

"Only an old riddle I've just remembered," Bobby replied. "When is a knife not a knife? I've forgotten the answer. Perhaps there isn't one."

Respect for Bobby's reputation and his position in the London police alone kept back the sharp retort that was on the tip of Nixon's tongue when he heard what he considered this ill-timed piece of frivolity. Instead he said crossly:

"This thing's getting me down. Everything contradicting everything else. I'll send a report to the Home Office. If there's anything in this uranium field story and those old fellows doing the vanishing act round here, I suppose they ought to know."

Bobby nodded agreement.

"Though I don't see what they can do," he said.

"What they will do," Nixon grumbled again, "is to acknowledge receipt of my report, which is receiving attention, and then push it in a pigeon-hole, where it'll stop till next office clean-up. I must go and see if my lads are ready to pack up. Done about all we can here."

"I'll slip across to Freres Lodge," Bobby said, "and see if I can get a chat with Dewey James. Unless it was one of those vanishing and probably non-existent Negroes, who else can have been smoking cigarettes that evening in the old burnt-out ruin?"

"Claims he was asleep in bed all night," Nixon pointed out. "If he sticks to that, how are we to prove he wasn't? And if he wasn't, does it help? He wasn't one of those there when it happened?"

"No; I know," Bobby admitted. "Only if it was Dewey, it may have been because he thought something was going to happen. If it was that, then we want to know why and what."

Nixon grumbled that he supposed so, but didn't see how it could be managed, Dewey not being the sort likely to break down under questioning.

"Not even if we could put the heat on, which we can't," he added; and went off, while Bobby made his way by the foot-path running round the Tower and the ruin to Freres Lodge, where he found some half-dozen journalists hanging about in a lugubrious group, waiting, as newspaper men, detectives and soldiers have so often to do, for something to happen and if it does, and you not on the spot, probably the end of your career. Not so bad, of course, if there's a bar handy where you can exchange gossip and buy drinks for each other, but in this case only the wind and the drizzle and the open road. So Bobby's appearance was hailed with enthusiasm as a possible harbinger, not of spring, but of news, consequent release from waiting about, and then a gallop full speed to the nearest telephone box. Their disappointment therefore was profound though resigned when Bobby told them there was nothing fresh and his present errand was merely to check up on one or two unimportant details.

"Better mind your step, then," one reporter warned him. "The old lady nearly laid the lot of us out with that crutch of hers."

"Shut up, you ass," a comrade exclaimed. "If you had held your silly tongue, we might have got a story out of that: 'Old lady empties pail on high-up police officer.' Would have rated banner headlines."

"Poked Bill in the tummy with the end of the thing," a third man remarked with sadistic pleasure.

"A super poke," confirmed the first speaker, who was apparently 'Bill'. "And then twirled the thing round her head as if she meant to brain the lot of us."

"Would that be possible?" Bobby murmured; and, under a barrage of indignant and bitter retort, escaped to the Lodge, where, when he knocked, Mrs James appeared, a pail of dirty water in one hand.

"Oh, it's you, is it?" she said. She put down the pail, though with an air of slight disappointment. "I told those jackanapes outside if they came worrying any more, they would get what they wouldn't like. Come in. They seem to think no one has anything to do but talk about things you only want to forget, but you can't. One of them had the impudence to ask if I wouldn't like my picture in the papers. I gave him what for."

"Bravo," applauded Bobby. "You can't give those chaps what for too often."

Pleased apparently by this expression of sympathy, Mrs James repeated her invitation to enter. Not without some hope that the watching journalists would note the difference between the reception accorded to him and that they had received, Bobby followed her into a most comfortable-looking, well-kept kitchen, all glamorous with shining brass and gleaming polish. Clearly Mrs James did her best to compensate for the loss of one leg by making her two hands do double work. The table was laid for tea, but not for one of your frivolous four o'clock affairs. A man-sized meal indeed, with sausages keeping hot in a frying-pan, an egg or two in the offing, a pile of buttered toast on the hob. Bobby indeed, whose chief nourishment since breakfast had been a meat-pie—not his favourite article of diet—surveyed these preparations with a touch of envy. Mrs James having laid aside her crutch, carefully balanced across the table with the end pointing towards him—perhaps a warning, he thought, that he, too, might get a 'super poke' if he didn't mind—made one of those prodigious hops of hers to the stove. There, balancing herself on her one leg, with a hand on the mantelpiece for additional support, she poured out a cup of tea. By the aid of a chair-back, she brought it to him, swung back to her own chair and pushed over to him a plate of scones.

During all this she had not spoken a word, but equally she had not ceased to watch him. He had never noticed before how bright and keen and searching were those rather hard, clear light blue eyes of hers, how intent and questioning. But perhaps they had not been so before. It might be that only since what had so recently happened had they gained this new strange intensity of vision. But now she broke into the thanks he was beginning to express for tea and scones, saying:

"It's Dewey you want, isn't it?"

"Well, yes," Bobby admitted. "But I should like to ask you a question or two if you don't object, just so as to get things clearer in my own mind."

"I told the police all I could," she grumbled. "A statement, they called it. I thought they would never stop asking questions—most of them silly or the same thing over again. They've been at Dewey, too, though what can he say when he was asleep in bed all night?" She paused and stared at Bobby, apparently challenging him to reply. When he did not, but remained silent, she went on: "You're police too, aren't you?" He nodded. Still staring at him in the same challenging, defiant way, she said: "One of us six, that's what you all think, isn't it? Which?"

"Well, that's exactly it—which?" Bobby agreed. "Often there's a very limited circle of suspects. But this time, just the six, and it seems certain it must be one of them."

"It certainly wouldn't be his wife or the girl," declared Mrs James positively. "There is one thing I do remember, though, that I don't think I told the other police with their note-books and their pencils and all the rest of it—taking your finger-prints, too. What for? We were all there, weren't we? I don't expect anyone else bothered to say so, but in all the flurry and scurry someone, I don't know who it was, knocked me down—you're not too steady on one leg. So there I was on the floor and I could see under the table and I saw Ludo Manners bending over Mr Outers and slipping a hand into his pocket. I don't know if he took anything out. I don't think he did; he might have. But why should he?"

"Yes. Why should he?" Bobby repeated. "Manners isn't a pick-pocket. Only, for that matter, why should anyone want to kill Val Outers? He had no enemies, had he? He was a newcomer in the neighbourhood—had hardly had time to, for that matter."

"Doesn't take some people long," she retorted. "Mind you, I'm not swearing to anything. It's what I thought at the time, but there I was on the floor, hardly knowing what was happening, only trying to get up before getting trodden on with all of them stamping round in the dark and shouting at each other to get a light."

"It's just possible some of them may have noticed something," Bobby remarked thoughtfully. "I expect Mr Nixon would like another talk with you as soon as he knows. He's sure to want to follow it up. You've not mentioned it to anyone else?"

"Only Dewey," Mrs James answered. "He didn't take any notice. He never takes any notice of his old mother or what she says, though I always try to do my duty by him. Look at the time. Long past when he said he would be in, and everything ready and waiting, and all the washing up to be done he never thinks of helping in. And what's he doing? Fiddling about outside, that's all. Never forgets it's me made him as he is so no woman will look at him twice without giggling or being silly scared."

CHAPTER XV
RESOLUTE IN SILENCE

ALL THIS LAST outburst had been spoken by Mrs James with such extraordinary bitterness, her features so contorted by the passion with which her words had been, as it were, flung at Bobby, that he was considerably startled. There came back to his mind his wife's dictum that Mrs James had never forgiven herself for her son's deformity. Gently, but also a little uneasily, for who could tell to what extremity such self-reproach, so long brooded on, might not lead, he said:

"Don't you think you exaggerate a little? I noticed Miss Outers talking to him. It was the only time I've seen her chatting and laughing like any ordinary girl."

"Oh, her," Mrs James said, and seemed with a casual gesture to dismiss her from consideration. "Showing off. That's all. To annoy her father."

"Why?" Bobby asked. "Has there been any ill feeling between them?"

"Not on Dewey's side," Mrs James assured him. "Mr Outers seemed to think Dewey was something so different, the girl oughtn't to talk to him. A black man was all right. Not Dewey the way he was born. We heard about his saying that people like Dewey often had minds as twisted as their bodies, and he didn't like his girl talking to him. Not that Dewey minded, or me either. We're used to being looked at as if we weren't the same as others. Freaks. Not by everyone, I don't mean, but some, like Mr. Outers. Dewey has a right to be treated as an ordinary human being, hasn't he? If you want him, you had better go and have a look round the outhouses. He'll be somewhere at the back most likely."

So Bobby thanked her for the cup of tea, and, taking her advice, made his way to the back of the lodge.

He went slowly, deep in thought, puzzled not so much by Mrs James's loquacity and her confidences as by the impression strong in his mind that behind her flow of words had been a clear and steady purpose. He knew well enough that those who endure such a shock as the happenings in the summit room of the Folly must have inflicted on them all, are often inclined to seek relief in endless talk. It was a trait well known to police, sometimes helpful to them, sometimes not. But that did not seem to Bobby to be quite the case with Mrs James. She chattered, or so he thought, with a purpose, for a reason, with a controlled aim in view. But what that might be he found it hard to imagine.

Difficult, too, to be sure what were her real feelings, her deeper feelings at least, towards her son, to whom her attitude seemed so oddly compounded of mingled devotion and aversion. He put the problem aside for further consideration and began to wonder instead if Dewey would prove as willing to talk as had all the others he had questioned. But when rounding the corner of an outhouse he saw Dewey standing there, leaning on a spade in a kind of heavy immobility, he knew at once that from him would come no easy flow of words. Not in talk would this man seek relief from his thoughts, no matter how much he might need it, but rather in silence and restraint. Of Bobby's greeting he took scant notice, but one could not say that his bearing was in any way hostile. He merely waited, and why that waiting was impressive Bobby could not tell.

"Mrs James told me I might find you out here," he began, and still Dewey waited, but again, not so much as in indifference, but only as if he were attentive not to what had been said but rather to what was going to be said. "You know I am an officer of police?" Bobby went on, and this direct question brought now a faint gesture of acquiescence, so that Bobby began to grow irritated at such persistent taciturnity, but which nevertheless, he felt instinctively, was not being deliberately adopted, but was rather an attitude habitual with one who knew that words are but light and transient and treacherous things whereby to express emotion. Perhaps, however, on this occasion there was also in this persistent silence of his, an element of defence. Against what? For of all of those directly or indirectly concerned, he alone, by the unanimous testimony of the others, could not possibly be implicated in any conceivable way.

Nevertheless, Bobby decided to try to break down this barrier of silence by sudden, abrupt assault. He said:

"There's reason to believe that someone was in what is left of the old house last night. Was it you?"

Slowly Dewey answered:

"Why should you think so?"

"Who else could it be?" Bobby asked in return; and in the same slow, deliberate, unemotional tones, Dewey countered simply:

"I do not know."

Bobby asked again:

"Who else could it be?"

This time, to this twice-repeated question, Dewey still made no reply. Bobby waited. In silence—a heavy brooding silence—the two men waited, Dewey leaning motionless on his spade, Bobby erect and equally motionless, looking down from his more than six feet on Dewey's less than five. But somehow this gave to Bobby no sense of dominance, nor, seemingly, to Dewey any feeling of inferiority. It was the first time that Bobby had been so close to him. That early impression, founded on a brief glimpse from some distance, had been of a body so oddly distorted as to be almost grotesque. Now he recognized that this distorted body was also solid, firmly knit, and that the great head, sunk between its shoulders showed features of a noble form, finely shaped. There was a contradiction, though, or so Bobby thought, between the sad, soft brown eyes, placed far apart, clear as a summer's dawn, yet pleading, too, like those of a faithful dog waiting its master's will, and the ruthless-looking mouth, set in such hard lines above the granite-like protruding chin.

Now it was Bobby who spoke first, asking for the third time:

"Was it you waiting there that night while a man was murdered nearby?"

"That is for you to say," Dewey retorted then, and to that Bobby retorted in his turn:

"You mean you do not wish to say?" and when Dewey still spoke no word, Bobby knew he must accept this silence as definitive—for the time at least. Further thought and further time for reflection, might, as often happened, make even those apparently most resolute in silence, decide to speak. Fear, doubt and, sometimes, conscience could frequently do their work best in a man's own mind and heart.

"If you change your mind, let us know," he said. "Murder has been done and truth must be made plain," and with that he turned and walked away.

As he went, though slowly, he glanced back over his shoulder and saw that Dewey still remained as before, motionless and brooding, wrapped in his own dark thoughts.

Bobby, too, went heavily, oppressed by many fears and doubts. When he came to the Lodge, the door was open and Mrs James was standing on the threshold, clearly outlined against the bright glow of the oil lamp she had just lighted now that it was growing towards night. When she saw him approaching, she called:

"Did you find him?"

"Yes," Bobby answered.

"Did he say anything?"

Bobby shook his head.

"Why did you expect him to?" she asked, and, without waiting for an answer, went back into the house, banging the door behind her.

From the Lodge, Bobby walked on to a road box he had noticed not far away, and, ringing up Nixon, informed him of what he had learned from Mrs James. Nixon sounded a little excited and seemed to think this 'pinned' the murder on Ludo Manners. Bobby, less optimistic, agreed, however, that it might be so and then hung up and returned to Constant House, where, when he entered, he was met by Rosamund, still looking like a distant thunder-cloud, still so closed in her own secret thoughts that when she spoke it seemed as though the words came automatically, without conscious purpose or intention. In this strange new, lifeless, voice of hers, she said:

"Your room is ready. It's the one you and Cousin Olive had. One of the policemen has stayed on. He said he would sleep in an armchair on the landing outside mother's room. He can if he likes, but I've made up a bed for him in the spare room next to yours, only it's not properly aired."

"Oh, he'll be all right," Bobby assured her; and he found something a little daunting in this careful thought for homely, household detail against the background of agony and fear he sensed lay hidden in her deepest self. He said to her:

"What do you think your mother meant by blood washing out blood?"

It was then that sheer terror leaped into her eyes. A dreadful panic so marked that he half expected to see her turn and fly. But that he knew was not her way; neither was she likely to seek refuge in tears or collapse. Her voice had even become steadier, more lifelike, though the fear was still in her eyes as she said:

"Did you hear her say that? You never did."

"No," he answered. "It is in a statement made in the course of this inquiry."

"Whose?" she demanded.

"It is what we call 'information received'," Bobby explained. "We never give names unless and until it has been decided to lay a charge."

"I suppose I was forgetting you are a policeman," she said bitterly.

"That is a thing no police officer can ever forget," Bobby told her. "It is because I am that I think I can help you and that I stay here to help get at the truth. You knew that. If you are afraid of the truth and would like me to leave, you have only to say so. But it is possible that I might be sent back, and then I should be more strictly controlled."

"You would be all policeman then, I suppose," she said, still more bitterly. "You may as well stay. Besides, I know. It was Mrs James. It isn't true. She hates me; she hates her son. How could it be true? The doctor said no one was to see her, and he gave her something to make her sleep. Mrs James did take her some coffee and toast, but she was asleep. She said so."

"Does your mother ever talk in her sleep?" Bobby asked.

"No; she doesn't," Rosamund answered quickly. "Never." But the confidence had gone out of her voice, to be replaced by a kind of nervous tension. "Never," she repeated. "She wouldn't say a thing like that even if she did. I'll get you something to eat. There's not much in the house. I expect there's some cheese and I can boil you an egg. Would you rather have coffee or cocoa? He had coffee."

Bobby thanked her, begged her not to trouble, guessed that the 'he' referred to the man left behind by Nixon, opted for coffee, too, and as she went off to attend to his needs, she said over her shoulder:

"It doesn't mean anything. How could it?"

Without waiting for an answer, she hurried off, and Bobby went upstairs to wash his hands and exchange his shoes for slippers. Then he went to visit the duty constable in the next room and found him lying fully dressed on the unaired bed, smoking a cigarette and filling up his football pool coupons. He jumped up as Bobby entered. Bobby said:

"Don't set the bed things on fire. I'm in the next room, but I shall go to bed properly. Not yet awhile, though. If there's any disturbance, call me at once. I don't think there will be. Having a go at that £75,000?"

"That's right, sir," the man answered grinning.

"Better fun than five bob on the favourite that never wins," Bobby said. "And all the same in the end—five bob down the drain. You've had something to eat?"

"Yes, sir. Very nice young lady, even if she does look as if she hadn't only just seen a ghost as been living with 'em. I hope it won't turn out to be her or her mum."

"I hope not," Bobby said and retired to seek his bread and cheese.

CHAPTER XVI
NO GLIMMER OF LIGHT

EARLY NEXT MORNING, Nixon arrived, all eagerness to follow up the hint of a clue that Mrs James seemed to have provided. He had had already an interview with her from which he retired in some disorder and from which he learned no more than he knew before. Next there was a consultation with Bobby, ending in agreement that for the present at least the available evidence was far too slender for any action to be taken on it.

"Not a glimmer of light anywhere," Nixon sighed; and Bobby did not think it necessary or desirable to say that for his part he did think that a very faint such glimmer, very far off, might perhaps be discerned by the eye of hope.

"Got to wait and see if anything turns up," Nixon resumed after lighting a cigarette, that ever-present help in moments of doubt and of perplexity. "Got to have something stronger to work on than dabs on an old bureau and a story about an unknown gold-mine that most likely isn't one at all. There's one thing I've noticed, though. When Manners was searched two sets of keys were found on him. He said one was for home, one for the office. Unusual. No trace of a map or anything like that."

"It might have been there, but not noticed," Bobby said. "No one was bothering about papers. A knife was being looked for. And the only one of the six with anything like a chance to get away with it was B.B."

Nixon nodded a gloomy agreement.

"Had a chance yet for a talk with Mrs Outers?" he asked. "Or the girl?"

"She got us some breakfast," Bobby said. "I tried to help, but was badly snubbed for my pains. I'm afraid the only part of me she likes is my back, and yet I think in a way she wants me to stay on. What they call a split mind about me. She says her mother had a little tea and toast this morning. But she's taking jolly good care we don't get a chance to talk to her before the doctor turns up and says we may."

"Well, I must be getting on with the job," Nixon declared. "Very little we can do though in my view, unless we get some lucky break. A dead end, and that's a fact."

"Should you mind if I saw Mrs Outers by myself at first?" Bobby asked. "I have an idea she may be willing to talk more freely if we are alone. Of course, I'll make it quite clear to her I have to be a policeman before being a cousin."

Nixon was frowning now. Not at Bobby or at this suggestion, but at certain memories of his late interview with another elderly lady and of the 'what for' she had given him. No need to risk another interview with a second elderly lady if Bobby would take on the job.

"That'll be quite all right," he said. "Very difficult case. I've a letter about it from the Chairman of our Joint Committee. I'm relying a good deal on you, Mr Owen. There's never been anything like it before in this neighbourhood. When we do have a murder, it's generally quite a straightforward affair. Husband and wife doing each other in, or boy and the girl who turned him down, so he goes off his head—the young fool. That sort of thing. Money or sex. Simple. But this thing doesn't make sense."

"No; only a dead man," Bobby said grimly; but Nixon still looked unappeased, as if he felt it hardly fair that he should be confronted with such a problem.

They were talking in the room Val Outers had kept more especially for his own use, where, too, stood that old mahogany bureau round which, to Bobby's fancy at least, the shadows now lay less thickly. Nixon got up to go; saying gloomily that he supposed he must get along to see his Chairman and explain, or try to, why the guilty man had not already been arrested.

He opened the door to leave, and Rosamund promptly emerged from the kitchen, where she had been busy with domestic cares.

"Mr Peel's here," she said. "I put him in the sewing-room." She pointed to the door of a small room that once had been so used, at a time when sewing-maids were still to be heard of. "He didn't say what he wanted." She went with Nixon to the front door and let him out, and then came back to Bobby. "Is that other policeman staying on?" she asked him, and Bobby recognized a little feminine dig contained in that 'other'. "I want to know because of lunch."

"He will be going almost immediately," Bobby answered, "but there will be another to take his place. A relief. Please don't bother about lunch. He'll have sandwiches or something from the canteen. You don't have to board police as well as air their beds for them."

He made this remark smilingly, hoping to cheer things up, though indeed it had no such effect.

"He never slept in it," she said seriously. "I expect he remembered I told him it wasn't." And then, with that deep, sombre passion she sometimes showed, she said, "I hate their being here," and went back to the kitchen.

Bobby hesitated for a moment and then crossed to the room where Rosamund had told him Teddy Peel was waiting, a piece of information which Nixon had either forgotten or ignored—or perhaps thought there were more pressing matters to attend to than chatting to Teddy. Before Bobby could enter, however, there was a knock at the front door. Bobby opened it as Rosamund, immured in her dark little kitchen, built in days when the convenience of maids was not much considered, had apparently not heard. A stranger stood on the doorstep.

"Doctor," he said briefly, and then: "You police?"

"Yes," Bobby answered. "I was waiting for you to know if you consider Mrs Outers fit to give her account of what happened. She has made no statement so far, and it is important we should have one as soon as possible."

"Not to-day, I'm afraid," the doctor answered with a gleam in his eye Bobby noticed at once and recognized. Some doctors were always inclined to think their duty to their patients came before their duty to the law. And then this particular doctor had twice been summonsed and fined for small parking and speeding offences. "No, not to-day," he repeated.

"Possibly you would like a second opinion," Bobby suggested. "The police surgeon, for instance?"

But the idea was not very favourably received. Bobby even thought that he caught a murmur sounding very much like 'Antiquated old fool.' Aloud the doctor said stiffly:

"I see no need for a second opinion. Of course, if my patients wish it . . ."

"Oh, I'm sure they are perfectly satisfied," Bobby said in what Olive was wont to call his 'sugar and honey' voice. "Just police regulations, that's all. Red tape." He made an apologetic gesture that seemed to include all police forces all over the world—they and their red tape together. "I'll ask Mr Nixon to arrange it, shall I? To suit your convenience, of course."

"I suppose I can be allowed to see my patient first," growled the doctor, not—repeat not—pleased.

"So long as there is no undue delay," Bobby agreed, this time with just a trifle less of the honey and sugar in his voice, and the doctor, a retired Army man, looked very much as if he would like to order Bobby Number Nines and be done with him.

By this time Rosamund, hearing voices, had emerged again from her kitchen. She greeted the doctor, gave Bobby a disapproving glance, for she suspected there had been something like an argument between them, and to argue with a doctor is, in every woman's view, a kind of *lèse-majestè*—and Rosamund was all woman behind that dark, stormy cloud of reserve in which she wrapped herself—and so disappeared with the doctor up the stairs to her mother's room.

Bobby, left alone, entered the sewing room and found it unoccupied. Teddy Peel had evidently taken some opportunity to slip away unperceived. Bobby wondered why he had come and where he had vanished to and then sat down to smoke a meditative cigarette. He had not long to wait. Soon he heard the two—Rosamund and the doctor—coming down the stairs together. The doctor tried to ignore him, but somehow Bobby had got between him and the door, which could not be reached without pushing Bobby aside. Nor did that look as if it would be easy. Bobby was evidently waiting to hear the verdict. The doctor said:

"I've told Miss Outers her mother is sufficiently recovered to see you—but only for a very short time. Five minutes at the most."

"Is that final?" Bobby asked. "Or must I ask the police doctor to come over to confirm it?"

"If my professional opinion is not good enough for you, you can do what you like. Your responsibility," came the snarled response.

With that he flounced away, and when he had gone Rosamund turned to Bobby.

"You had better come up now," she said. "I don't think you were very polite to the doctor."

"It's so hard to be loved by all," Bobby sighed. "Even by all young ladies."

This was meant for a gentle hit back for her recent 'other policeman', and for the first time he managed to produce from her what was nearly a faint semblance of a smile, even if it disappeared again almost at once.

"Where is Mr Peel?" she asked, and then, without waiting for an answer, continued: "I told Mother I would bring you back. Please be as quick as you can. There's such a lot to do. I haven't even been in the bedrooms yet. Will the new policeman want to stay all night?"

"I shouldn't think Mr Nixon will consider it necessary," Bobby said. "I don't know. It's for him to say, and he didn't tell me. Can't you let the house go for the present? Surely you needn't worry about beds just now?"

"I've been through it all before," she said, "when my brothers—" She paused abruptly. Her face twisted. Then her back was towards him, her whole body shaking. He thought she was going to break down. It was two or three minutes before she had her voice sufficiently under control to allow of speech. When she turned to face Bobby again, he was standing at the window, apparently absorbed in contemplating the landscape.

"Thank you," she said. "It's all got to go on—cooking and cleaning and beds and everything. It stops you thinking too much."

"Yes," Bobby agreed from his post by the window. "It always has to go on. Everything. I've been wondering what's become of Mr Teddy Peel and what he's up to. I don't trust him a lot. May I ask—have you yourself any suspicion of anyone? It might help if I knew."

She shook her head.

"I suppose it must have been one of us," she said. "Only it couldn't be. So it must have been some one else. But there wasn't anyone else. So that's impossible, too."

With that she turned towards the door, leading the way up the stairs to her mother's room.

"It's Cousin Owen, Mother," she said as she went in. "He says he wants to talk to you."

CHAPTER XVII
IMPOSSIBLE POSSIBLE

MRS OUTERS WAS sitting up in bed, propped against pillows. She was wearing a woollen bed-jacket and looked pale and ill. Not to be wondered at, Bobby thought. But what struck him immediately, and far more forcibly, was a certain serenity in her expression, an air of peace as it were—or was it resignation?—that surrounded her, as if now she knew the worst had happened and there was nothing more to fear.

"The doctor," she said after a word or two of greeting, "told me I wasn't to talk to you for more than two or three minutes, but I don't think I shall mind very much about that. I feel quite strong, and then he seemed so much more fussy than he is generally."

"That's Cousin Owen," Rosamund put in, still disapprovingly. "He upset him terribly."

"All in the way of duty," Bobby explained with no great outward show of contrition. "Duty comes first."

"Dear Val used to say that, too," Mrs Outers agreed, "when he would go out on one of his inspection tours and I didn't think he was well enough. I expect you want me to go over it all again. Rosamund says so."

"Well, yes," Bobby said. "Statements have to be taken from every one who was there, but that's for Mr Nixon—a formal statement, that is, you will be asked to sign. All the facts, so to say. But facts can be so misleading. They can get interpreted all wrong. Often it's the apparently unimportant background you have to know to understand the facts correctly."

"I don't think I quite understand," Mrs Outers said.

"He means he wants to get into your mind and turn it inside out," Rosamund interrupted with another frown at Bobby. "You've got to be jolly careful."

"Oh, dear. I don't think he's like that," Mrs Outers protested. "Are you like that?" she asked him.

"It was put very clearly," Bobby admitted. "Not exactly what I should have said, though. You only need to be jolly careful if there's something to hide. If there isn't, why try to keep me out?"

"I would," Rosamund exclaimed. "It's my mind."

"Hush, Rosy dear," her mother said. "I'm sure we can trust Cousin Owen."

"He's a policeman. He keeps on saying so," Rosamund muttered, and subsided into her usual gloomy, frowning silence.

Bobby—who had had quite a shock when he heard her addressed as 'Rosy'—somehow it seemed as ill-fitting an appellation, as 'Rosamund' had appeared appropriate—began to ask his questions. All Mrs Outers said, however, was very much the same as that told by the others, nor had Bobby expected it would be otherwise. But it served to get her talking freely. He made no attempt to take anything down in writing. That is apt to inhibit any witness, no matter how anxious to be helpful. Gradually the atmosphere relaxed. Mrs Outers talked more freely, Rosamund began to seem less keyed-up.

"Thank you," Bobby said presently. "It's just the same, of course, only seen differently. That often brings out some fresh detail. A shift of emphasis. Now I must ask you this. Have you any feeling of suspicion against anyone? For any reason whatever, no matter how slight. Was anything different? The order in which you sat round the table? Was that always the same? It might be very important," he added.

"Oh, no," Mrs Outers answered immediately. "Nothing. We always sat like that. Mr Peel said it helped results. I do remember now Mrs James said her leg was hurting her. It's never healed completely. Splinters of bone keep coming away. That's why she can't wear an artificial leg, and has a crutch instead. Generally she leans it up against the wall and then makes one of those great hops of hers to the table. I think they are wonderful, though it frightens me sometimes. It doesn't seem natural the way she does it."

"She's always there, isn't she?" Bobby asked. "But not her son?"

"Oh, no, never," Mrs Outers answered. "He never comes. I'm afraid Val didn't like him very much and he's so sensitive. He's so deformed. Val used to say in any African village he would have been destroyed at birth. Of course, he didn't mean it was right to do that; only Africans do know a lot more than we do in some ways. Mrs James never misses. Mr

Peel says her being there helps with what he calls his electric magnetism. I've wondered sometimes if he was wanting to marry her."

"Oh, Mother," protested Rosamund, very much surprised. "Why, she's only got one leg."

"You don't marry people's legs," Mrs Outers retorted. "She's very active—those hops of hers. You never know who'll want to marry who."

"Well, I don't," Rosamund said—a remark Bobby found somewhat obscure.

To her mother, he said:

"Myra, there's something else that may be important. Apparently a story's going round that Val had a map showing where there's a hitherto unknown gold-mine or something of the sort in a native location in Africa?"

"Oh, that," Myra answered. "Oh, yes. Not in a location; somewhere right in the interior. It was in that thing he got from an old witch-doctor. Val, said probably it was notes of his travels by some European—someone meaning to write a book. They all do—such nonsense, most of them. Natives don't know much about books, but they all know about gold and how Europeans want gold more than anything."

"Val never looked to see?"

"Oh, no," she exclaimed. "No. You see . . . well, I can't explain exactly . . . of course, he didn't really believe . . . only you never know with those dreadful men."

"Father knew," Rosamund interposed, "and so did we, it was better left unopened."

"Scorpions and things," her mother suggested and repeated: "You never know."

"Now it's gone, hasn't it?" Bobby said.

"Rosy says so," Mrs Outers answered. "She says it was in the old bureau in his room. He always kept it locked. Rosy says the medicine bag was there, and now it isn't. I don't know how she can tell."

Rosamund offered no explanation and Bobby asked for none. He knew he would not be likely to receive any that the common-sense side of him could accept and use. If Myra's suggestion that the missing bag might contain a dozen or so living—and stinging—scorpions or any other form of poisonous insect, then no doubt it was most desirable it should be left unopened. Still more desirable perhaps that it should be promptly put in the fire. Breaking the silence that had followed Myra's last words, Bobby went on:

"There's another story I've heard, about two old Negroes seen dodging about here."

"So silly," Myra told him. "What for? Africans wouldn't touch a medicine bag, even an old one, for anything in the world. Besides, how could they possibly get here or get passports or anything? I told Val. He said it was most likely a bush or something by the side of the road, and it was taken for Negroes because of Val having been out there and not being quite like other people. He would never play golf or bridge and he was so interested in the Africans, and gossip got about. I never knew Home was such a place for gossip."

"All places are places for gossip," Bobby told her. "Good thing, too. Often how we get at the truth. About Mr Peel—do you think he can be trusted? He seems to have taken himself off somewhere now."

"Trusted?" Myra repeated, apparently somewhat surprised by so naive a question. "Oh, no. Not a bit. But Val always said there was something odd about him, and it was very interesting, like the witch-doctors out there. Only they claim it's because they can compel or persuade natural forces that aren't exactly either good or bad, but just powers—it's in the Bible, 'principalities and powers.' Mr Peel talks about electric magnetism and believes it's inside him and nothing to do with anything else, like poetry and things. Shakespeare," she concluded abruptly.

"He does produce results not easily explained?" Bobby suggested.

"Oh, funny things do happen," Myra admitted. "Floating tambourines. That sort of thing, and he tells you what you're thinking or things you had absolutely forgotten, only they're really true and you remember them when he tells you."

"Silly things," Rosamund interposed. "Like that once I went to have a shower and forgot to take all my things off. Mother says she remembers. I don't. He never knows what I'm thinking."

"He says you close your mind against him," Mrs Outers said.

"Do either of you see any possibility of his having had anything to do with the disappearance of the knife used?" Bobby asked them.

Rosamund shook her head. Her mother said, "No." Rosamund went on:

"How could he? He never went out of the room till the police came. None of us did. We were all together, all the time till then."

"Except Mr Baynham," Bobby reminded her gently.

"He only went to ring up the police," Rosamund explained; and seemed to think that fact ruled out any possibility of his having taken away the knife at the same time. "When the police came we were all searched. Mother and I were taken away to wait for a policewoman. There was a policeman with us till she came. They made the men strip to the skin."

"It was all horrible," Mrs Outers said. "The policewoman said it was only a matter of form, but she was very particular."

"I suppose it means Mother and me . . ." Rosamund said, looking at Bobby almost pleadingly, plainly seeking reassurance.

She did not finish her sentence, but her meaning had been plain through that deep reserve in which she lived, and Bobby said gravely:

"We have not been able to eliminate anyone yet. Nor find anyone else."

"There wasn't anyone else," Rosamund repeated. "That's why it's all impossible."

"It happened," Bobby said as he had said before. "And only the possible happens. Therefore . . ."

He, too, left his sentence unfinished. Nor did either of the two women attempt to answer that 'therefore', which to both of them had sounded like a word of endless doom. It was a minute or two before, a little sorry that that 'therefore' had escaped him, a little afraid that perhaps more might have been read into it than he had intended, Bobby spoke again. He said:

"You both heard this voice you've spoken about, the one that seemed to come from the top of the room above the table. In a native African language. You both know it well enough to be sure of the meaning?"

"Rosy speaks it like English," Mrs Outers said. "I know it well enough to talk to the servants. It's a very difficult language."

"But you're quite clear of the meaning?"

"Well, not at first," Mrs Outers admitted. "It was a funny voice."

"It said what you've been told," Rosamund said slowly and steadily. "That a death wish was loose among us, trying to get itself born into action."

"Ventriloquism?" Bobby suggested. "That's one explanation that's been offered."

"How could it be?" Rosamund asked. "Mr Peel has never been to Africa, never been out of England. I shouldn't think there are more than ten or twelve people in the world know it well enough to speak it. Europeans, I mean. We've thought of it, Mother and me—we've thought of everything."

Bobby made no comment. There was nothing useful he could say. Instead he changed the subject and asked:

"Is there any chance that what you heard could possibly have meant: 'Blood washes out blood'?"

CHAPTER XVIII
BY DEATH SET FREE

THE EFFECT OF this sudden question upon Mrs Outers was both marked and startling. Rosamund's expression remained comparatively unchanged. Only a slight increase in the intent watchfulness with which all the time she regarded Bobby seemed to show itself. Otherwise she might not even have heard. But Mrs Outers stared and flushed and stared again and became very pale. Till now she had been chatting freely as if some inner tension had been relieved, some barrier removed.

"What do you mean?" she asked in a voice not too steady. "Rosy?" Rosamund shook her head slightly, but did not attempt to speak. Nor did Bobby make any reply to the first question. Mrs Outers asked him now: "Who told you? No one knew."

Bobby remained silent. It was a way he had, a theory that if no answer were given to a question whose significance and meaning were not quite clear, then silence could often elicit a second question that might provide unconsciously an answer to the first. This time that did not happen, for abruptly Rosamund spoke.

"It was Mrs James told him," she said briefly.

"Mrs James?" her mother repeated, though now with less of the sheer terror that had seemed before to underlie her first surprise and bewilderment. "How could it be?" she asked. "She didn't know."

"She said she heard you talking in your sleep," Rosamund answered. "I don't believe her."

"What does it mean?" Bobby asked.

Neither mother nor daughter replied. They were staring at each other. It seemed that between them there was a mutual understanding, though to neither was it quite clear nor sure. Apparently they had completely forgotten Bobby's presence. He repeated:

"What does it mean?"

"We don't know," Rosamund answered, now, her attention still, however, on her mother.

"Val is dead, murdered," Bobby said, and his voice had become harsh and compelling. "Was it he or his sons' blood death was to set free?"

"We don't know," Rosamund said once more; and Bobby felt that that stark self-control of hers was on the point of cracking. "All nonsense," she said, a little wildly. "I wish it had been mine." With what seemed an extreme effort of self-control, she continued in a quieter voice: "When we were trying to find out what had happened to the boys, Father went to see an old medicine-man he knew of. Father said if anyone knew what had happened to the boys, he did. The Africans said he was older than anyone had ever been before. They said he was kept alive because the dark powers feared that if he joined the dead people they might become too strong and he would lead them back into the world again. But when Father found the old man he would not speak. He sat there and was still, as though he were dead himself, he was so old. Father came away and that night I went myself. I walked all through the night, and all day and all the next night as well, and then in the morning I came to the hut in the village where he lived. But he would not see me, so I sat by the door and waited, and when it was nearly night he sent his chief wife and she asked me if I had eaten or drunk since I started. So I said, 'No', and she said then it is well and she went back into the hut and presently he came out, and he went into a kind of trance. After a time he began to speak in a language I did not know and in a voice that was not his. And behind what wasn't his voice I heard two other voices, very low and faint, but I do not know whose they were or what they said. Then all at once he spoke in English, a very loud voice, and that is what he said: 'By death set free.' So I asked him what it meant and he did not answer. He could not, for he was dead."

"Dead?" Bobby repeated. "You mean he died as soon as he had said that?"

"Or else before," she answered simply. "I do not know. The villagers gave me food and drink and I rested and they helped me home. I think they were afraid because they thought my medicine must be stronger than his. I had left a note for Mother telling her where I had gone, and not to let Father know. She said I had a sick headache and mustn't be disturbed. I told Mother when I got back, but I never told Father."

"Why didn't you?" Bobby asked.

"I think it was because I was afraid," she answered, and after that there was for a time silence among them.

What bearing this macabre story had upon the investigation he had undertaken, Bobby was not sure, but he knew that for long—very long—there would remain in his mind a vivid picture of this lone English girl on her strange mission, battling her solitary way, by day and by night, through the darkness of the African forest. Little wonder perhaps that after such an effort, such an experience, as few of her age and sex had ever known, she had wrapped herself in such clouds of dark reserve as seemed at times to cut her off from common human intercourse. He could understand, too, that this tale of a white woman sitting waiting outside the hut of a native witch-doctor might well have aroused passionate repercussions had it become generally known. Probably, if any hint of it had got about, the authorities had taken pains to deny or suppress it, while Africans, though they might whisper it among themselves, would very likely not dare to repeat it aloud. At any rate, so far as he knew, no hint of it had ever reached Europe, or, if it had, its significance had not been understood and its impact negligible.

So was he musing, lost in thoughts darting hither and thither in his mind. When with a quick, abrupt movement Rosamund jumped to her feet. For a moment she stood still, then gave herself a little shake. Like a dog shaking off water from its coat, so she seemed to be shaking off thoughts and memories on which was she knew dangerous to dwell too long.

"I've got to see about lunch," she announced. To her mother she said, her voice, her whole demeanour, changing thus with startling suddenness: "You must try to go to sleep again. I'll bring you something on a tray. The fish-man has been this morning, and he had some turbot, so I got that, and I'll do an omelet as well."

"I don't want anything except a cup of tea," Mrs Outers said.

Rosamund was moving towards the door, at the same time glancing at Bobby to follow her. On the landing outside he said to her:

"It doesn't explain Mrs James's knowing."

Rosamund made no comment. It seemed now she had told her story she had lost interest in all but her household duties.

"Lunch ought to be ready by one," she said. "You can start laying the table—if you know how," she added doubtfully.

"I'm a married man—fully trained," he told her. "I'm wondering where Peel's got to, though."

"He's rather fond of turning up about lunch-time," Rosamund said over her shoulder as she led the way down the stairs to the hall. "Please don't go finding him. If you do I shall have to give him lunch, and I don't want to very much."

"I think I must try to find him," Bobby said. "But I won't invite him to lunch. I'll pack him off instead."

They had reached the hall now. She turned to look at him.

"You make people do what you want, don't you?" she said disapprovingly. "I expect you bully poor Cousin Olive dreadfully," and this remark so flabbergasted—it's the only word—Bobby that he could do nothing but stare and gasp at the mere idea of his bullying Olive, when it was so much, and so obviously, the other way round. "In here," Rosamund was saying now, leading the way into the dining-room. She showed him the sideboard standing against the inner wall. "Everything's there," she informed him. "There's a clean table-cloth in the middle drawer. If you must go looking for Mr Peel, mind you're back by one." She disappeared towards the kitchen, and then, before he had fully recovered from the slightly dazed condition in which she had left him she was there again, framed in the open doorway. "Now it's off my mind," she said and was gone, this time shutting the kitchen door behind her with considerable emphasis.

So Bobby set himself to complete the task allotted to him, decided presently that he had made a good job of it, and then, proceeding with some caution in case Rosamund called him back again to render her more assistance—peeling the potatoes perhaps—succeeded in reaching the Folly Tower unperceived. For it was much in his mind that there Teddy Peel was to be found, though for what purpose it was hard to guess.

He went in by what once had been the main entrance, though now it was little more than another gap torn in the nevertheless still solid shell of four walls. He picked his way with care through the jumble of debris and rubbish. Was there more of all this or was it simply that he was noticing it more? He didn't know. Leaving on his right the great marble stairway rising so bravely and so uselessly from the chaos and the ruin around to reach vacancy above, Bobby went on, listening, looking, searching for any sign of a recent visitor. He found none, though he did disturb a big black cat—it belonged to Mrs James, as he discovered later. It made a dignified retreat when he appeared—so dignified, in fact, that Bobby was tempted to expedite it by the help of a suitable and well-aimed bit of rubble. However, he reflected that neither the cat nor the ruin nor the rubble belonged to him, so he refrained. Nearby was what at first sight seemed merely a hole torn in the elsewhere intact flooring of the old building, but that on closer view showed itself as having been a way into the cellars, for there was a flight of stone steps, still firm and in position, leading downwards. It did not look a promising or an inviting field for further exploration. Not much likelihood that Teddy Peel would be seeking shelter there, and it was that gentleman Bobby was anxious to find—if, that is, he was there to be found.

It was while he was still staring meditatively into that deep Stygian darkness beneath that a sudden fall of plaster reminded him he was in a burnt-out building long since labelled 'dangerous' and marked for demolition. Had he heard something else as well—a hurrying and furtive footstep? He did not know. He jumped aside only just in time to avoid a heavier shower, not only this time of plaster, but of brick as well—a narrow escape from, at any rate, incapacitating injury. As it was he found himself enveloped in dust and dirt, and, tripping over another pile of rubbish, down upon his hands and knees. He cut his hand slightly in falling and it began to bleed. Another fall of brick and plaster followed and somewhat hurriedly he removed himself from the danger spot. He heard sounds as of someone making a cautious approach. He got to his feet and took out his handkerchief to wrap round his injured hand. A face appeared, peering through the gap above. It was that of B.B. Bobby said:

"Oh, it's you, is it?"

"Are you all right?" B.B. asked, and was there—Bobby asked himself this time—a faint note of disappointment in a question to which the answer was clearly "Yes"?

"You might come down here, will you?" was Bobby's response.

"As soon as I can get," came the reply. "Have to be careful. The whole place looks as if it might collapse any moment."

"I've just noticed that," Bobby answered.

CHAPTER XIX
FOOD FOR THOUGHT

THE DESCENT WAS fortunately accomplished without disaster, and once he was on the comparatively safe surface at ground level, Baynham made his way easily enough to where Bobby was still trying to brush away the dirt and dust with which he was covered. He looked round as he heard B.B. approaching, and perhaps in that quick and searching glance there was more of questioning suspicion than he fully realized.

"Been having a look round?" he asked.

"I thought I saw someone up there," B.B. answered. "I wondered who he was and what he wanted."

"Did you find out?"

"No. It wasn't you, I suppose?"

"It was not," Bobby answered. "I would like to know myself. It is always interesting to know who is poking about near the scene of a murder and why. Had you any special reason for returning here?"

"Is there any objection?" B.B. asked, belligerent now.

"At any rate," came Bobby's quick response, "there's a strong objection on my part to being nearly knocked out by a shower of bricks and plaster."

"Well, damn it, man," B.B. began angrily. "How was I to know? I nearly came through myself. Of course, I'm beastly sorry." He paused, for Bobby was looking at him rather hard. "I had no idea," he concluded, somewhat lamely. "You don't think I did it on purpose, do you?"

"The thought did just cross my mind," Bobby admitted. "After all, there is a murderer loose somewhere around here—one of six. As you are. And if the murderer begins to feel things are warming up it may occur to him that it would be rather a good idea to put one or two investigators out of action. You haven't told me yet if you had any special reason why you've returned?"

"Only to call at Freres to ask how they were—Mrs Outers and Miss Outers I mean. I've been out on business and I had to come back this way anyhow, so I parked my car near the Lodge and came round by the Tower track. That's all." He paused, hesitated, and then said: "It's hard to realize you're suspected of murder."

"Don't you suspect any of the others?" Bobby asked.

"No. No; I don't," B.B. answered, just a little too quickly perhaps, or so Bobby thought at the moment. "No," he repeated, now a little too firmly. "I did just think when I saw someone up there that it might be some chap looking for the knife. I've always thought it might be hidden there. I don't see how it could have been, but the police couldn't find it. It must be somewhere not far away. Now I suppose you'll say it was me trying to get it before there was another search?"

"It might be like that," Bobby agreed. "In this case anything is possible, except everything. You remember telling me there was talk in Midminster of Mr Outers possessing a map showing the position of an undeveloped gold-mine in Africa? Did he ever say anything to you about it or about an African witch-doctor's medicine bag?"

"He showed me what he said was a medicine-bag," B.B. answered. "It was because I gave him an old book I found in Father's library after his death, *The Night Side of Nature*. It was a collection of ghost stories by a Mrs Young, I think. I knew he was interested in that sort of thing and we got talking, and he got the medicine bag out of that old bureau of his and showed it me."

"Did he say what was in it?"

"He said he didn't know. I asked him why he didn't open it and see. He didn't seem to want to. He pushed the thing back in the bureau in rather a hurry. I thought he seemed a bit scared. I expect it was only my fancy. There may have been something infectious in it, or something like that. I didn't press him—couldn't very well. I remember thinking if it was mine I would have it open in a jiffy. I don't see what all that has to do with it."

"The bag seems to have disappeared, at least Rosamund says so," Bobby told him. "I suppose it may turn up somewhere. Rosamund says it's not in the bureau. Two things happening about the same time may be connected—cause and effect. Or, quite possibly, they may have nothing to do with each other. Was that all, or did he say anything else?"

"Well, he went on talking for a time. He said there might be anything in a witch-doctor's medicine bag, from a dead man's bones to the hairs from an elephant's tail. Just anything. An old torn copy of Tom Paine's *Rights of Man* in one case he heard of."

"*The Rights of Man*?" Bobby repeated. He had read the book many years ago and remembered it as a vigorous and effective answer to Burke's *Reflections*, but he had never thought of it as having any connection with the supra-normal—a development that would certainly have equally annoyed and bewildered its atheistical, free-thinking author. "What on earth makes them imagine it has anything to do with magic or anything of the sort?"

"Well, all the natives know there's a part of Africa—West Africa—where the African ruled and the Europeans were their servants, and they have heard, too, that it was all through this little book. Mr Outers said he thought they weren't so far wrong. It was doing in Africa what John Stuart Mill's *Liberty* did in India—making our position untenable by showing what we professed—and so what about a little practice as well?"

"Books always have been strong medicine in a sense," Bobby agreed. "Not much help here, though. You can't give me any idea who it was you say you saw just now?"

"I only had the merest glimpse, I couldn't possibly say," B.B. repeated. "It might have been anyone."

They had been slowly approaching the house as they talked, and now Rosamund appeared. Apparently she had been waiting for them.

"Lunch is ready," she began, and then interrupted herself with a quick exclamation of dismay. "Oh, Cousin Owen," she said, "whatever have you been doing to yourself?"

Bobby was greatly annoyed. He hadn't been doing anything to himself. He never had. It was always other people who did things to him. Somewhat tartly he said:

"Nothing."

"Whatever would Cousin Olive say?" demanded Rosamund, thinking but small beer of this excuse.

"Well, don't you try to say it for her," retorted Bobby, even more tartly; and Rosamund, probably feeling she had been warned off the matrimonial grass, went on:

"Did you find Mr Peel?"

"Has he been here?" interposed B.B.

"Do you think it could have been Peel you saw?" Bobby asked him, and this question alone of the three produced a reply.

"Well, at the time I did think it might be," B.B. admitted. "I didn't want to say so when it might just as well have been anyone else. The only thing is there was a bicycle leaning against the Tower wall. I noticed it was blue and I thought it looked like Peel's. He always uses a bicycle, getting about."

"Sounds like him," Bobby agreed. "No telling, though."

"Lunch is ready," Rosamund repeated. "Come along."

B.B. said with obvious sincerity that he was awfully sorry, but he couldn't stay, he had a business appointment in Midminster he must keep.

"I only called to ask how Mrs Outers was," he explained.

"The doctor's been," answered Rosamund. "He said I was to keep her as quiet as possible. She's asleep now." Rosamund paused and looked at Bobby. "He's trying to find out all about it," she said with the same odd mixture of trust and mistrust she had shown before, and then Bobby saw, or thought he saw, that B.B. was looking at Rosamund with very much of that same strange mixture of trust and mistrust.

"Until the truth is known," Bobby said, and now his voice had grown heavy and sombre, "this thing will always lie between you six," and the silence that followed his words lay like a cloud, heavy and sombre, too, upon the three of them.

"I must be going," B.B. said, though it cost him an effort to speak.

With no other word uttered, he turned and went. In equal silence Rosamund watched him go and then returned to the house. Bobby was left standing alone, and the sun that all at once broke through the heavy clouds above did nothing to cheer him. He was facing the possibility of a dénouement more dreadful than he had ever known before. He drifted away into the house, but avoided the dining-room. He went into the room the dead man had used and sat there. He had food for thought. There presently Rosamund found him.

"Lunch is waiting," she said. "The sauce is spoiled. Turbot needs sauce."

"I did not know if you would want me there," he said. "I think perhaps I ought to go."

"Wouldn't that be running away?" she asked. "Don't mind me. It's only that sometimes I feel I can't bear it any longer. I do so desperately want to end it all. There's always the top of the Tower. Don't look at me like that. I'm not going to jump from it just yet. There's still Mother. Come and get your lunch, or the fish will be ruined as well as the sauce. One must always eat and everything has to go on just as usual. If it wasn't for having to keep things straight, I think I should go mad. Can you go mad sweeping and dusting and polishing?"

Without waiting for the answer, Bobby would not anyhow have known how to make, Rosamund went back into the dining-room, where the turbot, grown cold, and the ruined sauce, awaited them, and where they ate a gloomy and a silent meal. Afterwards he offered to help her with the clearing away and the washing up. Those homely tasks completed, Rosamund vanished, and Bobby got out his car and was soon on his way to Midminster.

CHAPTER XX
IMPOSSIBLE MURDER

IN MIDMINSTER Bobby paid his first visit to the West Midshire Police Headquarters, where he found Mr Nixon flushed and excited after another talk over the 'phone with the Chairman of his Joint Committee. This gentleman, a bustling, 'go-getting' man of business, whose slogan was always 'Small profits, quick returns, or 'S.P.Q.R.', initials under which, as he was never tired of informing others, a great Empire had marched from victory to victory, though as the 'others' were never tired of telling each other it was the 'Quick returns' he was chiefly interested in.

"I gave him my personal assurance," Nixon complained, "that we were leaving no stone unturned, no avenue unexplored, and all he said was that everyone had heard that one before. I don't know what he meant. You can't do more, can you?"

"Oh, he was only talking," Bobby explained, and this seemed to satisfy Nixon, who continued:

"He got on to that yarn about old fellows seen hanging round the Constant Freres place. He didn't like it a bit when I told him I didn't believe there ever had been any. Do you?"

"No clear evidence as yet," Bobby said. "One way or the other. Got to follow it up, though."

"Yes; of course," Nixon agreed. "The Chairman had what he called a clue. About a fellow seen at a lodging-house here. Turned out to be an Italian on his way to try for a job in the North. The poor devil was scared half out of his life when he heard we were making inquiries. He thought the Miners' Union had ordered his arrest and imprisonment."

Having thus let off steam, Nixon now was prepared to listen to Bobby, who proceeded to give as full an account as he could of his own recent activities, laying special emphasis on Rosamund's account of her long walk through the African bush and also on his own somewhat narrow escape from death or injury in old ruined Constant Freres. To all this Nixon listened with close attention and then asked:

"Do you think that was just an accident or a deliberate attempt to do you in, or at least knock you out."

"If it was, and if it had come off," Bobby remarked, "it would have been what the papers like to call a perfect murder on top of an apparently impossible one. Prowling about an old tumbledown ruin—nothing more likely than an accident. I can't say I much like it. Luckily, it didn't come off, but I did let Baynham know what was in my mind. I calculated that if I did it might fluster him a bit. Just as well to fluster a suspect if you can; shakes his self-confidence."

Nixon said he supposed that was psychology, and the way in which he pronounced that word left no doubt of what was his opinion of it and all it represented. Then he opened a drawer of his desk and took out a small sheaf of papers.

"I've been jotting down some of my own ideas," he explained. "All ready to show the Chairman next time he buzzes in. First the three women, to get them out of the way."

"Can you?" Bobby asked doubtfully. "They were there."

"Yes; I know," Nixon admitted. "Wife, daughter, and a one-legged cripple, though. In my view, not very likely, any of the three of 'em."

"Even one-legged cripples can commit murders," Bobby commented. "Though I can't remember a case," he added thoughtfully.

"Yes, of course," agreed Nixon. "But it is a handicap, isn't it?" and to this proposition Bobby had in turn to agree. So Nixon continued: "So do wives."

"Murder their husbands, you mean?" Bobby asked. "Oh, yes; that happens. So do daughters their fathers. Much more rare, though."

"Almost always a history of bad feeling and quarrelling over money or something to give a pointer," Nixon observed.

He spoke carelessly, almost casually, as if speaking as much to himself as to Bobby, but Bobby knew that Nixon was watching him closely and trying to decide where Bobby stood, situated as he was between the claims of kinship and childhood memories and his duty as a member of a force that is never off duty for a moment by night or by day. Possibly, Bobby thought, the Chairman of the Joint Committee, evidently a busy gentleman, had heard that Bobby and Mrs Outers were relatives and had told Nixon to try to make sure which Bobby put first—kinship or duty. Very much what Rosamund had shown were her feelings, too. An equivocal position, Bobby reflected gloomily, but none of his seeking and not one he had felt he could avoid. So there it was, and he told himself he was not going to withdraw, unless asked to by Rosamund or ordered to by his superiors. Unless Rosamund and her mother were cleared, as they could only be by the discovery of the actual murderer, then they would have to bear such a load of suspicion as might well prove unendurable and drive Rosamund at least to the suicide at which she had already hinted.

But now or so at least it seemed to him he was caught in such a net of circumstance as he could not honourably extract himself from.

These thoughts, though in less coherent form, flashed swiftly through his mind, yet not so swiftly but that Nixon could see how deeply troubled he was. Not without sympathy, Nixon now said:

"It's a fair mess-up, isn't it? One thing and other. It's getting round that Outers deliberately sent off those two boys of his on purpose to discover what they could about secret native rites he wanted to describe in a book he was writing. So that Mrs Outers did him in, and serve him right."

"Well, that's a point of view," Bobby remarked. "There's something else I ought to mention, though it's only a personal impression. I got the idea somehow that Myra—" Here he paused for a moment. He had used the Christian name deliberately so as to make it plain that he had no intention of glossing over in any way the kinship between them. Then he resumed: "Nothing that could be called evidence or that could be put before a jury, but it did strike me that there was a curious air of relief she showed, a kind of peace and tranquillity, as though she felt now the worst was over and there was nothing more to fear. You get it sometimes when a sick person understands that at last the doctors have given up hope. It may have been nothing but my fancy, and anyhow I don't see that it need have anything to do with any feeling of guilt or innocence."

"No," agreed Nixon. "No. I don't either. But does it tie in with these stories of warnings that there was murder in the air or what the old witch-doctor said to Miss Rosamund?"

"No, I know," Bobby said. "That's got to be remembered. And it does sometimes happen that a person contemplating murder goes out of the way to attract attention with the idea that to attract attention is the last thing anyone guilty would do, and so it's a kind of reverse proof of innocence. All that has to be considered. But what does it all add up to? A kind of general atmosphere of suspicion, no solid fact. There is one fact, though, that points the other way. Physical strength was needed to inflict such a wound. A man's strength, not a woman's, to drive that knife home."

"If Mrs Outers is feeling like you say," Nixon asked, "do you think she might say something if she were pressed?"

"I don't think that ought to be tried," Bobby told him flatly. "It would be difficult to justify in her present condition. Her doctor would certainly protest strongly."

"Yes; I see that," Nixon admitted. "How about the girl, though? She looks as if she had the physical strength all right. That walk of hers. All day, all night, and all day again. Not so many men could have stood up to a walk like that."

"Endurance rather than muscular strength," Bobby suggested. "Endurance under great emotional stress."

"In my view," declared Nixon, evidently not much impressed by this argument, "she's the pick of the basket. It was her brothers she lost, and it must have gone deep if it was that held her up. Another thing. The women weren't searched immediately on the spot like the men were. Couldn't be till we got a woman officer to do the job. That means if one of them had the knife, she must have had opportunities to get rid of it."

"Defending counsel would get busy if you put that forward," Bobby remarked. "You would be asked, 'Do you admit your officers were so incompetent that the two women under their escort from the summit room to the room where they were searched could manage to get rid of the murder knife under their noses? If so, what value can you expect the jury to attach to their general evidence?' Almost enough to make the jury want to stop the case on the spot."

"That may be," admitted Nixon, though reluctantly. "All the same. In my view—sufficient grounds for suspicion to justify positive action." Bobby nodded agreement to this, though wondering what form the 'positive action' could take at this stage and Nixon continued: "Old Mrs James there too, but no conceivable motive. At the table she was sitting right opposite Outers, the furthest away from him. To get at him, she would have pretty well had to climb on the table, and she couldn't have managed that without all the rest of them knowing, could she?"

"She's astonishingly nimble," Bobby remarked.

"Well, yes, I know," answered Nixon. "But in my view—utterly impossible."

"The whole thing seems utterly impossible as far as that goes," Bobby said. "The impossible murder. There must be a way round somehow."

"Then I wish to God we could find it," Nixon exclaimed. "The whole blessed set-up is getting me down. Well, that's for the three ladies. Then there's the three men. Young Mr Baynham. Very popular, and being popular is a good cloak sometimes. Ludo Manners, pushing type, but in my view not likely to push himself into murder. And Teddy Peel. Doubtful character, very, but no actual record. In my view, if it's not the girl, then it's him, and how about it being the two of them acting together?"

CHAPTER XXI
NEW EVIDENCE

IT WAS NOT a possibility that Bobby much liked to contemplate. It was, moreover, altogether opposed to a theory at last beginning to formulate itself more clearly in his mind. But he had long been conscious that it was also a possibility that would have to be faced and to which would have to be given full weight and consideration. Nor did any one know better than he did himself how sadly often the most promising theory is killed off by even a single fact. He said now:

"Yes; I know. It has to be kept in mind. But I don't think it very likely. Miss Outers strikes me as one of those self-contained, self-reliant personalities who act by themselves and for themselves alone. I think that walk of hers through the

African bush shows that, though, again, she's a woman, very much a woman, and if she did surrender to another I fancy it would be absolute. I may be wrong, but that's how I feel, and I certainly can't see her making any sort of surrender to Teddy Peel of all people."

Evidently, Nixon, who looked wholly unimpressed, had either not followed all this or it had failed to convince. Bobby could almost see the fatal word 'psychology' trembling on his lips. However, he managed to suppress it. Instead he said:

"Well, I don't know. She goes about looking more like a cat in a thunderstorm than any ordinary human girl. Mrs Nixon says it's most likely sulks, unless it's indigestion. I'm thinking of having Teddy Peel pulled in. Even if he is tough, I may be able to get him talking."

"Worth trying," Bobby agreed, though privately of opinion that Teddy was not so much 'tough' as slippery, and it is easier to crack the toughest nut than to get a grip on a jellyfish. "Clearly," he continued, "if there is any link between them, Teddy may have learnt from her that phrase in the local African dialect they all claim to have heard. What common motive could they have had, though?"

"A share in the gold-mine or whatever it is for him and her brothers' death for her," Nixon replied promptly. "We don't have to prove motive; only fact."

"Of which last there seems at present to be precious little," commented Bobby. "Have you taken any further statement from Baynham?"

"I will now you've told me what happened at the Constant Freres ruin."

"Or from Ludo Manners?"

"I sent one of my chaps to ask him about those finger-prints on the old bureau Outers had in his room at Constant House. Well, he got on his high horse at once and said, of course, none of us—'coppers' he called us, trying to be offensive, not that we mind—would have been likely to notice that the bureau was a very fine piece of old furniture no intelligent person could help being interested in. All very la-de-da, you understand, nose-in-the-air stuff, and it was the bureau that interested him, not what was in it. If Miss Outers said something her father used to keep there wasn't there any longer, well, why ask him? What was he supposed to know about it? Of course, he had heard chaps talking of a gold-mine or something—a new diamond field, one man said—Outers knew about. Rot. Stands to reason. If you knew anything like that and had good backing evidence, you didn't lock it up in an old bureau. You took it to one of the big City swells and asked him to finance you. And now he had business to attend to and would our men go away, and stay away if possible."

"Had quite a lot to say, hadn't he?" Bobby remarked thoughtfully. "Just a little too much perhaps."

"In my view," declared Nixon, "it all sounded very like a carefully prepared statement. And now a little bit of fresh evidence has just come in though I don't know exactly what to make of it. Haven't had time to consider it properly as yet. But it may prove important if we can follow it up. *Re* motive."

"Yes?" said Bobby, interested at once.

"It's from the woman who was the daily help at Constant House. She's left now, because, she says of not caring for being mixed up in such goings on."

"One way of describing a murder," Bobby remarked. "Is it first-hand what she says, or does it sound more like hearsay stuff?"

"She claims it's what she heard with her own ears," Nixon explained. "Her story is that when she was sweeping the stairs, she heard Mr Outers shouting at the top of his voice, and it wasn't like him, as he was a very quiet gentleman. But this time he was shouting so loud no one could possibly help hearing especially," Nixon added, "if you had your ear to the keyhole, as I expect hers was. But that's neither here nor there. What she says she heard was Mr Outers shouting he wouldn't ever stand for such a marriage, not over his dead body he wouldn't, and he thought it was insolence even to think of it. Unluckily, according to her story, then Mr Outers seemed to calm down a bit and, the sweeping of the stairs being finished, she went to get on with her other work, so she didn't hear any more and didn't know who it was, except that it must have been one of the two young gentlemen, meaning Baynham and Manners, I suppose."

"Probably what happened," Bobby commented, "was that she heard Mr Outers beginning to move, and scuttled off as fast as she could for fear of being caught at the keyhole. But it certainly does suggest a possible motive. Did your man say anything to Manners about Mrs James thinking she saw him with his hands in Outer's pocket immediately after the murder?"

"Oh, no," Nixon answered at once. "I gave instructions that nothing was to be said about that for the present, not until we know a good deal more," and to this Bobby nodded approval, for he knew well that the effect and value of information often depends as much on the timing of its disclosure as on the information itself. Nixon was speaking again now. He was saying: "In my view, there's the makings of a good case against Manners. He was after the map, whether it was gold or diamonds or uranium or what-not. Once he had it, he could raise money for a trip to West Africa to look for it, knowing all the time where it was likely to be. He could easily memorize the map and destroy it if he thought it too incriminating to hold. It would all seem safe enough, and so it is unless we can get more evidence."

"The makings of a case certainly," Bobby agreed, "but so far no more than the makings. There's one other thing though with no direct bearing on the murder that I can see. Both young men turned up for tea the first afternoon I was here, and they managed to make it sufficiently plain that they were hating each other quite energetically—rivals for Miss Outers's favours, the two of them. Quite a natural, healthy hatred I thought at the time. I'm not so sure about that now."

"Well, that fits in a way, don't you think?" Nixon asked. "If Ludo could get the map by marrying the girl, much the easiest way. Nowadays you can always get rid of your wife if you want to—divorce, like scrapping an old car and buying a new one. I can't imagine anyone being really keen on marrying that girl. I would as soon marry a nightmare."

"My own impression," Bobby told him, "is that Baynham wanted to rather badly, and I thought Miss Outers was trying hard to snub him and encourage Ludo. As she's a woman, a contrary lot, as every nursery knows, it may mean she feels safe with Ludo because she knows she can handle him, but is frightened of losing out to Baynham. The important thing at the moment, though, is to try to decide who it was Outers thought was being insolent in wanting to marry Rosamund. Nothing serious against either of them, is there? They seem eligible. Both have good positions, apparently, and nothing against their characters?"

"Oh, no," Nixon responded quickly. "Both very well thought of. Only—"

"Yes," said Bobby encouragingly, for he felt there was more to come.

"Well, the fact is—we keep it very much to ourselves, of course—but the fact is Manners's father is doing a seven-year stretch for long-term frauds. Nothing to do with Ludo himself. His mother died when he was a baby, his father disappeared, and an aunt took the child and brought him up. It came out when your Yard people asked us for help to trace the old Manners's activities, as there were threads leading to Midminster."

"Does the young man know?" Bobby asked.

"No idea," Nixon answered. "He may or he may not. We dropped the whole thing, of course, as soon as we were sure he was in no way implicated. He was never questioned."

"Not very likely then that Val would know anything about it?" Bobby suggested.

"I don't see how he possibly could," Nixon repeated. "We took every precaution to prevent anything leaking out. Might have done young Manners a lot of harm if it had."

"Yes; of course. All the same, there's the off-chance. Got to be remembered. What about the other chap—young B.B. I hope he hasn't got a father in gaol?"

"Oh, no," exclaimed Nixon, more than a little shocked. "Old B.B. was always most respectable, most. But—"

"Yes?" said Bobby again, and even more encouragingly than before, sure this time that there was indeed more to come.

"Married," said Nixon.

"What?" exclaimed Bobby, really startled.

"Oh, he's got a divorce, or, rather, she got it. So it's on record that he was the guilty party, which he wasn't. It was when he was at Oxford. He got mixed up with his landlady's daughter and was bamboozled into marrying her. Compromised her good name and so was in honour bound. All that guff. Once she had hooked him she carried on regardless. If old B.B. hadn't come to the rescue the young man would have been ruined for good. Old B.B. offered her a thousand if she would consent to a divorce. She would only agree on condition that she was allowed to bring the suit and that it was not defended—to preserve her good name, she said."

"I take it all that would be well known and talked about," Bobby remarked. "You don't get a divorce on the quiet, not when your father's a well-known business man in your home town. I don't know what Val's views were though about divorce, but it seems going rather far to talk about insolence if it's true he did. It doesn't strike me as an adequate reason for getting excited and shouting and so on. And it hardly seems at all likely that Val could have heard of the father in prison."

"Well, it must have been one of them," Nixon said. "No one else after the girl."

"No, no," agreed Bobby. "Not that we know of. You can never tell, though, can you? 'Must, must,'" he repeated. "Just as the murderer must have been one of the six who were present. I don't like 'must' somehow—a dogmatic, thought-stifling, initiative-quelling, word. It ought to be banned. Anyhow, we must think it over," and Nixon looked at him curiously, wondering what he meant and deciding very reasonably that most likely he meant nothing at all—just talk.

CHAPTER XXII
LUDO'S THEORIES

WITH THAT OPINION firmly fixed in Nixon's mind, their colloquy came to an end. Nixon, indeed, had much else to attend to and Bobby had nothing more to say, though much to think about, for it did seem to him that from this prolonged and somewhat wandering talk there might well be presently distilled something more than merely the beginnings of a tenable theory. It was largely in the hope of getting to hear something that might strengthen this vague possibility that he now suggested his paying a visit to Ludo Manners. Nixon thought it would be well worth while. Ludo he said would very possibly prove more willing to be communicative to a man from distant London than to members of the local force.

To Ludo's office in the High Street, only just round the corner, Bobby therefore now made his way, though when he arrived he was greeted with no great show of enthusiasm.

"Are you taking over?" Ludo demanded. "I've had the local coppers here till I'm damn' well sick and tired of saying the same thing over and over again."

"Vain repetition," Bobby admitted. "I expect sometimes we overdo it, but all the same it's really necessary. Every detail has to be checked and then rechecked or else some vital clue may be missed and a murderer go free to have another try. That's detection routine, and a jolly dull routine most of the time, too. Only now we've got to know—from information received as we say—that Mr Outers was heard shortly before his death quarrelling violently with an unidentified person."

"Well, not with me," Ludo said, looking slightly puzzled. "Seemed a peaceable old bloke as a rule. Someone got in his hair, I suppose. Not me, though. I was doing my best to keep all hunkadory with him. For why? Well, I was, that's all.

He might have been having a row with Baynham—the chap they call B.B., you know. He was making himself a nuisance running after Rosy. Not that I blame him. She's a jolly fine girl, though she wants shaking out of the way she broods on what's over and done with."

"Over no doubt, but perhaps not done with—few things ever are," Bobby replied. "Done with, I mean. Didn't some-one once say that we all live both in eternity and in time?"

"What the hell does that mean?" demanded Ludo suspi-ciously.

But to this question Bobby made no attempt to reply. Pos-sibly because he did not know. Instead, he said:

"You may think it a question I've no right to ask and most certainly you need not answer it if you feel you would rather not, but were you and Mr Baynham in any sense rivals for the hand of Miss Outers?"

"Well, now, that's a question," Ludo said with a sort of would-be shy snigger. "She's O.K., but I'm not sure that she's my cup of tea, if you see what I mean. When it's a girl you've got to look before you leap. Once you're in, you're in for good, aren't you?" He sniggered again, quite unaware that Bobby was longing to throw something at his head, and continued: "She does rather grow on a chap. At first you think she's just sulky and you're apt to sheer off, and then you begin to see it isn't that exactly. I can tell you one thing, though, I'm pretty sure of—she's got no use for B.B., and I don't wonder. Forc-es himself on her like a salesman trying to push second-rate goods. She don't like it. Now, I don't do that. No need," and he grinned at Bobby in a way that intensified that secret longing Bobby was so increasingly aware of. "The truth is," he went on after a pause, "I haven't made up my mind yet. If it's O.K. Outers was having a row with anyone, it might be B.B., because of how he had been pestering the girl, and Outers was telling him to keep out where he wasn't want-ed. But don't take that from me and don't get it into your head I'm hinting it might be B.B. did him in, because I'm jolly sure it wasn't. Not his line. But what about Teddy Peel? Ever thought of him?"

"He's not been forgotten," Bobby said. "He's one of the six who were present. But we've found nothing to implicate him in any way."

"You wouldn't. He's a cunning little devil," Ludo said, and said it with an angry emphasis that Bobby did not fail to notice. Ludo had paused to light a cigarette and Bobby noticed also that his hand was shaking slightly. Something more between them, Bobby told himself, than Ludo wished to reveal. His cigarette safely lighted, Ludo was continuing to speak. He was saying: "I tackled him. I always go straight to the point. All cards on the table. That's me. In business too. I said: 'What made you do in the old man?' You ought to have seen him. He went pale as death. He started to swear at me. I told him to shut up. Then he said he would take me into court, and I said that was O.K. by me. He quietened down a bit then and I said: 'If you didn't, who did?' He had nothing to say to that."

"I'm afraid we haven't either," Bobby admitted. "All clear-cut and simple as far as it goes, and then the complete dead end."

"Well, but is it?" Ludo said. He looked at his cigarette, appeared to notice with some surprise that it had gone out, and threw it into the grate. "You police chaps go on and on about it must have been one of us six. Well, must it? You've been in the summit room over there at Freres. Ever notice the windows?"

"I noticed they all had closely fitting shutters, if that's what you mean," Bobby answered. "To keep out the light, I suppose."

"That's right," Ludo said. "Made the room dark as hell, but that's not what I was thinking of. They all had curtains as well, thick and heavy as they make 'em."

"Yes. Well, what about it?" Bobby asked, still slightly puzzled.

"What about," Ludo retorted, "some bloke being behind them, slipping out—it was dark as pitch, so he couldn't be seen, and the gramophone going like one o'clock so he wouldn't be heard—doing the job, slipping back again and then when Baynham opened the door and rushed off to ring a doctor and you blokes, slipping out again and off."

"Rather too much slipping in and out, isn't there?" Bobby suggested, not as much impressed by this theory as Ludo had evidently expected. "The idea was considered, I believe, but the curtains fit as closely as the shutters. No one could possibly hide behind them without it's being immediately obvious."

But Ludo stuck to his theory.

"Of course," he agreed. "If you looked you would spot it at once. The point is, no one looked or thought of looking except Peel. And he wouldn't because he knew and had helped fix it all up."

"Why should he?" Bobby asked.

"Well, just think," Ludo admonished him in much the tone in which he admonished prospective clients to think of all the advantages he was offering them. "There's that goldmine yarn, isn't there? And the map showing where it may be that Rosy says isn't now in the bureau drawer where it used to be. Maps of undeveloped possible gold-mines command a high premium in the City." He paused, and once more there had come into his voice that note of anger and resentment—even fear—Bobby thought had been there once before. "I happen to know Peel's not above a spot of blackmail, and blackmail's not so far off murder."

"A little more discreet, that's all," Bobby agreed, ready to keep Ludo talking so long as he remained in his present loquacious mood, for often there is more in talk than the talker knows. "Can you be a bit more explicit?"

But now Ludo seemed to feel he had said more than he had ever intended to, more perhaps than was altogether wise, and he shook his head in answer to Bobby's question.

"No," he replied at once, a little too loudly and too quickly indeed. "Nothing to do with me; not my pigeon at all. Just what I've heard. What I do say is: Find that gold-mine map and your man won't be far away." He paused and, when Bobby did not speak, went on: "All hunkadory? Anything else I can tell you? Only too glad to help. Means a lot to me to get it all cleared up. Horrible business altogether. It's funny, though. V.I.Ps. I couldn't get near before want to hear all about it, and after I've told 'em all I know and a bit more— well, they can't very well refuse to sign on the dotted line. What do you make of that?"

Bobby made nothing of it, and as he felt that there was no more to be learnt from Ludo for the present, he took his leave.

Back at the County Police Headquarters, Bobby asked for the rapidly growing dossier of what the papers were beginning to call 'The Impossible Murder' and whereto the latest addition had been the report of the two police officers Nixon had sent to interview Ludo. It was this which Bobby specially wished to study; and to it, aided by cups of tea from the canteen of an almost Herculean strength and a plate of toast most exceeding thick, he gave a prolonged, meticulous examination, weighing every word, considering every phrase, comparing word and phrase alike with those Ludo had used in talking to him, trying to distil from both the hidden significance that might mean so much—or so little.

Then he wrote his own report, added it to the dossier, sent it back to its appropriate pigeon-hole, and wrote a letter to Nixon, stating his opinion that there must be some deep underlying cause for the complete change in Ludo's tone and attitude that had taken place in the brief interval separating the two interviews—that he had had himself and that earlier one with the two police officers. For his part, Bobby wrote, he thought this change in tempo, so to speak, must be connected with the animosity shown to Teddy Peel, the suggestion that Peel might have been an active agent in the murder, the accusation that he practised blackmail. But all this, Bobby was careful to point out, might have nothing to do with the present investigation. It might mean that Peel had got to know of the elder Manners's imprisonment.

"Nevertheless," Bobby concluded his letter, "I should, I think, pay special attention to Ludo's remark: 'Find the map and your man won't be far away'."

All this took time, and it was late before he was able to return to Constant House. He had rung up earlier to say he had been delayed and was not likely to get back much before midnight, but he found Rosamund still up and still busy, though what with did not appear. She was wearing a big apron over an overall, rubber gloves, her hair tied up in some kind of wrapper. She emerged from somewhere in the back regions when he entered but she did not speak, and for the moment they stood still looking at each other in silence.

"You've got back," she said at last, and then he knew that she had been waiting with great fear, a great, consuming fear that showed so plainly in her eyes, in her whole still, strained attitude.

"I hope I have not kept you up," he said. "I would not if I could have helped it," and to this she made no reply, but he thought those few commonplace words had relieved the tension he had seemed to sense in her.

"There's some bread and cheese in the breakfast-room," she said. "Would you like coffee or cocoa—or beer? I think there is some left."

"I should like you to go to bed," he said gently, "where I think you should have been long ago."

"Bed?" she repeated. "Why? Bed's for sleep," she said and went away, returning presently with a jug of cocoa freshly made with milk. "It won't keep you awake," she said. "Coffee might. It's bad to stay awake and think all night."

"Will you tell me one thing?" Bobby asked. "How did you know the medicine bag wasn't in the bureau drawer any more?"

"There was always a smell," she replied. "Now there isn't," and turned and went, nor did he see her again that night.

CHAPTER XXIII
THE DARK ONES

Bobby slept late next morning. There was no alarm clock to waken him for a morning run round the park, and, for that matter, no park for him to run round. The first thing that struck him as he began to dress was that everything in the room had been redusted, repolished till it all shone and shone again, like the boots of a guardsman on inspection day.

In the bathroom it was the same. Everything shone, and so it was with the stairs and passages. It pleased him not at all. Rosamund must have spent the whole of the preceeding day cleaning the already clean, polishing the already polished, sweeping and dusting where there was nothing left either to sweep or to dust. He felt there had been on her part a frenzy of determination to allow herself no time to think. And what thoughts were they her urge was so great to keep at bay? He remembered then that deep-seated fear, that near-panic he had seen in her when he returned the previous night.

His mood was gloomy as he descended the stairs, for he dreaded the denouement almost more than he dreaded failure to resolve it; and now, as he reached the foot of the stairs, Rosamund appeared from the kitchen, carrying a tray with a dish of sizzling bacon and eggs on it.

"I heard you getting up," she said. "Would you like coffee or tea? The coffee's ready, but the kettle's on the boil if you would rather have tea?"

He did not answer for the moment. He was looking at her, shocked by her drawn and tense expression. At the corners of her usually firm mouth a nervous trembling came and went, and he could see that this proud and lonely girl was not far from a breakdown.

"Well?" she was saying impatiently. "Well?"

"Oh, coffee, if it's ready," he answered then, but stopped her with a gesture as she turned to go. "Rosamund," he said, "I could be more help to Myra and to you if you would be more frank with me. For I think something has made you more afraid then you were before."

"I'll fetch the coffee. Those eggs are our own," she said, and then suddenly, abruptly: "Mother saw a light in Freres last night."

"Is she sure?" he asked.

She hurried away without answering and returned with the coffee.

"Why aren't you eating your breakfast?" she said. "I got the eggs from the nests this morning."

"If you don't stop talking about those damned eggs, I'll throw them at your head," Bobby exploded in wrath; and Rosamund looked very startled and backed away, as if fully expecting him to put his threat into instant execution.

When he did not, she said indignantly:

"You needn't talk like that. It's very rude."

"I daresay it is," Bobby grumbled. "But when a fool of a girl works herself into near hysterics she needs talking to. If we're ever to get to know the truth, you've got to help for the sake of all concerned. Understand?"

"You think it was me, don't you?" she asked then, half sullen, half defiant.

"I'm not concerned with 'thinks' at present," Bobby told her. "I want facts, and one fact is that you're more panicky to-day than you were before and you haven't told me why."

"I'm not," she interposed, "and I never will, never."

"Another fact," he went on unheeding, "is that your mother says she saw a light in the Freres ruin last night. I want to ask her about that."

"Well, you shan't," Rosamund said. "I won't let you. Never."

"A third fact is that you say the medicine bag your father had gave out a strong smell and it was because you missed this smell that you knew it wasn't there any more."

She had seated herself by now and was listening intently with both elbows on the table. Her sole comment was a muttered:

"Well?"

It was quite plain she did not mean to be helpful. Probably, Bobby thought, because of what she had seen or heard or learnt the previous day and that had apparently so intensified her fears. Not in all probability anything directly involving herself, for to that, he felt, she would react with defiance rather than with terror. Nor yet B.B., if, as Bobby believed, she was fighting against a dawning attraction drawing her towards him, for that would help her in her resistance. Her mother, then? On the whole this seemed more likely. Perhaps simply the light Myra claimed to have seen in the Freres ruin during the past night? But why should anything her mother had seen so much distress Rosamund.

He was busy with his eggs and bacon while these puzzling and disturbing thoughts were passing through his mind, and he still took no notice of Rosamund's questioning 'Why?' She also was silent, watching him intently, evidently puzzled in her turn by his silence. Then she got up and began to move towards the door. He called after her:

"I must have a talk with Myra this morning. You might tell her, will you? As soon as possible. There are things I must ask her."

"You can't. I won't let you. She's not fit," Rosamund repeated, still defiant.

"Don't be a little fool," Bobby snapped. "Do you think you can stop her being questioned? I suppose you know an inquest will be held? Or don't you? Mr Nixon will need to take a formal statement, and I'm sure it would be better if I had a quiet chat with her first. Now run along and tell your mother, and don't make any more difficulties, or I shall be wondering still more than I am now what it is you are trying to hide."

She did not answer, though she had paused to listen. Still silent, she closed the door behind her, leaving him to finish his breakfast alone. He lighted a cigarette then and settled down to think things over and to wait for Rosamund to return—if she meant to, that is. He would give her, he thought, half an hour, but no more. He had to wait only half that time.

Then she returned bringing with her the morning paper just delivered.

"I've told Mother about you," she said. "She's getting up. I don't think she ought to, she's not really fit, but she says she will. I expect our doctor will be furious. I asked her if she was sure she saw the light and she said of course she was. It was quite bright and kept moving."

"Did she say if she heard anything?" Bobby asked. "A car for instance?"

"I didn't ask her," Rosamund said. She put the paper on the table and picked up the tray, on which Bobby had piled the crockery ready for removal. "I'll let you know when Mother's ready," she said.

"I'll come and help you wash up, shall I?" Bobby asked.

But Rosamund, though much subdued, had not gone as far in submission as that.

"No, thank you," she said coldly, and added: "Those reporter men were here all day and people staring. I had to get Dewey to ask them to go away, but they all came back. There's a horrid picture of him in that paper, and one of a girl, and they've put my name under it. I don't know who it is, but it isn't me. Do you think it could be someone like that with the light Mother saw?"

"Well, it's possible," Bobby admitted. "Newspaper men are up to anything. I'll inquire."

Rosamund went away then, taking her tray with her. This time it was longer before she came back to say her mother had come downstairs and was in the front room. So thither Bobby proceeded, followed by Rosamund, who evidently had no intention of leaving him alone with her mother. As soon as he entered the room he was again struck by the air of calm and tranquillity that surrounded her as of one who had come to journey's end and now could rest.

"It was certainly a light I saw," she told Bobby in answer to his questions. "It went out occasionally and then came on again. I thought it might be you. Rosy says you told her it wasn't. It's dangerous—Constant Freres, I mean. Bits of it are always coming down."

"I know," Bobby said, grimly enough. "Mr Baynham very nearly landed a chunk of it on my head."

"Such a good thing it wasn't worse," Myra said. "Rosy says you looked such a sight. What was Mr Baynham doing there?"

"He saw someone," Rosamund interposed quickly. "I expect it was Cousin Owen trying to find out things. It's what he's doing all the time."

"Yes, dear, I know," Myra answered her. "I expect he will. I am sure I hope so. So much better for everyone."

She said this as simply and brightly as before. Bobby did not quite know what to make of it, but felt the remark troubled Rosamund. There was a silence neither of the two women seemed inclined to break, and then Bobby asked:

"I'm rather wondering about the medicine bag Val had in a drawer of his bureau. Did he ever talk to you about it."

"Well, no, not exactly," Myra answered. "Of course, I knew all about it. Rosy says it's gone. Someone must have taken it. Such a silly thing to do."

"Why?" Bobby asked.

"There are things best left alone," she answered slowly, and for the first time seemed a little troubled.

"Rosamund says it gave out a peculiar smell? Have you ever noticed that?"

"Oh, yes, indeed. When Val first got it. After that you got used to it."

"I didn't," interposed Rosamund.

"Did Val ever say what could cause it?" Bobby asked.

"I think he thought it was probably some sort of poison. The Africans make all sorts of horrid things from plants in the bush Europeans know nothing about. Sometimes they do wonderful cures."

"Val told me," Bobby went on, "there was a map in it showing where there was a new uranium field? Did you know that?"

"Well, not a map exactly. It wasn't, was it, Rosy dear?"

"I don't know," Rosamund answered, not too willingly, Bobby thought. "Something of the sort. I asked him once and it made him cross and he said more likely it was only rough notes, and anyhow no one would ever know and I wasn't to say anything about it, and I never did. I hated the beastly thing."

"There's a dead man's hand in it," Myra said. "At least that's what Val was told. Some of the Africans say—but only whispering among themselves—it's the hand of a white man who had found out something they thought he oughtn't to know, so when he went on a trip alone they got hold of him and buried him alive as a sacrifice to the Dark Ones. Then they reported he had died of fever, and nobody could prove anything else. Afterwards they dug the body up and took the heart and the right hand, and cut off the feet so he wouldn't be able to run after them, and buried him again and no one ever knew."

"Good Lord!" Bobby exclaimed, and was silent.

"It's what they believe," Myra said as placidly as before. "They don't want to, but they feel they must to save themselves from the anger of the Dark Ones. They wouldn't hurt a fly generally. That's how it was with my boys. They had to be given to the Dark Ones to make the world safe. It's a little like that hydrogen bomb thing everyone's always talking about, only different, of course. But the boys are safe now. Rosamund told you of what the old medicine man said before he died, didn't she?"

CHAPTER XXIV
CRUTCH AND CAMERA

NOW, HOWEVER, came an interruption, for the doctor arrived, and showed himself much annoyed at his patient's having got up and dressed without his permission. If his advice wasn't to be followed, he grumbled, he might well withdraw from the case. Myra at once became extremely apologetic; Bobby much less so, and then Rosamund, who had vanished on some household errand, returned to say all the reporters were back again, the crowd of gapers bigger than ever, and Dewey, trying to keep them of, on the point of losing his temper.

Bobby said that would never do—losing your temper was always the biggest mistake you could make—and he would go and see if he could help. He was only just in time. Dewey and one of the Press photographers were by now on the point of blows, and, as Dewey possessed an unusual physical strength of the extent of which he was hardly conscious, and as the photographer was a tough six-footer, always ready 'to mix it', as he called it, the situation was threatening to become serious. It was all Bobby could do to separate them. He had to warn the photographer that he was trespassing, so adequate force to remove him would be in order. Fortunately, a sudden heavy shower intervened at this point. The reporters, photographer and all, fled back to the shelter of their cars, the gapers dispersed on the run, and Bobby and Dewey retired with equal speed to the shelter of a nearby shed, one of the old outbuildings of Constant House. To Dewey, Bobby said severely:

"What's the sense of losing your temper with a crowd like that?"

"He called me a misshapen dwarf," Dewey answered. "I know I am. He asked me if I wasn't the murderer myself. I know I'm not. Perhaps you think I am. Do you?"

"Well, you weren't there," Bobby observed. "You aren't one of the six who were."

"It comes over me at times," Dewey said. "Something seems to go in my head. If you hadn't got between us, I believe I might have killed that chap."

"Well, watch it," Bobby said. "Watch it," he repeated. "There's been enough killing round here for the present."

"I know," Dewey said. The heavy rain seemed to have passed now and a clap of thunder in the far distance suggested that it was only the tail end of a thunderstorm they had experienced. Dewey opened the shed door and looked out.

He said: "I caught that photographer fellow trying to sneak round to the front of the house to get snaps of Mrs Outers and Rosamund. He offered me a pound note to let him through. That started it. I think the rain's stopping."

A sudden gleam of sunshine appeared. It shone directly on Dewey's face, and again Bobby was struck by the calm, serene nobility of those beautifully shaped features, Grecian in their perfection and yet in a way so terrible a contrast to the twisted and distorted, almost ape-like body. It was as though Nature, having planned a masterpiece, had then forgotten and produced an abortion. Understandable that some, seeing so distorted a body, were inclined to think, as they had done throughout the ages, that so twisted a form must contain a mind equally twisted.

Dewey began to walk away. Then he turned and said:

"I think I should kill, I'm sure I should, if it were for the sake of someone I cared for. Why should life be sacred when it is so soon over?"

He did not wait for any answer nor did Bobby attempt to give one. But he was deeply troubled. It sounded so much like a deliberate, even defiant confession, and yet was it meant to be so? Or was it put forward as a possible defence of probable guilt? Impossible to say. Difficult, more than difficult, to tell what thoughts were going on behind that broad forehead, those clear, deep-set eyes. Meanwhile, there was the problem of the reporters and the gapers to be dealt with. They were all beginning to drift back now that the rain had almost stopped. Dewey seemed to have abandoned his post. Rosamund had previously objected strongly to a suggestion that Mr Nixon should be asked to supply a uniform man to ward off unwelcome intruders. Then Mrs James appeared, swinging along on her one leg and her crutch at a speed at least as great as any one still blessed with both legs would have been likely to show.

"Dewey says," she explained to the surprised Bobby, "you want that crowd of gaping idiots kept out and he can't stay here any longer. There's things to do, stuff to be got ready for market. Leave it to me. I'll attend to 'em."

"Do you think you could?" Bobby asked doubtfully.

"I've got my tongue, haven't I?" Mrs James retorted.

"That may not be enough," Bobby said. "At Constant House they're in no state to be bothered by all that lot."

"If it isn't, there's always this," she told him. She held up her crutch. "Put the end down hard on anyone's toe and they won't ask for more. If they do"—levelling her crutch like a spear, she made a sudden, thrust forward—"in the tummy," she said through a brief cackle of laughter, "and he's out for keeps. Didn't think I had it in me, did you? I lie low. I keep quiet. Like Dewey. He knows a lot, but he keeps it to himself. He's not telling."

"He knows a lot about what?" Bobby asked.

"That would be telling," she replied. "Ask him. Ask Dewey. Tell him he can if he likes for all I care. Up to him."

Bobby was watching her closely, and she returned his gaze with an equal sharp intensity. He felt there was much behind her words she was not allowing to appear, though what that 'much' was, impossible to say. A formidable, secret, strange old woman, he told himself.

"Do you mean," he asked, breaking at last the silence that for those moments had hung between them like a cloud, "Dewey knows or suspects who it was killed Mr Outers?" But to this he got only the same reply, "Ask him," emitted through a fresh cackle of laughter.

She began to move away then, towards the shrubs and evergreens that bordered the path giving direct access to the house. He called after her, but she took no notice. She now appeared to be hobbling along with some difficulty, in curious contrast to the almost uncanny agility she so often showed. She vanished behind the screen of rhododendrons and evergreens that lined the approach to the front of the house. Bobby waited, puzzled. She's up to something, he thought. Next moment there was a roar of loud, masculine rage and Mrs James shot out from behind the rhododendrons, swinging along on her crutch in one of those fantastic leaps of hers that always made Bobby think of some story-book witch and her broomstick. There followed her that same tough, six-foot photographer, shouting and furious, Bobby had seen before.

"Here, what's all this?" he exclaimed, running towards them.

"She's smashed my camera, my new camera, my brand new camera," the photographer shouted. "I'll . . . I'll . . . I'll . . ." and his voice trailed off into a kind of whimper like that of a small child who has just seen his favourite toy inexplicably destroyed. "My camera," he repeated.

"I caught him trying to sneak through to the front again," explained Mrs James, now safely ensconced behind Bobby. "I told him to stop it. He thought I was a poor, harmless, crippled old woman. So I am. So I am." She paused to giggle delightedly. She resumed: "He said, 'That's all right, mum. Don't you bother. Just doing my job.' I said, 'So am I,' and I knocked that camera thing of his for six, as Monty used to say in the war."

"You old devil," the photographer snarled. "I'd like to wring your damned old neck."

"Now, now. Naughty language before ladies," the old woman rebuked him. "And if you try you'll get a poke"—she illustrated—"that'll lay you out, young man, in double quick time."

"That's enough," Bobby said authoritatively. "Mrs James will have to answer for what she did if you care to press it," he added to the photographer. "I wouldn't advise it myself, but that's your affair, and that of your paper. The *Daily Whirl*, is it? I guessed as much. It would make good headlines for all the other papers. '*Whirl* Man and Crippled Woman.' I think I should let it go if I were you."

"I was only doing my job. We've all got to, haven't we?" the photographer asked in a very injured tone. He began to walk away. Then he turned and said: "If I do let it go, you won't tell the boys?"

"Certainly not," Bobby replied at once. "Mrs James, too, I'm sure."

"Of course," declared Mrs James. "Only too glad. I can see now my conduct was not really ladylike. I regret it," but the effect of this conciliatory speech was rather spoiled by the snigger with which it concluded.

The photographer gave her a glance of ineffable hatred, but said nothing as he went away. Bobby said:

"I don't think I like that crutch of yours."

"I don't think I do either," she answered, and to his utter surprise he saw tears gathering in her old, sharp eyes beneath their wrinkled lids. "One does what one can," she said.

Bobby made no comment. Leaving her on guard, he returned to the house. The first thing he did was to ring up the Midminster Police Headquarters and ask for a uniform man to be sent to keep away intruders. Neither of the Constant House ladies, he repeated, was in any state to be bothered by newspaper men, or by anyone else for that matter. Rosamund, who had heard him come in, appeared in time to hear what he was saying. She began to renew her former objections, but he told her somewhat brusquely that it had become necessary. She was evidently surprised at the sharp authoritative tone he used, but made no further protest. Instead she said:

"Mother wants to talk to you as soon as you have time. You'll be in for lunch, will you? Not that there is anything. Mr Peel has been. He wants his money."

"What money's that?" Bobby asked.

"He always had five pounds when he came," Rosamund explained. "I don't think he ought to have it, but I suppose he must. Only I haven't got any, and he says he can't wait. I haven't even enough to pay the butcher and the milkman."

"Well, I can give you enough for that," Bobby said. "Enough to carry on for the present. I've been wondering about money?"

"I don't know," she answered doubtfully. "I don't think Mother does either. There was only the pension, and there was a lot of money went trying to find out what had happened when the boys didn't come back. We shall have to sell this place, only there's a mortgage, I think. I shall have to get something to do. I think it's what Mother wants to talk about."

"I'll go to her at once," Bobby promised. "She was saying some strange things this morning before your doctor came. Something I didn't understand about your two brothers being safe now, safe from what she called the 'Dark Ones', whatever they are. And about what the old medicine man said to you before he died."

For a moment or two it seemed as if Rosamund was not willing to reply. He had a feeling that she was frightened and she was trembling slightly. It was with a visible effort that she said, almost whispering: "Through death set free."

CHAPTER XXV
AGAINST ALL CREDENCE

HERE AGAIN their talk was broken into by a loud knocking at the back door. Rosamund hurried away so quickly to answer it that Bobby felt the interruption had not been unwelcome to her. He even had an uneasy feeling that she might not return. However, he had not long to wait.

"It was only the butcher," she said as she came back. "I got some chops. They'll do for lunch. I'll get it ready while you are with Mother. I told her you were coming."

"Could you explain things a bit more first?" Bobby asked with no idea of accepting this broad hint to go. "Who does death set free? Your brothers? But you say there's no hope that they are still alive. Who then? Set free from what?"

"How can I explain what I don't know or understand?" Rosamund asked. "What that old, old man said to me, he said, and then he died, and that is all."

"And the Dark Ones—who are they?" Bobby asked; and somehow as he said this he was aware of a distinct feeling of discomfort, though it passed almost immediately, even before Rosamund could reply.

"They are some of the Unknown Powers the Africans believe in," she was saying now. "I mean, believe in all the time, not merely on Sundays and never again all week. They believe some are good and some are bad. Of course, it's the bad ones you have to worry about, because the good ones aren't likely to do you any harm anyhow, though some of them may be a bit touchy, and you have to look out for fear you offend them without meaning to; and very likely there is a big power like a big chief, but you can't expect it to bother too much any more than you can expect a tribal council every time there's a quarrel about something or another. The Europeans all laugh and call it silly superstition, and the missionaries talk and talk, and I daresay it is all very childish, but I don't see that it's so very different from saints in Heaven and devils in Hell and a Supreme Being no one is very sure about. I dare say they've got it all wrong, but then perhaps all the other religions have got it all wrong, too."

"Yes," Bobby said. "Yes. But haven't you been talking rather round and about what I asked? I don't quite see how all that explains about your brothers and the Dark Ones or what was meant by 'Death sets free'."

"I've told you all I can," she answered angrily. "What else do you expect me to say?" But when he still waited, watchful and expectant, somehow making his strong will felt on hers, she burst out in a new hard voice. "I can tell you what the Africans say, only not out loud, whispering round the fires at night. They say because of how the boys died they came under the power of the Dark Ones, the Evil Ones, those that hate men and do them mischief, and that unless the boys can be set free, very soon they will become the servants, the agents, of the Dark Ones, and then they will be lost for ever. I didn't mean to tell you, but you've got it out of me. I think you are good at getting things out of people, aren't you?"

"Surely you can't believe all that?" Bobby asked, still a little bewildered by what seemed to him so monstrous an idea, too horrible, too outrageous, to deserve even a moment's serious consideration. "I don't believe it could happen, not if there are what you say they call 'good' powers."

"Why should they interfere?" Rosamund asked, and her voice had grown heavy and sombre and her young face a tragic mask. "They don't seem to while they are alive. Why should we expect them to afterwards? We do things on our own and what happens is our own look-out. Why should we expect it to be different—afterwards? I've only been saying what the Africans believe. I've talked to them and I've talked to the missionaries, and I've thought and thought, and now I don't any more. No one knows anything, anything at all, so what's the use?"

"Well," Bobby insisted, "I don't believe anything like that could happen or would be allowed to happen. It would be against all ideas of justice. There was no guilty mind. Your brothers meant no harm."

"Is justice a thing of this world?" Rosamund asked him, echoing, though she did not know it, a modern philosopher. "How can there be when anyone like Dewey James can be sent into the world as he is, all crooked and misshapen, so that when you see him you want to cry and yet you want to laugh too? What did his mother think about justice when she saw other babies and then looked at her own? Justice?" Rosamund repeated, almost with scorn.

"How did your father look at it?" Bobby asked after a momentary pause. "Or your mother?"

"I think Father was frightened, deep down in him, but I don't know. How should I? I was afraid sometimes he meant to follow the boys and try to find them, but he never did. He used to say primitive people knew things we others have long ago forgotten, and it might be the more you knew of this world the less you knew of any other. You must ask Mother yourself. We never talked about it. We daren't," and Bobby knew that what she meant, but did not say, was that that way madness lay.

"She seemed to me quieter somehow, more composed, so to say," Bobby said. "More restful than she was before."

"Now it has happened, she knows it can't happen again," Rosamund answered steadily, and added: "She's waiting for you. I told her you wouldn't be long."

"Yes. I'll go," Bobby said; but all the same still hesitated, deep in troubled and uneasy thought, nor did he either look up or speak when Rosamund went quietly away.

He roused himself then and went into the hall. A clatter of dishes told him that Rosamund was again seeking relief, as she had done before, in a flurry of household tasks—her way of avoiding brooding. He crossed the passage to the room where Mrs Outers was waiting, sitting by the window. She greeted him with a faint smile and explained that she didn't quite know what to do, and could he help her? It soon appeared that she had only the vaguest idea of how things stood. She knew that the pension stopped and she knew that there was a mortgage on the property. She knew also that the last instalment of interest had not been paid, but of what money there was available she seemed to be entirely ignorant. Bobby gave her what advice he could and suggested her best plan would be to have the help of a lawyer. He promised to try to get the name of a reliable one for her to consult. Then he went on:

"I've been having a talk with Rosamund. I don't understand a lot of what she's been saying."

"Poor child," Myra murmured; and he thought she was looking at him warily, as much as to say it was just as well he didn't. "It's all been so dreadful. She's too young. What has she been saying?"

"Well," Bobby explained—or tried to, though he thought that Myra had probably guessed already—"she seems to be taking seriously some fantastic native superstition or another. Do you?"

"When you have lived so close to the Africans as we did for so long," Myra answered, "you can't help wondering. Everything sounds so different back here from what it does in the African bush. You may laugh here at home. You don't out there. It's so quiet there, so noisy here. No wonder you can't hear what's so loud and clear out there."

"Then you did take seriously the stories the natives were telling?" Bobby said, not liking it. "Did Val, too?" Myra made no answer, and he did not press her. He went on: "Rosamund says the old witch-doctor told her 'Death sets free' just before he died himself. What did he mean? What can it have possibly meant?"

"Val thought he was telling us that only the dead can help the dead," Myra replied. "That's what he told me. But you have to wait till you are sent for and your path prepared. Or you may miss your way and be lost yourself."

Bobby was silent then. He felt confused, even angry, but most of all bewildered, by ideas that all his education and training, all his instincts, innate or acquired, taught him to disregard as fit only for the nursery, but that the father, the mother, the sister of the dead boys seemed to be inclined to accept to a greater or less degree. However, he reminded himself that for him the question was not whether these stories had any truth in them, but simply what effect they might have on those who did, to some extent at least, believe. It was Myra who spoke first, saying quite calmly, gently, even with a faint smile:

"I expect you think we were all mad. We weren't really. It's hard for anyone to understand who hasn't lived out there in the deep bush."

"Well, I don't pretend to understand," Bobby admitted. "Fortunately, I don't have to. It seems to me a monstrous idea, even a wicked idea. All I've got to do is to try to clear up how Val died and why; who murdered him? I am sure that must be your wish, too. Are you quite certain you can't help in any way?"

"But I've told you everything I know, you and Mr Nixon, too," she protested. "I've told Mr Nixon I don't think it could have been anyone there. It's no good his going on saying it must have been, if it wasn't, is it?"

"I have to take it, then, you don't suspect anyone," Bobby said. "Do you think Rosamund does? Could she have seen or known something only she was aware of? I've got the impression once or twice that there was something on her mind."

"She hasn't said anything like that to me," Myra answered. "It's all been such a terrible shock. I think often she can't quite believe it really happened. Of course she knows it did. It's just like a nightmare, and you know all the time you'll wake up soon and it'll be all right. Only this time you won't. It's funny how you can believe two different things at the same time."

"Rosamund has never said anything definite, has she?"

"Oh, no. She won't unless she chooses to. Even when she was quite a tiny you couldn't budge her once she had made up her mind."

Bobby gave it up then and asked instead:

"Rosamund says you saw a light in the old Constant Freres ruin last night. About what time would that be?"

"I looked at my watch and it was soon after twelve," Myra told him. "Do you think it could have been Mr Peel? He's been here this morning. I do hope Rosamund doesn't give him any lunch. I don't like him very much. I don't know what he could be doing if it was him. You could ask him."

The door opened then and Rosamund appeared to say lunch was ready, and would they come at once, or the omelet she had made would be spoilt.

CHAPTER XXVI
PRESSURE OF EVENTS

A GLOOMY AND a silent meal it proved to be for all three of them. It was indeed as though there weighed upon them, and not least upon Bobby himself, a sense of a heavy and impending doom. As soon as the meal was over—the omelet was a masterpiece—Bobby explained that he wished to go into Midminster, and went off to get out his car. While he was busy doing this, Dewey James came up and stood for a time silently watching, as if he found this operation of great and unusual interest. But to Bobby, himself silent, it seemed that Dewey's generally impassive features, calm as those of a marble statue, showed plain signs of strain. Indeed, for all his air of close attention, he was in fact hardly conscious of what Bobby was doing, so deeply was his mind engaged with its own problems. Not till Bobby was in the driving seat and ready to start did Dewey speak, and then it was only a mumbled remark to the effect that the reporters and the gapers seemed to have alike departed.

"I expect the rain discouraged them," Bobby said, always ready for one of those apparently irrelevant chats from which so much useful information could so frequently be gathered. "Looks as if it was coming on again," he added, glancing up at the rapidly darkening sky.

"I told my mother to go back in," Dewey said. "Is it true she knocked out one of the reporters?"

"Well, not exactly," Bobby explained. "But she smashed the camera of one of them with a swing of her crutch. She can make good use of that crutch of hers."

"She has to," Dewey muttered, and not as if the fact pleased him. He put one hand upon the car, gripping it as though he meant to try to hold it back, and the thought flashed into Bobby's mind that this gesture came from a deep-seated wish, strong within him, to hold back the investigation in conflict with his inner knowledge that he could no more do so than he could hold back the car by physical force. As if more consciously recognizing this, he took his hand away, his manner grew less strained, his voice more normal as he went on: "Yes; she is wonderfully active. I tell her sometimes she ought to have been an acrobat, the things she does. We match, don't we? Me as I was born and she as unlucky chance has made her. How is your inquiry going?"

"Well, it's hard to say," Bobby replied. "We don't find it easy, and I can't say that we seem to be getting much help. Nobody seems to know anything, and what they do know seems to add up to the impossible. Personally, I don't happen to believe in the impossible. I have my own private theory, and I believe I know who it was." He paused and he saw that Dewey's glance, hitherto wandering and restless, sometimes as if searching the far horizon, sometimes fixed upon the ground, had now become firm and clear, fastened upon Bobby himself.

"Who?" he breathed rather than asked. Bobby made no answer. Dewey said: "You don't . . . you can't. . . ."

"Can't what?" Bobby asked. In his turn he got no answer. Then he said: "Can't prove it, you mean? No satisfactory evidence. Well, not yet, but it may come. Or the murderer may confess when he feels the pressure is getting too strong and the strain becomes so great he feels it intolerable, and yet knows that it will never end till the truth is known."

"Especially," Dewey said, and not too pleasantly, "when the pressure comes from Bobby Owen."

"Not my pressure," Bobby answered gravely, "but the pressure of events of what has been done. That is always there, except for the few who are more nearly brute than human."

"There may be those who kill who feel that they are justified, that they had a right or even a duty to do it," Dewey said. "What then?"

"All the more likely," Bobby told him, "that confession will result. If there is no sense of guilt—no guilty mind, as the lawyers say—why not tell all? The urge to tell is always strong and the urge to justify yourself still stronger." He paused. Dewey was looking straight at Bobby and in his eyes there had come a strange, troubled expression. Bobby felt he knew exactly what was being suggested and that this disturbed him greatly. Bobby resumed: "Mr James, are you sure there is nothing on your mind you feel you ought to tell us? Remember, it is not only the guilt of one, but the innocence of others. If this is not cleared up, there are some who will live under a terrible suspicion for the rest of their lives, and that may prove a burden too heavy to bear."

"And do you think," Dewey asked with a slow and formidable anger, "that I have never thought of that—or of anything else indeed since it happened?"

With that he turned and began to walk away. Bobby watched him go and it seemed to him that Dewey was perhaps faced with a dilemma too great for mortal strength. Then he seemed to change his mind and turned again.

"Mr Peel has been here all morning," he said. "Did you know? I think now he is at the Lodge, talking to my mother. Mother," he repeated, it was not quite clear why, for he had spoken the word clearly and loudly.

"Do you know what he wants?" Bobby asked. "I would like a word or two with him myself. I was thinking of looking him up in Midminster."

"I'll tell him, shall I?" Dewey offered; and it was not long before Teddy Peel himself appeared, wheeling the bicycle which seemed to be his invariable companion.

"How's it all going?" he demanded as he greeted Bobby with a cheerfully casual wave of the hand. "But there, you won't tell. I know. Mum's the word till ready to pounce. I don't blame you. It's doing me no good. I can tell you that. Consultations being cancelled by every post nearly. They all know I was there, and so I'm in the front line of suspects. I shall be on the rocks soon unless you can make an arrest. What about Ludo Manners? If you ask me, he's your best bet."

"Doesn't seem very likely, does it," Bobby remarked, "that he would murder the father of the girl he was making it clear he wanted to get engaged to?"

"Ah!" Peel said, and repeated an "Ah-h!"—this time much more long-drawn. "But supposing he hadn't an earthly? And, if you ask me, he hadn't. What he was after was a map of a uranium field Mr Outers knew of, but was keeping strictly Q.T."

"How do you know about it?" Bobby asked sharply, and Teddy grinned and winked.

"You would be surprised," he said. "The things my clients tell me. And then their eyes near drop out of their heads when I tell it 'em back again. Mind you, things do happen. Only, take it from me, there's no spirits to it. Just electric magnetism and people ready and wanting to believe."

"It is said that man is first of all a believing animal," Bobby agreed. "I expect you know too that the bag Mr Outers kept it in has vanished?"

"And who has got it?" demanded Peel. "Take it from me, find it and there's your murderer."

"Someone was in the Freres ruin last night," Bobby said. "A light was seen. Looking for it, perhaps. Was it you?"

"Me?" Teddy asked in a voice a little too full of injured innocence. "I was in bed and asleep, same as per usual. But I could tip you off where it was hidden after the murder. Only what's the good when it isn't there now and nothing to show who put it there?"

"How do you know all that?" demanded Bobby. "Electric magnetism?"

"Smell," came the prompt response; and Bobby remembered that Rosamund had spoken of the strange odour that had seemed to emanate from the medicine bag. "Funny sort of smell, too. Brought the prickles out all down your back, and that's a fact. There's things I've seen, and some I didn't like too much, but this was different, and I tell you straight I wouldn't be the one to open that bag, not for all the uranium fields in or out of Africa. There's some things best left alone." He gave a sickly and uneasy laugh. "Poison or germs or something of that sort, it might be," he concluded.

"If we could find the thing, I would risk that," Bobby said. "Can you show me exactly where you noticed this smell or whatever it was?"

"Oh, yes," Teddy answered at once. "Not that I'm anyway keen on catching another sniff. It may have gone off by now, though. There was a heap of rubble I noticed, heaped up together like as if someone had been at it. I gave it a kick, casual like, and that smell fair leaped out like a cork out of a champagne bottle. But nothing to show what made it."

"What sort of a smell?" Bobby asked.

"Like a dead man mouldering in his grave," Teddy answered.

"Oh," Bobby said, rather taken aback by this reply, noticing, too, that Teddy had gone a little pale. "Oh, well. Well, when was this?"

"Yesterday afternoon," came the prompt reply, "when I was having a dekko on my own, just in case. I don't know as I was expecting anything, not knowing even what to look for, but I got an urge, as I do sometimes. Come on sudden like, they do, and often a dead loss, but then again sometimes it comes off."

"Electric magnetism?" Bobby asked. "Or what your clients have already told you without knowing it?"

"Oh, you can laugh," Teddy said.

"Sure it wasn't last night?" Bobby asked again. "If it wasn't you, who was it? Never mind. It's not an offence to take midnight strolls even in rather dangerous ruins. I would like a look round myself, though, if you will show me where it was."

"If you like," Teddy said, though with no great show of eagerness. "Safest way is up Folly Tower and then through the old communicating door. Can't say I much like messing about up there. If you ask me, what I say is, the whole caboodle ought to have been pulled down long ago, and if it isn't then it'll come down of its own doing first time there's a bit of wind."

CHAPTER XXVII
ROSAMUND'S FEAR

THIS WAS A prediction Bobby was inclined to agree with, and it was with some degree of apprehension that both of them surveyed those uncertain ruins of what once had been the great house of the neighbourhood. However, Folly Tower itself was still solid enough, and, picking their way with care, they reached safely a spot, where, in front of and partly sheltered by what had evidently been a recess in an inner wall, lay scattered plaster and rubble that did undoubtedly give the impression of having been swept or raked or gathered together from elsewhere, since here walls and ceiling were alike comparatively intact, though part of the flooring had gone.

"There you are, Mr Owen," Teddy said, pointing. "All in a neat little pile it was, kicked together, if you see what I mean, and when I kicked it, idle like, wondering who had taken the trouble and what for—well, as I said, that smell flew out and took me by the throat, so as I nearly choked, and that's a fact. Gone now," he added, sniffing the air. As he spoke he bent down, turning over as he did so some of the bigger pieces of plaster. One of these he lifted, putting it to his nose. Instantly he dropped it again with a loud exclamation and jumped hastily back. Had not Bobby caught hold of him he might easily have fallen.

"What's the matter?" Bobby asked.

Teddy, pale, gasping, still not quite steady on his feet, seemed for the moment incapable of speech. He gestured towards the lump of plaster he had been smelling at and had now let fall. Bobby picked it up, examined it, looked closely at it, half expecting to find bloodstains, smelt it. It seemed to him in no way different from any other lump of plaster or rubble, entirely innocuous. Teddy panted:

"Can't you smell it? You can't help."

"Smell what?" Bobby asked suspiciously.

"Strong enough to knock you down," Teddy insisted. He seemed to be recovering now from whatever it was had so affected him. "Nearly did me. Mean to say you can't smell anything?"

Bobby shook his head. He brought the plaster lump as close to his nose as possible and sniffed vigorously.

"Not a thing," he declared.

"You aren't a sensitive," Teddy told him. "Not like me."

Bobby did not attempt to dispute this verdict. But inwardly he wondered if 'sensitive' in this instance was not the equivalent of the common phrase, 'putting on an act'. He repeated that he could find nothing unusual about this very ordinary bit of fallen plaster, either by touch or sight or smell. Teddy was beginning to walk away. He said over his shoulder:

"I'm getting out. I've had enough."

Bobby followed him, and, once more by way of the Tower, so reassuringly solid a support to the tottery walls of the old ruin, they reached the ground without mishap. Teddy at once disappeared, almost at a run. Gone to get his bicycle, Bobby supposed. He himself returned, but more slowly, to Constant House, where his car was still waiting. He went into the house and found Rosamund, busy as usual, as though only thus could she keep her thoughts at bay. To her he handed the fragment of plaster he had brought away with him and asked if she noticed anything peculiar about it, any scent clinging to it, or anything like that.

"No. Why?" she asked, puzzled. "Is it from the old ruin?"

Briefly Bobby told her what had happened.

"The thing is," he explained, "was it all eyewash, or did Peel really smell something that rather scared him? He certainly seemed a good deal shaken."

"I don't think you can ever trust him," Rosamund said. "But he does often seem to know things, and you can't imagine how. But why should he pretend about a piece of plaster smelling if it didn't, and, besides, how could it?"

This was one of those questions to which there seems no possible reply. Bobby, at any rate, did not attempt to offer one, and Rosamund took advantage of the pause to smell 'something burning in the kitchen', so went off in a hurry to attend to it. Not the first time Bobby had noticed that she had a certain faculty for discovering 'something burning in the kitchen' when she wished to avoid further questioning. An innocent manœuvre? Or possibly not so innocent? Anyhow, there it was, and so he too went off in his turn to get his car and start at last on his delayed visit to Midminster.

There at Headquarters he found Nixon in a gloomy mood he was attempting to alleviate by the aid of strong tea and buttered toast from the canteen. Bobby's appearance he greeted with mingled hope and resignation.

"Got anything?" he asked. "Stuck, we are. Nothing to go on. Nothing to get hold of. Nowhere to start. Just like that."

"Well, there is one small development," Bobby told him. "There was someone prowling about the old Constant Freres ruin last night. Mrs Outers is quite clear she saw a light there," and he went on to repeat Teddy Peel's story of the strange odour he had noticed. Nixon did not seem much impressed.

"You can't offer a smell to a jury," he pointed out. "What could you expect them to do with it?" Bobby admitted that once again here was a question to which he had no reply, and Nixon went on: "Sounds to me like a red herring to put us off. What the guilty chap would want to do. Means Peel himself is the man we want? You agree?"

"Might be like that," Bobby agreed. "Peel is a slippery character all right, but that's still a long way from murder. If he did it, then the motive would be possession of Outers's medicine bag that was kept so carefully locked up. But Peel did seem really scared of the thing. I doubt myself if he would be very keen on opening it. There's a lot of humbug, and even downright fraud for that matter, but I do believe there is something about him he doesn't understand himself and is more than half-frightened of."

"Well, I don't know about all that," Nixon said doubtfully. "Not a police matter, anyhow. Do you think it was his light Mrs Outers says she saw?"

"He claims he was in bed all night and hints most likely it was Ludo Manners. That does link up with Mrs James's story of having seen Manners taking something from Outers's pockets after the murder. And I did get a strong impression when I was talking to Manners that there was something going on between him and Peel. My own idea is that Peel suspects Manners, but is not sure, and was feeling his ground, possibly with blackmail at the back of his mind. But Ludo strikes me as a tough customer, and he might retaliate by suggesting, as he did, that Peel is the man we want."

"If it's Manners," Nixon said, "then it would be this medicine bag thing, or, rather, what's in it, he was after. I don't see any of these old wives' tales scaring him from opening it. And there's evidence of Mr Outers having had a bad row with someone unknown shortly before the murder. Could that be Peel if Outers had caught him out in some of his tricks?"

"Well, it could be," Bobby agreed. "But nothing to show it was, and, of course, if the quarrel was with the murderer, he's not going to admit it."

"Another dead end," commented Nixon, as gloomy as ever. He took a drink of his tea, now not only strong, stronger, strongest, but also stone cold as well. "Mrs Nixon says it's poison," he remarked. "The tea I mean. The chaps like it that way. Always get so far and then stuck. The closed door. If it was Ludo Manners in the old ruin last night, it would be the medicine bag he was looking for. Precious little medicine about the thing as far as I can see. Anyhow, how did it get there?"

"Someone—perhaps Manners—took it after the murder and hid it where Peel says he noticed a queer smell when he was having what he calls a 'dekko' on his own. But it could be that the murder was only the occasion of the taking of the thing, not the cause. It has to be remembered too that Baynham—B.B., as everyone seems to call him—was the only one of the six out of the summit room after the murder. He would have ample opportunity to get at the bureau while he was supposed to be ringing up police and doctor, and it would have been easy for him to get a duplicate key made for the bureau drawer. Whoever it was would soon realize it was too risky to keep it on him, and would hide it till there was a chance to remove it again."

"What sticks in my throat," complained Nixon, "is all this crazy stuff about 'Death sets free', and those two dead boys being under some devilish power or another. You're not going to get anyone outside a lunatic asylum to believe that."

"Well, for that matter," Bobby observed, "there's a good deal now that fifty years ago no one outside a lunatic asylum would have believed possible, but common form now. Besides, it's not what we believe. It's not even what is or isn't fantastic Stone Age superstition. It's what other people may have believed. I have it in mind as a possibility that the motive behind all this hasn't been any uranium field and the millions it might mean, but some deep-seated emotional urge. I don't know, of course. Just an idea."

"Well, there's a lot of feeling between them," Nixon agreed. "B.B. and Ludo Manners. If one of them had been killed, I should have looked at the other at once. But it wasn't."

"No," agreed Bobby. "It wasn't anything like that I meant. But the Outers, husband, wife, daughter, have all been living under a very great emotional stress. Val Outers felt himself responsible for what had happened and knew other people put it more strongly. His wife had not only lost her sons, but there was also the rather horrible suggestion, however absurd and even impious as it would seem to many people—I don't like it myself—of the children's fate after death. I think it's certain that all that had worked on her a lot. Then Rosamund. She took that tremendous journey on foot through the African bush to ask the old witch-doctor's help, and got the message 'Death sets free', made all the more impressive by the old man's own death immediately afterwards. And then on top of it all there's what they all say they heard at one of Peel's sittings and that made my cousin write to me. One of Peel's tricks perhaps. No telling, but it may well have brought things to a head."

"Rosamund, Rosamund," Nixon was saying, half to himself. "You know, there's not much I would put past her. She has a way of looking at you. You never know with a woman. Meek and quiet as a mouse one moment and like a volcano on the loose the next. A Lady Macbeth in the making if you ask me. She's been the one for me all the time. Only how did she bring it off?"

"That's a question," Bobby said. "How did any one bring it off, for that matter? But, personally, I am sure of one thing. There's something very much on her mind. My idea is that all the time she's trying to prevent herself from thinking because she daren't, and what she's thinking is that it was her mother killed her father."

CHAPTER XXVIII
B.B. QUESTIONED

Nixon had listened in silence; nor did Bobby attempt to say more. The two men sat still, staring at each other across Nixon's desk, and the same picture was in both their minds, that of a young girl, driven by such a fear, struggling against such a doubt. Or was it—for this, too, was a fear running in both their minds—not doubt but certainty?

"If it's that," Nixon said at last, "we'll never bring it home to her or anyone else. I'm beginning to think no one did it at all. No good saying that to our Chairman or the Press—or the public either. Give me a good, clean, healthy murder. Chap doing another chap in because he's been messing about with the first chap's girl, or something like that. Or a gangster, meaning no harm; just after a bit of easy money. It's all this damn' witchcraft that's getting me down."

"I'm beginning to feel like that myself," Bobby admitted. "It's like trying to get into things beyond knowledge or understanding where you are all lost and helpless. Hard enough to get to grips with this world without trying to barge into the next."

"That's what Mr Jones would say, I'm sure," declared Nixon, as if citing authority. "All wrong to try, he would tell you."

"Who is Mr Jones?" asked Bobby, puzzled by so sudden an introduction of this new name.

"Our parson," Nixon explained. "Parsons ought to know."

"Oh, well, yes," Bobby said. "Yes. No more than the rest of us, perhaps."

"All the same, witchcraft or none, it must have been one of the six of 'em," insisted Nixon, this time with the air of a man struggling hard to return to common sense and sanity.

"Well, there's always the chance of an X turning up," Bobby told him. "The unknown quantity."

"What's that?" Nixon asked, now vaguely hopeful.

"I've worked out a theory," Bobby explained slowly. "Pure theory. Not a shred of solid fact to support it, but it might suggest a line to follow up. I've one or two other theories as well—all very much in the air at present. The one that's most in my mind at present would bring in one of the six as a helper, but possibly one ignorant of what was really intended. We've got to accept it that the door of the summit room was locked and bolted. But it would have been perfectly easy to have a duplicate key made. The room was in pitch darkness, the gramophone blaring away full tilt, and the other five of them all keyed up, all waiting for and expecting—well, whatever it was they were expecting. It wouldn't have been too difficult—I'm afraid all this points to Teddy Peel, though I hadn't intended to mention any names—to slip away from the table controls, draw the bolts and leave the way open for an X to slip in and do what he did. I said there wasn't a shred of evidence to bring forward in support. Well, there is, light and insubstantial, though, as the ash on which the whole theory starts from. You remember I told you I had noticed a cigarette butt in the Freres ruin, near the old door communicating with the Tower. Someone waiting there that night. Why? What for?"

"Dewey James?" suggested Nixon and repeated the name, this time with less of a note of interrogation in his voice. "Dewey James."

"Can you imagine him working in with Teddy Peel?" Bobby asked.

"Why not?" demanded Nixon. "Teddy would work in with anyone, cash or credit, and why shouldn't James want to be a uranium millionaire as much as anyone else? Or more. It wouldn't count then that he's the way he is. Women running after him then instead of running away. You know there are stories about him and the Rosamund girl? Well, he might have a hope there, too. I expect it's been done before now."

"Killing the father to get the daughter?" Bobby asked. "Well, possible, I suppose. Anyhow, it seems we have one more suspect to add to the six who were present. Or should we say two more, if we still keep in mind an unknown X—someone who up to now has managed to keep under cover.

Let's ignore that. Six present, and another, probably Dewey James, waiting outside and what for? Then Mrs Outers. And is that new manner of hers of peace and tranquillity she seems to me to show so plainly mean that she has accomplished the task she feels laid upon her to save her two sons in the next life from something even worse than their ill luck in this?"

"If it's that," Nixon said, "then it'll be Broadmoor for her and not hanging. Can't say I like hanging. Not for women, anyhow."

"Then Rosamund," Bobby went on. "And what is it on her mind that's driving her to such a frenzy of activity? Is that so she won't have time to think?"

"She's my man," declared Nixon. "Blamed her father and brooded on it till she felt he must go the same way, and up to her to send him. You've only got to look at her to feel it wouldn't be beyond her. It might be Broadmoor for her, but most likely not. I don't like hanging, but there's cases and cases, and when it's a father . . ."

He left the sentence unfinished and Bobby continued:

"Get on to the three men. Take Teddy Peel first. He seems the only one who knew from Val Outers himself about this uranium field map. And what is it that's between Ludo and him? I'm certain there's something—each hinting it's the other. I should say Ludo is the one among them all the most likely to go to any length to obtain possession of the thing. Finally, Baynham, who seems to be keeping very much in the background, which is exactly where any intelligent murderer wants to be."

"I've heard say the most unlikely suspect is the one to watch," Nixon commented. "Is that it? A decent sort, B.B."

"Murderers often are," Bobby said. "I always tell my chaps that murder's the worst of crimes, but murderers not always or often, the worst of criminals. Well, there they all are, all in line. And which is it?"

"Pick the loser," Nixon said dismally. "Yes. All right. But how?"

This poignant question Bobby left Nixon to wrestle with while he himself went on to visit B.B. at the offices of B.B. United, Ltd.

"Sorry if I seem to be going once again over the same old ground," he began, "but there are one or two details I feel it might help to try to get a fresh angle on."

The questions he asked were all unimportant and to all appearance aimless. B.B. began to show signs of impatience, but he replied to them all fully and carefully, and presently Bobby switched the talk to Constant Freres.

"You haven't called at Constant House since I saw you there, have you?" he asked.

"No," B.B. answered. "Why? Is that suspicious?"

"Oh, no," Bobby said. "I just wondered. That's all."

"I wonder myself," B.B. retorted, "if you ever say 'that's all' till you've got it all fixed up in your own mind."

"Which I certainly haven't," Bobby assured him. "I do believe I know who it was and even how it was done. One thing, though, to think you know and quite another to prove it, even to yourself. I fancy Mr Manners has been over at Freres once or twice, hasn't he?"

"How should I know?" growled B.B. "He mayn't have been told to keep away," and this was a remark that interested Bobby more than anything else—it wasn't much that had transpired during their talk.

So he drove back to Freres, not wholly dissatisfied with what he had learnt and not learnt. There the first person he saw was old Mrs James, who came hopping out from somewhere—he did not see exactly whence—and was at his side before he knew of her presence.

"Well?" she said. "Well?" and, when he did not immediately reply, added: "Got your eye on the right one at last?"

"I wouldn't go quite so far as that," he answered then. "Is there anything you could tell us to help?"

"Oh, I could," she said with her thin sardonic laugh. "I know. But I'm not telling. Not me."

"Why not?" he asked.

"Why should I? Your affair. Not mine. What you're here for, isn't it? Anyhow, you would only have my word for it."

"Anything you chose to tell us," Bobby assured her, "would certainly be followed up with the greatest care. We neglect nothing."

"It's all about here," she said, ignoring this, "how some papers of Mr Outers have been stolen and that's what he was killed for, to get hold of them. Means a fortune, they say."

"Who are 'they'?"

"Everybody," she told him. "Everybody."

"Who is everybody?"

"The milkman," she answered and gave him a queer twisted grin. "Milkmen know it all."

"I wish they would tell me, then," Bobby retorted. "Why are you saying all this?"

Instead of answering, she took out a police whistle and blew it loudly.

"That's for Dewey," she explained. "To let him know he's wanted. There's times I tumble over and can't get up so easy if my crutch is out of reach. He tries to do his duty by his old mother, but deep down inside him, there's hate. Oh, I know."

"Why should he?" Bobby asked. "I haven't noticed anything like that."

"Wasn't it me brought him into the world the way he is?" she asked in return. "More like a gorilla than a man." And for a moment, a moment only and no more, her old face seemed to break up as it were and then immediately change again to its normal expression.

Dewey had joined them now. To his mother he said:

"I thought I heard you whistle."

"I was talking to Mr Owen," she said. "I told him I know who did it. I shouldn't be surprised if you didn't know, too. But I won't tell him. Not me. Why don't you? You ought to, oughtn't you?" And now she spoke with a faint, mocking imitation of what Bobby's wife was accustomed to call his official voice.

"You know very well, Mother," Dewey answered, "that even if I knew for certain, and I do not, I should never say." And Bobby remembered. It was the first time Bobby had heard him use the word 'Mother' to her, and Bobby fancied that even now there had been a hint of rebuke in his tone, as though Dewey felt that in some way she had been taunting him, issuing as it were a secret challenge Bobby himself was not meant to understand. Uneasily he wondered why. "I was busy with the asparagus bed," Dewey was saying now after a momentary silence. "There was no need to call me away for that."

"There are those papers people are saying Mr Outers was killed to get hold of," Mrs James said. "I expect if Mr Owen can find them, then he'll be sure whoever has them was the murderer."

"It might very well be thought so," Dewey agreed and walked away.

Bobby made no comment. Behind all this he felt there was something he did not understand, something he had not been meant to understand, some hidden significance to which he had no clue and this troubled him deeply.

"Whoever it was didn't ought to get away with it," Mrs James said more to herself than to him. "I don't expect she will." And with that she turned and followed her son to their own part of the Constant Freres land.

CHAPTER XXIX
INTERRUPTED SUPPER

IT WAS MRS JAMES'S use of the feminine 'she' in what she had last said that stuck in Bobby's mind as he watched her go more steadily and slowly than was her wont, for indeed that old and crippled woman seemed often to use her crutch more like a witch's broom than like an ordinary, awkward substitute for a lost limb. It was as if, consciously or unconsciously, she were in perpetual protest against her disability, to show to all the world that she made nothing of it.

Soon she was out of sight and Bobby turned away, still wondering about that 'she'. Had the word slipped out accidentally? Or 'accidentally' on purpose, to use a common phrase? Or had it been uttered with the deliberate intention of suggesting that the guilty person was a woman? But only three women were involved—Mrs James herself, Mrs Outers, and Rosamund. And then Mrs. James's strange, defiant challenge to her son to name to Bobby whom it was they both 'knew' to be the killer, a challenge she apparently equally 'knew' Dewey would not, could not, accept? And whom was it that both seemed determined to protect?

Questions hard to answer, and yet for certain the answer was there for him to find if he could.

Now he had come to the house and as he entered Rosamund was crossing the hall. She saw him entering and she must have thought he looked strangely at her, for she stood still, evidently expecting him to speak. When he did not she spoke herself.

"Is there anything new?" she asked, and then again "Is there . . . ?"

"No, no," he answered. "No. I was only thinking I would give much to go back to London and leave the rest to Nixon."

"You mean you want to give up?" she said. "If you do, we shall never know. No one will ever." And now he wondered if it was with fear or with hope that she spoke, or perhaps with both together.

"Would that be best?" he asked in his turn. "That none should know?"

"There is no best," she said. "There is only bad and worse"; and, saying this, she disappeared into her fastnesses of the back regions of the house, whence sundry sounds soon announced that she was seeking relief—forgetfulness, perhaps—in ceaseless activity as others might perhaps in drugs or drink.

Bobby lingered, listening, for a moment or two, and then went to his room, there to sit for a time in solitude, in one hand his cigarette he had forgotten to light, not so much lost in active thought as in slow, steady contemplation of the whole of recent events in their entirety, hoping that somehow there would presently emerge something either to confirm or to deny the tentative theory he was half unconsciously formulating to himself.

It did not. The only result was a kind of mental vacuum, as if he had emptied his mind of its whole content.

From this he was presently aroused by certain interior promptings reminding him that the hour for the evening meal had arrived. So he went downstairs to the dining-room, found the table laid for one only, while from her inaccessible retreat at the back of the house Rosamund's voice informed him that her mother had retired to bed, that she herself was busy cleaning out the boot and broom cupboard, and that his supper was ready and waiting. She had heard him coming, she explained, and so had taken it out of the oven where it had been keeping warm and popped it on the table—two pork chops, and she hoped he would enjoy them and wouldn't mind having his meal alone.

Bobby replied sourly that pork chops was his favourite dish, that it was all very kind of her, that of course he didn't mind having a solitary supper, and then banged the dining-room door behind him as hard as he could to indicate extreme displeasure—not that he felt Rosamund was likely to take much notice. But before he had done more than convey one of the chops to his plate he heard the 'phone ring. As it went on ringing, as Rosamund was either too far gone in the depths of her boot and broom cupboard to hear, or else had decided to take no notice, he went to attend to it himself in case the call was for him.

As it was, for Chief Constable Nixon was on the line and seemed rather excited. A new startling development, he said. It seemed that an A.A. scout on his usual round had been stopped by a man who had asked him to ring up the police and give them a message to the effect that the 'Holy thing' was back whence it came, that the curse had been lifted and now all was well.

"I know the A.A. man," Nixon went on. "Very reliable, trustworthy. He says he thinks it was a coloured man, but the chap went off so quickly on his bike that he can't be positive. It was getting dark, too. He says the chap spoke in an odd, high, squeaky voice and broken English. Is this your Mr X, do you think?"

"Shouldn't think so," Bobby answered. "Holy thing? Holy fiddlesticks more likely. Holy red Herring. Coloured man? What about black gloves and burnt cork?"

"Oh, well," came Nixon's voice, sounding much less hopeful now. "May be important, though. What I always say is, follow up every line. Besides, you remember there were those earlier reports of coloured men appearing and disappearing like so many jacks-in-boxes. Worth seeing if there's anything in it. You agree?"

"Oh, yes," Bobby answered at once. "Certainly. Follow up everything. Anything may lead anywhere."

On this profound reflection the conversation ended. Nixon rang off and Bobby went back, past the dining-room, where his two pork chops were slowly congealing, and on to the green baize door that guarded regions unknown—unknown to Bobby that is.

"Rosamund," he shouted imperiously. "Rosamund. I want you."

"I'm busy," came the muffled reply, emphasized by an extra clattering of pans and pails.

"Never mind that," Bobby roared back, determined to make his voice heard though all the pots and pans in Christendom defied him. "It's important."

A reluctant, somewhat dishevelled Rosamund then appeared and looked at him sulkily.

"Well?" she said.

Bobby returned her sulky look with a scowl as serious and menacing as he could contrive, for though he thought he understood the dreadful fear that lay behind it, none the less he found her lack of co-operation exasperating in the extreme.

"Listen to me," he said sharply, "and don't try to dodge. That's no good. There's always been a chance there was someone else in all this—a Mr X. Somebody no one knew about. Mr Nixon thinks that he has now got supporting evidence. A man, described as coloured, otherwise unidentified, asked an A.A. scout to ring up the police and tell them that the 'holy thing' had been returned, the curse lifted, and all was well. What I want to know is if that is the kind of message any African coming here specially to recover the medicine bag that keeps popping up all the time would be likely to give? Or even the kind of language he would use?"

"He wouldn't even know what such a word as 'holy' meant," Rosamund replied. "To him, the 'Unknown Powers' simply represent something you had better keep away from. Witch-doctors may help if things are going wrong—but that's a kind of magic. Nothing to do with holiness or anything like that."

"Supposing the African's a Christian convert?" Bobby asked.

"If he is, he probably takes his Christianity much more seriously than most Europeans. He would be horrified at the very idea of calling a witch-doctor's medicine bag 'holy'. But there, again, he would be as frightened of it as any other African, especially if the medicine in it was said to have gone bad. He would be sure it would bring the worst of luck. Well, it has, hasn't it?"

"I don't know about that," Bobby answered. "I'm no great believer in luck, except what you make for yourself. Most of what you've been saying, I rather thought myself. It looks as if we had a Mr Y on our hands, not a Mr X at all."

"How do you mean?" Rosamund asked, puzzled and a little suspicious as well.

"A Mr Why," Bobby repeated. "Why has whoever it is chosen to send us a faked message? It may be merely a silly hoax, someone trying to be extra clever. There's hardly ever a difficult case but some fool of an exhibitionist jumps in. Or it may be one of the six who were present trying to confuse issues and send us off on a false trail. If it's that, then it must be one of the three men as the A.A. scout says it was a man spoke to him. Which of the three—Baynham, Ludo Manners, Teddy Peel? Young Baynham? I don't somehow feel it's an idea likely to occur to him."

"Oh, no," agreed Rosamund.

"Or Ludo Manners?"

"I don't know. I don't think so," Rosamund answered, but this time more doubtfully.

"Or Teddy Peel?"

Rosamund made no reply, and this Bobby interpreted as meaning that she, too, thought the cyclist might well have been Peel. Bobby continued after a minute or two's pause:

"He seems to have all the qualifications. We know he is a bit of a ventriloquist. He gets tambourines and so on floating in the air, and that's evidently faked. Means he is used to playing on the credulity of his clients, so why not try it on other people as well? He almost picks himself."

Rosamund had not been listening very attentively to all this. She had been following her own line of thought instead. She said:

"If he has the medicine bag, does that mean he did it?"

"Well, at any rate," Bobby answered, "he would have to give a very convincing explanation of how the thing came into his possession and why he didn't inform us? Holding back vital evidence is one way of becoming an accessory after the fact."

Again Rosamund did not reply, but as she stood there in silence and deep thought, Bobby got the impression that there had come to her a great relief, greater even than that all pervading fear he had sensed in her before, though whether that fear had been for herself or for another he could not tell. He was on the point of making that attack by sudden direct question, pressed home, which does so often succeed in breaking down the most obstinate silence, when she said, as if indeed anticipating this:

"I must go to Mother, she will be waiting," and with that she went, nor did Bobby try to stop her.

CHAPTER XXX
FOLLY TOWER BY NIGHT

IT WAS LATE NOW, and presently, as Rosamund did not re-appear, he went upstairs to bed. But he made no attempt to undress. Instead, he sat still and tried to think out the implications of this new development. After all, here was at last a break in that apparent dead end which had produced in Nixon a kind of defeatism and had at times made even Bobby himself wonder if he would ever be able to find certitude. But now had come proof that the guilty person—or at least an associate—was sufficiently disturbed by the investigation to try by action of his or her own to divert it into other channels. And when that happens this fresh action opens of necessity a new point of attack.

Yet still to be determined was whether it was more concerned with the murder or with obtaining and retaining possession of the medicine bag and its contents of such, by all accounts, great potential value: or, again, it might be with both, so closely interwoven did they seem. A question to which at the moment Bobby saw small hope of being able to supply an adequate reply.

It was this tumult and even indeed confusion in his mind, as much as anything else, that presently moved him to put on again his shoes he had just taken off, creep out of his room, and tiptoe down the stairs. He knew where the front door key was usually kept, found it, as softly as possible unlocked the door and drew the bolts, paused a moment to make sure there was no sign of his having disturbed either Rosamund or her mother, and then let himself out, locked the door again, and pocketed the key.

The night was singularly dark, with occasional showers of cold, driving rain. A gale was blowing up and seemed to be growing rapidly worse. Dark as was the night beneath its canopy of heavy rain clouds, Bobby was sufficiently familiar with the ground to be able, without too much difficulty, to pick his way towards the tower—the focus, as he felt, of all those strange and menacing activities he sensed gathering around.

As thus with care he groped his way onward he became aware of a vague impression that in the all-pervading cloak of darkness around, he was not alone. The belief grew strong within him that he was following someone who was moving with a speed and surety of footing he could not rival.

"Who's there?" he called.

He got no reply save from the wind and the rain, but the faint sounds he had heard, or fancied he had heard, ceased entirely. He took out the electric torch—it was one larger and more powerful than most—he had taken the precaution to slip into his pocket and flashed it. Uselessly. In that darkness its ray penetrated no more than a yard or two and he switched it off again immediately. It was serving merely to proclaim his own presence, if indeed there had been anyone there at all. He began to think he must have been mistaken.

Nevertheless, he went more cautiously, listening more attentively, though the swiftly rising wind and the patter of rain made listening to anything but them almost impossible. It was a relief to reach the ruin, since the wind was coming from that direction and even its crumbling walls afforded some protection. But that relief was mitigated when close by there came crashing down a shower of heavy stone-work, dislodged by a gust stronger than most, and accompanied by pelting rain.

In some haste Bobby hurried to seek at least temporary shelter. Aided by his torch he flashed from time to time, he groped his way to the entrance to Folly Tower. That at least stood secure, invulnerable to anything except earthquake or high explosive. Not likely, he reflected, as he rested for a moment from that breathless struggle with the weather that anyone but himself would be out on such a night. For his own part, he was only sorry that on a mere restless, unreasoned impulse he had deserted the comfort of his room at Constant House and the near prospect of bed. He told himself that as soon as the present squall abated he would return to them with all the speed possible. Meanwhile, as no abatement seemed a near prospect, he climbed the stone steps to where there still remained on first-floor level the usable entrance between the tower and the old house. There he stood for a moment, telling himself that if the storm increased in violence, it was as likely as not that the whole of what was left of Constant Freres might collapse in one great final crash.

Fortunately, there was now a lull in the fury of the wind. The rain, however, was still as heavy as ever, and Bobby had no wish to get himself as thoroughly drenched as any attempt to return just now would certainly result in. He hoped the rain was too heavy to last for long. Probably for a time at least, it would be better to stay where he was. Idly he flashed his torch into the darkness stretching before him, reflecting that, strictly speaking, in deference to the strange uneasiness still at the back of his mind, he ought to explore that tangle of rotting floors, unsteady walls, passages and corridors where gaps lay waiting for incautious steps. Even so, he was still conscious of an impulse to make a search till common sense told him that the risk of a bad fall was too great and the chance of any such search being worth while too small.

He was on the point of returning to ground-level to see if the weather was showing any sign of improvement when he had his answer in the form of a flash of lightning and a clap of thunder just overhead. Not very hopeful. If the rain did not stop soon, he supposed he would just have to go through it and get drenched, since the only alternative seemed to be staying all night where he was—an even less attractive prospect. Then, in the comparative silence that had followed what seemed to be in that place of resounding echoes a loud and distant cry, or rather scream, smothered almost simultaneously by such a crash of falling masonry as to make Bobby feel that the whole building was about to collapse beneath the renewed anger of the storm.

Yet that scream, if indeed it was one, demanded investigation. If there was anyone else wandering about here on this tempestuous night, it was necessary to know who and why—and why that scream so immediately smothered by other sounds? It could very well mean that this other midnight prowler had met with an accident. Accidents might easily happen on such a night, here where footing was so insecure and treacherous, pitfalls so numerous, where what seemed perfectly safe might end abruptly in such a yawning pitfall as those many others he himself had left behind him. Fortunately, he had his torch and by its help he was able to pick his way with a fair measure of speed in the direction whence that scream had seemed to issue.

This aid, however, he discarded when at a little distance ahead he caught a glimpse of another light that shone brightly for a moment and then was gone again. An electric torch switched on and off apparently. Towards this then he hurried as silently as he could, but also with more speed than was altogether prudent, and indeed once his foot broke through the flooring, so that now there was another pitfall to be avoided and lucky it was no worse.

Again the light ahead shone out, now not so far ahead, though, by any means. The going was easier too, and he even risked a kind of tiptoe run. He turned a corner, dodged with difficulty, for he was intent to give no warning of his approach, a pile of debris of which the slightest touch might have disturbed the balance, saw where, crouched at the other side of a yawning gap in the flooring, peering down by the aid of an electric torch into the darkness below, was the crouching figure of a man. From both sides of this great gap, bits of debris were still falling off, as if in warning not to approach too near, from below clouds of dust were still rising, as if to conceal what it was had fallen. The gap, though thus continually widening by the still-falling debris, was not too wide for a jump. But the difficulty of the approach the uncertainty of a secure landing made Bobby hesitate. No help to the investigation if he himself went crashing down with more of this tessellated flooring, there to lie crippled or worse till morning came and he was found.

Even as these considerations flashed through his mind the crouching figure opposite straightened itself, stood upright, shone its torch on Bobby, revealed itself as Teddy Peel, and exclaimed:

"Oh, Mr Owen! I might have guessed you would be around."

"What are you doing here?" demanded Bobby.

"Don't try to jump," Teddy warned him, perhaps guessing from some instinctive movement Bobby may have made that such a thought was in his mind. "It's not too safe over here. I thought I heard someone cry out, as it might be he had come a cropper. It wasn't you, was it, as let out that yell I didn't half like the sound of? And then a smash as if half the place had come down. If it wasn't you, who was it?" and again, not waiting for an answer, he stooped down to flash his torch once more into the darkness of the hole at his feet. "I can't see more than a big heap of stuff," he said. "The chap may have got away safely."

"What are you doing here?" Bobby repeated, his first impression that Teddy was merely trying to put him off strong in his mind.

"Well, now," Teddy answered, rather with the air of someone trying patiently to explain something quite simple to an unusually dense person, "I just had a feeling like us sensitives have, or else we wouldn't be such, would we? Very strong it was, keeping on and on like a nagging woman, only if it's that you can go off to a pub, and there you are. But if it's a feeling you take it with you and it gets worse and worse. Sort of treachery to yourself, if you see what I mean, if you don't take notice. Bed was what I wanted, but what it said was, 'Get your bike and go along. Things happening.' So off I went, for peace's sake. That's all."

It was hardly an explanation Bobby was much inclined to accept at face value, but he felt this was no time for further questioning. That could wait. Instead, he said:

"I must make sure no one fell. I'll have to go round and out by the Tower. You get down by the stairway and wait for me. You'll be there first. If anyone has fallen through, we must get help first thing."

"O.K." Peel answered. "There is someone—must be. That cry I heard. And you don't have to be a sensitive—"

Once more he left a sentence unfinished, for Bobby was already hurrying away with all the speed permitted by surroundings so treacherous and doubtful. He turned to go, and by the time Bobby arrived he was standing by the side of a prostrate, unconscious man.

"I had pretty near to dig him out," Teddy said as Bobby came up. "He's bad. He's alive, but he's hurt bad."

"Who is it?" Bobby asked, and then answered his own question: "Ludo Manners." He knelt down by Ludo's side to see what he could do and recognized at once that that was little. "What was he doing here?"

"After that medicine bag," Peel said. "There's ill luck goes with it, but all the same—" and once more he left unfinished what he was saying.

"Go back to the house," Bobby directed him. "Here's the front door key. Call out there's been an accident and I've sent you to ring up for help. Hurry."

"Hurry no good," Teddy said. "He's past help."

Bobby was supporting Ludo's head on his knee. He had wiped away the blood, the dirt, the dust that had covered it, and he had wiped out Ludo's mouth with a handkerchief soaked in the brandy from a flask he always carried with him. He dared not try to give any to Ludo to drink for fear of choking him. Ludo opened his eyes. He seemed to recognize Bobby. He said quite loudly and clearly:

"I've had a fall. Damn tricky up there. I don't feel anything, but I think I'm hurt. She poked me. From behind." His expression changed. "Hullo, Mummy," he said and died.

CHAPTER XXXI
NO ESCAPE

SCARCELY HAD THE dread sound of the death rattle died away, scarcely had Bobby time to lay a handkerchief over the dead man's face, than the sound of approaching footsteps became audible. Teddy Peel heard them first.

"There's someone coming," he said with a kind of nervous giggle, for he was in fact much shaken. "Getting to be kind of a general meeting, ain't it?"

The footsteps grew nearer, hurrying a little now, as if speeded up by hearing voices. B.B. appeared. He said no word, but stood there, staring, as incredulously he took in the meaning of those two men in the small islet of light their torches made in the dense surrounding dark and of that still form with the shrouded face that lay between them. Neither did they speak, but looked at him strangely, doubtfully. Then he said, pointing:

"Who's that? What's happened?"

It was Peel who answered with the same nervous alacrity he had shown before, saying:

"Had a fall. Croaked. It's Ludo Manners. He said 'she'. Clears you and me. 'She' he said; plain he said it. Didn't he?" he added, appealing to Bobby for confirmation.

"What are you doing here?" Bobby asked, speaking to B.B.

But B.B., staring at the two of them and then at the dead man and then back again at Bobby and at Peel, seemed too bewildered to answer.

Peel said, repeating himself:

"'She', he said, plain as you like before he went. So it isn't you nor me. Or Mr Owen would have had us both in clink by now. Wouldn't you?"

Bobby made no answer to this appeal either. But the word 'she' seemed to catch B.B.'s attention and he said:

"Is Rosamund—Miss Outers—is she here?"

"Why do you think she might be?" Bobby asked. "What are you doing here? In this weather, at this time of night?"

"She's not at the house," B.B. answered, making an obvious effort to collect his scattered wits. "She rang me. She said to come quickly. She didn't say why. I was out. They told me as soon as I got back, and I came at once. I couldn't make anyone hear. Her room's at the back, so I went round to see if there was a light showing, but there wasn't. I thought it was funny, and I tried the back door. It wasn't locked. I went in, but she wasn't there. So then I thought she might be here for some reason, and I came to see." He paused, and again stared at them, outlined in their little patch of light which now his own torch had widened. "For God's sake," he cried out suddenly and violently, "what's happened? If—that—is Manners lying there, where's Miss Outers?"

"That's just it," Peel answered before Bobby could speak. "'She', he said, plain as tripe. Well, where do we go from here? What next?"

"Stop chattering," Bobby told him sharply and a little unfairly. "Do what I told you. And hurry."

"O.K. O.K.," Peel said, a trifle scared by that tone of angry authority that sometimes came without his knowing it into Bobby's voice, coming as it were spontaneously from that fiercely latent, inner force of which his general manner gave but small indication. Before it Peel scuttled away, as if blown by a sudden gust of the wind still howling without. To B.B. Bobby said, equally sharply, "You stop here," though, indeed, B.B. had shown no sign of wishing to do otherwise, and now was saying:

"What's been happening? . . . There's been an accident. . . . This place ought to have been pulled down long ago . . . dangerous. . . . It is an accident, isn't it? What was the poor devil doing here?"

"There's nothing we can do till Mr Nixon gets here," Bobby said.

He lapsed into silence and deep thought—nor were those thoughts happy. Dark was his mood, dark as the surrounding night. If only he had not obeyed the quixotic impulse to use all his long painfully acquired experience and skill to remove even the faintest suspicion from those who, after all, had some claim upon him, both of kindred and of childhood memories. Unless that could be done, doubt and fear, mistrust and whispering gossip, would follow both mother and daughter all their lives. But now it had come to this—that he would have to testify to the dead man's last words, and to the last words spoken by a dying man both law and natural feeling attach the utmost importance. Faced with the last verity, few men lie or none. It was an issue from which there was no escape. Not only he, but Teddy Peel had heard, plainly, beyond all possibility of doubt or misunderstanding. And Peel would certainly be no way inclined to keep silent. Nor was there any reason why he should.

He was still facing this unhappy prospect with ever-increasing dismay when he heard cars approaching. Nixon's men had not lost much time. Bobby braced himself to say what had to be said. It was Nixon himself who appeared first, called from a warm and comfortable bed, and, though the wind was now dropping, and the rain lessening, wet through, since in his haste he had brought no coat.

"Bad business," he said with brief greeting. "Now it's two. Ten to one whoever did the first did this as well. 'She pushed him', he said, didn't he? Can't be Peel or Baynham if he said 'she'. Peel says you'll confirm?" Nixon waited for a nod of assent, received it, went on: "Well, that Outers girl was always my first pick."

"There was no name," Bobby said. "Manners gave none."

"No. I know," Nixon agreed. "Just 'she'. No name. Might be anyone in a way. All the same, there you are. One thing and another. Clear enough to my mind, even if a bit more evidence would strengthen it. It'll come all right now we know."

Bobby made no comment, even though that last word seemed to extinguish all hope, since he felt that how Nixon saw it was how most people would see it. Now more of Nixon's men were arriving—those who conduct the preliminaries to the investigation proper: the photographer, the pathologist, the finger-print expert, the specialist in preparing those plans and models so necessary for the full understanding of the scene of any crime. All this busy, grim activity Nixon became fully occupied in supervising, making sure that everything was being done according to rule and method as officially laid down.

Bobby, who in spite of all his training and long service, had never got over a deep inner distrust of all rule, all method, all too strict adherence to the beaten path, though none the less admitting their absolute necessity, now slipped away; since in all that was now going on he had no part to play. The rain had ceased, though it seemed likely to start again at any moment. He noticed that no light showed at Freres Lodge, so apparently neither Dewey nor his mother had been disturbed, or, if either of them had heard anything had not thought it desirable to be again concerned in any further happenings. Very prudent, very sensible, Bobby thought, and not uncharacteristic of Dewey, who always seemed much to prefer to be a spectator rather than a participant in events. Hurrying on, Bobby found the Constant House front door open and entered. Teddy Peel heard him and promptly appeared. He said eagerly, not without a trace of satisfaction in his voice:

"Her outdoor things are in the kitchen. Sopping wet. She was trying to dry them. Shows she's been out to-night, and no use her saying she wasn't."

"Has she said she wasn't?" Bobby asked.

"Hasn't had much chance to yet," Peel retorted. "You see if she don't. Makes it a sure thing, even if that 'she' of Manners' didn't."

"It's a lot to build upon a pronoun," Bobby told him. "You've seen her?"

"She heard me on the 'phone," Peel explained. "Came to the head of the stairs and called down to know if it was you. Dressed she was, which makes it a safe bet she had a job to do and went and did it."

"I think it would be better not to talk like that till Mr Nixon has finished over there," Bobby said. "He'll want to take statements from both you and me. You told Miss Outers what had happened?"

"That's right, and she never turned a hair, just listened like a stone statue. Made you feel funny like, when it was her ought to have been feeling that way—and plenty cause, too."

"You didn't ask any questions?"

"No," Peel answered resentfully. "Somehow she made you feel you hadn't better, and if you did you wouldn't get any notice taken, and what she thinks you can't even guess. Oh, she's a deep one, and what I say is, she's got the medicine bag all right. Ludo Manners had it and that's why she went to meet him to-night. Only he wouldn't part, so she outed him and got it. You find it, and that'll show you. Ought to be enough for anyone," and when he had said this he looked at Bobby in a sly, sideways way, evidently already suspecting that Bobby meant to do his best for these two relatives of his—that they were of his kindred was now generally known and had been the subject of some behind-the-back whispering. He might even just possibly be open to the suggestion of what Teddy Peel himself was wont to call a 'gentleman's agreement'. If anyone had suggested that that was another name for a mild form of blackmail, Teddy would have been most virtuously and genuinely indignant. Besides, in any case, call it by what name may be preferred, there were only one or two such 'gentleman's agreements' in force between him and his clients. After all, a 'sensitive' can't help now and then picking up little things the client is not too anxious should be generally broadcast to the world. He tried a cautious gambit. He said: "I'm sorry about all this. I only wish there was something I could do to help. Not much I wouldn't if I saw a way."

Bobby made no comment. He did not choose to let Peel see that he had so much as noticed the veiled suggestion, not even to show, or still less betray, any indignation. Teddy, realizing quickly that his gambit had failed, himself lapsed into silence.

They had been standing in the entrance hall at the foot of the stairs as they talked. Now at the head of these stairs

Rosamund appeared. Slowly she began to descend them, almost like a woman walking in her sleep, so remote did she seem, so far away in a dark world of her own. At the foot of the stairs she paused, and when she still did not speak, but only stood there motionless, looking silently at them who in equal silence had watched her slow descent, Bobby turned and said to Peel:

"You go, will you, and wait somewhere? Mr Nixon may be some time yet," and when Teddy hesitated, plainly reluctant to obey, Bobby, whose mood was not one of patience and of tolerance, repeated: "Get out. And don't try to listen or any other tricks," and this he said with such a tone and manner as induced Teddy to depart with all convenient speed. To Rosamund, who had remained impassive, as if she had not even noticed this small passing interlude, Bobby continued: "I'm not going to ask you questions. That's for Mr Nixon. He will be wanting you to make a statement."

"Yes. I know," Rosamund breathed rather than spoke.

"But there's one thing I would like you to tell me. You've heard what's happened?"

"Mr Peel told me," she answered in the same dull, far-off voice. "I knew before," and Bobby was only too quick to see how those few words would sound if they were repeated in a court of law.

As well might be.

CHAPTER XXXII
COUNSEL FOR TRUTH

NOW THERE WAS a silence that hung between them like a cloud, a silence like the silence of the grave. Yet it was one to which Rosamund, standing there so motionless, to all appearance so far removed from present things, seemed hardly aware, or, rather, was to it utterly indifferent. All the same, it was she who broke it first, saying:

"Mother is awake. It was the cars coming that woke her. I said I would go and see what it was. It's the police, isn't it?"

"Yes," Bobby answered.

"They have been quick," she said musingly. "That was you, wasn't it? I want to warm some milk."

"Yes," Bobby said again. "Where were you? Out there I mean. How long? How much did you see?"

"I heard you go out," she answered, "and I saw a light in the ruin, and I knew then there must be some one there. There hadn't been time for it to be you, and I thought it must be Mr Baynham, sheltering."

"Why him?" Bobby asked when she fell silent again, thinking seemingly that she had said all that was required.

"I had rung up to ask if he could come," she answered in the same monotonous voice, almost as though a marble statue spoke. "He was out and they didn't know when he would be back. It got so late I thought he couldn't be coming. I went to bed. When I heard you and saw the light I thought I had better go, too. But it wasn't him. It was you and Mr Peel, and someone lying still between you, and you and Mr Peel looking at each other and I saw the man lying there was Mr Manners and I saw he was dead."

"How did you know it was him? How did you know he was dead?"

"There is a difference between life and death," she answered slowly. "I knew. And I knew who it was. I knew the suit he had on—the pattern."

"Why was it so urgent to see Mr Baynham? I mean, what made you ring him up like that? Don't say if you don't want to."

"Mr Peel had been again. Earlier. Soon after you went to Midminster. I expect he had been waiting till you were out of the way. He said Mr Manners had Father's medicine bag, and if I would promise to give him a half share in it and let him open it, he would get it back. I only wanted it to destroy it for ever. I said so. I said it brought ill luck with it—the worst luck, because the medicine in it had gone bad. He said he knew that, because he is a sensitive, and I think he is. All he wants is the money he thinks might come from opening it, and he doesn't understand that may make the medicine ever so worse—stronger and worse, too strong for him to deal with, at least when it's only himself and his own gain he is thinking of."

"I don't know about all that," Bobby said doubtfully. "It doesn't seem to help to find who killed your father. Or Ludo Manners. It can't have been Peel himself, or Manners wouldn't have said what he did as he was dying. It may show a motive. I don't know. You ought to have told me when I got back. Why didn't you?"

For the first time the frozen composure of her countenance was broken by a faint smile, or rather the semblance of a smile. It was gone again instantly, but a greater animation showed in her voice as she replied:

"I never know what you will do. I expect you would have rung up Mr Nixon at once. Mother says you are like Abraham."

"Abraham?" Bobby repeated, not for the moment quite certain which Abraham was meant—Lincoln or Biblical. "What on earth did she mean?"

"Abraham was ready to offer up his son as a burnt offering to his God. Your god is duty, isn't it? You would sacrifice your son to it, wouldn't you, if you had one? Anyone else as well."

"Hardly a fair way to put it," Bobby protested, deeply hurt, even though he knew it was true enough.

"Men are so impersonal," she said tolerantly, trying to soothe any feathers she had ruffled. "It's always like that with men. We think of persons first—persons are more important than rules and things."

But now they were interrupted by the arrival of Nixon.

"What a night," he said as he came in. "A bit better now, though." Then he said. "This is the second time." And he looked hard at Rosamund. "You've been out there, haven't you?" he asked, and when she made a gesture of assent he went on: "I'll have to ask you a few questions, if you don't mind. To clear things up. Anywhere we can talk?"

Silently she led him into the dining-room. Bobby watched them go. He did not speak. Plainly Nixon wished to be alone with Rosamund while he asked a few questions before taking the more formal statement that would be required later on. It might be he was merely being tactful, in sparing Bobby the embarrassment of being present at, and perhaps taking part in, the examination of one of his own family—one, too, to whom at the moment he stood as guest to host. Or, more probably, because he feared Rosamund might derive courage and support from the presence of a relative and prove more obstinate in her attitude—if, that is, there was anything to be obstinate about.

In neither case was there anything that Bobby could do. His position was so entirely unofficial that he could hardly open his mouth unless by previous agreement with Nixon. In a thoroughly depressed mood, Bobby wandered off to find Peel dozing by a kitchen fire, now surrounded by a collection of drying clothing. He looked up when Bobby entered and said:

"Putting her through it? Rather her than me. Watertight, and, if you ask me, her pa, too, most likely."

"There's nothing certain yet," Bobby said, speaking as much to reassure himself as to contradict Peel. "Nothing proved. Manners may have been mistaken."

"Well, he ought to know who it was, oughtn't he?" Peel grumbled.

Still speaking half to himself, Bobby went on:

"It's possible a third person crept up and Manners didn't know, hadn't heard anything, remembered who had been there, and thought it must be her. Or it might have been just possibly all an accident. If the floor gave way suddenly, and if Miss Outers was there and made a grab to try to save him, that might account for it. In his confused state of mind he might have taken it she had done the opposite."

"Lord, Mr Owen," exclaimed Peel, a little less assured now, "you might be counsel for the defence."

"Counsel for neither side; only for the truth," Bobby told him. "Miss Outers says you claimed that Manners had the missing medicine bag as they call it and offered to get it back from him. Did you?"

"Haven't had much chance to try yet, have I?" complained Peel. "All this happening, and I only put it up to her this afternoon, and how, if I did, then I wanted a fifty per cent. interest. Turned it down flat, she did."

"Both you and Manners were there to-night. Does that mean you were following him without his knowing it?"

"Lucky for me, he said 'she', before he went which I'm not, or you would be after me all right, wouldn't you?" complained Peel. "I had to keep an eye on him, hadn't I?" and now the one-time confidence he had begun to show had clearly become a distinct uneasiness. "Me being a sensitive—"

"Oh, cut that out," Bobby interrupted impatiently. "I want facts, not humbug like that."

"Which shows how little," retorted Peel with an odd touch of dignity that took Bobby entirely by surprise, "how precious little you know about it. Humbug I may be, but a sensitive I am, like it or not, and know things that others don't and never could. Not all the time. It comes and goes. The same as at cricket. One day you'll see the ball big as a pudding, and next day fumble at it as if you couldn't see straight any more. Believe it or not, there it is, and that's a fact."

"I meant as evidence given in Court," Bobby explained, half apologetically. "Mr Nixon will want a lot more than talk about being a 'sensitive'. He'll certainly take into account the possibility of an accomplice being there. A lot of digging to be done before we get to the bottom of it all. And there's something Miss Outers told me that may alter all our ideas. I'm not sure yet."

"Well, if anyone else—and I don't see who—did the pushing, it wasn't me, and that's a fact," Peel protested, and still not too comfortably. "And I'll tell you something else I'm getting to feel pretty sure about. But not a feeling like I meant before when you know without knowing how or why. The sort that only comes from brain work, logically, if you see what I mean, reasoning it out. I'm only trying to help. For why? Because it's doing me no good with half my clients holding off because it looks like I'm a suspect, and the other half because if I'm a sensitive and was there, but can't say who did it, then looks like I'm a humbug all right. Like a nut caught between the crackers I am. See?"

Bobby did see and said so, but added:

"You were going to tell me something? What was it?"

"I'm coming to that," Peel answered. "Only wanting you to understand first. What I reason is that, seeing someone got Mr Outers's bag, it was more likely Ludo Manners than anyone else. Up and coming chap. B.B.'s not that sort: slow and sure and more slow than sure, and that's a fact. I don't know how Manners managed it, but I reckon he did, and hid it somewhere in the old ruin, meaning to take it away on the Q.T. when he got a chance. Only then some other party found it, and went off with it, or else Manners forgot exactly where he'd put it. That's the way how I believe it happened, and if I'm right—and I'll bet I am—then I know who has it now."

"Who?" Bobby asked.

"Ah! That's telling," Peel replied, with a little knowing nod added for good measure.

CHAPTER XXXIII
ONE LINK NEEDED

BOBBY OFFERED NO comment. He allowed Peel's claim to know what Bobby himself was so anxious to know and did not to pass by him as though he had hardly heard it. For he was very well aware that a show of indifference was often the best and quickest way to induce most people to reveal what they knew, or thought they knew, and were inclined to keep to themselves. To feel they know what others are ignorant of seems to enhance their ego, while simply to ignore their claim tempted them to prove its value by revealing its nature.

So it was now. Peel was evidently both surprised and disappointed by his failure to impress Bobby, but then the door of the dining-room opened and Rosamund appeared. She came into the kitchen and stood for a moment in the doorway, looking at the two men as if wondering who they were and what they were doing, and Bobby was once more struck by the marble rigidity of her face and bearing, so that she more resembled a walking statue than a living, breathing woman. Then she spoke. She said:

"Mother's waiting. I must get her milk ready."

She went through into the pantry, presumably to get the milk. Peel got up and said to Bobby in a kind of muffled whisper:

"Gives you the willies, don't she? And that's a fact."

Bobby went into the hall and through to the dining-room. Nixon looked up as he entered and said:

"Looks to me as if we had it all sewn up now."

"You've decided to charge her?" Bobby asked.

"Oh, yes," answered Nixon. "Yes. Not at once. I've told her I shall have to get her to make a full statement, and she had better think over what she wants to say, and how she can have her lawyer present if she likes. We don't want to take her at any disadvantage, I told her. What you say yourself in one of those lectures of yours on C.I.D. work about giving suspects time to think things over, and what they say then often gives just the lead wanted. Very interesting, those lectures of yours. You ought to put them in a book. Why don't you?"

"Oh, I might some day," Bobby answered, secretly much flattered. "I don't know, though. Talking's not like writing. Besides, chiefly of technical interest."

"Oh, I wouldn't say that," Nixon protested. "Lots of men turn author when they retire—make a jolly good thing of it too. 'The Reminiscences of Bobby Owen.' Should go down well, and keep you busy when you retire." He reverted then to what he had been saying before. "Giving her time, that's the idea. She may come clean when she sees she's cornered. She might even try to make a get-away. I shouldn't be a bit surprised. Panic. Or do a suicide. She has a way of staring at you I don't like."

"I don't think she's that kind," Bobby said. "If you don't mind my saying so. I should wait a bit. I don't feel myself that the evidence is quite enough as yet. There's been too much happening too quickly to-night for it all to be thought out yet as it should be. I am inclined to think that a careful study of what's been said and done to-night might give a new conclusive lead."

"You don't mean you've an ace up your sleeve, do you?" Nixon asked, a touch of suspicion and distrust in his voice.

"No. No," Bobby protested. "Nothing like that. All cards on the table. But I'm not sure how to sort them out till I've had another good, long look at them."

"Well, tell me when you have," Nixon said. He blinked drowsily at the clock on the mantelpiece and then yawned mightily. "Might be time," he said, "to get an hour's shut-eye before starting again. Lord knows I need it. My chaps, too. Occupational risk, I suppose, having to work the clock round. If it hadn't been for Manners saying 'she', I don't deny I might have paid a little more attention to Teddy Peel. Don't trust him somehow. He says you'll confirm it was 'she' Manners said. You wouldn't say there was any chance of any confusion, misunderstanding?"

"None whatever," Bobby assured him. "Manners spoke clearly and strongly as men do sometimes at the hour of death."

"Not the first time everything has depended on the last words of a dying man," Nixon commented.

"No, indeed," agreed Bobby. "I do think that perhaps if you think them over . . . they may show . . ." He drifted away into silence, deep in a medley of thought.

"Show what?" Nixon asked, and, without waiting for a reply, went on: "Well, they do, don't they?" He paused again, and when Bobby still seemed lost in his own thoughts, continued rather uncomfortably, as if he wished to show sympathy but didn't know how: "I'm afraid you'll have to go into the witness-box. I've been thinking about that. I'm sorry, but I don't see any way to dodge it."

"There isn't any," Bobby said.

"A relative, isn't she?"

"Mrs Outers is a first cousin," Bobby explained. "We were children together. Miss Outers will be a second cousin, isn't it? I'm not sure. Anyhow, one of the family one way or another."

Nixon looked a little shocked, as if he felt Bobby's attitude rather callous, rather too carefree. Nothing to do with him, though. All he said was:

"Well, what must be, must be. What about bed for an hour or two?" and he yawned even more mightily than before.

Bobby looked at his watch.

"Not for me, I think," he said. "I want to have a talk with Dewey James and his mother as soon as I can. There's been no sign of either of them all night, though you would think they must have heard something was going on."

"Want to keep out of it most likely," Nixon suggested. "I don't blame them. I would myself if I could. I expect you would, too."

"Yes, indeed," Bobby declared with fervour. "Too late for that, though. Got to go through with it. Dewey might have something to say. Or his mother. I'll try and see them as soon as they show."

"Well, I'll be off," Nixon said. "Won't be long before I'm around again. Got to do a report, and I must ring up our Chairman and tell him it's in the bag now. As near as near can be," he added hastily, remembering that Bobby had hinted at the possibility of fresh evidence coming to light. "Not going to bring in an accomplice, are you?" he asked. "If there is one, most likely it's Teddy Peel. I feel he's up to something, or has been. I don't know which."

"I feel fairly sure no one else was in it," Bobby assured him. "It's a one-man job, carefully planned, carefully worked out."

"I'll leave you one of our chaps," Nixon promised through another yawn, the biggest yet. "In case you need help. Take my advice. Never mind Dewey. If he has anything to say and is ready to say it, he will, if he isn't, he won't; and nothing on earth will make him. By the way, Teddy Peel's gone off. Asked if he might, and didn't wait to be told; just buzzed off on his bike."

With that Nixon himself departed to find his car. Bobby sat down in the nearest chair. His watch showed it was five o'clock. Too early to expect yet those signs of activity at Freres Lodge for which he was waiting. Another hour perhaps. He closed his eyes, but he felt no inclination to sleep. His thoughts were in a ferment, seeking the more probable, seeking certainty, testing one theory against another, only to discard each in succession as each began to show those inner contradictions which deny validity. Always he found himself returning to his original belief he had never yet mentioned, since to do so might, if it became known, lead to the destruction of the one piece of factual evidence he needed to establish his theory on a firm, objective base. He glanced again at his watch. Six o'clock. He got up and went to the window. It was growing lighter now, in spite of the rising morning mist, and the storm of the previous night was subsiding rapidly. A light appeared in Freres Lodge. In the kitchen, Bobby thought, from what he remembered of the layout of the cottage. Preparations for breakfast probably. Soon the first of the day's outdoor activities would begin and then he would go across and have his talk.

Then as he watched he caught a glimpse of a figure, that of a man, hurrying at speed between cottage and outbuildings, into one of which it quickly disappeared, the one Bobby was nearly sure wherein a short time previously he had found Mrs James busy over some mechanical job and been struck by the dexterity with which she handled her tools.

Much puzzled, Bobby rubbed his eyes, wondering if, more sleepy than he knew, he had dozed for a moment on his feet and mistaken a passing dream for reality.

The mist, rising from the soaking ground, made it difficult to distinguish objects or be sure of their identity when at one moment they were shrouded in invisibility and at the next showed clear and distinct. All the same, he felt fairly sure it was a man he had seen, a man hurrying to seek shelter—or concealment—and that that man had not been Dewey James. Nor was it in any way likely that Dewey would be hurrying in so furtive, almost slinking, a manner to dodge into one of his own outbuildings. And then Dewey, as Bobby knew, seldom ran or even hurried. He was more accustomed to move with a certain grave deliberation, as of one who knew there was always time, since time is but the gloss upon eternity.

Who, then, and on what errand? The name that now began to run in Bobby's mind was that of Teddy Peel. But Teddy Peel according to Nixon, had 'buzzed off' in the small hours. And what could he be doing back again at an hour scarcely less small?

Matter for investigation, even though it might not be Peel at all. Some friend of Dewey's, perhaps, or one of the casual helpers he occasionally employed—when he could get them—or even Dewey himself, forgetting his usual non-hurry habitude.

Bobby decided it would be as well to go across to the cottage at once and see. He went out into the hall. Rosamund was there. She had just come downstairs. She saw him and said:

"Mother is sleeping now. Haven't you been to bed? You ought."

"Have you?" he retorted.

"I have been lying down," she answered. "I must get breakfast ready. Has Mr Nixon gone? He thinks I killed Mr Manners. You think so too, don't you? Mr Nixon wants me to say I did. Father, too. Mr Nixon says they wouldn't hang me, now it isn't done any more. They would bury me alive instead. Is it better to be buried alive than to die and be done with it all?"

It was a question to which Bobby knew no reply.

CHAPTER XXXIV
CONCLUSION

THE SUN WAS rising, the dank morning mist dispersing, as Bobby picked his way across the soggy, sodden ground towards the Lodge. From the direct path to it he turned aside to the tool-shed into which he had seen that hurrying figure vanish. Of course, whoever it was might not be still there, might have slipped out again as swiftly and as secretly as he had entered.

Hurriedly Bobby pushed on past the hen-run, where its inhabitants were noisily proclaiming their conviction that breakfast was much overdue, and arrived at the tool-shed. The door was shut and he noted that it was strong, as was indeed the whole substantial building. He saw that the key was in the lock. It was more a general feeling that a crisis was near at hand than any real sense of danger that made him cautiously remove the key and slip it into his pocket. Not likely that anyone would turn the key if he left it where it was. But if that did happen he would be a prisoner, nor would it be easy to break out quickly in case of necessity. He pushed open the door and entered. There was no one visible and nothing to suggest that anybody had been there that morning. Later on, he thought or imagined he had thought—he was never able to determine which—that as he entered he had been aware of a faint, all-pervading smell, stench rather, hovering in the air. If he had done so, he paid it now no attention. He gave a quick glance round, at the work bench, at the rough deal table near by, at the two tool chests, both padlocked. Why two? One for Dewey, one for his mother?

He stood there for a moment or two, slowly looking round. He was not fully satisfied, but for the moment he did not push his explorations further. Instead he said aloud, as if communing with himself:

"No one here, anyhow."

With that he opened the door to go and once outside two or three quick strides took him to the small side window by which the shed was lighted. One glance showed him a man crawling from under the table. It was Teddy Peel. While Bobby watched, Peel went across to where the two tool-chests stood. He seemed to be examining each in turn, bending over them and apparently sniffing at them, as though testing them with his nose. To judge by the little nod, as of satisfaction, that he gave he seemed to have found what he had expected. Taking some small tool or another from his pocket, he began operations on the padlock of one of them. Bobby judged the time had come for him to intervene. He went back to the front of the shed and pushed the door open. Teddy jumped round, all tense and ready. His hand dropped to his coat pocket. Then his attitude relaxed. His hand emerged empty. He said ruefully:

"I might have known your popping off like that was just a do. I might have known you would be sure to be around. And me thinking you would be in bed."

"What are you doing here?" Bobby asked, ignoring these lamentations.

"Trying to recover Mr Outers's bag that's missing and you can't find. No idea where to look, you police haven't."

"Do you mean it's in that tool-chest you were fiddling with?" Bobby asked.

"That's right," Teddy answered.

"How do you know?" demanded Bobby.

"Can't you smell anything?" Teddy asked.

"No," snapped Bobby, even though afterwards he came to feel that this prompt response had been given too quickly—the result perhaps of an unconscious resolve not to be put off by any other than an explanation in terms of common experience.

"I've told you before," Teddy was saying now, "that me being a sensitive—"

"And I've told you before," Bobby interrupted sharply, "to drop that sort of thing when you're talking to me. I want to know what you would say if you were in the witness-box. I don't advise you to start offering explanations of that sort there. Wouldn't go down too well with the lawyers, or the jury either."

"More fools they," Peel retorted equally sharply, and looked as though he would have liked to substitute a more personal pronoun for the 'they'. "As much use talking to a deaf mute as to some people. O.K. I'll tell them I worked it all out, reason, logic, all the rest of it, as there's plenty fool themselves there's nothing else. Slide-rule cranks, I call them. O.K. O.K. Only common sense that it must have been one of us six who were present as saw his chance or made it for himself purposeful like, to get hold of the bag as someone pinched for what's in it—and who did the pinching did the killing, too, and that's a fact."

"If you're right," Bobby said, though rather doubtfully, "and the thing really is in that tool-chest—"

"Oh, I am," interposed Peel. "This one," he said, putting his hand on that he had been busy with before Bobby's unexpected appearance put a stop to his proceedings.

"Why that one?" asked Bobby and got the reply:

"It's the smell, like dead men and vomit mixed. What about getting on with opening it?"

"It must only be opened in the presence of witnesses," Bobby told him. "What you say is enough for asking Mr Nixon to come at once and bring with him a magistrate if possible. I don't want to give any possible ground for a suggestion that the thing was planted by us."

From the door came suddenly the slow, deep voice of Dewey James. In one hand he held the pail he had brought with their morning feed for those still clamorous hens. He said:

"What's all this? What are you doing here?"

"Looking for what you went and pinched before you did in poor Mr Outers," Peel retorted before Bobby could speak. "Or how else did you get hold of it to keep it hidden? And don't go for to try to out us, too. Two of us and you only one."

"Only one of you that matters," Dewey said, quiet contempt in his voice. "You hardly count."

"Oh, don't I?" Peel snarled, and his hand went to that pocket which instinctively it had sought before, though this time when it emerged it held a small deadly-looking automatic.

But Bobby reached out a long arm and took the weapon from him, took out the clip, put that in one pocket, the pistol in another, and said:

"Mr James, a statement has been made by Mr Peel. It seems sufficient to justify me, acting as an officer of police, in taking charge of both these tool-boxes till they can be opened and examined in the presence of witnesses, and in asking you to remain here till that has been done. Have you any objection?"

"Need you be so very official?" Dewey asked with that slow, grave smile of his, and then added with a touch of irony in his voice: "Can't I even go and feed the hens? Never mind. Mr Peel is quite right. Mr Outers's medicine bag is there. I don't know how he managed to find out."

"Smelt it," Peel explained. "Stinks like hell. And why for not, seeing as that's what it is?"

But Dewey only looked puzzled.

"Smell?" he repeated. "I can't smell anything. You couldn't, not while it's in that chest." He turned to Bobby. "I've had it ever since the murder," he said, and again Peel interposed:

"If you put your ear close you can hear it wriggling," he announced. "It's the blood it senses that's woke it, and now it wants more."

Neither of the other two took any notice of this remark, and Dewey continued to Bobby:

"I suppose I can take it you mean to have me arrested? For murder? Very well. I'll say nothing now—except that I admit nothing, and that I think you'll have a job to prove it."

Privately Bobby was of the same opinion, but he made no comment, and indeed had no time to do so. For now they were joined by Mrs James, standing there in the doorway, where she had been in fact for a minute or two, unnoticed, regarding them with that cold, sardonic grin of hers as she balanced herself with such apparent ease on her one leg, using her crutch to point it at them.

"Quite a conference," she said. "Well, well." Speaking directly to Dewey, she said: "Well, my son, found out, haven't they, what you thought your old mother didn't know? But then you always were a fool about her. Well, it's all over now," and now that pointing crutch of hers was levelled at Bobby as she went on: "I know what you want. How did you know? I was a fool not to take the blow-lamp to it. I meant to and then to bury it deep, but some way I couldn't bring myself to touch it. It's there, waiting for you, and there's blood on it still. His blood."

"Don't try to knock me out," Bobby said, watching her warily.

"It wouldn't be any good," Dewey warned her, and came to stand by her side. "It's gone too far."

She nodded acquiescence, and to Bobby she said: "All your doing, and in the end—why, well done." She paused and her expression changed as she swung round upon Dewey: "Dewey, my son," she snarled, "if I had borne half a man instead of all a monster, you would have helped, and the girl yours by now."

With that she went as quickly and as silently as she had come, while the three men looked uneasily at each other.

"What's the old witch mean?" Peel asked of no one in particular.

"I think, perhaps," Dewey answered him, "as she said in the end—why, well done."

"I had better see," Bobby said.

He moved quickly to the door and opened it that Mrs James had shut behind her. She was already at some distance, hurrying, not towards the Lodge, but in the direction of the Folly Tower. She was using her crutch, not as a mere aid to walking, but rather as a pivot for those strange, prodigious hops of hers that enabled her to cover the ground with such uncanny speed. Bobby saw at once that the chance was small of overtaking her before she reached whatever goal she was aiming for. He snatched out the police whistle he always carried with him and blew it loud and long. Mrs James, startled by that shrill summons, stopped for an instant to look round. Simultaneously the uniform man Nixon had left in charge came tumbling out of the house. He had chanced to be in the hall, hoping for a cup of tea to have with his sandwiches.

"Stop her," Bobby yelled at the top of his voice. "Stop her," and then set off to run at utmost speed.

Doubtful if the constable heard, but at least he understood. He ran at an angle, trying to cut across her path. In turning to look round, Mrs James had lost a little of her momentum by so breaking the long rhythm of her hops. The constable was young and active. He was there first, standing between her and the entrance to Folly Tower he had seen she was making for.

"Look out. Look out," Bobby yelled, even more loudly than before.

But this time, even if the constable heard he did not understand. Hearing or not, he saw nothing to 'look out' for. Only an old crippled woman helping herself along by her crutch.

"What is it, missus?" he asked amicably.

She balanced herself for a moment and then without a word, delivered that poke or thrust of hers. Unexpectant, he took the full force of it below the belt and went sprawling. Mrs James left him there and disappeared within the Tower.

Bobby and Dewey arrived almost together, but Bobby by a yard or two, the first. Almost he threw himself up those steep, winding stairs, but not with the same wild energy Mrs James had shown, for he was driven by no such wild and fierce need. Yet at the end he was so close that his hand was outstretched to seize her as she fled into the summit room, banging the door behind her, shooting the bolts.

Baffled, he stood a moment. Nothing he could do to break down that door, so solid and so secure. He turned and began to descend. The sound of shouting reached him from below to tell him what had happened—nor did he know whether he regretted that he had failed in his purpose or to be glad.

At the foot of the Tower, a little group had gathered. Nixon was there and the uniform man and Dewey, supporting his mother's body in his arms. He looked up as Bobby came to join them. He did not speak. Nixon said:

"We saw her plain. She threw her crutch away as something she had no more need for, and then she jumped. She was still alive when we reached her. She said something. I don't know what. Then she died."

"She said, 'Goodbye, my son,'" Dewey answered.

Some hours later, Bobby, Mr Nixon, Dewey James were together in a room at the Headquarters of the West Midshire Police. On the table before them lay the crutch and something else that looked like a kind of lazy tongs with its interlocking levers. Apparently it could be put into action by a wire running to the head of the crutch. Nixon had just placed this wire back in position and had been showing how firmly, when the wire was pulled, the lazy tongs held, and held in its grip six inches of a kitchen knife, ground to a fine point. Here and there dull spots of a reddish hue dimmed the brightness of the steel.

"Deadly," Nixon was saying. "A spear! That's what it is." He repeated: "A spear, and a jolly fine mechanical job, too. Explains how a blow across a table could be delivered with such force. She knew how to use her tools all right." He turned to Dewey and said sharply, as he had said previously and more than once: "You must have known—couldn't help."

Dewey did not reply. He saw no use in repeating a denial already twice given. Nixon frowned. That was to show he did not regard such silence favourably. He turned to Bobby and complained:

"I still don't understand how you built up all that out of nothing at all as far as I can see," and in this there was, or so Bobby thought, an underlying implication that he had been keeping to himself facts, privately given that he ought to have shared equally with Nixon.

He felt himself bound to explain—a thing he always hated doing. Anyone, he told himself, ought to be able to follow a process so essentially simple and straightforward. For just as one straw floating by can show the way the wind is blowing, so a steady flow of straws can prove they point to one fixed compass point.

"Oh well," he began now, "the very first time I saw Mrs James she showed us a rather odd hostility. Not that I thought much of it. Just a grumpy old woman's bad temper. Later on, in the same way, the first time I was in the tool-shed she seemed very unwilling to let me see what she was doing. Trifles in themselves, no doubt, but I remembered them. They helped." He turned to Dewey: "Had you never seen that contraption of your mother's?"

"No," Dewey answered in his calm, untroubled voice. "I knew she liked to work at little mechanical devices of her own. I did suspect she had something on her mind. Something she felt she had to do, but didn't want to. I thought it was in her mind to leave me, to leave here altogether."

"What made you think that?" Nixon demanded. "Had you been quarrelling?"

"We did not quarrel," Dewey answered. "It was because she could no longer endure to see every day what she had brought into the world with such pain and effort. Me."

Nixon only looked puzzled. He clearly did not understand, did not believe or accept what Dewey had said. But he did not speak, and Bobby continued:

"Then there is the fact that the murder weapon—apparently a knife—could not be found. It seemed certain it could not have been removed and even more certain that it was no longer in the room. It was then that the old, childish riddle—when is a knife not a knife?—floated into my mind. I forgot all about it until presently it revived itself with the answer—when it's a spear. But that was after I had begun to notice, half-unconsciously again, the use Mrs James made of her crutch. As a kind of weapon, I mean. To thrust or swing like a club, or even to plank it down on someone's toe. A picture began to emerge. That of Mrs James standing against the wall, supporting herself unnoticed on the murder weapon because it was a knife that was being looked for, not a spear. And if anyone noticed the crutch was splashed with blood, what of that when everything in the room was the same?"

"Well," said Nixon. "Well. Beats me," he said, and collapsed into his chair.

"Of course, all the time I was trying to eliminate the others," Bobby continued slowly. "I was sure that what was secretly devouring Rosamund was her dreadful fear that it might be her mother who had killed her father. But then obviously if that really was her secret terror, as I was certain, she could not be guilty herself. Then her mother showed a most strange tranquillity after her husband's death that I could not reconcile with the idea that she had acted with such cunning, secret violence. I think what she felt was that her husband had been called away on a mission to save their boys—as any father might visit a far country to help his sons in trouble there, and that presently she would join them and all would be well."

"Psychology," interposed Nixon disapprovingly, but Bobby took no notice and went on:

"So I ruled her out and then I ruled out B.B. on the ground that you don't murder the father of the girl you hoped to marry. Ludo Manners was unscrupulous in business, a 'get there' man at any price almost, but not that of physical murder. It was the medicine bag both he and Teddy Peel wanted. Each suspected the other of having it, and each tried to throw suspicion on the other. That left Mrs James, but the final demonstrable fact I needed to link my theory to proof, only came with the last words of Ludo Manners—'she poked me'—not 'she pushed me' as Peel turned it into. The 'she' meant a woman, and it couldn't have been Rosamund, as I had locked the door behind me and she would have had to go out by the back, following, not preceding, me, as I knew someone had done."

"That's all very well," grumbled Nixon. "I know we haven't to prove motive, but juries like it, and I don't blame them. I like it myself."

"It was for me," Dewey answered him, "for my sake she did—what she did."

"For your sake?" Nixon repeated sharply. "When you've just been telling us you thought she was intending to leave you because she couldn't bear the sight of you any longer?"

"Is that so very strange?" Dewey asked. "I was her son, and therefore she loved me as mothers will. I was an ill-shapen monster—you heard her call me so. A living reproach. She convinced herself I held her to blame for—for me. Does the card-player blame the dealer for giving him bad cards and the other man all the aces and kings? But then she began to notice Rosamund was beginning to make a friend and confidant of me. It was because she pitied me. Pity is a hard thing to bear. But not hers. I loved her for it, but not so that she should love me in return. Love is not a bargain that you should expect it in return. It is a gift, a free offering. Then Mr Outers noticed that Rosamund and I were growing close together. He called me into his room over there in the house. He was very angry. He used words it was hard to listen to in silence, and the less I said the more loudly did he shout at me. He asked me if I wanted to bring more abortions like myself into the world, and he would rather see Rosamund dead than married to such as me. He said he would take care she never spoke to me again. He said he would send her away till she had got over her infatuation. That night I broke down. I put my head on the supper table and cried like any child, and Mother got it all out of me. I must have said something—I don't know what—that made Mother think I had really hoped Rosamund might marry me. But for Mr Outers. A thought to make the sun and moon and stars to dance with mirth. But Mother entertained it and accepted it and told herself it was for her to remedy what she had come to believe was the wrong she had done me in her failure to give me the normal man's normal hope of a happy married life, a complete life. So she did—what she did."

"That's all very well," grumbled Nixon. "But what it comes to in plain language is that you knew very well what she intended to do or else why were you waiting there that night? Hiding. Waiting to see how it went off?"

"If you like," Dewey said with one of those rare smiles of his. "I imagine a more experienced criminal would have known better than to leave that cigarette butt Mr Owen found. I expect it formed an important link in the chain of evidence he has been building up. In a sense, I suppose I did know. But not as a fact. Can you know what you only surmise?"

But this was a question Nixon did not attempt to answer. Instead, he turned on Bobby and demanded:

"Where does the second killing come in? Why should Mrs James kill Manners! If she didn't and there's still a second killer we haven't spotted yet, knocks your whole case end-ways, doesn't it?"

It was Bobby he asked, but it was still Dewey who replied. He said:

"I think that was accidental in a way. I think Mother was watching. I think she knew Mr Owen was drawing so near the truth he was sure presently to reach it. That meant that in removing one obstacle she had created another, for even if I had been different—I mean, even if I had been normal, no marriage would have been possible between the son of the woman who killed the father of the girl he had married, and killed him simply and wholly to make that marriage possible. But she still clung to the hope that Mr Owen might be less near the truth than she feared. So she watched, and when she saw a light—I dare say Mr Owen used a torch—and someone leave Constant House, she followed, but got there first by cutting across. She evidently had no idea how close-ly Ludo Manners and Teddy Peel were watching each other, and that the one of them who decided to search again for the medicine bag had been followed by the other. So when in the old ruin she saw the figure of a man standing over a recently formed gap she pushed him to make him fall through it. But not with any deliberate intention of killing, I think. To inca-pacitate so as to prevent Mr Owen from carrying on till she had had time to make it more difficult or indeed impossible for him to arrive at complete proof."

"How do you know all this?" demanded Nixon. "Sounds to me more what you and she had planned together?"

"She left on the kitchen table rough notes and scribblings. I found them and read them," Dewey answered.

"Where are they?" Nixon demanded.

"I burnt them," replied Dewey. "I did not choose that anyone but myself should ever see them."

"You mean you destroyed written evidence as well as never warned us of what you practically knew your mother intended—your plain duty."

"Is it a son's plain duty to denounce his mother?" asked Dewey in return. "Or for a daughter her mother? Rosamund did not think so. Never mind that. Will you read this?" As he spoke he put a letter on the table before Nixon. "It is from Mrs Outers asking you to hand over to me the African medicine bag belonging to her husband."

"Can't do that," Nixon said briskly. "It'll be an important exhibit at the inquest for one thing. Besides, national importance. A new uranium field. Just what we want."

"Bigger and better bombs," Dewey commented in his impassive way. "Exactly. That's why."

"What do you mean?" Nixon asked suspiciously.

"It may be of public interest," Bobby interposed, "but at present it is private property. Now the investigation is closed, there is no power to interfere. What does Mrs Outers want done with it?"

"Weighted, taken out to sea a hundred miles or more, and dropped overboard," replied Dewey.

"Good God!" exclaimed Nixon, dismayed.

"Oh, well," said Bobby approvingly; and to this day he is half-inclined to believe that he saw a quiver pass through it as it lay on the table next to the crutch, as though it—or its master—had heard and understood, and that for a moment, a moment and no more, there hovered above it the semblance, or, rather, the caricature, of a human face.

Anyhow, however that may be, there the medicine bag lies, many fathoms deep, and there presumably will lie till sea and land shall pass away and only eternity remain.

THE END

"Death on the Up-Lift"
An Introductory Note

"DEATH ON the Up-Lift", described as "a problem in detection", was the contribution of Ernest Robertson Punshon to a series of "original plays for broadcasting written by members of the Detection Club" for the British Broadcasting Corporation. For the series, the each contributor elected to set a challenge for his/her best known detective, in Punshon's case Bobby Owen. Others contributing to the series included the Club's irascible founder Anthony Berkeley, the poet laureate 'Nicholas Blake' (Cecil Day Lewis), H.C. Bailey, Gladys Mitchell and E.C. Bentley, whose novel *Trent's Last Case* is regarded by some as marking the beginning of the Golden Age of detective fiction. Unfortunately no recordings of this rare but important series of mysteries appear to have survived, and – most frustratingly – the script of one play is incomplete.

The Detection Club series was produced by John Cheatle, a stalwart of BBC radio drama, and each play was broadcast in two parts, the first as 'The Crime' and the second, a few days later, as 'The Solution'. "Death on the Up-Lift, Part 1" was broadcast on the BBC Home Service on 19 April 1941 and "Part 2" on 24 April 1941.

Death on the Up-Lift was not Punshon's only radio mystery. He also wrote *The Body in the Heather*, a short puzzle play featuring Dr Carteret, a wily coroner who appears to have been created by another member of the Detection Club, Margery Allingham. Carteret is unique in the Golden Age, a "round-robin" sleuth for whom cases were devised not only by Allingham and Punshon but also by John Dickson Carr, Gladys Mitchell, Freeman Wills Crofts and others. Under the title "A Corner in Crime", two series of Carteret's cases formed a segment within the popular British wartime radio series *Here's Wishing You Well Again*. After the first part of each play, the listeners, mainly members of Britain's armed services, were invited to send in a solution and compete for a cash prize. *The Body in the Heather*, broadcast on 2 December 1943, is the only one of Carteret's cases for which a recording survives, complete with Punshon's 'challenge to the listener'. In the first part Carteret conducts an inquest into the shooting of "a person of decidedly shady activities in the London underworld"; in the second Carteret, reflecting on the evidence of the various witnesses, identifies a small but telling inconsistency that identifies the murderer. Three astute soldiers were as quick as Carteret, each winning a prize of ten shillings and sixpence, equivalent to about $75 today.

Other radio plays by Punshon include *The Word*, "a fantasy in two dimensions", broadcast on 3 July 1946, *The Elderly Mrs Smith*, broadcast on 4 September 1946, *Sir John's Little Bit of Gossip*, broadcast on 31 January 1948; and *The Poet Answered*, broadcast on 25 February 1948. Like other members of the Detection Club, Punshon also made personal appearances and in 1945 he, together with Carr, Dorothy L. Sayers and others took part in the programme *Detective Quiz*.

Tony Medawar

DEATH ON THE UP-LIFT

This radio play by E.R. Punshon, the only one featuring Bobby Owen, was originally broadcast by the BBC in April 1941. It appears here in print for the first time.

CHARACTERS:
PAGE.
FIRST RECEPTION CLERK.
SECOND RECEPTION CLERK.
LIFTMAN.
SIR JOHN BRIGGS.
STEPHEN SMITH.
CHARLES CARTER.
DICK FULLER.
DOCTOR.
DETECTIVE-INSPECTOR BOBBY OWEN.
CHIEF INSPECTOR HUNT.
SERGEANT MARTIN.
THE ASSISTANT COMMISSIONER OF POLICE.
ELSIE WHITE.
LADY (KATHLEEN) WEEDON.
MRS. KATE SMITH.
VOICES IN HOTEL LOBBY.

The Scene is the lobby of a fashionable hotel – the Hotel Elegance – in the West End of London. There are heard the usual noises and scraps of dialogue common in such places. 'Get me a taxi'; 'I must have a room facing south'; 'Just got my bill, make you pay through the nose, don't they?'; 'Hotel de Luxe, I suppose'; 'Yes, I shall be staying another night'; 'I've asked at the desk and they say they haven't got it'; 'They do you well enough here but I don't call it any better than any other of the big hotels'; 'Bring my bag down, will you? Room 483'; and so on and so on. Conspicuous through the various noises is the voice of a page boy, calling 'Sir John Briggs, Sir John Briggs' very loudly and clearly. Another voice says, equally clearly: 'Is that the famous millionaire?' and a third voice replies: 'Some one seems to want him very badly'.

The page's voice dies away in the distance, still calling: 'Sir John Briggs'.

(The idea is that the page's voice is loud and these last two sentences spoken very clearly, so that listeners may guess they have significance.)

(a 'phone bell rings)

1ST RECEP. CLERK. "Hotel Elegance" speaking. Reception desk. Yes. No. I am so sorry my lord. It is most unfortunate, but we simply have no private suite free at the moment. All occupied. Not likely to be free just yet, I'm afraid, my lord. Yes, most disappointing, but I'm sure your lordship would find the accommodation we could offer very comfortable – I could offer one of our most ideally situated rooms. No, I'm afraid it's not on the ninth floor but in other respects unique – unique, I assure you. Thank you, my lord, we shall be most pleased to reserve it for you. Most gratified. Thank you. *(Hangs up)*

(sound of cups)

2ND REC. CLERK. Fathead. All the private suites are empty, except Sir John Briggs's. If the office gets to know you've turned down an inquiry for one, you'll be for it. Not so easy to get off these days, private suites aren't.

1st R.C.. Fathead to you and then some. That was old Lord Meanmines – hasn't got a bean to bless himself with and wouldn't spend it if he had. If I told him there was a private suite vacant, he'd say 'Oh, good', and that's the last we should hear of the old skinflint. Now he's hooked. Put him down for the cheapest room we've got. Show him others first of course, but he'll take the cheapest in the end. Only, mind, not on floor nine.

2ND R.C.. Why not on nine?

1ST R.C.. Good lord, man, use your brains, if you've got any. Sir John Briggs's private suite is on nine, isn't it? Have to be jolly careful who you put on nine. Half of 'em only want a chance to rub up against Briggs and get a Stock Exchange tip – especially just now if it's true he's putting through a fresh deal.

2ND R.C.. Ruining some more poor devils, I suppose.

1ST R.C.. Well, that's business, isn't it? ('Phone rings) Hotel Elegance speaking. Reception desk. I'm afraid we are very full, but if you will hold the line one minute I'll see what accommodation we have.

2ND R.C.. Lashings of it.

1ST R.C.. No wonder, seeing what the war's done to the hotel business, Heil Hitler, blast him. Wish I could get at him with my bare hands. Can't tell clients we're three parts empty, though. *(at 'phone)* Hotel Elegance speaking. I find we can just manage – I beg your pardon. Excuse me. Do you mind repeating. I am not sure I heard correctly. I am exceedingly sorry sir, but we have no accommodation – none at all – without private bathroom. We find that all our clients make that a sine qua non. Naturally. No doubt the class of accommodation you require could be found in one of the outlying districts – Bloomsbury, for example. *(hangs up)* Tommy, what do you think of that? Seems to think this is a Hoxton pub.

2ND R.C.. We do get some quaint inquiries and that's a fact.

('phone rings)

1ST R.C.. Reception desk, Hotel Elegance speaking. My God, Tommy, this is the limit.

2ND R.C.. What do they want now?

1ST R.C.. I am extremely sorry, sir. The Hotel Elegance is unable to quote lowest terms. The Hotel Elegance's lowest terms are its highest terms – I mean, its highest terms are – that is to say – no doubt, sir, you will be able to secure the class of accommodation you require in one of the more outlying districts. West Kensington, perhaps. *(hangs up)* Tommy, did you hear that? Rather a good touch, eh? West Kensington, I mean. Ought to settle him, oughtn't it?

2ND R.C.. Is there a West Kensington?

1ST R.C.. I daresay. Never heard of it, but there might be. *('phone rings)* Hotel Elegance speaking. Oh, very gratifying to hear from you again, my lady. The hotel is certainly very full, but it would have to be very full indeed if we could not find accommodation for your ladyship.

ELSIE WHITE. I. . . . I. . . . beg your pardon. . . . oh, please. . . . my name is White. . . . I mean. . . . Elsie White. . . . I. . . .

1ST R.C.. One moment, miss, if you please. *(at 'phone)* Oh, yes, your ladyship, we have very suitable, pleasant accommodation on the third floor. A unique room. Oh. Oh, I'm sorry. It must be on nine? Yes, the view from nine is certainly superb. Most superb. Some of our guests find the lift ascent a little tedious – oh, of course, exactly as your ladyship pleases. I will reserve accommodation on floor nine. Thank you, my lady.

2ND R.C.. Another of 'em wanting to rub shoulders with Johnny Briggs? Why did you let her have it?

ELSIE. Oh, excuse me. . . . I'm so sorry. . . . could you please. . . . please. . . .

1ST R.C.. Just one moment, miss, if you'll kindly wait. I'll attend to you in one moment.

2ND R.C.. Well, why did you?

1ST R.C.. That was Lady Weedon. Says she's been in town all day and it's got late and she doesn't want to go home in the blackout. So she wants a room. Dining, too.

2ND R.C.. Who is Lady Weedon?

1ST R.C.. Good lord, man, do you never read your gossip columns? Better, if you want to keep your job – a reception clerk has got to be au fait. Lady Weedon was Mrs. Briggs till she divorced him over the Billy Jacks scandal. After he left the sea and settled down to owning ships instead of sailing them and before he cornered the metal market. It was his first really big coup. I don't mean the scandal exactly. I mean the way he ruined Billy Jacks, diddled him out of his business, and got off with Mrs. Jacks as well. One of the smartest things ever done in the city of London where they are born smart. Billy Jacks had to be bound over to keep the peace for six months – he was threatening to murder Sir John. Of course, Sir John was only plain Mr. Briggs then. I expect he'll be Baron Briggs if this new deal of his comes off.

PAGE. (in distance) Sir John Briggs. Sir John Briggs.

2ND R.C.. Paging him again.

1ST R.C.. Some one does seem to want him pretty badly.

2ND R.C.. If she divorced him, what's the big idea? Putting her on the same floor. They're bound to meet on the corridor or the lift. She won't like it.

1ST R.C.. My good ass, that's her idea. Now she's a widow and he's stuffed with money, she's angling to get him back – him and his millions.

ELSIE. Please. . . . I'm so sorry. . . . if I'm interrupting. . . . but I must know . . . I must really. . . . I'm so sorry, but it is here where Sir John Briggs is, isn't it?

1ST R.C.. What about it if he is?

ELSIE. I. . . . I want to see him, please.

1ST R.C.. Have you an appointment?

ELSIE. No . . . yes. . . . I mean . . . not exactly. . . . will you please let him know I've come. Miss White. Elsie White.

1ST R.C.. All right. Take a seat over there, miss, I'll let you know.

ELSIE. Thank you – thank you. God help me.

1ST R.C.. Tommy, hear that? What's the matter with her?

2nd R.C.. Got the wind up all right.

1ST R.C.. If she were more of a high stepper, I should think she was one of his fancy women he's chucked.

2ND R.C.. She's not such a bad looker. Wouldn't mind having a date with her myself.

1ST R.C.. Not Johnny Briggs's style. He likes 'em – well, more lush like if you see what I mean.

2ND R.C.. Aren't you going to send her name up?

1ST R.C.. Oh, no hurry. Miss Elsie White can wait. No good worrying Johnny Briggs unless you have to. It's not safe – have your off as soon as look at you.

2ND R.C.. She said he was expecting her.

1ST R.C.. I've heard that one before. Look at her fidgeting there like a cat on hot bricks. Scared she is. Scared. If we wait a bit, very likely she'll take herself off.

2ND R.C.. She does look queer – excited. Been having a spot of drink, do you think?

1ST R.C.. Might be that. Anyhow, she can wait. She's no one. Not dressed even. Day clothes. Cheap gloves. Cheap shoes. Imitation pearl beads. You could buy her as she stands for five pounds. She can wait.

2ND R.C.. Think so?

1ST R.C.. Sure of it. At this job you soon learn to spot what people really matter. It don't do to make mistakes and I never do.

2ND R.C.. Strikes me there's something rum about her.

1ST R.C.. They often look a bit nervy when they want to see Sir John Briggs.

2ND R.C.. Hadn't we better tell the house dick to keep an eye on her?

1ST R.C.. Didn't you know? He's managed to fall down and twist his ankle. Wilkins has gone off to hospital with him. That reminds me. Wilkins left a message for No. 3 lift.

PAGE. *(in distance)* Sir John Briggs. Sir John Briggs.

1ST R.C.. Hi, boy.

PAGE. Yessir.

1ST R.C.. Who is on No.3 lift?

PAGE. William, sir. Just come on duty for the night shift.

1ST R.C.. William? What William? There's half a dozen Williams.

PAGE. William Johns, sir.

1ST R.C.. William Johns, eh? Well, why didn't you say so? Tell him I've got a message for him from Mr. Wilkins.

PAGE. Yessir!

1ST R.C.. Stand by the lift till he comes down.

PAGE. Yessir.

2ND R.C.. What's the big idea? The office sending that boy round paging Sir John. He's in his private suite, isn't he?

1ST R.C.. Lets people know Sir John is staying here, doesn't it? Why, I've known places send a boy round paging some swell – Lady this or Lord that – just to give the other guests a thrill – not that the Hotel Elegance would ever play a trick like that.

2ND R.C.. Oh, ye-ah. Correct is our middle name, isn't it? Why, when I said something in the office about the house dick, I got told off – wanted to know if I meant the hotel's private detective.

LIFTMAN. *(he speaks very badly, with a strong cockney accent)* Beg parding, that there boy was saying as 'ow there's a messidge for me from Mr. Wilkins.

1ST R.C.. That's right. You're on No. 3 lift, aren't you? You're to run it as an express to floor nine and keep a sharp look out too. The house dick has hurt his foot and Mr. Wilkins has taken him to hospital, and so it's up to you to stop any one trying to get up to nine unless they have business there. Sir John Briggs has been complaining at people hanging about the corridors and trying to speak to him.

LIFTMAN. Always complaining of, 'e is, the old swine. 'Ow can I stop 'em? Anyone as wants can nip up the stairs, can't they? The light's that bad up there, top floor, what with this 'ere black-out and the lights shaded, you can't 'ardly see nothink in a manner of spaiking.

1ST R.C.. There's a floorman posted on the stairs to stop that. You look after your lift and never mind the rest. Have you got new gloves? Sir John was complaining yesterday that your thumb was sticking out. Said it looked squalid and not the sort of service he expected here.

LIFTMAN. Weren't my fault. I put 'em on has issued. Pity some one didn't do a bit of complaining about 'im. I saw 'im a-kissing of one of the chambermaids yesterday. Wish I had a chance to drop the dirty old blighter down the lift shaft.

1ST R.C.. Don't talk like that unless you want the sack. The office wouldn't like to hear of its No. 1 guest going squash.

2ND R.C.. Squash! Squash! I bet they would put it on the bill, though.

LIFTMAN. Wouldn't be 'ard a do. Lummy, I like to think of it.

1ST R.C.. Did you report the girl?

LIFTMAN. Wasn't her fault.

1ST R.C.. It's always a girl's fault when she's kissed – if she's a pretty girl, that is.

2ND R.C.. Suppose she isn't pretty?

1ST R.C.. Then it's her bit o' luck. You get back to your lift, Mr William Johns, and don't get dropping hotel guests down the lift shaft.

LIFTMAN. All right. Quick and easy, though, it would be.

1ST R.C.. Look out, there's Lady Weedon just come in. Oh, Lady Weedon, such a pleasure to us all to see you again, if I may say so. I hope you will like your room. On floor nine, as you said. We are extraordinarily full, but I've transferred another guest to floor six. I shall have to say there was a mistake in the booking, I suppose. For such a valued visitor as Lady Weedon, we are always willing to do our best and you so specially said you wished accommodation on floor nine.

LADY WEEDON. On account of the view – a really remarkable view.

1ST R.C.. Yes, my lady, I often say, my lady, we ought to put that as an item in the bill – to one superb view over London, so much. Ha, ha. My little joke, my lady. But the office is seriously considering placing field glasses in every room on nine.

LADY WEEDON. Quite a good idea.

1ST R.C.. Boy, show Lady Weedon her room. No. 385, floor nine. Lift no. 3 remember. We are making it an express, my lady, express to nine for the convenience of guests on the floor.

LADY WEEDON. Very sensible – so boring if people crowd in all the time. I shall expect those field glasses, mind. I do so adore that view.

PAGE. This way, my lady.

1ST R.C.. Tommy, hear that; her and her view. View my foot. What she wants is a chance to rub up against Johnny Briggs and see if she can work the oracle again.

2ND R.C.. I thought you said he took up with some one else after a scandal there was.

1ST R.C.. The Billy Jacks scandal? Oh, that didn't last long. He never married her. She got weepy – remorse, that sort of thing. Well, of course, you couldn't expect Sir John to stand for that, could you?

2ND R.C.. I suppose not – not his line.

1ST R.C.. I daresay she hadn't much S.A. All he wanted anyhow was to use her to do in her husband's business – got all his business secrets out of her like that, and knew just what to do. She never spotted it. Never got on his game. And when she did she cut up rough and Johnny Briggs was only too glad of the excuse to drop her. I believe she went back to hubby.

2ND R.C.. Her husband took her back after that?

1ST R.C.. He must have been a softy. I suppose he was all gaga on her. She was all broken up. Dying she was. They went abroad and that's the last anyone heard of 'em. Probably she pegged out abroad.

2ND R.C.. Not a pretty story.

1ST R.C.. My good babe, millionaires don't have to be pretty.

2ND R.C.. I suppose not.

1ST R.C.. There was a lot about it in the papers at the time. Johnny Briggs worked it so most people thought Billy Jacks was to blame. Smart he is, our Johnny Briggs. ('phone rings) Reception desk speaking. Oh. Yes, Sir John. Certainly, Sir John. Very good, Sir John. No, Sir John, no one of that name. Miss Elsie White? No, she hasn't been yet. Certainly, Sir John, the very moment she comes. I'll instruct the Head Porter myself at once. The special menu shall be seen to – the best attention I need not assure you, Sir John. The very moment the lady comes in. I quite understand. Is that all, Sir John? Thank you, Sir John. Certainly, Sir John. Thank you. (hangs up) My God, Tommy, we're for it now, both of us.

2ND R.C.. What's up?

1ST R.C.. The sack most likely. My God, how the devil could we know?

2ND R.C.. What's wrong?

1ST R.C.. It's that girl, you know. The one who looked all worked up and said her name was Elsie White.

2ND R.C.. What about her?

1ST R.C.. Sir John's expecting her, wants to be told the moment she gets here. Going to dine her – in the restaurant – special menu, too.

2ND R.C.. Good Lord!

1ST R.C.. He was expecting her and we've kept her waiting. If he gets to know, he'll have us both kicked out.

2ND R.C.. She must be one of his fancy women, then.

1ST R.C.. She doesn't look it. How could we tell?

2ND R.C.. If she's that, why is he dining her in the restaurant, instead of in his own suite?

1ST R.C.. He may be only on her trail, the old devil; and until he's got her, he has to go slow.

2ND R.C.. That's why she looks so funny. Looks like – death, she does.

1st R.C.. I'll have to go and apologise. If she complains of being kept waiting, we're sunk, both of us.

2nd R.C.. Nothing to do with me.

1st R.C.. You were there. Special menu too. Perhaps I can talk her over. What about my tie? I'll have to lick her boots.

2nd R.C.. Don't look so jittery.

1st R.C.. The more jittery I look, the more likely she'll turn soft. Thank God, women are generally a soft lot. My God, what a mess. Sir John'll get us sacked as soon as not. I wish that lift-man had dropped him down that shaft. I wish I had a chance to put a bullet in his blasted back. Here goes. *(he approaches Elsie)* I beg your pardon. Excuse me. I am so sorry. Miss Elsie White, is it not?

ELSIE. Oh. Oh, yes. Yes. I – I – I – has he – I mean –

1st R.C.. I must apologise most sincerely. I do indeed, most humbly. I do hope you will overlook it. I can't tell how much I regret your being kept waiting.

ELSIE. Oh. Oh, it doesn't matter at all.

1st R.C.. Indeed, Miss, it does matter. It is not the sort of service the Hotel Elegance expects to render to its guests. We do pride ourselves on our service – especially our service to ladies. I can't even now understand how such a thing could possibly happen.

ELSIE. What – what thing?

1st R.C.. You being kept waiting even for one moment.

ELSIE. Oh, please don't bother about that.

1st R.C.. I do hope you will accept our most humble apologies.

ELSIE. Really, it doesn't matter a scrap.

1st R.C.. So very, very kind of you. You – er – excuse me – Sir John – you understand – you won't – er – think it necessary to inform Sir John?

ELSIE. Inform him. . . . ? Why? What of?

1st R.C.. I mean of the unfortunate delay.

ELSIE. Of course not. Why should I? I didn't mind waiting. . . . I was glad.

1st R.C.. Thank you very much indeed. Thank you. I will let Sir John know at once.

ELSIE. Oh, no – oh, must you? Oh, I mean. . . . yes, of course, please let him know.

1ST R.C.. Certainly, madam. Again all my regrets, madam. *(at the reception desk)* It's O.K. Tommy. The girl's a nit-wit, didn't even know there was anything to get peeved about. If you ask me, she isn't looking forward to meeting the old blighter one little bit. Something screwy somewhere.

2ND R.C.. Why are millionaires like God?

1ST R.C.. That's an easy one – because whom they will they exalt and whom they will they cast down.

2ND R.C.. No. Because they move in a mysterious way their wonders to perform. John Briggs is planning something on the Q.T., and it's got that girl scared out of her wits. If you ask me, he had better be careful, though. She doesn't look a girl it would be safe to push too far.

1ST R.C.. Perhaps she'll push a dinner knife into his throat. She might hang for it but lots of people would cheer.

2ND R.C.. See that tall, dark young chap staring at her?

1ST R.C.. Looks black as hell, doesn't he? Something else up. He's going to speak to her. Had I better butt in?

2ND R.C.. You've put your foot in it enough for one night if you ask me.

1ST R.C.. If the house dick were here, I would put him on it. Of course, he's sure to be missing when wanted.

2ND R.C.. Haven't they sent for his assistant?

1ST R.C.. Not got here yet. I say, the girl knows that tall, dark chap. Tommy, go and stand near. Be ready to interfere if you have to – not unless. I don't like the looks of it.

ELSIE. *(as tall, dark young man comes up)* Oh, oh . . . Dick . . . how you startled me.

DICK. Didn't expect to see me.

ELSIE. What are you doing here?

DICK. What are you doing here?

ELSIE. Dick . . . Dick Fuller, you've not been following me?

DICK. Haven't I?

ELSIE. You don't mean you've been spying on me

DICK. Yes.

ELSIE. How . . . how dare you?

DICK. I can dare a lot when you are concerned.

ELSIE. I . . . I . . . I think it's beastly of you. Go away at once.

DICK. Public place. Hotel. I'm dining here.

ELSIE. You can't. You can't afford.

DICK. I can now. I pawned my watch as I came along.

ELSIE. I'll never have anything more to do with you. . . . over. . . .
interfering. . . . impudence. . . .

DICK. All right. All right. Say just what you like.

ELSIE. Nothing to do with you. You've no right. . . .

DICK. I think I've a right to know why you are going to meet Sir
John Briggs.

ELSIE. It's no business of yours.

DICK. You're my business. You know that well enough.

ELSIE. Please go away. Please. You don't understand.

DICK. God in Heaven, Elsie. It's you who don't understand. He's
got you here by some trick or other. He's done that before
with other girls. They didn't understand. They do now.

ELSIE. Dick. . . . oh. . . . did you think – that? Dick!

DICK. What else? For goodness sake, don't start crying. Come
away with me. Come away at once. It's all right. All you've
got to do is to come away with me.

ELSIE. I daren't. . . . oh, Dick, I daren't. . . . I must see him. I
simply must. . . . I daren't. . . . Dick, please go away. . . . It's
not what you think at all.

DICK. Oh, yes, it is . . . don't be a fool, Elsie . . . he's pitched you
some yarn, I suppose. . . . you're too innocent to know what
it means when a man like Briggs asks a girl to dine with him
at a swell hotel like this.

ELSIE. It isn't that at all.

DICK. Oh, isn't it? Look here, Elsie, I'll tell you something. . . . if
anyone tries to play tricks with you, I'll kill him.

ELSIE. Oh, Dick, if it was only that. . . . I wouldn't care. . . . I
could manage then. . . . it's. . . . business.

DICK. Business?

ELSIE. Cocktails.

DICK. Cocktails! What on earth . . . ?

ELSIE. You know he's the chairman of Consolidated Metals?

DICK. What's that got to do with it?

ELSIE. Oh Dick, it's so awful, and it's all my own fault . . . only
I never meant. . . . I told you I was secretary now to Mr.
West. . . . you see, we audit Metal Industries accounts. . . .

Mr. West does. . . . he knows all their confidential figures. . . . turnover, profits, everything . . . so do I.

DICK. Is Briggs trying to get it out of you? Well, tell him to go to hell.

ELSIE. Yes, I know and I will if I must, only I don't want to. . . . Dick, you'll despise me . . . so do I . . . I can't tell you how ashamed I am. . . . I. . . . I went to a cocktail party. . . . I never have before. . . . not a real one. I mean. . . . cocktails don't look anything . . . they aren't even nice. . . . only everyone was having them and so was I. . . . I suppose I got saying things. . . . a man was there and he asked me. . . . questions. . . . I don't remember. . . . it's all like a haze. . . . I did feel so awfully sick next morning. . . . you can't possibly imagine how sick . . . there wasn't simply anything left in me . . . I thought I should die. . . . I hoped so . . . and a man came to see me. . . . the man at the cocktail party who asked me questions. . . . he said I had given him some figures but they were a little confused and he wanted them made clearer. . . . I got so angry. . . . then he said if I wouldn't. . . . then Sir John Briggs would let Mr. West know his confidential secretary had been talking secrets and I should be sacked and never get a job again and starve and of course I shall and serve me right, too.

DICK. Do you know how much he got out of you?

ELSIE. Only a little. I suppose I wasn't so drunk I had lost all decency. That's why they want me to tell them more. What I did let out isn't much in itself, only of course it's the principle of the thing, and Mr. West would never overlook it, and of course he oughtn't to. . . . it's the unforgivable thing . . . telling confidential figures. . . . and oh, I was so proud of being secretary.

DICK. Well, if you got sacked, we can get married, that's all.

ELSIE. No, we won't, Dick. Ever. I won't ruin you, too. I've got pretty low when I can be offered a job as a business spy, but I won't let people say you married a girl sacked for betraying her employer's secrets. Everyone would know. That's part of Sir John's plan.

DICK. The. . . . The. . . .

ELSIE. Don't look like that, Dick. You frighten me. It's bad enough. Don't make it worse. I've been a fool. . . . only, Dick, really, really, I never knew cocktails were like that. You see, I had never, never even tasted one before.

DICK. My poor darling.

ELSIE. Don't call me that . . . I've been a fool, worse, and now I'm paying . . . there's only one chance. . . . I'm going to ask Sir John please not to . . . he can't really mean it. . . . no one could . . . not to be so awful. . . . he just thinks he'll try . . . because of course, I shan't ever do what he wants, and when he sees that, then he'll just give it up, won't he? Because, you see, it wouldn't do him any good to ruin a girl like me. . . . he can't want to. . . . no one could ever possibly be so awful a to try to ruin a girl only because she wouldn't be a spy. . . . I'll tell him about Mum. . . . and what a hard time we had when Dad died. . . . and about Sis at school. . . . Dick, per-haps . . . perhaps I'll even tell him about us. . . . you see, Dick, it just isn't possible anyone would want to be so awful because I wouldn't be a spy . . . not when they understand . . . of course, it's only business to try. . . . so when I was rung up and they said my only chance was to come here and have dinner with Sir John, I said I would because when he under-stands. . . . why should he ask me to dinner if he didn't want to be friendly . . . it'll be all right, really, because he can't really mean to be so dreadful to a girl like me who doesn't matter a bit to anyone.

DICK. You happen to matter to me. And to him. It would be worth a lot to him to get a confidential agent into West's of-fice. . . . your people do a lot of work for other firms besides Metal industries. . . . you could give him a lot of information. He wouldn't go to all this trouble, dinner and all, if he didn't think it pretty big. He means to try to talk you over or he'll turn nasty. Suppose he does. . . .

ELSIE. Then I'll kill myself. . . . only I might kill him first.

DICK. Leave that to me.

ELSIE. Oh, Dick, there he is. . . . look, getting out of the lift. . . . go away . . . Quick. . . . let me have this last chance.

DICK. All right. But I'll stay around. I'll be there if you want me. Or even if you don't.

SIR JOHN. Ah, there you are, my dear. . . . I didn't see you at first. . . . it is Miss White, isn't it? I remember you at West's office. . . .

good job there, eh? . . . well, I can offer you a better. . . . now, now, nothing to look frightened about.

ELSIE. Sir John. . . . oh, please. . . . please . . . I want to explain. . . .

SIR JOHN. Yes, of course. That's the idea. Explain it all. Nice and friendly. Over dinner. Dinner first and business next, hn, hn. And a cocktail to start with. Hi, you there, two White Ladies.

ELSIE. Oh, no. No. I'll never, never, touch a cocktail again.

SIR JOHN. Very wise, too . . . very prudent. Only a little late in the day. You have tasted them, you know. Ha, ha. Remember? Good heavens, girl, don't look as if you thought I wanted to eat you. . . . come along and eat your dinner instead. . . . I've ordered something special. . . . we'll have our chat afterwards. Arrange everything. Friends together. Who is that tall, dark young man over there, scowling fit to split his face in two? Do you know him?

ELSIE. A . . . a little.

SIR JOHN. Jealous? Is that it? Well, never mind, let him scowl. You know, my dear, I always enjoy dining with a pretty girl, and you know I can offer a good deal. Look at this. Know what it is, eh?

ELSIE. Is it. . . . is it a diamond?

SIR JOHN. Ha, ha. Bless the child. It's the Blue John diamond. Got it cheap. It's worth three thousand any day. I didn't pay that much though. Fellow wanted some money. I let him have it – the Blue John as security. Of course he meant to pay it back, but I took my little precautions to see he didn't. So I got it for just exactly one tenth of its value. Make a nice pendant, wouldn't it? for a nice little girl. Now, now, nothing to look like that about. We'll keep the whole thing on a strictly business footing if you like. For you to say. Now you wait here a moment while I lock the diamond in its case and put the case in the hotel safe. I shan't keep you a minute.

ELSIE. Please God, make him kind . . . please God, make him kind.

SIR JOHN. Miss White. . . . round this way. . . . quick. . . . there's a woman over there I want to dodge. . . . Lady Weedon . . . I had to divorce her and now she wants to come back . . . not if I know it. . . . what the devil is she doing here tonight? Oh, damn, she's seen us. Why, Kathleen, a real pleasure to run across you again.

LADY WEEDON. Good gracious, John, is that you? What a surprise . . . Now, I call that real luck. . . . I was looking forward to a lonely miserable evening. . . . do be a sweet and dine with me. . . . it's so long since we met. . . . but what are you doing here, of all places in the world? Do tell me all about it over a poulet a la reine Marguerite . . . such a coincidence . . . I happened to remember we had one here once, and how you enjoyed it.

SIR JOHN. Delighted. . . . nice of you to remember. . . . bit of bad luck though. . . . may I introduce a ward of mine, Miss Elsie White, daughter of a very old friend . . . I've promised to give her some advice on her private affairs. . . . confidential, of course. . . . I'm sure you'll understand. Another time it would be the greatest pleasure in the world. . . . but this evening Miss White and I. . . . you understand, I'm sure.

LADY WEEDON. Of course . . . really, John, you are very lucky in your – wards. Charming girls, all of them.

SIR JOHN. Yes, quite so. . . . See you later, Kathleen.

LADY WEEDON. Miss White. . . . was that the name? . . . . charmed to make your acquaintance. . . . So your father was an old friend. . . . I never heard John mention the name I think. . . . but John has so many friends. . . . all charming. . . . so pleased to have met you, Miss – er – White. So delightfully unconventional, the modern girl. See you again, Johnny. I'm stopping here for the night. I'll have to ring up some one else to share a widow's solitary meal. Oh, page, where's the 'phone?

PAGE. This way, madam.

SIR JOHN. Pertinacious old girl. She'll have another try.

ELSIE. She was horrible. . . . she thought. . . .

SIR JOHN. Jealous, that's all. She always was as jealous as the devil. Hard up, now, too. She worked it to meet me tonight and it was a bit of a facer to find a pretty girl there already. Liked to have poisoned us both, she would, and I wouldn't put it past her to try something of the sort if she got half a chance.

ELSIE. Please, Sir John. . . .

SIR JOHN. Now, now, my dear, dinner first, if you please, and then I'll listen to anything you want to say. But dinner first. Come along. That's the restaurant over there. . . . see how careful I am when young ladies dine with me. . . . generally I eat in my private suite, but tonight with you – the restaurant. I thought you'd rather.

STEPHEN SMITH. Boy. . . . you. . . . boy. . . . is Sir John Briggs here?

PAGE. All inquiries at the reception desk, please.

SMITH. Where is it? Oh, I see. . . . no, I don't want a room. Is Sir John Briggs here?

1ST R.C.. Have you an appointment?

SMITH. No . . . no . . . but. . . . I . . . I must see him. . . . it's important.

1ST R.C.. If you'll give me your name, I will send it up as soon as possible. At present Sir John is at dinner.

SMITH. My name is Smith – Stephen Smith, of Smith Brothers, base metal dealers. He'll know. It's particularly important.

1ST R.C.. I'm afraid we can hardly disturb Sir John at dinner. If you care to write a note, I could send it in.

SMITH. Very well. Give him my card. I've written a word on it. I'll wait.

1ST R.C.. Very good, sir. Page – take this to Sir John Briggs.

PAGE. Yessir.

SMITH. I'll wait.

MRS. SMITH. Stephen.

SMITH. Kate . . . what are you doing here?

MRS. SMITH. Come away. Why are you here Steve? . . . I mean. . . . where have you been? They said at the office they didn't know.

SMITH. Shut up. . . . don't make a row. . . . people are looking.

MRS. SMITH. Come home.

SMITH. No. I've got to see Briggs. . . . I've got to.

MRS. SMITH. Don't look like that.

SMITH. Like what?. . . . like the way you were looking at him that night at the Duncans.

MRS. SMITH. I wasn't.

SMITH. I suppose you didn't have lunch with him next day.

MRS. SMITH. Stephen. . . . don't be silly. . . . it's ridiculous to be jealous. I'll cut him dead if you like next time I see him and then you'll turn round and say I've ruined you.

SMITH. He's done that already.

MRS. SMITH. Stephen!

SMITH. I got tipped off tonight . . . that's why I've got to see him . . . I must know . . . Briggs has got hold of some inside information . . . a spy of his . . . it'll bring down Metal Industries . . . his big rival . . . If they go, we go too . . . only he'll make terms with them. We're only a small concern and he'll let us go bankrupt . . . smash for us. So now you know.

MRS. SMITH. Stephen . . . it isn't true . . . it can't be . . . you're only frightening me.

SMITH. True enough my dear. Time to quit the sinking ship and get off with Johnny Briggs, isn't it?

MRS. SMITH. You've been drinking . . . or you wouldn't say such things . . . you can't possibly believe there's anything between Sir John . . . and . . . and me . . . I've only tried to be civil to him for your sake.

SMITH. That's an old story. Remember Billy Jacks? I know him . . . years ago . . . met him in business. Same line . . . Mrs. Jacks began by trying to be civil to Johnny Briggs for Billy's sake . . . next thing she was letting out all his business secrets – Billy ruined, and Mrs. Jacks Sir John's mistress.

MRS. SMITH. Oh, how horrible.

SMITH. Not for long though . . . Johnny chucked her when he had got all he wanted from her, and Billy was fool enough to take her back . . . and they went abroad and she died and he did, too, I suppose, and that was that. Well, it's not going to be like that this time. I'll put a bullet through him first.

MRS. SMITH. Stephen . . . don't say such things. Stephen . . . why have you got your hand in your pocket all the time?

SMITH. Don't be a fool.

MRS. SMITH. Where's your old service revolver . . . it wasn't there last time I looked . . . you've got it . . . give it me . . . give it me at once.

SMITH. Shut up . . . you're making people look.

MRS. SMITH. Give it me this instant . . . or I'll make them do more than look.

SMITH. I tell you I haven't got it.

MRS. SMITH. Why are you keeping your hand in your pocket?

SMITH. I cut it this afternoon . . . that's all . . . if you had any sense you could see I hadn't my service revolver . . . you can't hide a service revolver . . . too big . . . if you want to know, I got rid of it . . . sold it in a pub this afternoon.

MRS. SMITH. Thank God . . . in a pub . . . why did you . . . let me see your hand.

SMITH. It's nothing. There you are then . . . it's all tied up. If you must know, it was a bit of a shock . . . what Johnny Briggs is doing I mean . . . I did take the revolver . . . I don't know whether it was for him or for me . . . I went into a pub and a chap there offered to buy it . . . I thought I had better get rid of it.

MRS. SMITH. Thank God, you did.

SMITH. I got plastered and they threw me out . . . I cut my hand on a bit of broken glass . . . that's all . . . I got as far as a doctor's and he was very decent about it . . . he tied up my hand and let me sleep it off . . . that's all.

MRS. SMITH. It's a mercy it's no worse . . . come home now.

SMITH. No. I must wait and see Briggs . . . nothing for you to get scared about, but I must see him . . . I must know what he's up to . . . if I have to choke it out of him.

MRS. SMITH. You did really sell the revolver . . . you haven't got it with you?

SMITH. Anyone but a fool could see that. You can't put a service revolver in your pocket without it showing, can you?

MRS. SMITH. Well then. Stephen, come home . . . please.

SMITH. I tell you I must see him . . . I'll wait till after dinner. Perhaps he'll be in a better temper then. I sent him in a card . . . he hasn't taken any notice . . . he'll have to see me all the same.

MRS. SMITH. Come and sit down.

SMITH. Not there . . . here. I can watch the lift then . . . it's express to his floor . . . he'll take it and I'll go up with him.

BOBBY OWEN. Hi, Boy! Boy! No, I don't want a room. I want to see Mr. Lewis. He's your house detective, isn't he?

PAGE. He hurt himself tonight and he's off duty.

BOBBY. Oh, that's a bore . . . isn't there someone in his place?

PAGE. The Reception Desk would know.

BOBBY. Oh, that's all right . . . I don't want a room, thank you. There's my card.

1ST R.C.. Detective Inspector Owen, Wychshire County Police . . . I've heard our house dick talk about you . . . at the Yard together, weren't you? Bobby Owen, he called you. He's not here tonight, hurt his ankle and had to go to hospital.

BOBBY. That's bad. You have Sir John Briggs here, haven't you? He's one of our big pots up Midwych way.

1ST R.C.. That's right. Not going to pinch him, are you?

BOBBY. No such luck. The fact is, we've information . . . information received – one of our contacts – that there's going to be a try to lift a big diamond Sir John has just bought the Blue John diamond. I wanted to tell your house detective to keep his eyes open and warn Sir John to be careful.

1ST R.C.. He has just put something in our safe . . . in a locked case. If that's the diamond it's all right.

BOBBY. While it's there. But I suppose he'll take it out again. Meanwhile he had better be warned. Unluckily we don't know who it is . . . all we've heard is that it isn't one of the regulars. An amateur who thinks he sees his way to an easy job, name said to be Dick Forman, described as tall, dark and young.

1ST R.C.. (whistles) There was a tall dark youngish chap here just now. I noticed him because he seemed excited and nervous. Talking to a girl . . . she called Mr. Fuller, and then Dick.

BOBBY. Did she though . . . sounds interesting.

1ST R.C.. The girl's having dinner with Sir John . . . do you think it's put up job with her as a decoy duck?

BOBBY. It could be like that.

1ST R.C.. I'll bet it is . . . you know what Johnny Briggs is with girls . . . any good looking piece can get off with him . . . her job is to keep him busy and get a chance for the tall dark chap to grab the diamond . . . that's the idea.

BOBBY. It might be that way.

1ST R.C.. What'll you do? Pinch 'em both? For God's sake keep it quiet. If there's any scandal, the only thing the office thinks of is to sack everyone within a mile.

BOBBY. We'll be careful. Anyhow, there are no grounds for taking action yet . . . have to wait . . . the initiative is always with the criminal. Hitler has taught everyone that much. I think I'll stick around a bit till your relief man gets here. You've sent for him?

1ST R.C.. Oh yes.

BOBBY. Where is Sir John's room?

1ST R.C.. It's on nine.

BOBBY. I think I had better have a look around.

1ST R.C.. Right. Take No. 3 lift. It's express to nine. Sir John insisted on it. I'll show you. William! William!

LIFTMAN. Sir?

1ST R.C.. Take this gentleman up to nine. He has business up there.

LIFTMAN. Very good sir. Mind the step. We 'as to be a bit careful like . . . there's some what 'as no business on nine what's allers trying to get up along of wanting a word with Sir John about them stocks and shares of his.

BOBBY. So I've heard.

(Lift ascends)

(In Restaurant)

SIR JOHN. Waiter . . . confound the fellow . . . oh, there you are . . . never in the way when wanted . . . give me the bill, I'll sign it. Hope you've enjoyed the dinner Miss White . . . what did you think of that ortolan in aspic?

ELSIE. I . . . I don't remember.

SIR JOHN. Don't remember . . . My God, I shall remember them for the rest of my life – a speciality here. Do you remember the river trout then? No. Or the mushroom and champagne sauce . . . or the caviar?

ELSIE. Was that the greasy black stuff?

SIR JOHN. My dear young woman . . . Oh, well, beauty sufficient to itself, no doubt.

ELSIE. Please don't say things like that to me.

SIR JOHN. And don't you start putting on your gloves . . . we've got to have our little business chat now.

ELSIE. I've been trying to all the time. You wouldn't listen.

SIR JOHN. Never mix business and dinner . . . the two most serious things in life, but they don't mix. Hn. Hn. Besides someone might have been listening. Confidential, you know – our talk, I mean.

ELSIE. I must go.

SIR JOHN. Oh no. Oh dear no. I've been watching you all the evening. You're worth having. I can see that. And I'm going to have you, or smash you, you and all that is yours. Mind you, when I smash people, I do it thoroughly.

ELSIE. Like Billy Jacks – Mr. and Mrs. Billy Jacks.

SIR JOHN. What do you know about Billy Jacks?

ELSIE. I've heard about them.

SIR JOHN. Have you? Then you know I wiped them out . . . as you would wipe a crumb from your sleeve. Why, they've been done with so long I had quite forgotten them . . . quite. Thought everyone else had. They went abroad . . . vanished . . . died or something. That's what happens to people who get in my way, my dear.

ELSIE. I . . . please let me go home.

SIR JOHN. My good girl, you are coming to my suite to talk business . . . business! Don't be a little fool . . . you don't suppose anything can happen to you in an hotel like this, do you? Everyone perfectly safe here, everyone.

ELSIE. Are they?

SIR JOHN. Of course. Perfectly safe. You've nothing to look scared about, not if you do what you're told. I'm going to put a perfectly simple sound business proposition before you. That's all.

ELSIE. You mean you want be to be your spy?

SIR JOHN. Not at all. Confidential agent. Quite different. So you needn't look as if you would like to kill me. You know you've got to do what you're told. No way out.

ELSIE. There is always one way out.

SIR JOHN. That's our lift . . . express to nine. My suite's on the top floor, out of people's way. Dammit, there's Kathleen again.

ELSIE. It's Lady Weedon.

SIR JOHN. Shut up. She heard you.

ELSIE. I meant her to.

LADY WEEDON. Oh you're going up? So am I. Your little friend too, John – I forget her name . . .?

SIR JOHN. Miss White and I have some business to talk over.

LADY WEEDON. I'm sure you have. He. He. Business, just a little late for business . . . not for all kinds of business perhaps, though I'm sure Miss – er – I can't remember your little friend's name . . . oh, dear, there's my bag unfastened again.

SIR JOHN. Look here, Kathleen, try and be sensible . . . or do you want to make a scene? That won't do you any good, or me, either.

LADY WEEDON. Oh, no, of course not . . . quite strangers now, aren't we? Perhaps I ought to ask your little friend to introduce us. Just wait one moment . . . I can't get this bag to fasten . . . it will keep coming undone . . . and there's all my money in it I got from the bank today.

LIFTMAN. Beg pardon, sir, not this lift sir. This is express to nine only, reserved for guests on nine, sir. Next lift, sir, if you please.

SIR JOHN. Don't let anyone else in here, my man.

LIFTMAN. No, sir.

LADY WEEDON. Oh, one minute . . . my frock's caught.

SIR JOHN. Dammit, Kathleen, you're doing it on purpose.

LADY WEEDON. Oh, no, John. Now don't you go and make a scene . . . oh, look, there's that tall, dark young man who was scowling at you all through dinner. He was so interested he upset the salad all over himself and the table, too . . . watching you and not what he was eating. Why, he is coming in here.

SIR JOHN. Here, you, liftman, what's your name . . . keep the fellow out.

LIFTMAN. Next lift, sir, if you please . . . this is reserved for residents on floor nine.

DICK. That's all right. I'm waiting for Miss White. I'm going to see her home.

SIR JOHN. You needn't worry young man. I'll send her home, in a taxi or my car perhaps.

DICK. I'll wait all the same.

SIR JOHN. Do you know who I am? Who the devil do you think you are?

DICK. You're Sir John Briggs. I'm Dick Fuller. Now we know each other. I'm waiting to see Miss White home. If you like to provide us with a car, that's all right. I don't mind.

SIR JOHN. Confound your insolence. I'll . . . I'll . . .

LADY WEEDON. Now, John, dear, you don't want to make a scene, do you? Here's someone else.

LIFTMAN. Beg pardon, sir, not this lift, sir, this is express to Nine, for residents only. Next lift going up on the left, sir.

SMITH. I want to see Sir John . . . you remember me, Sir John? . . . my name's Smith. Stephen Smith.

SIR JOHN. No, sir, I don't remember you, sir, and I don't want to either . . . this is an outrage . . . Liftman . . .

SMITH. Rather I rang up the Financial News? I don't want to interfere, but I'm desperate . . . my firm's in the base metal line . . . which is it to be, Sir John? . . . a word with you to-night, or do I go to the Financial News?

SIR JOHN. Are you trying blackmail? Quite absurd. It wouldn't make any difference to me or any one else whom you rang up. I'll hear what you have to say if you like, but you'll have to wait.

SMITH. All right, I'll wait.

LIFTMAN. Beg pardon, ma'am, not this lift, ma'am, this lift is express –

MRS SMITH. My husband's there . . . I'm with him.

SMITH. Katie, you wait down here.

MRS SMITH. No. I'm coming with you.

SIR JOHN. You . . . Liftman . . . what's your name? You're deliberately letting these people crowd in . . . I shall complain to the management to-morrow . . . you're letting people in in flat defiance of my orders . . . very well, I shall see you are discharged to-morrow – without a character, if I have to take it to the board of directors.

LIFTMAN. Beg pardon, sir, not my fault. I can't 'elp it, so I can't . . . I ain't no bloomin' chucker out . . . I can't throw hotel guests out on their ear, can I?

SIR JOHN. Your delay was deliberate.

LIFTMAN. It weren't my fault, it weren't . . . I begs your pardon most humble, Sir John . . . I do indeed . . . I've often told 'em as 'ow this 'ere lift did ought to be marked private so as a gent like you, Sir John, could get what he did ought to 'ave.

SIR JOHN. Never mind sniffling . . . get on with it . . . good lord, here, you, sir, keep out . . . this is private.

CARTER. Keep your hair on old boy . . . no private lifts in an hotel . . . and anyway, this is pretty crowded even if there's still room for a little 'un.

LIFTMAN. Beg pardon, sir, this lift is express to Nine.

CARTER. That's O.K. by me. I've just registered – Charley Carter my name is. They've given me a room on Nine. My bag's following. Start up, laddie, or there'll be more of 'em crowding in, and we're enough for comfort.

SIR JOHN. *(as lift ascends)* Disgraceful . . . outrageous . . . never in all my experience . . . I shall take steps . . .

CARTER. What's bit the old boy in the corner? Who is he anyway?

SIR JOHN. Dammit, sir, do you know who I am, sir?

CARTER. Well, I was just asking, wasn't I?

LIFTMAN. Floor Nine – please mind the step.

LADY WEEDON. Oh, my pearls – the string's broken.

LIFTMAN. Mind the step, please.

SIR JOHN. You, girl, Elsie, come on, don't stand there.

LADY WEEDON. Oh, my pearls . . . don't tread on them . . . my pearls.

(Confused Voices)

Mind where you're stepping. There's one. Oh, I beg your pardon. Can't we have a light. Mind the step.

SIR JOHN. Damn your pearls, Kathleen, you did it on purpose . . . Elsie.

(Two pistol shots are heard)

(Confused Voices)

Oh, what's that? What's happened? What's that noise? Shot? Oh, my pearls. God in heaven, he's dead. Who's dead. What's the matter? I tell you he's dead. Someone shot him.

(Bobby Owen comes running up)

BOBBY. What's going on here?

LIFTMAN. Someone shot Sir John Briggs in the back as he was getting out of the lift and now he's dead.

BOBBY. I'm a police officer . . . stand back all of you . . . stand back, I say.

SMITH. How do we know who you are?

LIFTMAN. He is Inspector Bobby Owen, here on police business. It's all right . . .

BOBBY. The man is dead . . . he must have died immediately, two shots in the back . . . who did this?

(Silence)

BOBBY. One of you is guilty. Which?

(Silence)

BOBBY. Can none of you help me? What's the matter?

LIFTMAN. The young lady has fainted.

BOBBY. One moment. She won't hurt for a moment. Listen. One of you must have seen something.

SMITH. I didn't . . . The light's bad. It was all confused.

LIFTMAN. Some were pushing to get out and some were turning back because one of the ladies called out that her necklace had broken.

LADY WEEDON. The string broke. I was stooping to pick them up. I didn't say anything. I couldn't. How could I?

MRS SMITH. I didn't either. I was helping to pick up the pearls – look. I have two in my hand.

DICK. You can ask your questions afterwards . . . I suppose it was one of us . . . I don't know . . . Miss White must be seen to . . . you can't leave her like this.

BOBBY. Very well. Take her along the corridor there . . . one of the other ladies can see to her . . . not you . . . you stand away . . . here, you sir, come back . . . you, I mean, come back at once. What are you trying to do?

CARTER. Carter's the name. I want a drink . . . that's all . . . I feel a bit sick . . . I've nothing to do with all this . . . I suppose it was one of that bunch, but I don't know anything about it. I never saw any of them before to-night.

BOBBY. Your drink can wait. Please all of you stand back against the wall there . . . and remember that one of you is a murderer and I've got to know which. And don't talk to each other. Liftman, see none of them speak to each other. If any of them tries to get away, call for help at once.

LIFTMAN. Very good, sir.

BOBBY. I sent to ring up Scotland Yard the moment I heard the shots . . . and for a doctor . . . they'll be here immediately . . . meantime, you must just wait where you are.

DICK. We can tell you nothing. We know nothing.

BOBBY. One of you knows it all.

ELSIE. I'm better now.

LADY WEEDON. It wasn't me . . . I know nothing about it . . . if we've got to stop here, can't we have some chairs?

BOBBY. No. No one must come near . . . not till they get here from Scotland Yard . . . please stand apart . . . and please don't talk to each other . . . it must have been one of you . . . go back, you, sir, I said no one was to be allowed –

DOCTOR. I'm a doctor . . . I'm staying in the hotel . . . I heard someone had been hurt . . . shot . . . is it an accident?

BOBBY. No. Murder. Will you look at the body? Please disturb it as little as possible. Photographs will have to be taken. I'm afraid there's nothing you can do.

DOCTOR. What's that lying there?

BOBBY. Don't touch it . . . there may be finger prints . . . it's a two two automatic . . . I suppose the murderer used it.

DOCTOR. You're a police officer?

BOBBY. In charge till help comes from Scotland Yard. They will bring a doctor but if you would make a preliminary report it might be useful. Will you notice if the bullet wounds look like they were fired from a small automatic like that one . . . if not, another weapon may have been used. You see, one of these people must be the murderer and if that is not the weapon, the pistol used may be still in his possession – or in here.

DOCTOR. Pleasant thought.

BOBBY. Ladies and gentlemen, I must ask you to let me make sure none of you is armed. Thank you. That seems all right. I imagine then the little two two automatic is the weapon. Now I should like to ask you all a few questions. I'll take the liftman first. What's your name?

LIFTMAN. William Johns.

BOBBY. That's the door of Sir John's private sitting room, isn't it? Go in there. I'll join you in a minute. Try to remember every detail. Doctor, have you noticed anything?

DOCTOR. Well, not much, only –

BOBBY. Come over here . . . to the end of the corridor . . . where no one can hear you.

DOCTOR. Death must have been practically instantaneous. The wounds are consistent with shots fired from a small pistol like the one near the body. They were fired in close contact, the muzzle pressed against the body. The dinner jacket has no holes in it, so the murderer must have pushed his hand under it and fired two shots in an upward direction. Both shots penetrated the heart and made their exit over it, through tattooing marks – a 'K' and a 'J' entwined within a heart.

BOBBY. Is it a fresh tattooing, doctor? I remember Briggs was a sailor at one time, mate on a tramp steamer.

DOCTOR. Oh, no, they are old marks . . . done when he was a young man . . . his first sweetheart most likely . . . done thirty years ago. They can't have anything to do with this.

BOBBY. I suppose not.

DOCTOR. Want me any more?

BOBBY. I think not, thank you. I expect the Yard will ask to see you later . . . shall you be going out again to-night?

DOCTOR. No. I'll be on hand if wanted.

BOBBY. Good. I'll see you to the stairs. I've got some of the hotel staff there to see no one leaves. There's a murderer here and I don't mean to let him get away.

DOCTOR. Shivery idea.

BOBBY. Let the doctor through, will you? Lucky you were staying in the hotel, doctor, and could help us at once. Good night and many thanks. I'm going to talk to these people now and see what I can get out of them while it's fresh – perhaps before they've had time to think up any lies. The liftman first.

(Goes back along corridor)

Ladies and gentlemen, I'm going to ask the liftman a few questions and then I shall ask each of you to tell me what you know. I'm using Sir John's private sitting room.

(Enters sitting room)

Your name is Johns, isn't it? William Johns?

LIFTMAN. Yes.

BOBBY. What can you tell me?

LIFTMAN. Not very much, I'm afraid. The lift was rather crowded. Sir John was very annoyed about it. He threatened to report me to the management and get me discharged.

BOBBY. Oh. Oh, of course, you understand I'm taking a shorthand note of what you say and that it will be used in evidence?

LIFTMAN. I quite understand.

BOBBY. Were you upset at all by this threat to report you?

LIFTMAN. Not enough to make me want to murder him, even if I had a pistol handy. Of course, it's a terrible affair and won't do the hotel any good and you can guess how I felt – seeing a man shot dead like that right in front of me. All the same, I don't think the staff will feel inclined to shed many tears. Within the last month or two he has had two waiters, one page and the girl at the 'phone exchange dismissed.

BOBBY. Know their names?

LIFTMAN. The management could send them up, if you like. I expect they're all on duty.

BOBBY. I thought you said they were sacked?

LIFTMAN. Oh, the management always sacks any one an important guest complains about. Pleases the guest and doesn't hurt any one, because if you're sacked like that you're always taken on again, same job, same wages, same length of service, only somewhere else in the hotel. The guest sees a new face, the employee carries on as before, and everyone is happy. Naturally, sometimes there's a serious complaint and that's different. Oh no! If Sir John had complained about me for allowing the lift to be too crowded, they would simply have put me on another lift. That's all. I can assure you there's no sacking in the hotel business just now without good reason. Bad staff shortage with all the younger men called up and the older ones itching to get into the army . . . only, of course, you want influence for that.

BOBBY. I see. Sir John's threat didn't worry you then. Did Sir John think it was your fault the lift was over crowded?

LIFTMAN. Well, if I've got to speak the truth, the whole truth, and nothing but the truth – well, I'm rather afraid it was a bit like that. Only please don't tell the management so. They mightn't like it and I might get the sack in earnest. Sir John ... well, he's dead now, and so it can't do him any harm to say so, but he wasn't very popular with the staff ... too fond of throwing his weight about and bullying ... most of us would have done anything we could with safety to annoy him. Well, I knew Sir John liked to have the lift to himself and I did rather delay starting so as to give people a chance to crowd in. I could have gone up more quickly if I had wanted to. Still, after all, my job is to take people up in my lift. I was never told it was to be reserved for Sir John's personal use.

BOBBY. I see. Just a little trick to annoy?

LIFTMAN. It did annoy, too – rather more than I meant. I was ... on perfectly safe ground ... the management couldn't say I ought to have thrown people out of the lift that was there for their service. But Sir John did fly off the handle rather more than usual. I rather got the idea he was nervous about something.

BOBBY. Something scaring him?

LIFTMAN. That didn't strike me at the time. I just thought he was in a worse temper than usual. I didn't know why and I didn't much care. Dinner disagreed with him perhaps.

BOBBY. I see. Well, the lift was crowded – more so than usual. Sir John was in a bad temper – also more so than usual. Possibly cause and effect. When the lift stopped – ?

LIFTMAN. At Nine, the lift overshot a bit. It did sometimes. A bit too high. I told them to mind the stop. Then one of the ladies called out that the string of her pearls had broken and they were all on the floor. Some of them turned back or stopped to help pick them up. The light's bad with this blackout business and there was some confusion. Then the shots were fired.

BOBBY. Take it easy.

LIFTMAN. I'm sorry ... it was ... upsetting ... I think it's worse to remember ... I think at the moment I was more surprised than anything else ... one moment he was standing there, pushing out with the girl ... hurrying her along ... the next he was lying there ... I knew he was dead at once.

BOBBY. How did you know that?

LIFTMAN. I hardly know . . . I was sure, though . . . I could see his coat pushed up and the way he was lying . . . and the wounds behind . . . that's how it was, wasn't it?

BOBBY. From behind . . . yes . . . from the lift, upwards . . . the points of issue were just over the heart.

LIFTMAN. Near the tattooing he had done when he was a sailor for his first woman? I wonder how many he has had since? Good thing he didn't want all their initials done like that. I don't know if you'll think it funny, but just at first I never thought of wondering who had done it. I think I was just dazed. It was all so sudden. I don't think I shall sleep too well to-night, remembering him lying there. I never liked him, no one did, but now's he dead, you can forget all that.

BOBBY. Yes, Death closes all accounts. You have no idea who had fired the shots?

LIFTMAN. No. It might have been any one. It was so sudden, so confused.

BOBBY. Can you say how they were all standing?

LIFTMAN. It's a little difficult. There was a good deal of confusion, especially with one lady calling out about her pearls. I'll do my best. I was standing in the left hand corner, where the lift controls are. The bald elderly gentleman I think I heard called Mr. Smith was standing next to me. He was rather pressed against the wall and I noticed he kept his right hand in his pocket all the time. Afterwards I saw it was bandaged.

BOBBY. Yes, I noticed that. How to look into that.

LIFTMAN. It did strike me afterwards it might have been a dodge to keep that little two-two automatic hidden. Sir John was pushing to get out first – a great one he was for pushing to be first. The girl who fainted was with him. He had her arm. Both the other men were close behind. The two ladies were further back. They were stooping down to pick up the pearls.

BOBBY. Do you think one of them could have straightened up, fired the shots, then stooped again?

LIFTMAN. I'm sorry, but it all happened so quickly and was all so confused, it's very difficult to be sure exactly how things happened or in what order.

BOBBY. That's the best you can do?

LIFTMAN. I'm afraid so.

BOBBY. All right. Well, quite a clear statement. The Yard men will want you to repeat it when they get here. Oh, by-the-way, has the hotel a swimming pool?

BOBBY. Yes. Prides itself upon being the most up-to-date hotel in London, doesn't it?

LIFTMAN. I don't know that there's any hotel in the West End with a swimming pool. At any rate we haven't got one.

BOBBY. Well, much obliged for a very full statement. I hope the others . . . oh, here they are from Scotland Yard, I believe.

(Door opens)

Hullo, Sergeant Martin.

SERGEANT MARTIN. We heard you were here, Mr. Owen. Chief Inspector Hunt will be along – Oh, here he is.

HUNT. Ah, it is you. When they rang up they said Bobby Owen was on the spot. You've been at the Yard to-day, haven't you?

BOBBY. Yes, Chief Inspector. We had information some one was after a big diamond Sir John Briggs bought the other day. A tall, dark young man, we were told, probably named Dick Forman. And of these people in the lift, two are tall, dark young men, and one of them is named Dick Fuller.

HUNT. Good lord, is that the motive then?

BOBBY. I don't know, but if it was, it failed. Sir John put the case containing the diamond in the hotel safe before dinner and it's there still.

HUNT. Perhaps they didn't know that.

BOBBY. Perhaps not. This is the liftman. He has given me a very clear preliminary statement. Also a doctor staying in the hotel has examined the body. I've got a note of his report.

HUNT. Right. You're the liftman, are you? Cut along and wait outside. Don't go home yet. I shall want you again. First we must hear what the others have to say though. We'll take the ladies first. Martin, you might ask Lady Weedon if we can see her now.

HUNT. Look at the time . . . half past two in the morning . . . we've seen them all, and how much further forward are we? They've all talked, every blessed one of them has a motive of sorts and all of them could have done it. Only which?

BOBBY. Is that a complete list of those in the lift?

HUNT. Yes. Here it is.

Sir John Briggs himself, poor devil.

Elsie White.

Lady Weedon.

Mrs. Stephen Smith.

Dick Fuller.

Charles Carter.

That's the lot and it's certain Sir John was shot by someone in the lift. I did play with the idea that someone else might have been hiding somewhere but that's impossible. It couldn't have been anyone firing from the roof, for instance, because the shots were fired upward. Besides, the muzzle of the pistol was close up against the victim's body. So there we are. That's all.

BOBBY. Except that the two two automatic found near the body was the weapon used, and that it's small enough to go in a woman's handbag or a man's pocket.

HUNT. Yes, and a fat lot of help, too, unless we can trace it to someone, which isn't likely. Number filed off and American make. Most likely bought over there and smuggled in.

BOBBY. If only there were finger prints.

HUNT. There never are . . . now-a-days, if a five year old wants to pinch Mummy's jam he puts on gloves first.

BOBBY. Only smudges . . . smudges . . . look more like gloves, though, than a handkerchief or anything like that.

HUNT. We may take it the murderer wore gloves. Well, take the lot of 'em in turn and see what we get. Read your notes, will you?

BOBBY. Lady Weedon. Married Sir John when he was a young man, immediately after he left the sea to start business on his own. Divorced him at the time of the Billy Jacks scandal, re-married, now a widow, said to be badly in debt and anxious to try for a reconciliation with Sir John. Probably why she was at the hotel to-night. Showed anger and disappointment at finding he was dining with a young, attractive woman. The breaking of her necklace caused the confusion during which the murder occurred. The wire holding the necklace didn't break, it was cut. A look at the ends makes that clear. A possible theory is that she is jealous, desperate for money, decided that if her former husband wouldn't have her back, he shouldn't have any one.

HUNT. A jealous woman is capable of anything. Crazy, they get. I've seen it.

BOBBY. She was in full evening dress, wearing gloves. Her handbag fastening was loose and she says she had thirty pounds in notes in it. They aren't there now.

HUNT. Perhaps she had a two two automatic in it as well that isn't there now either.

BOBBY. There was nothing else in the bag of any interest, only powder puffs and that sort of women's truck. But I suppose with the bag coming unfastened all the time she could easily have slipped the pistol out if she had it there. Her story is that she was picking up her pearls at the moment the shots were fired. She admits she understands pistols and she knew all about the tattooing – says the 'K' is the initial of her first name, Kathleen, the 'J' stands for John, and it was done when they were first engaged, while he was still going to sea.

HUNT. There've many stood in the dock on less evidence.

BOBBY. Next. Miss Elsie White, the young woman who fainted. She admits Sir John was trying to blackmail her into acting as a kind of business spy for him and that if she refused, and she meant to refuse, she says, he could have made her lose her job in such disgrace she would never have got another. His death has saved her.

HUNT. Very convenient, too.

BOBBY. Also one of the hotel staff reports having heard her making threats about killing Sir John. That was in the hotel lobby before dinner. She was in outdoor clothes, hat and gloves. She denies knowing anything about pistols and from the way she handled the one we showed her it seemed like it. Even when we showed her the safety catch, she didn't seem to know what it was for. Questions about tattooing drew blank but she is fond of bathing and swims well.

HUNT. I notice you always asked that.

BOBBY. It may be useful to know. You remember the liftman said there was no swimming pool here.

HUNT. Yes, but what's that matter? What's swimming and bathing got to do with it?

BOBBY. I'll come to that later, Chief Inspector, if I may. But first, there's another possibility about Miss White in connection with Dick Fuller. He is tall, dark, and young. That answers the description of the person reported on the track of Sir John's big diamond. His name sounds like the name 'Dick Forman' our contact gave us. He and Elsie White were seen talking excitedly together before dinner. She dined with Sir John. It might be that she and Dick Fuller were working together to get hold of the diamond. He was certainly in a very nervous, excited state. At dinner he upset a bottle of olive oil over the table and himself, too.

HUNT. Sticky stuff, olive oil.

BOBBY. His own story is that he was there to protect Miss White.

HUNT. The jealousy motive again. Possibly Sir John had got off with her and our young man knew it and that's why. Considering Sir John's reputation it is almost a wonder no one's done him in before.

BOBBY. He admits he is a good swimmer and fond of bathing. Denies knowing more about firearms than any one else, but knows the difference between an automatic and a revolver and looked for the safety-catch at once. We drew a blank about the tattooing. He didn't seem to know what we were driving at. He had loose chamois leather gloves in his pocket, gloves easily slipped on and off.

HUNT. He's on the list of suspects all right.

BOBBY. Then there's the older man – Mr. Stephen Smith. You said you had something on him?

HUNT. Yes. Report just came in. From a pub where it seems Mr. Smith sold a revolver in the private bar. Nice sort of thing to do. The barmaid didn't know there was anything wrong about it, but she told the landlord, and he thought he had better report it. Did Smith sell the big service revolver or did he exchange it for that jolly little automatic that'll go into any one's pocket? The landlord says Smith was a bit plastered and they had to throw him out. All very suggestive.

BOBBY. His story now is he came to see Sir John on business – urgent business. When we asked what it was, he let out that

Sir John was putting through a big deal that might wipe Smith off the map.

HUNT. So did he wipe Sir John off instead?

BOBBY. He admits having used threats. He was certainly in a very excited state. He had gloves in his pocket, loose gardening gloves. He says he didn't know they were there. He supposes he put them in last night and forgot them. He hasn't swum a stroke or bathed out of doors for years. Weakish heart and doctors forbade it. His army service has made him familiar with firearms. Didn't respond to the tattooing question at first but got excited when he knew one initial was 'K', as his wife's name is Kate. It seems he thought she and Sir John were a bit too friendly. He knew once a Mrs. Billy Jacks who ran away from her husband to go off with Sir John and he thought the same thing might happen again and he didn't mean it to.

HUNT. Added motive, jealousy. Hang it, we can't put half a dozen different people in the dock, all charged with the same crime.

BOBBY. Then there's his wife – Mrs. Smith. She says she followed her husband because she was afraid what he might do. She was in outdoor dress, hat and gloves. Her christian name begins with a 'K' but the tattooing seemed to mean nothing to her and she gave up open air bathing when her husband did. She admits understanding firearms.

HUNT. If she's guilty, the idea is she did it to save her husband? Or because Sir John had chucked her as he chucked that other woman, Mrs. Billy Jacks. Which?

BOBBY. Neither perhaps. But she's one of those in the lift. Then there's Carter. He refuses to answer questions till he has his lawyer present. Probably bluff, as he declined to give the name of any lawyer. He wanted to refuse to turn out his pockets but finally produced a wad of pound notes looking very like those Lady Weedon says are missing from her handbag. He is tall, dark, and youngish. He had a pair of smart hogskin gloves in his pocket and also a pair of loose cotton ones.

HUNT. Ah. Loose cotton gloves – that smells.

BOBBY. He says he can swim and often does. He doesn't understand firearms, so he says. The tattooing didn't seem to mean anything to him. He has a copy of the Midwych Guardian on him. Nothing else much. He swanked a lot but was plainly nervous and I should expect him to break down under further questioning.

HUNT. We'll have a try. It stands like this then. It must have been one of those in the lift and there's a case against them all. Against Lady Weedon is the discarded wife planning a come back and apparently finding a younger rival in possession. Against Elsie White, to save herself from Sir John's attentions and blackmail. Against Mrs. Smith, to save her husband with possibly jealousy as a secondary motive. Against Mr. Smith, with a history of pistols and his admission that Sir John's death saves him from a business smash. Against Dick Fuller, who may be in with Miss White and may be identical with the 'Dick Forman' reported as after Sir John's diamond. Against Carter, for refusing to account for himself, for these suspicious cotton gloves, for being in possession of a wad of pound notes that look like those Lady Weedon says are missing. Hang it all, Owen, that means there's a case against them all, and we know it must have been one, and yet I'll be hanged if I can see why it should be one rather than another. Can they have all been in it together?

BOBBY. Hardly that, chief inspector, surely.

HUNT. No. I suppose not. But there it is. It must be one. A case against each. Only which one. What do you think?

BOBBY. Well, chief inspector, now we've been through it again it seems to me that there are three vital points to remember. Gloves. Voice. Tattooing.

HUNT. Gloves. Voice. Tattooing.

BOBBY. Yes. Gloves. Voice. Tattooing. That's three points. Add to that that the evidence seems to show pretty clearly the innocence of the others, and then I think myself you will be perfectly safe in arresting and charging –

PART 2
THE SOLUTION

(Phone rings)

HUNT. Hullo . . . yes . . . chief inspector Hunt speaking . . . oh . . . oh, is he? Oh . . . yes, certainly . . . very pleased indeed to hear it . . . delighted . . . difficult case . . . very gratifying to know I'm to have his assistance . . . most gratifying . . . thank you . . . goodbye. *(Hangs up)*

BOBBY. Who was that?

HUNT. Damn and blast . . . of all the lousy luck . . . it's the A.C. . . . he's coming along . . . I did think I should have a chance to clear it up on my own . . . and now here's the A.C. poking his nose in . . . what the hell . . . I hope he breaks his blasted neck before he gets here. What is it, Sergeant?

MARTIN. It's the Assistant Commissioner himself, sir. He's coming down the corridor.

ASSISTANT COMMISSIONER. Well, chief inspector, making any progress? Ah, there you are, Owen. I heard you were down from Midwych. Going to make a splash, this case, chief inspector, important man, Sir John Briggs . . . got to clear it up quick or the press'll be raising a howl . . . I had a short report over the 'phone. Shot in the up-lift, eh? Must have been one of the people in with him.

HUNT. Yes, sir. That much is certain.

A.C.. You were on the spot at the time, Owen, weren't you?

BOBBY. Yes, sir. I was at the end of the corridor, talking to one of the hotel staff.

A.C.. Yes, yes. Well, if it was one of those in the lift, it ought to be easy enough to sort 'em out. Sort 'em out. Let me see, who were they?

HUNT. Lady Weedon. Divorced wife of Sir John's. Possible motive, jealousy and disappointment as she was trying to stage a come-back and apparently he wasn't having any. Also she caused confusion by spilling her pearl necklace. Mrs. Smith. Possible motive to protect her husband whose business was threatened by Sir John's new deal. Also hint of possible intrigue with Sir John and fear husband might discover it.

Miss Elsie White. Possible motive, blackmail attempt by Sir John to force her to act as a business spy. Those are the three women. They all wore gloves and the small two two automatic could easily have been hidden in a hand bag. The three men are:- Dick Fuller. Possible motive to protect Miss White. Not engaged to her but wants to be. Another complication is that he answers the description of the tall, dark young man, Bobby Owen here had information was after a big diamond in Sir John's possession. Also his name, Dick Fuller, resembles the name, Dick Forman, reported to Owen. Possibly concerned to steal diamond with Miss White as decoy. Admits having used threats. Stephen Smith. Also overheard using threats. Possible motive, a fear of being driven out of business by Sir John's new plans. Or, again, jealousy, if there's any truth in the suggestion of an intrigue between his wife and Sir John. Finally, there's this man, Carter, who is more difficult to account for. He refuses to answer questions. He objected to being searched but — well, we did search him.

A.C.. No force used, I hope, chief inspector.

HUNT. Oh, no, sir. We shouldn't dream of using force, sir. Carter – er – well, he was persuaded to agree. He was found to be in possession of a wad of notes. Lady Weedon says she had a similar wad in her hand bag and now it isn't there. Carter's story is that he picked them up in the lift and was just going to ask whose they were when the murder occurred and he was so shocked and upset and excited he forgot all about them.

A.C.. Thin. Very thin. But it might go down with a jury.

HUNT. Anything will go down with a jury. All juries suffer from softening of the brain.

A.C.. He answers the description given the Midwych police, too, doesn't he? Tall dark and young. Sounds promising. Only we've got to have more proof.

HUNT. Yes, sir.

A.C.. Not so easy to sort 'em out.

HUNT. No, sir.

A.C.. Not so easy at all to sort 'em out. Looks like Carter to me.

BOBBY. If I may say so, sir, the evidence chief inspector Hunt has got together seems to prove the innocence of all in the

lift – except one of them of course. Then there are three sep-
arate clues that point very clearly to exactly the same person.
A.C.. Eh? What clues are those?
BOBBY. Voice. Gloves. Tattooing.
A.C.. But . . . hang it all, they've all got voices.
BOBBY. Yes, sir, only –
A.C.. The three women were wearing gloves. The three men had
gloves in their possession. So where do gloves come in?
BOBBY. Well, sir, you see –
A.C.. As for the tattooing. Hang it all, how does tattooing done
twenty or thirty years ago help to clear up a murder committed to-night? Tell me that, young man.
BOBBY. Well, sir, may I take them all in turn. I think the evidence shows that Lady Weedon and Mrs. Smith were both at
the back of the lift picking up the pearls fallen from the broken necklace. Mrs. Smith had two in her hand at the time.
She showed them to me. I examined the gold wire on which
the pearls were threaded. It was cut by some sharp instrument. Lady Weedon had no such sharp instrument in her
possession. Furthermore, if Lady Weedon had brought the
automatic with her, she would have taken care the fastening
of her hand bag was secure. Again if she had the automatic with her she must have planned the murder in advance.
But the evidence suggests that she wanted a reconciliation,
and only on her arrival just before dinner was upset to find
her former husband dining with Miss White. She had, therefore, since she must have thought a reconciliation possible,
no motive for even thinking of murder. Taking all that with
the other facts, especially the liftman's evidence that both
women were at the back of the lift picking up the scattered
pearls, I suggest it is impossible even to think of charging
either of them.
A.C.. No. I don't see any answers to that. Very well. Those two,
Lady Weedon and Mrs. Smith, are out of it. What about the
White girl?
BOBBY. She is entirely ignorant of firearms. Even when we
showed her the safety catch she had no idea of what it was
for. More important, is the elder evidence that Sir John was
pushing her out of the lift in front of him. It would not there-

fore have been possible for her to twist back her arm to shoot him in the back, more especially as she was on his right and the shots were fired from the left.

A.C.. Yes. I see that. Well, then she's out. Good thing, too. I hate bringing in a woman. So it must have been one of the men.

BOBBY. Yes, sir. For that leaves only men in the lift. Take Stephen Smith. His right hand was bandaged. He had cut it rather badly. The liftman's evidence is that Smith was standing to the right of Briggs, between him and the left wall of the lift, with his left arm pressed against the lift wall. He could neither have used his right hand nor twisted himself round far enough to push his left hand under Briggs's dinner jacket. Another physical impossibility.

A.C.. Yes. That clears him. Leaves the two young men, Dick Fuller, isn't it? And Carter. Looks bad against Mr. Dick Fuller, friend of the girl and threats and all.

BOBBY. Yes, sir. I think he would have been in a bad hole but for having spilt the olive oil at dinner. Olive oil is sticky stuff. Naturally he wiped his hands but they are still greasy and his handkerchief is covered with the stuff. He couldn't possibly have touched the pistol, put on his gloves or used his handkerchief, without leaving oily traces. But there are none. So I think he is out, too.

A.C.. You mean it was Carter? Very suspicious, his conduct.

HUNT. There was the way he barged into the lift at the last moment.

BOBBY. Could you see your way, sir, to letting me ask him a few more questions?

A.C.. Right. Chief inspector, tell one of your men to bring him in.

HUNT. Sergeant, ask Mr. Carter to come here.

MARTIN. Very good, sir. This way, Mr. Carter, please.

CARTER. What's the game now? Still trying to pin it on me. I tell you I had nothing to do with it.

HUNT. So you say.

CARTER. Why should I want to bump off the old geezer? I didn't know who he was. Never seen him before.

BOBBY. May I ask a few questions?

A.C.. Yes. Go ahead. Carter, you understand you needn't answer if you don't wish to but that anything you do say is required for use as evidence, and that my present intention is to charge you with the murder of Sir John Briggs unless you can give a very satisfactory account of yourself indeed.

CARTER. I tell you it wasn't me. My God, why should you want to pick on me . . . it wasn't me . . . it wasn't . . . you damn cops, you don't care who you hang so long as you can fix it on some one. I was a cop once myself and I know. All you want is some one with a record you can pick on, but I've never been before a beak yet so you don't get me there.

BOBBY. Pull yourself together, man. Cops don't hang any one. That's for judge and jury. If you are innocent, you've nothing to be afraid of, if you will answer a few questions. Are you willing to do that, or would you rather wait till you are actually charged with murder?

CARTER. You can't do that, you can't . . . I'm innocent. I –

BOBBY. Shut up. Don't be a fool. Are you willing to answer? I'm giving you good advice when I say it will be best to answer – and to tell the truth.

CARTER. What do you want to know?

BOBBY. Were you dismissed from the Midwych police because there were too many housebreaking cases on your beat?

CARTER. What if I was? How do you know?

BOBBY. Well, you told us, didn't you? You said you had been a cop yourself and you're a Midwych man. You had the Midwych Guardian in your pocket.

CARTER. Bought it in London.

BOBBY. Funny you bought the Midwych edition then and not the London edition. You hinted you had a record but said you had never been before a beak. That meant, if the police had a record and you had never been prosecuted. It must have been because there had been a police board of inquiry. Dishonest police generally go in for burglary and housebreaking, so it was a fair guess that was the trouble with you.

CARTER. Know it all, don't you?

BOBBY. We had information there was going to be a try to get off with the Blue John diamond. You answer the description given us – tall, dark, young. The name we had was Dick Forman. That seemed like the name, Dick Fuller, of one man in the lift. I think now there was a mistake and what was really meant was 'a dick formerly', a former policeman. A misunderstanding. Former policeman suggests you. And you lied when you said you had just registered here.

CARTER. All right. Smarty, you are, aren't you? Put it all together neat as ninepence. I only said that about having a room on Nine to get into the lift. But I didn't murder any one. I may pinch things when I get a chance but I'm no murderer. I was hoping to have a go at the Blue John diamond. Just watching for a chance. But I saw it put in the hotel safe so I knew that was off. I hung around to see if anything else turned up. A fellow's got to live and I didn't want all the expense and trouble of togging up to pass in a swell hotel without something to show for it. I heard the old girl who came up in the lift say her hand bag came loose and she must mind she didn't lose her money. You've got to think quick in my line, so I pushed into the lift, bluffed the liftman I had a room on Nine, and I snipped the wire holding the old girl's pearls. That's always a good wheeze. They got excited, with their pearls spilling all round, and then you get your chance. She dropped her bag to grab her pearls, just as I thought she would.

BOBBY. And you opened it and stole the money?

CARTER. No. It wasn't that at all. The handbag burst open itself. Weak fastening and the wad of notes fell out and I picked them up. Of course, I was going to give them her back for the reward, only with the murder and the excitement I never got a chance. Murder does put things out of your mind, you know. You've got nothing on me. It's not theft to pick things up. Not as if I cleared out with 'em.

BOBBY. I think I remember you tried, only I stopped you.

CARTER. That's neither here nor there. I ask you. Suppose I had pinched that wad of notes and meant to do a bunk with them, should I have corpsed the old boy and spoiled my chance of getting away? If it hadn't been for the murder, I would have been out of that lift, got the down lift, been out of the hotel, and off with a good night's work done, before any one knew a thing. That old boy's being done in has cost me a good thirty pounds. Well, I ask you.

BOBBY. Anyhow, I think that's all I want to ask you.

A.C.. All right. Chief inspector, send him back to the others but don't let him go yet.

CARTER. I've told you the truth. You've nothing on me.

HUNT. Sergeant. Take him back to the others. None of them are to go yet.

MARTIN. Very good, sir. Come along, you.

BOBBY. I think, sir, we must accept Carter's story. The wire of Lady Weedon's necklace was certainly cut as he described. I don't see how he could have known that unless he had done it himself. He had her money and as he says his guilt of the theft is clear proof of his innocence of the murder.

A.C.. Guilt proof of innocence, eh? Well, well.

HUNT. But, hang it all, man alive, you've proved the whole blessed lot are innocent. Owen, all the same, it's perfectly certain one of them is guilty. Unless there was an invisible man in the lift.

BOBBY. Not an invisible man. There was some one else in the lift though, wasn't there?

HUNT. But all the time you've kept saying no one else could possibly have been near except that lot.

BOBBY. Yes. That's so. Quite certain.

HUNT. Well, then.

BOBBY. You see, we've forgotten – the liftman.

HUNT. The liftman? What on earth has he to do with it?

BOBBY. Well, he was in the lift, wasn't he?

HUNT. Yes but . . . but . . . well, why should he? You can't think he murdered Briggs because of that threat to report him he said himself didn't amount to anything. A transfer to another lift at the most. Not likely the management would be keen on sacking him with the staff so short through the war.

BOBBY. No, but he did he say he might be moved to another lift.

HUNT. Well, what about it?

BOBBY. He would have lost his chance of being alone with Sir John as the lift went up and down.

HUNT. Yes . . . but . . . I mean to say . . . why should he?

BOBBY. May we have him in again? I think there are a few questions we could usefully ask him now.

A.C.. All right. Chief inspector.

HUNT. Sergeant, tell the liftman we should like to see him again.

MARTIN. Very good, sir. He's been fixing the lift as high as it'll go, in the free space above this floor. To prevent any risk of interference. I told him that had to be seen to and he said that was the best way.

HUNT. All right. Fetch him in.

MARTIN. The liftman, sir.

LIFTMAN. The sergeant says you want to ask me some more questions.

HUNT. That's right.

BOBBY. About your livery or uniform or whatever you call it. Do all the liftmen here wear gloves on duty.

LIFTMAN. Yes. Yes. I suppose so. Yes. The management makes rather a point of it.

BOBBY. Yes, I noticed you wore gloves. I wondered if it was usual.

LIFTMAN. Oh yes, quite usual.

BOBBY. That means that you yourself and the three ladies were the ones in the lift who were actually wearing gloves?

Liftman. I . . . yes . . . well, what about it?

BOBBY. Gloves were point one. The voice was point two.

LIFTMAN. What voice? I heard no voice. What do you mean?

BOBBY. I mean that when I heard you talking at first, you talked very bad grammar with a strong cockney accent. When you were giving your evidence you talked like an educated man.

LIFTMAN. What about it?

BOBBY. Only that it made me wonder why an educated man should be content with a job like running a lift. Unless of course he had some reason of his own.

LIFTMAN. What could that be?

BOBBY. I'm wondering. I'm wondering, too, how it was you knew there was tattooing on Sir John's breast, above the heart, where the bullets that killed him made issue?

LIFTMAN. Wasn't a secret, was it?

BOBBY. Hardly a thing he would be likely to chat about, I thought. I wondered if it had been noticed when he was bathing – having a swim. But you remember you told me there was no swimming pool here so that didn't seem likely. We asked all the others about bathing and swimming and about the tattooing. We drew blank. Except that Lady Weedon knew about it. After all she was his wife. I wondered if you had been told of that tattooing by some woman who had also had chance and opportunity to see it.

LIFTMAN. I don't know what you mean.

BOBBY. I think you do. How long have you been working here?

LIFTMAN. Five years.

BOBBY. That's a long time. Jacob served seven years for a wife, didn't he? Would five years be too long to serve to avenge a wife?

LIFTMAN. How should I know?

BOBBY. I thought you might. When Sir John Briggs threatened to report you, were you afraid you would lose your opportunity of being alone with him sometimes?

LIFTMAN. Why should I? Why should I care which lift I worked?

BOBBY. You said your name was William Johns. William Johns is not unlike Billy Jacks. Is Billy Jacks your real name?

LIFTMAN. What do you know of Billy Jacks? I thought everyone long ago had forgotten Billy Jacks.

BOBBY. Some memories are long. You are Billy Jacks?

LIFTMAN. How did you find it out? I thought I had got away with it. I meant to kill the swine. I always did. But I didn't want to hang for him. Not that I cared about going on living. Why should I? He took it all from me. He took my business. He took my wife. He chucked her out into the street and then she came back to me. She told me about the tattooing. We went abroad. She died there. I let them think at home I had died too. I think perhaps I had. But I made up my mind to see Briggs paid. I found out this hotel was his London headquarters. I got a job here. I worked it to be put on the lift he used – the up-lift to Nine. I had a little automatic I bought in America and smuggled in when I came back. I used to finger it when we were alone in the lift, thinking about pushing it in his face and letting go.

BOBBY. Why did you wait so long?

LIFTMAN. I don't know. It's not easy to make up your mind to kill a man. Besides, I didn't want to hang for it, because I knew how he would have grinned at that.

BOBBY. You were willing enough to let some one else hang for it. A very little more one way or another and any one of the others in the lift might have hanged for what you did.

LIFTMAN. I never thought of them. They had to take their chance like everyone else.

BOBBY. I might have been sorry I had to bring you in for doing what you did to any one like John Briggs. But not when I think of your putting six other people who had never harmed you in peril of their lives, making them suffer the agony of mind they must have gone through to-night.

LIFTMAN. When you have memories like mine going round and round in your head, you don't think of other people. But I shan't hang. I've taken my precautions. Good-bye. And good luck and no hard feelings.

BOBBY. Stop, you fool, you can't –

HUNT. Stop. Hi. Sergeant. Sergeant.

A.C.. Here, you, come back.

HUNT. It's all right. He can't get away. The lift's hung up out of reach. The corridor's guarded at both ends.

(Shouts are heard)

MARTIN. It's the liftman, sir. He ran out and he's jumped down the lift shaft.

THE END